SPLINTERED

Niamh Caldwell

For my Nana, thank you for letting me write at your dining room table and reminding me I am enough.

For Josh, who has loved me more than I deserve, and who I love beyond measure. I could write a thousand books and never depict a love like yours.

Author Notes

This book has been a labour of love for over ten years. These characters have gone by many names, have lived many lifetimes, and now they're here, still broken and burning but at least their names aren't Chaz anymore.

I'm sat here at a loss for words really, which is ironic considering I've just written 114,000 of them. All I can say is thank you. Thank you for believing in me, believing in this story.

Calluna comes from such a dark place inside me, a place that has always felt insecure, has always longed for traditional beauty, but through Calluna's journey I started to realise that the pursuit of perfection is a painful and horrific journey. I wrote this book for all the people who felt trapped, who needed to know they could be whatever they wanted to be.

I hope you know that you are loved.

See you on the flip side,

Niamh

TRIGGER WARNINGS

Please read these:

1. Domestic violence
2. Physical abuse
3. Sexual assault
4. Death
5. Parental neglect

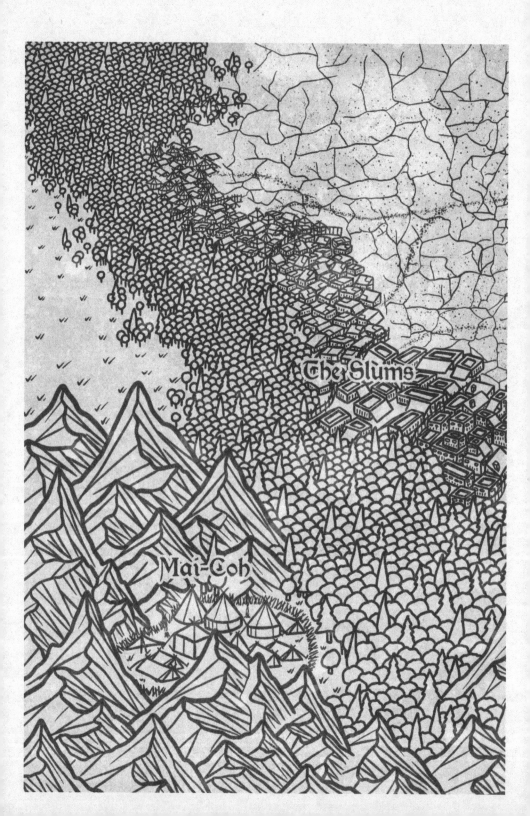

'Fear not the darkness, for Perfection is the light that guides us

Fear not corruption, for Perfection bares the eyes that watch us

Fear not transgression, for Perfection is the hand that holds us

Fear not destitution, for Perfection is the wealth that nourishes us

Fear not Perfection, for it is the life inside us'

-Book of Light, The Emperor's Promise

Chapter I

When you know one wrong answer could be the end of your life, you study pretty hard.

Even the word test is like the breath of some ferocious animal. *Test.* The hiss of a snake as it coils to strike. *Test.* A burning, wretched, life-threatening formality to separate the weak from the strong.

How many precious stones line the Emperor's driveway?

The question loomed as great as any foe; written in gold and intended to draw blood. I chewed on the end of my pencil as I tried to think back to a history lesson I should have been paying attention to, then stopped myself. I peered at the dented wood, smoothed my thumb over the place my teeth had been. I looked up at Mrs. Leath to check if she'd seen, but her eyes were elsewhere. Chewed on stationary would incur a punishment that really would ruin my chances of passing this test.

'Fear not the darkness, for Perfection is the light that guides us, and if it is his will, he will guide you to the right answer." Mrs. Leath said as she settled behind her desk.

She smiled out at the classroom, hands folded on the desk, a rehearsed pose of poise and beauty. She caught my eyes, and I looked back down, cheeks ablaze, pushed my ruined pencil into my pocket and took another from the line I'd made on my desk. Sweat slicked my dress against my back as I read the question again.

How many precious stones line the Emperor's driveway?

It was an easy question, something I'd learnt as a child. I took a deep breath and closed my eyes, tried to force myself to relax. I had to get this right. I had to pass this test. There were people counting on me, people that needed me to do well. My brain sung with a thousand thoughts as I tried to will it into submission. My fingers shook against the new pencil, and I pressed my lips tight to stop the tears that threatened to spill. Then, like sunlight through leaves, the answer fell into place.

Three million twenty-five thousand four hundred and eighty-two precious gems and jewels made up the driveway to the Emperor's keep. I let out a shaking breath as I rushed to scribble the answer down before it fled again.

The sound of scribbling pencils was deafening; it echoed off the pristine white walls like a thousand footsteps. I risked a peek across at my neighbour and sworn enemy, hoped I'd see her as stuck as I had been.

Olivia Dune was already on question nine. She caught me looking and cast me a condescending smile, mouthed the word 'loser'. I frowned at her, pursed my lips in an effort not to mouth something back. I turned back to my test, toes clenched into the soles of my shoes.

Damn Olivia.

It was a simple test of knowledge, one that under ordinary circumstances I would have at least scored close to one hundred. Yet the pressure of this test, the final test before our Appraisals, the one that would cement our intelligence for the rest of time, made my stomach swirl.

I looked at the mantra etched into the marble plaque on my desk, the curving gold words that served to remind us of what we did this for.

Fear not transgression, for Perfection is the hand that holds us.

The words were meant as a comfort, a cornerstone to rub in times of hardship. A warm, loving, guiding hand to grip and to follow. I grazed the words with my fingertips, traced the letters and tried to internalise them, but they were as cold as the walls that trapped us here.

I recited the words regardless, over and over until they were a jumbled hum of white noise. The test would not get the better of me; I couldn't let it. I would not be weeded out like some week-old begonia. I couldn't let the lure of a perfect assignment, of the Inner Ring, make me lose face this late in the game.

I pushed all doubt to the back of my mind, focused solely on the paper in front of me. The next few questions were as easy as breathing. The smell of ink, books and sweat hung heavy in the air as I focused on making my handwriting legible. The sound of breathing, of stifled coughs and half hidden sneezes faded to nothing as my mind eased into focus.

Halfway there, halfway to freedom.

I was approaching question eleven when I heard the sniffling.

Unlike the sniff of a tickled nose, this sound was harsh, loud, almost violent. I looked up, scanned my peers. Everyone else had their eyes glued to their tests; Philippe Must, his tongue stuck out of the corner of his mouth, hurried to get his words on the page. Olivia had finished already and was busy running her dainty fingers through her lustrous ash blond hair. I stared daggers at the back of her head as I moved past her.

Mrs. Leath sat in her chair, her shoulders straight and her smile unwavering as she sharpened some pencils. She lined them up along the desk in perfect uniform, her attention momentarily averted. I risked a look over my shoulder, and there, behind me, was the source of the sniffing.

Carolynn Crestly was staring at her test, her pencil laid down on the desk in dismay. Her milky blue eyes were filled with tears as she stared at the very first question. Carolynn was a pretty girl.

Simple, but pretty.

Her pale almost white, blonde hair fell around her face in a sleek waterfall, her doll like face red from tears. She stared at the page in utter distress, blank eyes unseeing. I bit my lip as a tear rolled down her cheek.

I turned back around and tried to focus on my test. Every few minutes I heard the shallow breaths and sniffs of Carolynn as she continued to cry. Olivia looked over her shoulder and pulled a sour face at Carolynn's distress. I scowled at the test instead of at her.

I read the same question over and over again, unable to concentrate. A nagging guilt rose in my chest; Carolynn was a sweet girl, she'd always been nice to me. If she did terribly on this test, she'd completely ruin her chances of a good appraisal, and end up either doing manual labour, or worse, cast out completely. It wasn't uncommon for low scoring girls to be carted off to the Riven Dens in Slum Five; pretty girls whose only use is to serve the Emperor and his elite guards as mistresses. Whores. Slaves. Carolynn didn't deserve that.

No one did.

I chewed on the inside of my cheek as I blinked the thought of those lost girls away. I looked up at Mrs. Leath, who was now stood with her back to the classroom. She was writing on the board with grand, sweeping gestures. Her hair, pulled into a knot at the back of her head, bounced as she wrote. I turned back to Carolynn. Tears streamed freely down her pale cheeks, and for the first time I thought she looked rather ugly.

I shook my head and looked out the window instead.

No. I couldn't risk helping her. Emperor knows that would get me in deep trouble.

A team of Pioneers from the Inner Ring were carting barrels of flowers from a LeviVan on the green. Their protective gloves shone as bright as pearls in the high afternoon sun. Men and women in white glossy suits brandished shovels and trowels like instruments of art. Some had already begun to dig up the month-old flowers from their beds, making room for the new arrivals.

A man I recognised by his bushy brows and accompanying thick beard was Peter Sole. He carried a container of staple breeds; tulips, pink and unspoiled as virgins' lips, dahlia as red and pungent as the rarest wine, and magnolia, always the centrepiece, as pure as the Emperor's unblemished skin. He lumbered across the grass with heavy steps, his brow creased as he struggled with the weight. His deep-set eyes were scrunched against the bright midday sun.

I smiled as he dropped the container of flowers on the ground with a thump, wiped the sweat from his brow. He picked up a handful with little care for the petals he sent flying; they were a new creation I had seen in one of my mother's workbooks.

I spotted the Boneset, bred under microscopes with Bloodroot to give the tall, wild plants more delicate, dainty flowers. DaffoDaisies, with petals so voluptuous and wide they dwarfed the toddler legs of its small stems.

The flowers were almost enough to distract me from Carolynn.

Almost.

She choked, and the sound of chairs screeching and pencils ceasing filled the room. I refused to turn around; I kept my eyes trained on Peter as he dug a hole for the DaffoDaisies, but I no longer found entertainment in his actions. Once the sound of writing returned, I found myself unable to resist peeking back at Carolynn. Her head was braced in her hands as she sobbed into her chest. The tear marks on her paper caused the golden ink to bleed. She shook her head back and forth, muttered to herself in a voice that bordered psychotic. Snot bubbled from her nose, but she didn't wipe it away. I clenched my hands tight, but I already knew I couldn't stop myself.

I looked at Mrs. Leath, who was still writing on the board. I waited a second or two to make sure she didn't turn, before I leant down and opened my bag. I drew out a piece of paper and pushed it underneath my test. My heart thumped as I leant forward, tried to shield what I was doing from prying eyes, aware that Olivia had nothing better to do than spy on her classmates.

The shake of my fingers almost rendered my words unreadable as I wrote the answers on the piece of paper. Sweat slicked my palms, and the same clarity that had shown me the answer earlier choked up to blackened, angry smoke. I ignored it and tried to concentrate on making my handwriting neat. I wrote the answers up to question seven; enough to get her a decent placement, but not enough to cause suspicion. If we were found cheating, there would be no leniency.

I folded the piece of paper and looked around to see if anyone had caught on to what I was doing. Olivia was too busy admiring her perfect nails to care, and everyone else was still working away. I turned in my chair and dropped my pencil onto the floor. Carolynn looked up at the noise, her eyes puffy and swollen. She reached down to pick it up at the same time as me, and as she handed it to me, I pressed the paper into her palm.

She cocked her head to the side, her brows furrowed as she sat up. She unfolded the piece of paper and her eyes widened as she read what was on it. She looked up; her mouth agape, snot still bubbling from her nostrils. I smiled, filled with a sense of pride and satisfaction. I nodded to her as if I were some sort of hero, and I allowed myself to feel that way.

I gripped my pencil with a newfound sense of confidence as I filled out the next question. My whole body sang with energy despite the fear of being caught. It hardly seemed to matter anymore, because I'd done it.

I'd gotten away with it.

Mrs. Leath turned around as if drawn by something, chalk still poised between her bony fingers. Her gaze zeroed in on something behind me, eyed narrowed to slim lines as her lips puckered.

"Yes Carolynn?" She asked.

My heart stuttered in my chest, and I almost choked on my breath. Every ounce of light and happiness that had been flowing through my body turned cold as ice. I couldn't turn to look at her. My body refused to move, refused to meet whatever was coming my way.

Maybe her pencil needed sharpening. Maybe she needed the toilet. Maybe she needed a tissue. Maybe she needed a new test paper, after all, hers was wet and bleeding.

"Calluna just handed me the answers." The words sliced through my back as harshly as any knife.

The weight of everyone's eyes was almost enough to collapse my lungs as I looked back at Carolynn. She held the piece of paper up for everyone to see, and there was no denying my handwriting. She was smiling at me, her eyes cold and unfeeling.

I wanted to scream. I wanted to throw myself at her. I wanted to get on my knees and beg for forgiveness. Deception of this kind had landed citizens of Sadon in Slums. Had left them handless or tongueless or worse.

"Is this true, Calluna?" Mrs. Leath asked, a note of betrayal in her voice.

I fixed Carolynn with one final stare. I hoped to see regret flicker in her eyes, but she met me with icy triumph. I turned, my fingers wrapped tightly around the edge of the desk to stop myself from throwing something at her.

16

Olivia could barely contain her laughter, her face lit wickedly as she leant back, revelled in my pain. I met Mrs. Leaths eyes, and despite every instinct in me that said to lie, I nodded. Mrs. Leath's jaw flickered as she took in a sharp breath, her eyes flashed with something dangerous and almost feral. My heart dropped into my stomach as an overwhelming shame consumed me.

I knew what the Emperor demanded of me, what he expected in return for his kindness, and this act of defiance went against his rule. Went against everything this city stood for. My hands tightened against the desk as my limbs shook, the fear finally settling in.

"Calluna. My prize pupil, my dearest student. How could you do such a thing? After everything Emperor Emercius has afforded you?" She turned her gaze to his painting.

The painting covered the entire wall. Several of his portrait, side by side, over and over he watched us. Law demanded his presence in every room, so he may preside over our daily lives. He loomed as ethereal and immortal as the moon. His eyes, devoid of any pupil or iris, only flecked with gold, were endless ivory voids that linked our room to his sight.

I shook my head, tongued my teeth and wondered if they'd rip them out.

I should have let her fail. I should have let her lose her future, lose her dignity, maybe even lose her life. I should have let her wail and cry until she was escorted from the room. I opened and closed my mouth, unsure what to say, because despite what Carolynn had done, I knew I couldn't have let that happen to her. Even if it meant that I might be face the same fate.

Mrs. Leath shook her head, her own calloused hands firm on the whip that hung from her belt. An instrument of torture, of order and retribution, one I wasn't unfamiliar with. She turned her eyes on me, and despite how often I had seen them, they still managed to make me squirm. They gaped at me as black and depthless as a winter's night. With no trace of white, they were perfect onyx circles. Her crimson pupils sat nestled within the darkness, like Mars sat swollen in the nights sky. The eyes that stared at me held unimaginable powers within, the power to know things that were unspoken, to walk freely within the confines of our fragile minds, to break and bend and meld what we were forced to give.

My lip wobbled as those eyes blinked, and I knew what would come to me now. After all my preening, after all my pretending, after everything I had given, I was going to lose it all over one dumb test.

"Do you have anything to say for yourself?" She asked, her voice perfectly even despite the flickering of her cheek.

She moved towards me slowly, as if wary of what I might do. There had been dissent in the air, even if those who chose to sin were few and far between. The Mai-Coh rebels had become audacious with their attempts to corrupt the perfect citizens, sneaking into homes and flaunting their arrogance. Most had died, but not without rebel success.

Only last week two Lower Ring citizens had been caught trying to sneak out of the city walls, smuggling medicine and food to the Mai-Coh who lingered somewhere far beyond the Emperor's reach. Their flogging had been public and gruesome, but a message as clear as day. Dissent will not be tolerated.

"No ma'am. There is no excuse for what I have done," I said, my voice barely above a whisper as she knelt in front of me, forced my gaze to meet hers.

"Dearest Calluna, my child." She touched my face, her fingers cold and smelling of chalk, and despite my training I flinched.

She looked upon me with a caution that was heart wrenching. I'd worked my whole life to achieve perfection. I'd kept my head down, followed the law, sacrificed my own needs for others. To see her look at me like I was the enemy, it made my stomach lurch.

Her brow creased; the corners of her lips turned down. A tear slipped down my cheek as I thought about my family, as I thought about the fact that this morning might have been the last time I ever saw them. She brushed the tear away with a tentative thumb, gripped my chin with a firmness that shot pain down my neck.

"The Emperor would be so disappointed in you, child. Your clear dismissal of his will is insulting." With wounded eyes, she looked to the painting again.

I looked to him too. I looked into his endless eyes, and my heart tightened. A paralysing fear clasped at my throat so viciously I thought I might choke. Life in the slums was a punishment worse than death. There were enough supplies and food to make them labour for our luxuries, but no medicine, no warmth, nothing but work and death.

I wouldn't last the year.

"Emperor please forgive my sins. Deliver me from darkness and into your welcoming arms. Do not reject me as we reject those who are unfaithful to your name. Protect and forgive me as you always have and always will." The words left my mouth in a practiced rush.

I pinched my thigh under the desk and forced myself to cry. If she saw my tears, she might pity me. Mrs Leath watched on in silent apprehension. My classmates all bowed their heads and said their own muttered prayers. Maybe for me, maybe for themselves. Sin by association was almost as bad as the sin itself.

"We are in your eternal debt," I whispered, my fingers numb against my leg.

"We are in your eternal debt," the classroom whispered in unison.

Mrs Leath deliberated; her fingers toyed with the strap of her whip. I watched it knock back and forth, back and forth, and hoped that I would be lucky enough to escape its lash. She pulled her whip free with a flourish that squashed my hope beyond repair.

It was a relatively small thing, standard issue to educational staff. Only the length of her forearm, it glistened as white and wondrous as the flowers being planted outside. I winced as the memory of my last lashing surfaced, the look on my father's face as he'd delivered three strikes to each knee for not cleaning my room to the perfect standard.

"Your mind must be searched. Do not make me struggle through it." She said sternly.

I wiped my nose and nodded despite the fear that threatened to render me paralysed. I sat up straighter, tried to relax my mind to make it easier for her to pass through. I knew better than anyone that facing your punishment with dignity and poise was highly praised. I had learnt from a young age that when my father deemed to punish me, as the Emperor advised, I was to take that punishment without crying, without anger. That he would never hurt me, that none of them would ever hurt me, unless the Emperor deemed it necessary and within the law to bring us back to Perfection. We all had to do our part in keeping up appearances, none of us did it out of choice.

"Relax now."

The room was deadly silent. I could feel Olivia's gaze burning deep into the back of my head, her smug, gloating smile painted on the back of my eyelids. We had always had a rivalry, always vied for the most competitive opportunities. Everyone had an equal, a challenger, someone to motivate them through hate to become better. She didn't fear that I had been led astray by the Mai-Coh scouts who had begun to slowly penetrate our borders, like most of the class did. She didn't worry that they had come in the night like thieves and persuaded me to the darkness. She relished in my deviation and cared little for my reasons.

Any thoughts I had of Olivia fell from my mind like water through leaves as Mrs. Leath tore through the first gauze of my mind. There was a deep nagging sensation in the pit of my stomach as she pushed through my mind, and I squirmed, tried not to jerk away. No matter how many times they did this to me, it always felt wrong. It always broke something inside me, tore from me the small part of this world I could keep for myself.

She broke through the layers of mush and goo and the pain peeked to something hot and sharp, the classroom faded from sight, and I was blinded by light.

I stood in a room without corners or limit. A never-ending white pocket of nothingness. Mrs Leath stood too, her back to me. She gazed through a frame without a door; a black hole of flashing colour and sound that represented my very consciousness. Something compelled me to call out. I opened my mouth, but no sound came. Mrs Leath peered into the whirlpool, her face reflected the roaring rainbow within. That nagging, uneasy feeling in my stomach rose into my chest as she poked a finger into the colours. They shied away from her touch, coiled and curled in on themselves like a burning piece of parchment. I opened my mouth to beg her to stop as she pushed a whole fist through the swirling mass of my consciousness. Her hand disappeared, then her elbow, as she pushed her way inside.

I watched the cacophony of colour absorb her, turn from a kaleidoscope to blackened char, and finally found the strength to scream.

I was in the classroom again, completely unmoved. My jaw was slack as Mrs Leath stared at my hands, which had come free from the desk and landed limply on its surface. How long we'd been gone, what she had seen, they were unknowns. My toes curled deep into the soles of my shoes as I waited. I couldn't tell what she was thinking; her brows were drawn low over her eyes as she worried at her lip. My stomach twisted painfully at the thought of punishment, of jeopardising my family, of my one shot at small freedoms fading to nothing.

"Dearest Calluna," the words fell from her lips in a breathless gasp.

She was flustered. Her chest rose and fell frantically, her forehead lined with worry. I looked around in confusion, my heart hammered hard against my ribs.

What had she seen?

Mrs Leath raised her whip, her eyes filled with something I couldn't understand. She bought it down with a slap against my forearm. I cried out like a silly child as pain spread like heat up my arm. I knew better than to whimper, I knew better than to cry. When she raised the whip again, I made sure to bite my lip until blood pooled under my tongue. The pain was unbearable, it radiated up past my shoulders, sent a shock up my neck that made my lips twitch. Mrs Leath was crazed with her strikes. They weren't calculated or precise like they should have been, but erratic, fearful.

Once the final lash had been dealt, Mrs Leath took a step back, as if pulled from a terrible dream. Some of her hair had sprung free during the punishment, and she slicked it back as she composed herself. Blood slipped down my chin where my teeth had sunk into my lip. My arms were red, small welts raised against the pale skin. I looked up at her, swallowed the anger and fear that threatened to make me do something I'd regret.

"I'm sorry," I stuttered despite the fact I didn't know what I was apologising for.

Mrs Leath turned and walked to her desk, where she picked up her Commniglass. The small ball of glass hummed

22

under her fingertips and misted over, a swirling orb of white and silver.

"Your father will be notified so you may be punished accordingly at home," she said curtly.

I nodded without a word, knew better than to argue. I looked down at my arms, blinked past the tears in my eyes. What had she seen? What was she afraid of?

The whoosh of the Commniglass made me look back up. Mrs Leath had sent my father her findings, whatever they were. Her whip laid on her desk, stained red with my blood. I looked up at Emperor Emercius and shame pressed down on my shoulders. Without him, we would be dead in a wasteland, still lead by selfish tyrants. I had to be grateful for what he'd given us, but I'd bitten the hand that fed me, and that hand turned to a fist quicker than a blink.

"I've placed you on the Register as an additional precaution. For the next 24 hours, your every move will be watched, documented, and any infraction will be treated with double the punishment. Understood?" she asked.

A rush of panic filled my veins as I resisted the urge to speak. I had never been on the Register, only potential defectors ended up on the Register. Repeat offenders, those suspected of treason. People that end up on the Register often ended up dead. I couldn't be on the Register, not so close to my Appraisal. I needed to get to the Inner Ring, I needed the freedoms it would give me. I had to win, and being on the Register would ruin my chances.

My breath lodged in my throat, my eyes burnt as I nodded. My sadness and shame rose like bile in my throat, but I choked it down. She gave me one last lingering glance before she took a deep breath and turned back to the board.

"Everyone, back to your tests. Now."

Chapter II

As soon as the bell chimed for the end of class, I packed away my things in an orderly fashion. My arms burnt at the slightest movement, but I couldn't show my weakness. I smiled through the pain, pulled up the façade I had perfected over the years, and as I stood, Mrs Leath fixed me with a stare.

"A word, Calluna."

I stepped up to the front of the class, forced on the mask that had always won me approval. The rest of my classmates filtered out slowly, whispered to each other. I caught dregs of their conversations as they fled.

"Poor Calluna, on the Register,"

"I wish I would have caught her; it's been ages since I got a gift from the Emperor,"

"Do you think they'll… you know, 'Cut her off?'"

"I can't wait to see what I get for reporting her."

The last voice was Carolynn. She hadn't stopped grinning. Many of my classmates were following her blindly, asking her how it felt, speculating what the Emperor would deliver her for her service. When I looked at her, something black and ugly rose in my chest, something that worried me.

"I'm concerned for you, Calluna." She didn't face me as she talked.

She stared at the board; her eyes focused on the historical photos she had put up for tomorrow morning's class. There was one of Emperor Emercius, stood in front of the Keep when it was first built. He towered over the others in the photo, the tallest man you will ever see. He grinned with perfect white teeth as he shook a smaller man's hand. The white marble walls reached up to the sky until they disappeared into the clouds, and the thick golden gate was sealed with the most intricate and beautiful locking system.

"I promise, Mrs Leath. I will not disappoint you again," I replied adamantly.

I was going to prove myself; I had to, for everyone's sake. I was going to strive for Inner Ring perfection, she wouldn't ever have to show me the light again.

Mrs Leath wasn't moved by my promises. She continued to stare at our Emperor with wistful sadness.

"I'm afraid... afraid you may slip from His Eye," she whispered the words as if she couldn't bear to say them.

The breath left my lips in a woosh. This was not a statement to be taken lightly, it was a statement that could land me cut off, or dead, or a Riven. I shook my head so hard pain lanced through my temples, rippled down the bridge of my nose.

"I would never," I tried to reassure her.

Finally, she looked at me. Her eyes were creased, her shoulders slumped as she looked me up and down. She reached out and pressed her finger into one of the splits in my skin. I forced my smile to remain as blood oozed down my arm and pain lanced up my arm. My lips twitched as she gave one last poke, and at the crack in my composure she withdrew her hand. My blood ran down her fingers, but she wiped it away as if it were ink or chalk.

"Go now. For your mother's sake, do not slip again," she waved me away.

I nodded despite the venom in my throat, eager to protect my family. My mother was responsible for raising me into perfection, for shaping me into a servant for the Emperor, and if I failed, it would be her that would be punished. That's how they got you; with threats against your loved ones, with competitions against friends, reasons to hate and calculated and betray. When you fake long enough, you start to forget what parts of you are real. What parts they made you.

I tried to remember which parts of me were real, as I emerged into the hallway. End the end of the hall stood Alfie, his pale orange hair slicked back and glinting under the fluorescent lights.

"Calluna!" He cried as he saw me.

"Alfie,"

I ran towards him, desperate for familiarity. He opened his arms and hauled me into them with a grin. He spun me around a few times before he set me down, his hands warm against my back.

"There's my perfect girl," he planted a kiss on my forehead.

The corners of my mouth dropped as he stared down at me. He could sense something was wrong, he always could. We'd known each other since birth, there wasn't much I could slip past him.

"What? Am I too handsome to bare?" he joked to bring the smile back to my lips.

I gave his shoulder a half-hearted thump. He feigned hurt, gripped his shoulder as if in total agony as he staggered over to the wall, crumbled to his knees like a fool.

"Oh, I'm hit. I'm down. Tell... My parents... To destroy my Commniglass," with a final breath he gasped and sat lifeless on the ground, tongue lolled out of his mouth.

I snorted despite my best efforts, nudged his knee with the toe of my shoe, ruffled his hair until it stuck up at all ends.

"Get up will you," I smiled as he opened one eye and smirked.

"I'm wounded, woman! Show a little sympathy," he pretended to cry, and I held out a hand to help him up.

"Sorry, guess I don't know my own strength," I played along as I pulled him to his feet, held my fists up in mock combat.

He held up his hands in surrender as he pulled a scared face.

"Please! Please, mercy I beg you," he begged.

Alfie was the only real thing about this place, the person that I anchored my real self to. He put an arm around my shoulders as we walked towards the school gates. I smiled at every classmate as we walked, waved even. I needed to prove myself after what had happened today. I couldn't afford to slip, not now that everyone was on the lookout.

"I got a very interesting message on my Commniglass," Alfie began as he pulled out the ball.

He swiped his hand across it, and my face was projected from the glass. The word 'REGISTER' was stamped in gold beneath my portrait. I looked up at Alfie through my lashes, unable to meet his gaze head on.

"I'm sorry Alfie. You know Carolynn? She was failing her test, and she was crying, and... I felt so bad for her. I slipped her the answers, I know I shouldn't have. I know it was wrong, okay?" I said, swallowed that part of me that wanted to complain about Carolynn and call her every horrible name.

Alfie listened in silence. His narrow shoulders were tight as we walked, his smooth, pink lips pressed into a line as he mulled over what I had done. I worried at my injured lip, tongued the bite marks as I waited for him to say something.

It would take only a handful of words from him to the officials to end our life mate agreement. He was my life mate, the boy the Emperor had assigned me at birth.

Everything I did reflected on him. He could claim I was damaging his reputation, ruining his perfection, and he would be free of me, and I would be served to the Riven.

"I can't bear the thought of you being disappointed in me. Please say something," I gripped onto his shirt with both hands as I stared up into his eyes.

Alfie tutted, gave me a frown that didn't reach his eyes, before he grinned, the pale freckles creased on his nose. His deep chocolate eyes were so bright that they chased away any shadow that dared to hang over us, and I relaxed as he patted my head.

"I could never stay mad at you," he reassured me as he kissed my head again.

I gave a sign of relief, linked my arms with his as we continued on. Alfie really was the Perfect mate for me; he was handsome and kind, clever and very reasonable. He was the logical choice; the Emperor had paired us well. I could always depend on him, depend on his familiarity, find comfort in the knowledge that things were easy here. Easy with him.

Even if I didn't feel the attraction for him that he felt for me.

We emerged into the courtyard, where Pioneers still bustled back and forth with handfuls of bulbs and flowers. Our classmates were all chatting, excited the school day was over. Carolynn was long gone, probably already opening her gift from the Emperor. It wouldn't matter that she had failed her test now, she'd done Sadon a great service, and she would be rewarded accordingly. I kicked myself for falling into such a trap. I should have known better. My father had not raised me to be anything less than Perfect.

"You don't half scowl when you're thinking, Calluna," Alfie teased, imitated my scowl.

I gave him a nudge with my elbow. It was so unusual for life mates to get along as easily as Alfie and I, and even more unusual for one or the other to feel something real. I was lucky that Alfie truly loved me out of choice, and not duty. I wished I could make Alfie as lucky, but most of the time it just didn't work that way. I was fond of him, I cared about him, but love is not the same as fondness, at least that's what I had gathered from my small understanding of love.

I adored his big brown eyes that under the sun, revealed veins of copper. I found his freckles, smudged across his cheeks like pollen from a lily, unbearably cute. I cherished his lopsided smile and soft jaw, but none of those things made my stomach tighten, or my heart flutter, or any of the other things Alfie described he felt when he saw me. I looked at him now, at the vibrant flame like mop of hair that fell over his pale forehead, at his sunshine filled smile, and felt empty in my stomach.

He caught me staring and cocked a brow. I turned away, hid behind my hair as I blushed. As I tried to hide my embarrassment, a cascade of raven hair caught my attention.

Polly, my designated best friend, sat hunched over something she was reading. Her onyx hair fell around her face like a shawl, hid her from view. I walked over to her, with Alfie mumbling complaints under his breath, and tapped her shoulder.

She spun around, clutched whatever she had been reading tightly to her chest. Her eyes were wide and filled with terror, her face ashen and drawn. I took a step away from her as her breath rattled, startled at her reaction. Her eyes softened as she focused on my face, and she let out a shuddering breath.

"Oh, it's you," Polly sounded relieved, but her fingers didn't relax on the book she was holding.

Through her white knuckled grip I saw a white cloth bound book. It was unlike any book I had seen before, tied closed with blue velvet ribbon. Colour wasn't afforded to many citizens of Sadon, not even those within the Inner Ring. Colour was for the immediate inner circle of the Emperor, and for Polly to hold such a thing was... unsettling. I gestured to it, my curiosity getting the better of me.

"What's that you're reading?" I asked.

She peeked down at the book, barely glanced at it, before she looked back at me. Her narrow face was unusually pallid, and much thinner than usual. Her cheeks were sunken, her lips cracked. When I tried to call to mind the last time I'd seen her, I drew a blank.

"This? Oh, it's nothing, something I picked up from the library," she rushed to say, unconvincing as always. "I saw you on the Register, what happened?"

She bundled the book up and pushed it deep into her bag. I knew she was lying; she had always been a terrible liar, but the look on her face, the bags beneath her eyes, told me not to push it. Polly could be sensitive sometimes, and provoking her into one of her episodes would only draw negative attention to me. Attention I didn't need.

Wow you're selfish.

"I helped Carolynn cheat on the test today," I replied.

"A minute lapse in judgement, really," Alfie added gently, rubbed my back.

Polly nodded wordlessly, as if it didn't matter at all. She looked between the two of us, her eyes as wide and cautious as a wild animal. She had never warmed to Alfie, for a reason I didn't know. Polly was an unusual girl in many ways. She kept to herself, rarely talked to anyone apart from myself. She looked at me now as if she ached to tell me something, but her eyes kept moving back to Alfie, watching him as if he were about to strike.

"Is everything alright Polly?" I asked.

She opened her mouth, then shut it immediately. Alfie rolled his eyes.

"Oh come on Polly. Out with it. Let me guess, Jorius asked for some under the shirt action again?" Alfie teased, and I jabbed him in the stomach.

I shot him a warning look as my face flushed red. Polly had told me that in confidence, I wasn't supposed to tell him, but keeping anything from Alfie was like drawing blood from a banana.

I looked back at Polly apologetically, but it was as if she hadn't even heard him. Her eyes slid from my face and behind me. I followed her gaze to where two Inner Ring Pioneers were standing. They were looking towards us, talking too quiet for us to hear. The taller of the two met my eyes, his violet pupils glistened in the sun. I smiled at him, raised my hand in a wave. Alfie mirrored my gesture, waved enthusiastically. They didn't return our pleasantries.

"They're watching us," Polly muttered worriedly.

"Come on Polly, why would they do that? They're probably looking at that tree or something, you know what gardeners are like. Excited by leaves and dirt, right Calluna? Tell her she's being silly," Alfie nudged me.

I wanted to agree with him. I wanted to brush it off, but I couldn't. Their eyes *were* on us, not the tall oak tree. Their interest was not on the birds that swooped overhead, or the lilac flowers that bloomed around our feet. I looked back at them again, narrowed my eyes, tried to place their faces.

They weren't like the other gardeners; they were taller, broader. They bore the hardened faces of our soldiers, our protectors. They had no reason to be here, at our school, not when the Hollow had the lowest number of Mai-Coh incidents. They should be in Penn, or Gallow.

31

I turned back, met Polly's frightened gaze. Alfie waited for my agreement, his eyes growing more bored by the second. Much like Polly had never warmed to Alfie, Alfie hadn't taken a liking to Polly either. She wasn't... perfect. She was outspoken and always in trouble, and I found it endearing, but most found it off putting. Associating yourself with trouble is a sure way to court death. I looked between Polly and Alfie, and found myself nodding despite how unsure I was.

"He's right Polly. They have no reason to watch you," I replied.

I waited for her to tell me I was wrong, to burst out with whatever she was hiding from me, but she nodded instead, crushed by my betrayal.

"Yes... Yes, I'm being silly." She pulled her bag over her shoulder and stood up, "I should get going."

She turned and took a few steps. I followed her despite Alfie's protests, caught her by the wrist and pulled her towards me. She refused to turn, her elbow locked, her muscles taut. I looked at the back of her head, willed for her to tell me what was going on. I gave her wrist a gentle tug.

"Where are you going? Come on, walk with us." I urged.

She snatched her wrist from my fingers and turned to face me. She fixed me with a defiant look. She was not frightened now, she was the headstrong and fierce girl the officials feared. She was the difficult girl who shied from no punishment.

"No. I'm being silly, right? I need to go home. You know how much my mother worries," she said, her voice sharp.

She made as if to turn again, but I moved closer, blocked her path. I tried to catch her eyes, but she averted my gaze. her anger was worse than her fear. My stomach roiled at how I'd failed her, at the stubborn set of her jaw. I was supposed to be her friend, regardless of how it hurt me.

"Come on, Pol. We're going to swing by the Palladium, check our scores. Maybe we can all hang out at Alfie's place after. Right Alfie?" I looked to Alfie, who shot me an irritated look.

I shot him an equally irritated look, nodded at Polly, tried to convey that she needed us right now. He rolled his eyes, ran a hand over her face, and nodded reluctantly.

"Yeah. It'll be fun," he said unconvincingly.

Polly shook her head, cast Alfie a venomous look.

"Don't do me any favours. I have to go," She turned before I could say anything more and headed off.

"Polly, wait!" I went to follow her, but Alfie placed a hand on my shoulder.

"Just let her go, Calluna. You're causing a scene," He jerked his chin back to the two Pioneers, who still had their eyes trained on us.

I sighed as I watched Polly go. Her small frame seemed so fragile as she retreated through the large golden gates. Something wasn't right, I could feel it in my stomach. Polly was always strange, but never feral. Never angry towards me.

"Come on, let's go to the Palladium before it gets too dark," Alfie patted my shoulder, and I nodded absently as Polly disappeared from view.

He held out his arm with a charming smile, and I took it without hesitation. We walked in silence. We looked so Perfect together, it was stupid not to show off our pairing. For many, we were the golden standard. The leading example.

A knot twisted in my stomach as I thought again about how being on the Register would affect our lives. For months now, Alfie and I had been going out of our way to show off how Perfect we really were. Alfie had been going door to door, offering a helping hand to anyone who needed it. I had taken a leaf from my mother's book and started to garden for our neighbours. We both desperately wanted a shot at being transferred to the Inner Ring, that little bit more security, little more leniency.

"Did you look where we were in the tables this morning?" I asked as we made our way down the street.

Alfie nodded, but there wasn't the excitement in his eyes I had been hoping for. Each year, three couples were offered a transfer to the Inner Ring. Alfie and I had been hopping from third to fourth for two weeks, in direct competition with Olivia and Aston.

"I checked last night. Olivia and Aston had third." He shook his head.

My fists clenched at the mention of Olivia. In three weeks, the scores would be set, and there would be no changing the verdict. I didn't want to have to see Olivia standing on the podium with that sly grin plastered on her face as I watched from the crowd. I would do anything to beat her, and I suppose that was the whole point.

"Now Alfie, you said it yourself. You're way too handsome to be rejected," I teased.

He smiled, but it was merely for show. His eyes fell flat, and for a moment there was a glimpse of anger there. A spark of pure rage. It fell as quickly as it appeared and was replaced by fake happiness.

"Well, we better make sure your deviation hasn't thrown us out of favour." He tried to play the accusation off as a joke, but the words conveyed what I had seen in his eyes.

I didn't say anything. I simply nodded. I couldn't afford to cause a scene. It was my duty to make him happy, and I owed him that.

We made no effort to converse, we had nothing more to say to each other. Although we were best friends, we spent a lot of time in silence. I assured myself that was because we had an unspoken bond that words would merely tarnish. Most of the time, Alfie was the one who spoke. He had a charisma and energy to him that demanded my attention at all times. I found myself in awe of him on most days. He was everything the Emperor had intended when he had envisioned the perfect Man.

The streets were abuzz with action. Each house had its doors flung open wide to invite any passers-by inside. Wives and mothers in white frocks tended to their front gardens, pruned their roses, trimmed their grass, added an extra layer of paint to their white picket fences. Each front garden, much like my own, had a round, ornate white table and four matching white chairs. Atop each table sat pitchers of water, juice, homemade lemonade, accompanied by homemade cakes, cookies, loaves of bread. The spread lay waiting for guests, for children to return home to their families after school. Even now, there were small children carrying large white backpacks walking into their gardens and sitting gracefully at the tables, waiting for their mothers to pour them a glass.

The sight made my stomach churn. One day, this would be expected of me. One day, I would be one of them; pouring drinks, rearing each child to be more perfect than the last. I had never been sure I wanted children, but that wasn't my choice to make. The Emperor knew what was best, and he had deemed Alfie and I would bare three happy, healthy children one day.

I hoped they would have all of Alfie's charm, and none of my misgivings.

The Palladium building loomed ahead, reflected silver in the bright afternoon sun. Placed in the centre of our sector, it was our place of worship, the place our meetings were held, the place our Pioneers were elected, the place where defectors were publicly punished, and, on rare occasions, the place where Emperor Emercius came to speak words of wisdom and encouragement.

The windows emitted a constant warm light, they hadn't been dark since its opening. Some of our classmates were milling on the steps, chatting idly as they waited for the misery to spill from the score boards. I recognised a girl, Lillian, weeping loudly on the shoulder of her life mate. She could barely stand; her body shook with sadness, her shoulders sagged as she stumbled blindly away from the Palladium, much to the delight of the gathered crowd.

She looked up as we approached. Her red-rimmed eyes focused on me as she gave a sniff. I gave her a soft smile of encouragement; I knew how hard she'd tried. She'd taken a secretary job at the medical centre, stayed long into the night to go through patients' papers, to write reminders and organise folders. Rumour was she'd even serviced a high-ranking Pioneer to ensure her place. She was a hard-working girl, from a hard-working family. Her life mate, however, was less so.

I went to take her hand, to offer her sympathy, but something in her eyes made me stop. Amidst the sadness and the pain, there was pity. She looked upon me with pity as Alfie guided me towards the steps.

"Poor Lillian. All Viktors fault, as you can imagine. I had to report him the other day for stepping on Mrs Zanders tulips," Alfie muttered in my ear as we walked up the stairs.

As if he weren't talking about ruining their lives.

I nodded absently as I tried to understand the look Lillian had given me. I thought about the tables, about what my position on the Register would do to Alfie and I. I toyed with the sleeve of my jumper; my stomach fluttered and swayed as Alfie pushed open the large doors.

The familiar smell of apricots and burnt parchment greeted me like an old friend. At first, there was nothing but the brilliant whiteness of the lights and decor. Alfie didn't wait for me to recover, he tugged me forward through the lingering crowd. The first thing I noticed were the lights; hundreds of white, glowing orbs were suspended from the ceiling by golden wires. The lights rolled on and off much like a wave lapping at the shore. Every so often there was darkness, and then immediate light as the bulbs powered on, one by one, and as they did, they emitted a beautiful, harmonic hum, as if souls lived within. My breath caught in my throat as I stared up at them in wonder.

"Alfie," I breathed, nodded up at the beautiful artwork.

Alfie barely raised his head. His eyes flicked up and down briefly; he'd never been too interested in art, not even my own. He jerked his head to where a golden plaque was hung on the wall. On the plaque were engraved the following words;

THE LIGHTS OF LIFE

A PIECE CREATED BY ADRIELLE BRIEKS

'FEAR NOT THE DARKNESS, FOR PERFECTION IS THE LIGHT THAT GUIDES US'

My fingers grazed the immortal words as I breathed it in. Adrielle Brieks was an esteemed artist, someone I had looked up to ever since she got her placement. She was allowed entrance into the Emperor's keep, a privilege very few were given, to study the Emperor, create the beauty that he envisioned. She featured prominently in his Gallery, an honour I dreamt of having. I closed my eyes, and as I listened to the beautiful humming of the lights, I wished harder than I ever had that I would make it to the Inner Ring. That Alfie would be granted the status of Pioneer, that I would walk through the Emperor's halls and live only to create art. At least if I had that, I could be happy with the rest of the things decided for me.

"Calluna!" Alfie cried.

My eyes snapped open, and I scrambled to catch up to him. He waited with a smile just shy of the entrance to the grand hall. The large white doors had been propped open; all the other eligible couples of our year gazed up at the projected tables. There was no worry in Alfie's eyes, only excitement, and I feared that soon he would never look on me with such happiness. He raised a curious eyebrow at my hesitance, gave me an expression that bordered on ugly. I took his hand, smiled until my cheeks hurt despite the pounding of my heart. I didn't want him to see me worry.

He tugged me through the crowded bodies, each step bringing us closer to our fate. The weight of a hundred eyes was unbearable as I wove through my lifelong friends. They stared and waited for me to prove my Register like behaviour, waited for an opportunity to advance their own positions. I hung my head, tried to edge out of their view as we neared the front. I'd messed up with Carolynn, and now I had to suffer.

As with most things in Sadon, when we finally came face to face with the tables, I realised I would not suffer alone.

"That's not possible." The words left Alfie's mouth in a rush.

I stared at the tables; my heart caught in my throat.

NO 1 - WILLOW AND GIDEON

NO 2 - APHORA AND BRENDAN

NO 3 - OLIVIA AND ASTON

NO 4 - VIVIENNE AND QUINN

NO 5 - PENELOPE AND DOMER

I kept searching, and searching, past eight, past ten. My eyes raked down the list of names. Lillian and Viktor had twelfth. Milla and Bradley had thirteenth. I couldn't breathe. With every number, my heart clamoured in my ears. A flush of embarrassment drowned my cheeks and slipped down my neck.

Then, there we were.

NO 16 - CALLUNA AND ALFIE

I couldn't even look at him.

I had disgraced us both. It was near impossible to climb that many places. I had ruined his future, his dreams, for one stupid test. He would hate me, even if not overtly. I would no longer be lucky to have a life mate who loved me. No, I would be lucky to have a life mate who even talked to me after this.

After a world of silence, I risked a peek at his face. He looked at the tables with emotionless eyes, his cheek taut. His hand on mine didn't waver, but with each passing second his fingers tightened.

"Well," he paused, took a steadying breath as he finally met my eyes.

There was a conflict there, a swarm of regret and anger and pity and affection within the confines of his eyes. Whenever I looked at him, I felt inferior. He was so beautiful, and I was so painfully average. Even now, so confused and broken, he was unimaginable. Alfie looked to the crowds around us, who didn't hide their amusement at our downfall. They were a step closer to the Inner Ring themselves, they had no care for what fate fell on us.

"I suppose we better try twice as hard, darling. Do things we must. I'll talk to Doctor Lynn, reason with him about the Register. I can be quite persuasive when I want to be..." He trailed off with a charming grin that didn't reach his eyes.

I squeezed his hand, grateful he hadn't caused a scene, and planted a kiss on his cheek. His face flushed at the contact, and it was as if the last day hadn't happened at all. I suppose its cruel, to use his feelings for me against him, but sometimes it's worth being selfish to make life a little easier. For both of us.

We walked from the Palladium, our score on the tables weighed heavily on both our minds. Alfie put on a smile, he nodded and waved to all the friends we passed. He thanked the Pioneer guards who were stationed in the hall for protecting our sacred Palladium. I smiled and nodded and kept quiet. I didn't need to be outspoken, I needed to be loyal, dutiful, gentle. All the things a perfect woman should be.

Despite how the thought made my fists clench.

Alfie didn't say much to me as we walked back to our homes. Each time I looked at him, I saw the wheels turning behind his eyes. He was constantly thinking, calculating how many points we needed to gain, who we could surpass and how. I admired his determination, although it was daunting at times. He caught me looking and gave me a cheeky smile.

"Admiring my beauty?" He teased as we neared his house.

We only lived a few doors from each other, our houses identical. The same sofa and lamps adorned his living room as mine. The same white rug and white painted walls. Yet his house always seemed darker. No lights were lit to welcome Alfie home. The table in the front garden was empty and bleached yellow from the sun; it had long seen its last baked cake.

His mother wasn't much of a homemaker, she was far too busy. She spent most of her days in the Inner Ring, an information clerk at the heart of Sadon. His windows were shut tight against the world, and I felt bad for him. Alfie rarely had either of his parents to care for him. His father, much like his mother, was often away on business, and his brother was almost never home.

"You know you're always welcome at my home. Mother adores you," I tried to be subtle.

It wasn't custom for the woman to look after the man in the relationship. Once we married, Alfie would take over from my father as my protector. He would approve or decline my decisions; he would do what is right for me. Despite how awful it sounds, I longed for those days. Alfie had no intention of ordering me around, he'd never even so much as tried. Being out of my father's house, away from his rule, I would allow Alfie the illusion of power for that freedom.

Alfie shook his head politely at my invitation, and a weight lifted from my stomach that was akin to gratitude.

"That's alright darling, my father returned home," He pulled a face at the mention of his father, and I gave him a frown.

"That's great news, then. Your father is a spectacular man," I reminded him, but he simply imitated me as I said it.

"So, when did your dad get back? How was he?" I asked, tried to coax Alfie into telling me what had him so bent out of shape.

"Early morning. We waited up till two to give him a welcome home party." At the memory he rolled his eyes, "you know dear old dad. Didn't appreciate it one bit. Just waltzed in, ranting about how 'only Arthur is doing anything worthwhile' and 'I go away to sea to keep this family afloat and you can't even live up to my expectations'. He didn't even realise how stupid he sounded with the boat talk," he shrugged it off like it didn't hurt that his father saw him as a disappointment.

Alfie dreamed of a teaching position in the history department, his father dreamed of a son in the guard, just like his brother Arthur. The thought of Arthur made my lip turn down. It wasn't just that Alfie's father revered his elder

41

brother, and therefore scolded Alfie at every turn. It wasn't even that most of the time, Alfie's parents barely noticed his presence when Arthur was home. It was how deadly cold Arthur was, how sadistic, how terrifying, how… evil.

I swallowed past the sour taste in my mouth.

"So is Arthur home as well then?" I inquired out of politeness.

Although Arthur was their father's pride and joy, he took a different approach to Perfection than most. He was often rude and impolite, which was excused due to his rank in the Guard. He'd risen from Cadet to Lieutenant in the first year due to his unorthodox tactics. What he was known best for were his search and recovery triumphs. He specialised in tracking down those crazy enough to attempt escape. He often mutilated those he found; brought them back without limbs, or branded, or barely clinging to life.

I shivered at the thought, swallowed the bile that threatened to burn my tongue.

"Yeah, he came back too, but I haven't really seen him much. He was supposed to be heading out over the bridge, but he found some defectors hiding in a supply truck on its way to Slum 4. Bought them back for punishment. I think the ceremony is in a week or so. It would mean a lot if you would come." His eyes glistened with something that made my heart flutter.

I never liked going to the punishment ceremonies. Some revelled in the torture of others, made spectacular events out of it, but I had never had the stomach for it. Being branded for saying the wrong thing, killed for falling pregnant when you were allotted no children, none of it was right, and I hated going. It didn't really matter what I wanted though, I owed him this for what I had done to our future.

"Of course, Alfie. Anything for you." I promised.

He wrapped his dainty fingers around my own, mercifully didn't remark on the damage that marked me as deviant. His hair fell into his eyes, flames against white satin, charcoal lashes against chocolate eyes. His hand found my face, and he stared at me with all the love and goodness that existed in the world. His affection was pure, unbridled, so natural and real. I had wished for so long that I could look upon him with the same effortless adoration. It was cruel, how the world worked. How someone can be perfect in every way but never make your heart skip.

I leant into the strength of his hands, let out a sigh. If it weren't for Alfie, I would have lost my mind long ago. His fingers left my face and landed on my waist, and I shivered. This was the part of our situation I could never allow myself to give into. The physical side, the side that made my stomach twist. Luckily, Sadon had strict rules on celibacy, on purity.

Despite that, his grip was firm, warm. His eyes were dark, unbothered by the consequences he was tiptoeing towards. His fingers tightened on my waist, and the breath left my lips in a gasp.

"Alfie, we shouldn't." I pulled myself back, straightened out my clothes.

"You're right, of course. I would be helplessly lost without you, darling," He said, but he couldn't hide the frustration that winked in his eyes behind gilded words.

His eyes lingered on my where his hands had been only second before. He smiled the way only he could smile. With such beauty, such kindness, such light. He seemed to consider something, a brief tilt of his head, before he seized me by the wrist and kissed me.

My stomach lurched at the touch of his lips. It lasted only a few second before he pulled back, but it was enough to turn my blood to ice. I stared at him, mouth open, face burning. He shrugged at my unspoken questions, ran a hand through his hair.

"You best be off then, Calluna. Before I push our rankings right down," he pulled an overly dramatic face, and maybe I would have said more if it weren't for the neighbours who were watching from their windows.

I wanted to ask him why he'd kissed me. I wanted to ask him what he felt. I wanted to know everything, to get angry at him for kissing me without asking. I could do none of that though, so I smiled instead.

"You can be so silly, Alf." I said as I turned, waved goodbye over my shoulder.

His eyes on the back of my head burnt like fire, and I had half a mind to turn and chastise him, but Mrs Peterson had emerged onto her porch and was watching our exchange. She gripped her Commniglass in her hand; she'd seen my portrait stamped with the Registers Sigel. I gave her a large smile and waved.

"Hello Mrs Peterson, I hope you're enjoying your afternoon," I called.

She barely smiled. She nodded but didn't retreat back into her home. She watched me, just like Alfie, all the way to my front door. As I reached it, I turned and waved to them both. Alfie waved back enthusiastically; Mrs Peterson grumbled. I took both as a victory.

Chapter III

My father's study had always been my favourite room while growing up. I used to sit on his panelled floor and gaze out the glass wall at our garden. I used to watch my mother plant daisies and bluebells as my father worked at his desk. The mere thought of the room brought back the warmth of the summer sun through the glass, the smell of ink and parchment. But then I'd grown up and realised that my father was no different to the rest of Sadon.

Cold and unforgiving.

It had not changed in all these years; boxes of papers were littered across the floor, books half read were left forgotten on the side cabinet. The bookcase was overflowing, bursting at the seams. A portrait of the Emperor, beaming widely, sat opposite my father's desk, to remind him always of the great man he worked for. The smell of ink lingered heavily in the air like an expensive perfume, and my father, unchanged from the day I was born, sat hunched over his desk, scribbling away.

I lingered at the threshold, unsure of my next steps. At dinner, my mother had informed me he wanted to speak to me. He often skipped family mealtime. The plate of steak we'd had for dinner sat on the corner of his desk, untouched. My palms were clammy as I stared at the top of his head. He would have seen my position on the Register, would have received Mrs Leaths report. He was responsible for me, responsible for returning me to the light, and I could only imagine how disappointed he would be in me.

He looked up, met my hesitant stare, and I froze. I had always thought my father had the most beautiful eye modification; his pupils were the colour of tepid pond water, the colour of moss on a warm spring morning. Uniquely designed for him alone. His jaw stiffened, his brows drew down low over those beautiful eyes as he gestured me into the room. Stepping through the door, I was five years old again. I small, helpless, stupid. I was unformed and fragile, vulnerable to how he would shape me.

"Come sit, Calluna." He nodded to the chair, and I sat without further delay.

My father was a very handsome man. Although I inherited so much of my physical beauty from my mother, I shared his thick, auburn hair. Even sat behind his desk, his height was obvious. His slim shoulders tightened as he looked at me, his lips thinned as he laced his fingers together atop the desk.

"I got a very disturbing message from the Register Office," he started, each word an effort.

I squirmed under his stare, fisted my hands into my skirt. His face was scored deep with lines, his hands, calloused and worn, reached for the Commniglass by his side. He swept his hand across it, projected the message between us.

"'Dear Mr Morano, after being caught helping another student cheat in class, an examination was performed by Mrs Helen Leath, the results of which resulted in one Miss Calluna Morano being appointed a position upon the Register for the next twenty-four hours. Please find a list of appropriate punishments for you to choose from to be carried out at home. One, a series of whippings, to be dealt out over the next twenty-four hours in intervals. Two, removal of all food sources, and a tripling of all water intake. Three, isolation within a cupboard, wardrobe, or adequate hole...'" He trailed off.

I hung my head, my eyes trained on my feet. My father had always followed the letter of the law, there was no mercy, not even for his own children. I shivered at the thought of being locked in my father's cabinet; I'd been six the last time I had spent time there, and even then it had been cramped.

"My boss has requested a meeting with me, Calluna. To interrogate me on your behaviour. Do you not realise that your actions have consequences?" He didn't raise his voice, he didn't need to.

He was daunting enough as it was.

I shook my head as tears pricked my eyes. I had cost Alfie and I so much, and now my father too. A father whose stern hand had always guided me to the light.

"I tortured the truth out of a little slum boy today, Calluna; one no one else could crack. I broke his spine in three places. It should have been one of the happiest days of my life. I was set to receive an Inner Ring visitation privilege; I was going to take your mother to see the Emperor's gates. Now I'm under investigation for your actions." His voice rose despite his efforts.

He looked away from me, hissed in a breath through his teeth as he tried to compose himself.

"I can't even look at you." He spat.

"I'm so sorry Dad," I whispered as I stared at the side of his face.

His cheek tightened as he continued to stare at the garden. It was a gesture I remembered all too well, a look he always had before he had to make a hard decision.

A soft breeze tickled my arms as the sky edged towards darkness. The house was silent. My father had requested, when the study was built, for it to be completely soundproof. It was easier for him to concentrate that way. I waited for him to turn back to me, prayed for him to look at me like I was his child, not his duty. He continued to look out the window, seemingly beyond the garden fence, at something no one but him could see. Finally, he sighed, and turned back to me.

"Apologies don't fix the wrongs you have done." He reminded me.

He sighed again as he ran a hand through his hair. His fingers trembled, before he flattened them on the desk. His fingertips were stained black with ink, his nails short and well kept. He had such delicate hands, dainty and slim. They had caused so much pain, served so much justice, and today, they would do so again.

He stood; his eyes trained on the door, as if checking no one would disturb us. He clicked his fingers at me, gestured for me to stand. I did so despite the hollowness in my legs. I wiped my clammy hands down my skirt, awaited the punishment I knew was required.

"Come. Here, now." He gestured sharply to his side, and I darted around the desk, desperate to please.

I looked up at him, saw the man he was outside this house. The torturer who had volunteered to interrogate deviant children, a job not many could stomach. A killer and a hunter, a man who lived and breathed pain. The Emperor, in all his wisdom, had provided my father with punishments, and they would be served. My stomach lurched at the thought. That feeling of wrongness, that feeling that this just wasn't right, returned in full force, threatened to make me do something I would regret.

His eyes were unusually dark as he touched the top button of my shirt. His ink-stained fingers brushed against my throat, left a streak of darkness behind. He took my collar in his hand, and I closed my eyes, swallowed past my fear and submitted to whatever was about to come to me.

With one swift motion, he tore my shirt from collar to hem. The sound of my buttons falling onto the hardwood floor made me think of rain. Of the pitter patter of a light storm on a winter's day. I opened my eyes, tried to pull the torn fragments of my white shirt across my bare skin, but my father slapped my hands away.

"Hold still," he instructed.

"Exposed flesh is a sin. Our Emperor-" the words were struck from my mouth before I could finish my train of thought.

My cheek burnt as I stared up at the man who had raised me. He looked back at me with an anger I had never seen before. He no longer looked like the father who had read me the Emperor's sacred texts. He no longer looked like the father who had bandaged my knee after I fell down the stairs. He no longer looked like a man at all, but a monster. Tears wet my cheeks as he flexed his hand.

"Punishment sometimes has to lie outside the law," he replied coldly.

I shook my head. My ears were hot, my forehead slick. I opened my mouth, then closed it. The law was the law. Breaking it, no matter the reason, was beyond the Emperor's plan. He would never advise deviance.

My father pulled the shirt from my body. I didn't move, my limbs locked as goosebumps rose across my flesh. Purity, chastity, celibacy until marriage, they were the defining qualities of Perfection. He must be testing me. A test to determine my devotion to the Emperor. There could be no other reason.

"I won't allow you make a fool of me. I will not break the promises I have made to our Emperor." I turned towards the door; jaw tight despite the pain that still stung my cheek.

My father's hands clamped around the back of my neck, swung my head towards the desk so quickly the world around me blurred. My forehead met the old oak with a dull thud, and for a moment my vision was completely white. The taste of blood stained my tongue as I blinked rapidly into the parchment and ink, pain as bright as the sun rocked my whole body as I tried to rise. His hand was clasped firmly over the nape of my neck, and he held me down as I

49

struggled, confused, hurt, my head spinning. I could faintly hear him talking, but the words turned to rushing water in my ears. I tried to turn my head to look up at him, but I couldn't move.

"Stay still. I order it. If you wish to atone for your sins, you will submit," he said as he rustled through his desk draws.

"But-" He grabbed me by the hair and bought my head up, wrapped a hand around my jaw, forced my stare forward.

My eyes met the eyes of our Emperor. He stared back at me, his grin unwavering. Through the eyes of that painting, the Emperor watched over us; he watched as my father pushed something cold and metallic against my skin and pressed down hard. The tip of the penknife pierced my flesh, and I let out a scream.

"Be a good girl. The Emperor is watching," He hissed, and through the fog of pain I thought I heard amusement in his tone.

I didn't struggle. I laid very still as I stared at our Emperor. I'd heard stories, of people committing crimes in front of the Emperor's portraits. Almost instantly, a squadron of Pioneers would appear and take away the deviator. The Emperor was always watching. He watched as my father yet again sliced the blade neatly through the flesh of my back.

I looked towards the door, teeth dug into my lip to contain the screams that displeased my father so much. I kept my eyes focused on it as pain washed over me until every muscle trembled. With each passing second, I grew emptier, purged by regret and agony and betrayal. The pain was more than anything someone should be made to bare, and yet I bore it.

It slid through every fibre of my being, slipped through my veins and become a part of me that I could never erase. My fingers gripped the edge of the desk as my entire body shook, fought to lash and run. Heat rolled over my body in waves of nauseating agony, my head pulsed with the effort of keeping myself awake. His hand pressed my neck down once more, pushed my face into his papers until my breath fluttered the parchment. His fingers left smudged prints on my skin as he worked, sadistic in his art.

The door opened, and my heart filled with hope. My mother walked in and stopped dead as her eyes landed on us both. She stood there, her delicate mouth hung open. I met her eyes, mouthed the word please. My father didn't seem to notice her presence, either that or he didn't care. My mother's eyes momentarily filled with sadness, and I watched her hand twitch, as if to help me. The desk shook relentlessly as she took a step backwards. I wanted to call to her, I wanted to ask her why this was happening. I wanted to ask why father had broken the law, and why nothing was being done about it. I wanted to know if this numbness inside my chest was ever going to go away.

For an eternity, she met my gaze. Then, as if she had never seen a thing, she turned and walked away, left me to drown.

I closed my eyes against the tears that threatened to spill.

I would not let him make me weak.

I laid there and waited for it to be over. The blinding pain in my back was all I had. I could feel the strokes of letters being permanently etched into my skin. Over and over he carved away, but my mind couldn't focus on the lines long enough to decipher what he wrote.

When he finished, he pulled away and admired his handiwork. I didn't move, I wasn't sure I could. The rustle of cloth against the knife was almost inaudible over the ringing in my ears. He sat down; his knees brushed the back of my thighs. Blood pooled on the small of my back. Hot and thick it dripped down my waist to stain the table.

"I don't expect to hear that you've deviated again. You've brought great shame on this family. You're going to have to do a lot of favours for a lot of people to get back to where you were." He paused.

His words hung around my head limply. It didn't seem to matter; the life in the Inner Ring, Alfie, the tables, Olivia and our rivalry. My world had been splintered, shattered, carved apart. Failing the Emperor didn't seem important anymore. Not when he'd failed me.

I loosened my grip on the desk; my nails had broken against the wood and blood oozed from my thumbs. My legs were limp, and I was unsure whether they would carry my weight out of this prison.

"Get up," he ordered.

I tried to pull myself up from the desk despite the trembling of my limbs. My back pulsed unbearably, and I crumbled back onto the wood, whimpered despite my best efforts. My whole body throbbed; my hands shook as I pushed myself up. I wouldn't let him see how he'd broken me.

I wouldn't.

My father's papers were sprawled messily across the desk, mottled with blood; some had fallen onto the floor. An ink well had tipped over, stained both the wood and my right breast black. My father tutted at the mess, and I found some sick comfort in knowing I had messed something up for him too.

"Look what you've done." He shook his head.

My legs buckled as I bent to pick up my ruined shirt, regretted the movement as the new wound strained against the gesture, skin pulled taut. I gripped the desk to stop myself from falling.

Rise. Don't let him see you falter.

My father ignored me as he sorted through the papers on his desk, dabbed at the ink and blood with a handkerchief.

"This was my favourite." He held the cloth up and pointed to the embroidery.

"It's ruined now," He muttered sadly as he dropped it into the bin.

I stood and stared at him, swallowed the words that bubbled like acid in my throat. I looked down at my hands, at the cracked nails, at my scratched palms. Black fingerprints littered my pale skin as dark and ominous as the plague. Blood dripped down my back, and I twisted to try and trace the letters. The skin was jagged and raw, and as my fingertips grazed the wound, I let out a hiss.

He raised an eyebrow and gestured to the messy desk.

"Unless you have anything else to add, I suggest you leave me be so I can clean up this mess you've made." He nodded to the door.

I turned and looked at the Emperor's portrait; he smiled back at me. I didn't try to smile back, my hands curled at my sides. I moved to the door and stopped to look over my shoulder. My father was already scribbling away, as if I had never set foot in the study. For a moment, I could imagine I hadn't. I could feel the warmth of the sun through the windows against my skin as I read childhood stories. I could hear my father's laughter as he listened to my crazy stories.

I blinked past the memories and shut my father's study door. I stood in the corridor, on the brink of the past and the present, with the world unchanged but suddenly so different.

I could hear my mother upstairs in Lavenders room; she was reading her a story, her voice soft as cotton. I walked up the stairs towards her voice despite the pain that radiated down my spine and deep into my stomach. I stopped at the top of the stairs and peered into my sisters' room.

Lavender was tucked into bed, her dark orange hair fanned around her head in unruly waves. She grinned as my mother did the voice for the talking dog, a part she always looked forward to.

My eyes burnt as I looked at my sister. Barely ten, she was still a child. A tear ran down my cheek as I thought about her sweet laugh and her lilting voice, and about my father hurting her the way he'd hurt me. I sniffed, and Lavender looked up.

"Callie!" She called, suddenly wide awake.

My mother turned to look at me. She smiled, but her eyes were hard with pain.

"You look tired. I suppose the talk with your father went well?" Her voice wobbled on the words.

Lavender sat up, her eyes on my bare torso, her head cocked. I curled in on myself, leaned heavily on the door frame; I didn't want her to see what my father had done. My mother's gaze was unwavering, unbreakable, as if she couldn't take her eyes off of me. Off of what he'd done. Tears streamed down my face, but I smiled and nodded despite the agony and confusion that wracked my chest.

"Of course," the words were barely above a whisper, "extremely well, thank you."

My mother smiled, but I saw the unshed tears that still lingered on her lashes. Her lips parted, as if she wanted to say something. I wanted her to come to me, to hold me, to sink to her knees and cradle me and make me feel whole again. I needed her to tell me everything was going to be alright.

54

Her hand twitched, and I thought maybe she would pull me from the tumultuous waters of grief and betrayal that threatened to swallow me whole. The moment passed, and she cleared her throat, nodded to the bathroom.

"I believe Chrys is out of the bathroom now. Why don't you bathe before bed," she suggested as she turned back to Lavender.

"You can use my special flannel," Lavender offered.

I smiled, but it was broken and cracked now.

"Thank you, Lav." I paused.

I waited to see if my mother would turn back around. To reassure me. To help me understand.

She didn't.

I let my smile drop when I turned. Chrys was stood in his doorway, hair as dark as burnt wood. He held one of our towels in his hand, soaked and dripping onto the hardwood floor. We stared at each other silently as our mother's voice filled the tense air around us. He held out the towel to me, and I took it with shaking fingers. He didn't say anything, but his eyes flashed with sympathy.

He gestured for me to turn around, and I did so. He hissed as his eyes landed on my back. He reached out with tender fingertips and grazed the wound. At the slightest touch, I was back there, being sliced all over again. The pain was unbearable; my knees shook as I struggled to keep upright. He removed his hand, and I turned around just in time to catch the anger in his eyes. He smoothed his face quickly; he couldn't risk our father's wrath. He nodded me to the bathroom, gave my shoulder a gentle squeeze. There was nothing more he could do for me than show his sympathy, and I nodded my understanding despite the fact I wished he would hold me.

The bathroom air was heavy with heat, the mirror steamed up, and I was glad. I couldn't face myself, not yet. I closed the door; my fingers lingered over the lock. I had never locked the bathroom door before, I hadn't ever felt the need, but now that added security was comforting.

I locked the door, let out a shaking breath. I stripped off my tattered clothes as the bath filled; every movement sent a twinge of pain down my back so harsh it made my vision blur. I held the ruined remains of my shirt; black and red splotches mottled the once white fabric; one solitary button clung on by a thread. I took it in my fingers and pulled it free, held it in my fist so tight it punched through a layer of skin. I turned off the hot tap, didn't add any cold. I needed to burn the feel of him away.

I slipped my feet into the scalding hot water. My skin screamed at the heat, but I lowered myself into the bath regardless. As the water lapped my injured back, I let out a whimper. I bit down on my fist as tears spilled anew down my cheeks. My skin hummed as I lowered myself deeper into the water, every inch a painful reminder. I kept the button gripped in my hand as the water crept up my neck, past my ears, my cheeks, until it reached my eyes.

I took a deep breath and sunk fully into the water. All I could hear was my beating heart, thudding hard against my ribs. I laid there, alone, concealed, until my lungs burnt as much as the rest of my body. I closed my eyes and let my lungs ache. In the darkness, all I could feel was pain, and in that moment, I couldn't help but feel I deserved it. That I deserved what my father had done to me, that I deserved to be on the Register, that I deserved every horrible thing that could be thrown my way for such deviation.

I resurfaced and sat up, shook my head.

No.

What my father had done was unthinkable, was against the laws the Emperor himself had set out, and yet, under his eye, I had suffered. It was all wrong, and for the first time I did not allow myself to slip into self-blame. I let the button drop into the water as I rushed to grab a flannel. I scrubbed angrily at my blotchy skin. The inky fingerprints and splatters of blood faded, but there were bruises already beginning to surface over my arms. I didn't dare touch my back, which had begun to ease with the water.

I scrubbed and scrubbed until my skin was red and raw, and then I scrubbed some more. My skin burnt with the memory of his hand, and no matter how hard I tried, I couldn't get clean.

I screamed, threw the flannel at the wall as hard as I could. My chest heaved as the mirky water dripped down the polished tiles. I dropped my head into my hands and let the tears flow freely.

I want the world to burn. I want the world to break and suffer like I have. I want everyone, everything, to turn to ash.

I sat and cried for a few minutes, let the feelings wash over me as soothing and dangerous as waves. I allowed myself a moment of weakness, before I looked up, smoothed my face over. I stared at the wall and forced the anger, the betrayal, the weakness to fade to nothing. My chest grew empty with practiced poise, and I stood.

I climbed out of the bath, let out the red tinged water. I focused on one action at a time, moved from one to the next with rehearsed poise. I wrapped a towel around my body and walked to my bedroom, each step thoughtful. I tried to avoid the full-length mirror of my wardrobe, not ready to look at myself just yet. I turned my back on it as I towelled myself dry.

I gripped my towel tight between my fingers as I stared out into the night. Its inky darkness was somehow comforting, the few stars dull under the night clouds. I stared out at the perfect houses and felt nothing at all, and I was glad.

I turned back to the mirror and let the towel drop. I stepped closer and stared at myself. I had never seen myself naked. Even in the bath, I never spent a long time looking at my body. Exposed flesh was a sin, it was wrong to gaze upon even yourself according to the Emperor. I had once believed that; I had once believed that the law was final. Now, I stared at my bare flesh without the feeling of guilt that usually consumed me.

I traced the lines of my waist with my fingers. I was up to the Perfect standard, but I was overwhelmingly average in comparison to some. In the dim light of the moon, I explored my body. I gripped my thighs and jiggled them, traced the dimples there. I had never noticed that they were chunky, rounded, womanly even.

I pinched the fat of my stomach, the chunk of my hips. I wasn't slim, or fat, somewhere in between, just satisfactory by Sadon's standards. I avoided the part of me I couldn't even name. My breasts, which were disappointingly small, always a matter of self-consciousness. Olivia had always called me flat chested, and I had always felt lesser than because of it. I hesitated, teetered on the edge of the unknown, before I turned and looked at my back.

The flesh of my back was red and swollen, the letters scored deeply into hot skin. Just above my waist was the punishment my father had inflicted. Still oozing blood, the jagged letters read: *Disappointment*

I stared at the word for a long time. I expected tears, but none came. Finally, I turned back and stared myself in the eyes.

I could pick out a million things wrong with me, with the body they had constructed for me. I no longer felt Perfect, something inside me had broken, and now I could never go back to how things were.

My breath caught in my throat as a sudden shame washed over me. I averted my eyes from my naked body and rushed to open the wardrobe door. I pulled out a full-length white nightgown and yanked it over my head.

I didn't look into the mirror again as I climbed into bed.

Chapter IV

"Calluna! There's someone at the door for you!" My mother's voice startled me from my sleep.

I groaned into my pillow, still half caught in dreams. I closed my eyes for a few more precious seconds, sleep already trying to claw me back into darkness.

"Calluna! I've been calling you for ten minutes," My mother hissed, closer now.

I shot up, heart stuck in my throat at her sudden closeness. I winced at the pain in my back, reached back to touch the still fresh wound. Scabs had formed, but the cuts were still angry and tender. I blinked through my sleepy haze, looked out the window through bleary eyes. The sun had barely risen, the sky still grey and as sleepy as I was. I looked to the clock; 5:13.

My mother stared at me expectantly, arms folded over her chest. She looked as put together as she did any other time of the day; she was wearing a white pant suit, her dark auburn hair twisted atop her head in a delicate knot. She was so extremely beautiful that the sight of her made my heart sink in inadequacy. She tipped her head towards the door.

"Let's not keep your guest waiting." She pushed impatiently.

She walked towards the door, all grace and beauty. The sight of her retreating, the delicate lines of her back, made me think about last night and her refusal to intervene. I leant forward; my stomach squeezed at the memory.

"Mum," I called.

She stopped and turned, her face soft, but her eyes betrayed her. There was fear behind the moss green of her eyes, the knowledge of what she'd done, of what he'd put me through. That I would ask something that, as a wife, she could not answer. I grasped the duvet in my hands, and although I wanted answers, although I wanted her to console me, I knew I couldn't be selfish. She was hurting too, and I couldn't bear to deepen her pain.

"You look beautiful today," I smiled.

She nodded, but I could see in her face she was not happy. She looked deflated, like a balloon left in the sun; flat and lifeless. She bent down, kissed me lightly on the top of the head. I closed my eyes as she held my face in her hands.

"Thank you. Now come on, your friend is waiting," she whispered.

I opened my eyes and stared up at her as if I was five years old again. I longed for her to hold me, to sing me to sleep, to brush my hair and patch up my wounds, but I was not a child anymore.

She stroked my cheek with her thumb, then turned and promptly left. I waited, savoured the comfort of my sheets. If I stayed in bed, I wouldn't have to face the day. If I stayed in bed, I wouldn't have to pretend to everyone I loved that everything was normal. If I stayed in bed, maybe I could pretend that what had happened last night was all a terrible dream.

I knew though, no matter what I did, the events of last night would remain unchanged.

I got out of bed and the ache in my back reminded me of that very fact. I rushed to pull on my most full coverage clothes; a high necked, long sleeved, buttonless white blouse and a pair of wide legged trousers. Professional and respectable, sure to pull us up at least one place in the tables. I pulled my thick hair up into a ponytail, too tired to bother with anything intricate. I didn't check my appearance in the mirror, it just didn't seem to matter anymore.

I was surprised at who I found waiting for me at the bottom step. Polly stood fidgeting in the hallway; her eyes kept darting to my father's study door, which was locked shut. When she heard me coming, her eyes flicked up, and she pulled the smallest of smiles.

"What are you doing here so early?" I asked.

I had expected Alfie, here at the crack of dawn with a crazy scheme to get us back to the top three. I hadn't thought Polly would come knocking; we hadn't walked to school together since her sister went missing.

"I thought it would be nice to take an early morning stroll. Two best friends, in polite company." Her words were forced into lightness.

Her face betrayed her. There was a feral franticness that stopped any questions in my throat. Her face, paler than usual, was almost skeletal. She looked hungry, tired, like she was just barely hanging onto life. Her hands were balled at her sides, but I could still see the scratches on her arms.

"Alright, as long as we stop for breakfast on the way," I joked, tried to lighten the mood.

Polly just nodded; her bottom lip stuck between her teeth. My mum came from the kitchen with a glass of water in hand. She smiled kindly at us both.

"Don't forget to have a drink before you go." She held the glass out to me.

I was about to take it when Polly gripped onto my wrist.

"We've got to go, Mrs. Morano. Thank you for having me," Polly said hurriedly as she tugged me towards the door.

I stumbled, tried to keep up with her as she rushed down my front garden.

"I was thirsty," I complained as she let go of my wrist.

Polly shook her head, her jaw tight.

"Just… come on," she said as she walked down the street.

I followed, confused beyond anything. Polly had always been odd, but this was out of the ordinary, even for her. She was on a mission, each step full of purpose, her eyes narrowed at the pavement in thought. She didn't look at me as we made our way through the labyrinth of streets. I wasn't sure where we were going, but it seemed Polly knew. It wasn't until we turned onto Plythe Street that I realised our destination.

The graveyard loomed in front of us, its glimmering white gates locked. We stood in front of them and stared through the bars at the white and gold tombstones. I looked over at Polly, expected her to be sad. She had never bought me here, to the place her sister was buried.

"Polly…" I broached, but she turned and walked down the edge of the fence as if I wasn't even there.

I followed her in silence, something about the silence of the graveyard commanded mutual muteness. Polly came to a stop next to a large bin, turned it over as if she had done this a hundred times before. She climbed on top and pulled herself up over the fence. She paused as she straddled the fence and looked down at me as if only just remembering she'd bought me along.

"It's easy," she encouraged, held out her hand for me to take.

I hesitated. The punishment for getting caught would be severe, double because of my position on the Register, and I couldn't risk jeopardizing mine and Alfie's future any further. Yet I couldn't deny my curiosity. Something in Polly's face, an urgency, a desperation, made up my mind.

I took her hand and hauled myself up onto the bin. I jammed one of my feet into the fence and managed to pull myself up, teeth gritted through the pain in my back and the weakness of my arms. We faced each other, and for the first time in a long time there was a hint of happiness on Polly's face. She smiled at me, a remnant of who she had been before her sister died. Her smile faltered as she looked back out at the graveyard, and the old her vanished as quickly as it had come. She jumped down from the fence, and I followed suit.

The morning was unusually cold, a soft breeze rustled the leaves in the great maple trees surrounding the lot. I shivered as we walked past the dead. I looked at the back of Polly's head; her hair was dishevelled from the climb, and I saw bruises around the nape of her neck. I pulled at the collar of my own blouse and wondered how many of my classmates had injuries like ours. How many felt the way I felt now.

Polly stopped, stared at the grave in front of her. I followed her gaze, and my heart sunk.

Here lies Klio Kane

Beloved Daughter and Sister

Taken too young by our worst enemies

May the Emperor give her peace.

Polly stared at her sister's grave; a small bouquet of daisies laid against it. I expected her eyes to water, for her to burst into tears and wail, for grief to spill down her cheeks as harshly as blood.

Her expression didn't change.

I reached out and took her hand, gave it a squeeze. She looked up at me, her face twisted into ugly anger. She yanked her hand out of mine.

"It's a lie," She hissed.

She jerked her chin towards the grave, her eyes ablaze with fury.

"What it says, on the grave. It's not true," She spat.

I rushed to calm her, stepped forward and took her shoulders in my hands. I forced her to look at me.

"Your parents loved her. No matter what the rumours are, I know they loved her, just as they love you, Pol," I assured, but she was barely listening.

"Not that. The Mai-Coh didn't take her. The Pioneers did," she hissed.

Polly had always been a conspiracy theorist; a sniffer dog on the lookout for trouble. Despite what had happened last night, despite the pain that had planted itself deep in my gut, I couldn't bring myself to believe that the Emperor would lie about Polly. He didn't make a habit of killing perfectly good young women. Their fates were often the Riven Dens.

"Polly, you know the Mai-Coh took and killed Klio. They sent a ransom letter to the Emperor-" She cut me off with a short, angry scoff.

"They lied, Calluna. They lied! Klio found out something she shouldn't have, and they killed her for it." She hissed.

I stared at her, unsure what to say. I had seen her be many things; crazy, uncontrollably emotional, inconsolable, but I had never seen the loathing in her eyes that I saw now.

"Why would the Emperor lie?" It was the only thing I could think to say.

Polly turned to me and fixed me with narrowed eyes. She looked unpleasantly surprised.

"Are you serious? He needed someone to take the fall for Klio's murder, and the Mai-Coh are the perfect scapegoat." She looked me up and down as if I were some stupid, foolish child, before she returned her gaze back to her sister's grave.

"They killed her, the Emperor and his men, and now I know why," as she said this, she pulled out the book I had seen her reading yesterday.

She held it close to her body as she continued to stare at the grave. I fidgeted, peaked over my shoulder at the gates. Sooner or later, the grounds keeper would come, and we would be found trespassing. My time on the Register wasn't up, and I couldn't bear the thought of any more punishment.

"We should go," I took a step back, but it didn't look like Polly had heard a word.

She stroked the book as one solitary tear fell down her ivory cheeks. She wiped it away as she unravelled the book from its casings.

"When Klio was taken they swept her room. Tore it apart. Took most of her things to the labs," she opened the book and let her fingers graze the pages.

"It didn't even smell like her in there anymore. I... I like to lie in her bed sometimes when I really miss her. Mum screams at me for it, but I do it anyway."

She paused to look back at the grave momentarily, and I wished I could help her with her pain. Klio had been an intelligent, kind young woman. A little off, like Polly, but a good person. Her disappearance had rocked the Hollow to its core. I couldn't imagine losing Chrys, or Lavender. The grief, the sadness, the never-ending pain.

"About a week ago, I felt something in the mattress. I took off the sheets and turned the thing over. I almost crushed myself underneath the damn thing. There was a slit, one they must have missed. This fell out." She gestured to the book.

I could already see Klio's messy handwriting scrawled over the bright white pages. My chest lurched as I realised what it was, and I reached out once again to take Polly's hand. This time she let me, and there was silence between us.

"So, I read it," she said it so simply, as if she wasn't talking about reading her dead sisters diary.

"What did it say?" I said, unable to contain the question.

I knew whatever was in that diary would be trouble, or Polly wouldn't be showing it to me. In that small white book was the reason Polly was so sure Klio had been killed by our own Emperor.

"I... I can't say. If you knew, they'd come after you too. But... I need to ask a favour of you. I need you to take it," She held the book out to me.

"Polly, no one is coming after you, and the Mai-Coh killed your sister, not the Emperor. We should go," I turned and went to walk away.

She ran to catch up to me, flung herself in my path. I folded my arms, observed her desperation carefully. If she wasn't going to tell me what was in that book, then why tell me any of this?

"Look, I know this is weird, but you need to take this. I don't think it's safe with me anymore. Please, Calluna. You're my only friend," she begged.

I hesitated, looked at the pages, so tempting with their mystery. My fingers itched to take it, rip it open and pour over its secrets, but if Polly thought it wasn't safe with her, then it would surely get me in trouble too. I couldn't afford any more trouble.

"I don't want any part of your conspiracy theory. I won't do that to Alfie," I said, but she shook her head.

I tried to move past her, but she placed her hands on my shoulders, forced me to halt. In the distance, the hum of an approaching Hovear broke the peaceful morning. I shot her a look and tried to move forward again, but she refused to budge.

"Please. Calluna, please. Can't you trust me? Please, just take it and hide it. Please," she pleaded.

She pushed the book into my chest. The hum of the Hovears engines grew louder as it drew near. I debated for a second or two, tongued the inside of my cheek as I tried to decide what was best. I looked into Polly's desperate, frightened eyes, and seized the book.

"Fine. Fine, but we really need to go," I nodded towards the fence as Polly exhaled in relief.

We moved to the large tombs near the entrance of the graveyard, carved from alabaster. We hid, our breaths rapid as the Hovear pulled to a stop outside the looming gates. A short man in a bright white shirt and tie eased out of the vehicle. He whistled as he twirled the keys around his fingers, head bent low as he walked. He unlocked the gates, ambled down the path towards the other end of the plot where the maintenance equipment was kept.

Polly and I darted out of the gates and didn't stop running until we were a few streets away, legs filled with acid. We slowed to allow ourselves to catch our breaths. I clutched the book in my hand. It was like electric between my fingertips, dangerous and powerful. I looked down at it and found myself drawn once more to its contents. Polly caught me looking and gave a smile that didn't reach her eyes, pushed a loose strand of hair behind her ear as she cast her eyes back to the pavement.

"I know it's tempting, but you can't read it. It's not safe for you. I just need you to look after it for a couple days until they stop watching me," she said.

I nodded despite the curiosity that had wormed its way inside my brain and pushed the book into my bag. I could feel its presence even out of sight, like the burring heat of a fire in a hearth. It laid in my bag like a weight, but I pushed down the temptation to pull it out. The thinness of Polly's wrists, the sunken circles of her eyes, told me that whatever was in there wasn't worth the risk.

We walked to school without another word about the diary. We chatted, but nothing we said was of any importance. She talked about her mother and father considering an appeal of their marriage, but this was their third try, and nothing looked promising. I talked about what I ate last night. Polly was the only person I trusted, but I couldn't tell her about what had happened in my father's study.

Some things were better left unsaid.

When we arrived at school, Alfie was waiting for me. He beamed when he saw me, but his smile faded when he saw Polly.

"Hey." He looked between us and raised a brow.

"Your mother told me you left early this morning," He continued with a confused look.

I kissed him on the cheek to ease his annoyance. Polly's eyes moved frantically between us, considering whether she should have trusted me. Whether I'd tell Alfie.

"Polly and I took a morning stroll. Two best friends, out in public. I thought it would be good for people to see." The lie was so smooth it surprised me.

He nodded as he stroked my ponytail, gave it a gentle tug. He took in my outfit, ran his fingers along the collar of my shirt.

"You look lovely today," he said.

69

Heat rushed into my cheeks as his fingers brushed my neck and travelled down my back. I closed my eyes as my heart thrashed erratically against my ribs. I couldn't let him find out; I couldn't let him know I was marred. Fear struck me harder than my father had the night before. I flinched away from Alfie's hand, played it off by straightening my trousers. Polly had been silent up until this point, but the gesture made her open her mouth.

"I should go. We should talk after school, alright?" She squeezed my wrist between her fingers.

I saw in her eyes that she could sense something was wrong, and I was grateful. I nodded, enough of a reassurance for her to walk away.

"Goodbye to you too, Polly," Alfie called over his shoulder, pulled a face.

He turned back to me and held out his arm.

"Shall we?" He grinned, but today, his smile didn't ward off the darkness that clouded my mind.

Chapter V

The diary occupied my every thought. As the days passed by, I found myself sitting and staring at it for hours. I had tried to hide it in the depths of my wardrobe, but every time I opened the doors it beckoned me with a sultry voice.

Read me. Come on, you know you want to. Think of what lies beneath these pages. Read me, Calluna.

I hid it between the slats of my bed, but every time I laid down it burnt into my spine as hot as the knife my father had wielded.

I even tried to hide it in the garden amongst the tallest bushes that my mother had not yet got round to trimming, but every time I looked out the window my eyes were drawn to where it sat.

When I had run out of ideas, I took to keeping it by my side. I slept next to it in bed, so that maybe by some sort of osmosis I would gain access to its information without breaking my promise. I kept it in my bag at school. I took it on walks and stroked its pages as I sat in the park.

Damn, I'm going crazy.

Polly hadn't spoken to me since. She'd ignored my numerous messages via Commniglass. Yesterday, she had missed school. When I went to her house, her mother had barely opened the door. She'd told me Polly had come down with the flu, but I could hear the scratching of nails against wood in the background, the whimper of a trapped animal. I had turned away without further questions, clutched the diary tightly in one hand as tears burnt behind my eyes.

I sat in bed, the diary on my chest, barely visible in the dim night. I stared at its silky wrappings, tinted silver in the moonlight, and my fingers twitched involuntarily. I had never felt so strongly about anything in my life. I knew it wasn't perfect to want something so badly, I knew it wasn't perfect to keep secrets either, but it no longer seemed important what was perfect or not.

As I stared at the diary, I heard a low mewl. I waited, squinted into the darkness. It came again, a pained whimper, followed by the sound of something hard hitting something soft. As I continued to listen, I realised that the crying was coming from my parents' room. I frowned at the wall that stood between me and them, squinted until my vision fizzled with spots, as if by some miracle I'd be able to see through the stones. My father and mother were the perfect couple, they always had been, but that didn't mean my mother was free from his temper. As long as the bruises were covered, it didn't seem to matter to anyone else what he did to her.

My bedroom door swung open, and I rushed to push the diary under my mattress. Lavender traipsed into my room, stuffed bunny in hand.

"Daddy's punishing mummy again. Can I stay in here with you?" She asked.

I nodded as my heart leapt into my throat, the diary barely hidden. I scooted up the bed and Lavender eased next to me. She was so small, so fragile. Her shoulders were slim, I could have wrapped my fingers easily around both of her wrists. She settled into my shoulder and wrapped her arms around me, and I stroked her hair. It had been a long time since we'd shared a bed. She'd always come in when we were younger; I would tell her stories and she would fall asleep, and I would have to carry her back to her own room. I missed those day. Simpler days.

"What do you mean again, Lav?" I asked.

Lavender looked up at me, her large grey eyes shining. I had always thought she was untouchable by reality. That she lived in some separate sphere, away from all the evil and darkness that plagued the rest of us. Yet here she was, tears in her eyes, cowering as our mother was being hit.

"He does it a lot. I can't sleep when he does," she stated plainly as if this was common knowledge.

I pulled her tightly to my chest and held her as my mother's whines filled the house. Her bony elbows pressed into my stomach, and revulsion rose in my chest at the thought of her suffering through this night after night.

Another reason to hate him.

After a minute or two, my door opened again, and Chrys wordlessly slipped into bed behind me. As his knee brushed my back I flinched out of habit. The letters had puckered; scabbed, oozed, burned as it healed, but the pain had almost dissipated. I moved up so he could edge in.

All three of us huddled under my duvet, tried to soothe away the pain of hearing our mother's cries.

"Tell us a story, Callie," Lavender whispered as she sniffed.

I looked to Chrys. He was bathed in shadow, but I saw the tears in his eyes. Reflected in the moonlight the weight of his own secrets was blinding. There was a fear of our father there too, that one day he would be subjected to the same fate as my mother, the same fate as me. I reached for his hand and gave it a squeeze. He held on tightly as he put his other arm around the both of us. I turned back to Lavender, wiped away her tears and forced a smile.

"Alright. What do you want to hear about tonight?" I asked.

She thought on it long and hard, chewed on her bunnies' ears, before she cracked a genuine smile.

"I want to hear about the Emperor's conquest," she said.

73

I hesitated. Everything Polly had said, what my father had done to me, what he was doing to my mother right now, it made me question things I never had. I didn't want to talk about how the Emperor had saved us, had given us the gift of perfection, when my mother was being beaten by my perfect father. Lavender looked up at me expectantly, and Chrys gave my shoulder a reassuring squeeze.

"Sure Lav." I said as she sunk deeper into the sheets, closed her eyes in anticipation.

"Once, a long time ago, our world was broken. The men and women in power only wanted to kill each other, they wanted to take each other's lands, and they didn't care how they did it. They built weapons so large they could be seen from space. They filled the air with toxic gas from their tanks and their bombs. The people starved as the soldiers burnt down their homes. Our people wept into the bodies of their loved ones, and their cries were so loud, our Emperor heard them across the galaxy." I paused as Lavender yawned and fidgeted.

She rolled onto her side, wrapped her arms more tightly around my waist. Warmth spread through my chest as I watched her eyelids flicker. I bent and kissed her forehead and she smiled, gave me a nudge to prompt the continuation of my story.

"The Emperor was moved by our struggle and called all his people to come to our aid. When he arrived at our world, he was met with hostility. Our people, the pure and perfect, rejoiced at his presence, but the others, the leaders, and the dark followers, the Mai-Coh, they didn't want to be saved. They enjoyed destruction, they revelled in death and bathed in the blood of their enemies-" Chrys elbowed me in the back and I let out a whine as my scabs crack under the pressure.

Blood trickled from the wound anew, and I shifted uncomfortably as Chrys shook his head. A warning. Lavender would be told the true gory parts of this story

74

soon enough, she would see the videos in class of the dead Pioneers on the field.

"The Emperor tried to reason with the Mai-Coh, to come to an agreement, but they were ruthless, and they killed many of his brothers and sisters. The Emperor wept for fifteen days and fifteen nights at the cruelty of our world and made a promise to liberate us. The Liberation War raged for years. The leader of the Mai-Coh rode into battle on the back of a large wolf, and won many battles with his wild magic and brethren. Finally though, a man rose from the ashes to end it all. Sadon Yen, a simple carpenter, charged into battle with only a spear that he had fashioned from the bones of his dead wife and children-" there was another elbow to my spine, but I ignored him this time.

"and killed the leader of the Mai-Coh in one swoop. The battle was won, the war was over. Most of the Mai-Coh were captured, tortured and killed in public for their crimes, but some managed to escape past the wilderness. Sadon Yen was the first man to receive the eye modification, to bring him into the realm of the perfect for his bravery. The Emperor named our new city after him, and gave him his own land, which became the Yen district of the Inner Circle. The Emperor has been protecting us from imperfection ever since," I finished, and Lavender snored.

Chrys stretched behind me, groaned as his joins clicked. He too looked at Lavenders sweet, sleeping face and shook his head.

"We have to protect her," He whispered.

Silence had fallen in the house. I played with a lock of her hair as I thought on the story I had just told. All we had ever been taught was that the Emperor loved us, that he cared for us, wanted nothing but perfection for us. How could I believe that after what had happened with my father? How could I believe any of it?

75

"The Emperor will protect her," the words left my mouth out of habit.

There was a long silence between us as we thought about the words I had spoken. I turned my head to look at Chrys more clearly. He was deep in thought, his eyes distant. His jaw clenched, a seriousness that didn't suit his youth, before he turned his gaze back to me. He looked me in the eyes and I felt safe. He took me in his arms and held me against his chest, and before I knew it I was crying.

I wept as silently as I could, but strangled sobs escaped my lips no matter how hard I tried to contain them. I clung to him, listened to the steady thump of his heart, the rise and fall of his chest. He was alive, he was safe, at least for now.

Chrys pulled back and held my shoulders steady. I sniffed as my final tears fell. My eyes were swollen and sore, my nose ran, and my cheeks were raw, but I didn't care.

Screw perfection.

"You need to make it to the Inner Ring. Take Lavender with you. Okay?" He asked, and when I didn't reply, he gave me a shake.

"I can't leave you here," I said as I wiped my nose on the back of my hand.

He shrugged.

"I'll be fine. I've got people to take care of. I'll be out of here in no time, but you need to get to the Inner Ring. If you stay in the Hollow, you're never going to escape him," he told me.

I nodded, unsure what else to say. He didn't know how far Alfie and I had dropped down the tables, but mentioning it wouldn't help either of us.

When Chrys was satisfied that I understood, he nodded and stood. He moved around the bed, scooped Lavender up in his arms. He walked towards the door, gave me one last look. He looked so much older than fifteen, and I wondered what had happened to him that had forced him to age, and why I hadn't noticed before.

Maybe I had been too blind and selfish to care.

He left, closed the door behind him. I laid back in the bed and stared at the ceiling with a renewed determination. Chrys was right, all I had to do was get to the Inner Ring, and things would be alright.

They had to be.

~

I sat at breakfast, pushed my muesli round my bowl as I glared at my father across the table. He was reading through a notebook, pencil balanced behind his ear thoughtfully. My mother had her back to us at the sink as she scrubbed at the dirty plates. Her red hair fell down her back and around her face, and she wore multiple layers of full coverage clothing. Despite how hard she had tried, the bruises that circled her neck in the shape of hands was too evident to miss.

"Mummy, are you sick?" Lavender asked as she munched on her toast.

Our mother stopped scrubbing the plate in her hand. She didn't turn to face us.

"Mummy's got the sniffles, hunny. She's staying home today," our father replied, not bothering to look up from his notebook.

Lavender looked at mum with worried eyes. I sat up straighter in my chair and put on a smile.

"It's alright Lav, mummy will be just fine in a few days, won't you mum?" I addressed her back, my tone sharper than I intended.

77

My mother nodded. Lavender didn't seem convinced, but she went back to eating her toast anyway. I reached across the table and gave her cheek a reassuring squeeze. She attempted a smile, but the expression fell flat. Desperate to prove I could conquer the gloomy mood that had settled over the breakfast table, I tried to address my father.

"So, Alfie invited me to Arthur's award ceremony tonight. We should all go," I looked to Chrys for support, and he nodded despite his mouth full of porridge.

We had to get out of this house. If we could just spend a few hours out, then maybe my father would spare my mother. Maybe he would get too caught up in the punishment of others to hurt any of us.

"It's been a long time since we went out as a family," Chrys added, sprayed porridge across the table.

My father nodded without looking up from his work.

"Yes. Well, some of us have more pressing matters to attend to. You two may go. Your mother, Lavender and I will stay home," he decided.

My hands balled into fists on the tabletop. I wouldn't leave Lavender here with him alone. Not when he was so consistently letting his punishments fall outside the law. He had never raised a hand to her, but I didn't put it past him.

I looked to Chrys, who shook his head ever so slightly, asking me not to challenge him. I couldn't help it.

"But Lavender has never been to an awards ceremony before, and you know how much Alfie loves her-" my father raised his hand up to silence me.

I closed my mouth as he finally lowered his book and fixed me with a hard stare. My stomach twisted into unfathomable knots; my head spun at a dangerous speed. All I could think about was the feel of oak against my cheek, the searing pain of betrayal and sadism in my back, the smell of parchment and blood. I averted my gaze to ward off the surfacing memories.

"Do not test me, Calluna. You and Chrys will go alone, and you will represent our family name. You will act accordingly, and maybe you'll be able to climb those places you lost in the tables," he reminded me, and I felt Chrys staring at me across the table.

I didn't look at either of them. I wanted to argue further, but then there was a hand on my shoulder, and I looked up to find my mother standing over me. Her eyes were red rimmed, and one was beginning to grow dark with a bruise. Her lip was split on one side, and the bruise I had spotted earlier on her neck spread endlessly under the neck of her blouse. I swallowed the horror that rose in my throat and tried to act as if nothing was wrong.

For the sake of all of us.

"Listen to your father. He always knows what's right," She shot me a look I didn't quite understand, but it stopped any further complaints I had.

I nodded wordlessly before I stood up. I could no longer look upon my mother's bruises or tolerate my father's scolding.

"I'm off to school," I announced, all efforts of cheeriness gone.

As soon as I was out of my house and on the street I released a breath, flattened my shaking hands on my thighs. I walked instinctively to Alfie's house, needed the comfort of his easy-going personality.

As I walked up his front garden, I saw his house as I had rarely seen it before. In the living room Alfie and Arthur were watching a projection from a Commniglass as they demolished their cereal. They commented on whatever they were watching animatedly, laughed and jeered like the best of friends. Through the glass front door I saw his mother in

79

the kitchen, preparing lunch bags. She was wearing a beautiful dress, one clearly made in the Inner Ring, already dressed for Arthur's award ceremony. It was the most exquisite thing I had ever seen, encrusted with small diamonds and pearls. Although I couldn't see Alfie's dad, I could hear him, shouting down the stairs for one of his favourite ties. It was strange, seeing it so full of life.

I lingered on his porch, unsure whether to knock. His family didn't like me much. They didn't know me, but they'd already made up their minds. They were never around, and when they were, they didn't usually like to host guests. His mother always tried to put on a show of affection, but she was as cold as the fridge she was pulling butter out of.

Alfie looked to the window and spotted me loitering on the threshold. He beamed, gestured for me to come in.

I smiled nervously, raised my hand in a half wave, then kicked myself for looking so stupid. I tried to steady myself, my lungs burnt from holding my breath as my hand hovered over the doorknob. I knew I had to enter, and yet it was as if my blood had turned to ice. They would have seen my status on the Register, they would have seen how far we had fallen. They would blame me, and rightly, for ruining their sons' chances. I didn't want to face the dark hatred in their eyes and the venom in their voices, not today. I swallowed hard, allowed my fingers to rest on the handle, and opened the door.

Mrs. Clarke looked up instantly; a wolf alerted to the proximity of prey. She looked surprised to see me, her nose pulled up in dislike, her brow crinkled, before she put on a fake smile and strode towards me, arms open.

"Calluna. How lovely to see you! Come in, come in," she said, her tone too high and pleasant to be genuine.

She threw her arms around me, smothered me against her large, perfumed breasts. I managed to wrap my arms around her for only a second before she pulled back and took my face in her hands. She tilted my head side to side, inspected me. Her eyes were sharp, watchful, and despite the pleased hums she let out, I saw the waves of anger and blame that toiled behind her perfect mask.

"My my aren't you shaping up to be a beautiful young woman. What a terrible shame about that business with the Register," she tutted as she gave my cheek a slap.

I resisted the urge to snap as my cheek stung. I balled my hands behind my back, dug my nails into my palms until my eyes watered to keep myself from lashing out at her. My father had raised hell in my veins this morning. My limbs shook with the effort to contain all the feelings that spiralled in my chest.

"Yes, well I'm off it now, and don't intend to be back on it again," I reassured her, the edge to my voice sharp enough to cut through flesh.

She laughed, a condescending, belittling smile that made my toes curl in my shoes. I could picture it; lunging at her, slapping her back. The image frightened me, the clarity of it, the viciousness of it. Alfie's mother had always irritated me, but never tempted me to break the law. I wondered if maybe who I had been, the simpering, quiet, just-trying-to-get-by girl I was, had died on my father's desk, and what had risen in my place was something unknown and rough and filled with fire.

"Oh my dear no one intends to be on the Register, do they. Some of us are just more suited to Perfection than others." She gave my nose a tap as Alfie emerged into the corridor, and I was glad for the interruption.

I didn't know how much longer my patience would last.

"Stop fussing over her mum, she's not five anymore," Alfie swooped in, slipped his hand in mine, and I quietly thanked anyone who might be listening that he'd come.

She cooed over Alfie, took his face in her hands and squeezed his cheeks. Alfie rolled his eyes, allowed himself to be subjected to her affection in the name of sparing me. I watched it with absent emptiness. It had been a long time since anyone had fussed over me.

"My baby is all grown up. You better take care of him, Calluna, or I'll have to make a complaint," she laughed loudly, but her eyes conveyed the severity of her words.

Mr. Clarke came clambering down the stairs, held a tie in either hand. He looked flustered, his brown hair uncombed, his round face flushed.

"Silvia, which tie is better?" He asked, then his eyes landed on me.

He pulled that same, displeased face, before he forced a tight-lipped smile. Mrs. Clarke had always been better at faking it than he had.

"Calluna," he acknowledged my presence sternly, "are you here to walk with Alfie to school?" The mention of school gave me the excuse to leave I had been looking for.

I grabbed Alfie by the arm and managed to smile genuinely.

"Yes! Yes, we better be going. We don't want to be late," I tried to pull Alfie towards the door, desperate to get out of this poisonous house, but he pulled in the opposite direction.

"Yes, well you made sure Alfie can't make a single mistake with that deviation in class. It'll be hard enough to make up the places you lost him," Arthur said.

The Clarke family fell silent as I stared back at Arthur. He leant languidly against the living room door, challenged me with his stare. He had gotten much bigger since the last time I had seen him. His shoulders were so broad it was a miracle he could even fit through the doorframes. He'd grown at

82

least an inch or two, and he now towered over Alfie. His face was sharper, more defined, as were his muscles. His daunting presence, however, was unchanged from the day we first met.

I swallowed down the words that threatened to end everything I had worked so hard to achieve, bit my tongue. Arthur raised an eyebrow, the corner of his mouth turned up in amusement at my speechlessness. Mrs. Clarke looked between the two of us as she ran her hands over her dress, smug that her brute of a son had silenced me. Mr. Clarke had the faintest of smiles on his lips as he observed his Lieutenant son. Alfie moved towards his brother and gave him a hard slap on the back, ever the peace maker.

"And how many places did you lose when you threw that kid across the field?" Alfie reminded him.

Arthur smiled at the memory, threw an arm round Alfie's neck, pressed against his windpipe. Alfie elbowed Arthur in the stomach, broke free of his grasp with a grin. Mrs. Clarke fussed around the both of them as they stared to brawl in that way only brothers can.

"Boys! Not in the house," She begged as Arthur tripped Alfie to the ground.

Alfie spluttered, laid on the carpet breathlessly. Arthur held out his hand to help him up, and Alfie took it. The brothers smiled at each other, and Arthur returned the slap on the back that had begun it all.

"I'll make a man of you yet," Arthur praised, but Alfie rolled his eyes as he grabbed his bag.

"What am I now then, a woman?" Alfie jested as he came back to my side.

He kissed me on the cheek, brushed a stray strand of hair behind my ear. I managed a smile, but my eyes never left Arthur, who watched us with growing annoyance.

"Near enough," Arthur muttered as he folded his arms.

He stared at me again, but there wasn't the same hostility this time. Alfie always managed to drag out the smallest sliver of light from within Arthur's black depths.

"Go on, before you're late," Arthur nodded to the door.

Mrs. Clarke ran to the kitchen and came back with lunch for Alfie. She gave him a kiss on the head, before she stood next to Arthur. Mr. Clarke chose a tie, and fixed Alfie with a pointed look.

"Don't be late tonight, son. It's a very proud moment we're going to share," He reminded him.

Alfie nodded, stood taller as he addressed his father. His arm fell from around my shoulders, and he held his head up high. I couldn't help hating Mr. Clarke then, for what he made Alfie. I hated the way Alfie grew so distant in his presence, I hated the way that no matter what he did, it wasn't enough. I cut Mr. Clarke with my stare, hoped he saw how I loathed him.

"Yes sir. I won't disappoint."

Chapter VI

No one could concentrate at school that day, there was too much excitement surrounding the Ceremony tonight. Both teachers and students alike gave up on professionalism and opted for a day of Appraisal meeting practice. I managed mine well, answered the questions perfectly, but at the end Mrs. Leath reminded me that my previous position on the Register would influence the overall results. The Appraisals were the last option to bring up your scores on the boards, and despite the endless practice with Alfie, I knew that there would be more scrutiny that usual.

Polly hadn't come to school. I'd stared at her empty chair until my eyes burnt with fear. I wanted to believe that she was ill, that her mother was making her soup and wrapping her in blankets. I wanted to believe so badly that she was hunched over the toilet spilling her guts into it, but there was a part of me that kept repeating: *they know, they know.*

I stood in the kitchen, flour caked over my clothes and hands as I proceeded to make the fifth Victoria sponge of the day. The ceremony invitation stipulated that it was a cake party, and therefore there I was, batter under my nails, sweat on my brow as I mixed in the last of the flour. Lavender was at the table, icing the cakes that had cooled, licking jam off her fingers excitedly, and Chrys was putting each finished cake into a box.

"Don't you think you're going a bit overboard?" Chrys asked as I poured the mixture into a cake tin.

I shook my head, wiped my forehead with my shoulder as I scraped the last dregs of mixture out of the bowl. I needed to go above and beyond if I wanted to get Alfie and I to the Inner Ring. We'd already climbed from No. 15 to No.11, and as I stood here shoving the cake into the oven,

Alfie was across the street helping Mrs. Peterson move around the furniture in her living room.

"I want to do my best. I want to be the best for our Emperor," I said plainly, the words like ash in my mouth.

Despite all that had happened, I knew I had to keep up appearances. There was no telling who was listening at any given time, and the paranoia of it all was causing a thundering headache to batter my temples. I sipped at my water, and as the water slipped down my throat, my vision wobbled. I gripped the counter, blinked through the spots in my vision as the roiling rage that had burnt my throat quelled. I tried to clutch at it, summon it back, but it slipped through my fingers like silk, left me feeling deflated and smooth.

"Done! I wish I could come," Lavender whined as she passed the cake to Chrys.

I went over to her and smoothed a hand over her hair, tried to concentrate on the flutter of her lashes over what my father might do to her in my absence. She giggled, her mouth covered in icing and jam, face sticky with her mischief. I took my sleeve and wiped her clean as she squirmed. Mother walked into the kitchen, her face half hidden behind her hair. She looked me up and down and gave me a frown.

"Shouldn't you be getting ready? You don't want to be late," she moved past me and began to wipe down the kitchen counters.

"Just finishing up, need to wait for this last cake," I said.

She didn't look at me as she filled the sink with water. She looked frail, broken, the bruises on her arms had grown in multitude and severity. It hurt to see her that way, it hurt to think that because of what I had done, she was being punished.

"Mum…" I moved towards her and took her arm in my hand, desperate to say something, to say anything that would make it better.

She turned and gave me a look that stopped me dead in my tracks. Her eyes were wild with fear as she shushed me; a feral, wounded animal chained in the cold. Her hands found my own, her nails dug into my wrists.

"Don't," she hissed. "He'll hear you."

Her eyes flicked over my shoulder, watching for him, before she met my eyes again.

"Don't say anything, or he'll come for you again," she whispered.

My stomach twisted at her warning. I pulled my hands from hers, met her eyes with an intensity that made her skirt my gaze. Where was this protective streak when he was mutilating me? Where were her warnings at the dinner beforehand? I took her chin between my fingers, gripped it so hard her lip curled, but I didn't care.

She would look at me. She would look at what he'd done to me.

"And you'll let him," I hissed.

Her eyes stopped flickered, and she finally looked at me. Her face fell, and there was a depth and darkness to her sadness that almost made me regret my words. After it became apparent that she wasn't going to say anything, I turned away from her, no longer sorry.

"Chrys, keep an eye on that cake. I'm going to get ready," I said as my eyes filled with tears.

I didn't give him the chance to argue. I walked out of the kitchen, past my father's office door, which was propped open. I caught a glimpse of him at his desk, and the sight made my head burn. I shook my head as I stumbled blindly up the stairs.

Shame and emptiness raged inside my chest, made my throat swell closed as I struggled against my tears. I fell into my room and slammed the door. I leant against it as my chest heaved, sunk to the floor before I could stop myself. My lungs burnt with the effort of holding in my tears, but with every passing second the agony and betrayal of what my father had done, what my mother had failed to do, splintered my heart.

I sat on the floor for a long time, stared at my desk chair as if it could give me all the answers. A million thoughts coursed through my mind at first, about what I knew, and what was true, and if everything was as it seemed, but after a while my mind went blank, and I was alone in my silence.

My Commniglass buzzed in my pocket. I ignored it until it stopped, but then it began again. I sighed, wiped my eyes, pulled it out. Alfie's name and portrait projected in the air, and I patted my hair down, practised smiling for a few seconds before I answered.

"Hey Alfie," I said.

Alfie's annoyed face came into focus, and he stared at me.

"I've been calling you for ages! Are you almost ready? Are you? Because I can't wait, I can't be late. Dammit where are my shoes?" He moved in and out of focus as he searched through his room.

"Yeah, give me five minutes. I'm almost ready," I reassured him.

He came back into focus and finally looked at me properly, his eyes narrowed. He frowned, squinted at my face.

"You little liar," He said, only half joking.

I pulled on the largest smile I could muster despite the pain in my cheeks and chest.

"Five minutes. I promise." I held up my pinkie finger.

He huffed, but then held up his own pinkie finger.

"I hope you're telling the truth, because I really don't want to have to break that cute little finger," he gave me a grin.

I forced a laugh, then hung up. I pulled myself to my feet and went to my wardrobe, stripped my flour caked clothes off and looked at my back, peeled the gauze away. My skin was slick with sweat and whitish yellow liquid, the gauze covered in blood and gunk. I grabbed a tissue from my dresser and gently dabbed at the wound, tried to clean myself up the best I could. I hissed at the pain, grit my teeth as I wiped away the last of the blood. The scabs had fallen away, left the letters open once more. I took another gauze from my desk and plastered it on.

I reached for the nicest thing I owned; a beautiful knee length lace dress with long sleeves and small pearls around the neckline. I yanked it over my head and found that where it used to cling to my skin, it now suffocated me. I poked my hips, pinched the flesh curiously. I looked in the mirror; I did look bigger. 'Plump with wealth', as Mrs. Clarke had once sniped about a girl in our class.

I sucked in my stomach and tried to smile through the pain. I dropped the smile as I let out my breath. I had once been perfect in this dress, unquestionable and beautiful. Now I was hollow, a bad imitation of who I once was.

I turned away from the mirror and slipped on a pair of heels, ran a brush through my hair, pulled it into a braid before I turned to the door. The flash of sunlight on the dairy caught my attention, and I wavered.

Don't be stupid.

Don't be stupid.

Don't-

I went around the bed and pulled it out. Polly had been right, Klio had been right, this place, the Emperor, they weren't what they seemed, there was something going on and I had to know the truth. I yanked off its wrappings, ready to open it, unable to resist any longer.

There was a knock at the door, and I let out a yelp, my heart in my throat. I dropped the diary and kicked it under the bed as Alfie stormed into my room.

"Come on now. Five minutes over." He came over to me and kissed me on the head.

"How did you…?" I looked between him and my bedroom door.

He paused as he looked me up and down. His hands stroked my waist, down my hips, and I shivered. He caught his lip between his teeth as his eyes met mine. His cheek feathered as he grazed my jaw with his knuckles, brushed a thumb over my cheek.

"You look so beautiful," he said, his voice thick.

He leant forward, captured my chin in his fingers and kissed me. One hand on my face, the other on my waist, he kissed me with an urgency I had never felt before. As his lips moved against mine, all I could think was how wrong this felt, how strange and sickening. My stomach roiled as I attempted to pull back, but his hand tightened on my waist, pulled me flush against him. My hands clenched into fists as his hands moved along my skin in a way that would have us both killed if we were found. As his tongue brushed my bottom lip, my chest cracked, and my fear and disgust won out over my hesitancy to hurt him.

I yanked back, turned away from him to hide the flush of anger on my cheeks. I was shaking. I couldn't see through the stars in my vision. I could distantly hear Alfie speaking, but the words turned to white noise as I tried to pull myself back to reality. The word carved into my skin burnt as if they were fresh, and it echoed over and over again in my ears. Alfie's hand was tentative on my shoulder as he turned me, but I couldn't take it. I couldn't look at him; my mate, my friend, the person I was destined to love yet who I couldn't even trust with the truth.

"No. I'm sorry. We should go," I managed to choke out as I tried to flee, unable to meet his eyes.

Alfie stepped into my path, his big eyes troubled and shining. His cheeks were flushed, his lips red and swollen from our kiss.

"Calluna, I'm sorry. I just… you look so wonderful. I… I shouldn't have been so forward. I'm so sorry my love. Please forgive me," he said, his lip wobbled as he spoke.

I swallowed hard past the bile that rose in my throat. I focused on Alfie, on his chocolate eyes and regretful stare. I focused on his slicked hair and his freckles, and my anxiety shifted, ebbed away as I detailed every feature. I took one breath at a time, let the flecks of gold in his eyes wash over me like sunshine. He waited patiently for me to finally come back to earth. I forced a smile, then let it drop. Alfie knew me too well to be fooled by an act.

"I'm sorry Alfie. It's just…" I stopped short and met his eyes.

I wanted to confide in him, to tell him everything, but there was always the possibility that this information could get us both killed. Polly had been frantic, had begged me to keep this secret, but would Alfie do the same? I looked at his kind face, at his expectant eyes, and the words rose like vomit in my throat.

"Do you ever…. ever think that maybe we don't know something… that something isn't right here?" I asked.

His eyes widened a fraction, his face paled, and for a moment I thought he was going to run. I saw what I had feared reflected in his eyes; that ingrained fear that I was falling out of the Emperor's eye, that I was rebelling, that I was becoming imperfect. That fear that was drilled into us from birth, that became instinct, that was essential to the function of this society. But then he shook his head, as if throwing the thoughts from his mind, and gave me a smile that didn't quite light his face.

"What are you talking about? Sadon is perfect. Everything here is Perfect, what could possibly be wrong?" He asked.

I didn't say anything more. I could see in his eyes that he believed completely in this world, and that nothing had happened to make him think anything other than what we had been told. I shook my head and smiled, tried to play it off.

"I think I'm just lightheaded. You can't spring a kiss on a girl like that and expect her to make sense after," I teased.

He chuckled; his cheeks red as he scratched the back of his neck. I gave him a nudge with my shoulder, linked my arm through his and gestured for him to lead the way despite the pain in my chest and the pounding of my heart. He smiled uncontrollably as we walked down the stairs, his hand tight on my forearm. Chrys was stood waiting at the bottom; he'd put on a suit and managed to tame his usually fluffy hair. He held a large white box in his hand, and another sat at his feet.

"Little help?" He nodded to the box, and Alfie rushed to pick it up.

He balanced it in his arms and gave me a wink.

"Can't expect a lady to do all the lifting," he grinned at me.

I smiled back and went to open the front door, glad for a night away from the house that had become so suffocating. As we were about to leave, my father emerged into the hallway, a shadow that threatened to pull me back into the pit. He looked at me, his eyes blank, and a cold hand of terror wrapped around my throat.

"Children. I expect you will behave accordingly tonight. If not, there will be punishment," as he said it, his eyes lingered on me.

Alfie put the box down and walked over to my father. He stuck out his hand, and they shook like lifelong friends. It was then that I realised how similar they looked. Both handsome with red hair, both tall. My stomach coiled as I looked away, disgusted by the realisation.

"Don't you worry sir, I'll keep them in line," Alfie joked as he came to stand next to me again.

He went to plant a kiss on my head, but I dodged, made as if I was holding the door open. Alfie's face fell, his eyes narrowed at my reaction, but he picked up the box of cakes anyway, gave my father one last winning smile.

"Goodnight Mr. Morano, you'll be missed tonight,"

~

The Palladium was abuzz with voices, the grand hall filled to the brim with eager citizens. White chairs trimmed with draping ivy and white roses were set up in lines in front of the raised stage. Three wooden chairs sat equidistant on the stage, all painted gold, with small piles of white fire stones underneath. Wreaths of white and gold flowers hung from the ceiling; long vines trailed above our heads. The chandelier was made from a million small diamonds and glistened as bright as the sun under the light of the Commniglasses.

Around the room, tables were set up and piled high with cakes; some were simple like mine, lemon cakes, fruit cakes, blueberry cupcakes and oat cookies. Some were so elaborate it was impossible to believe they were edible. Some were so tall that a small wind could have knocked them over. Some were decorated with real gems and jewels, clusters of rubies the size of babies' hands. Some were in the shape of trees, buildings, even one of the Emperor's Keep. The air was filled with the sickly smell of icing and sugar.

I stood patiently next to Chrys in the throng, took it all in. Alfie was up front with his family. Arthur was stood proud by the edge of the stage as his mother fused over him. Alfie looked out of place, perched to the side of his family like an awkward outsider. He caught my eyes and gave me a nervous smile. I gave him a reassuring nod, before my eyes left his.

I was searching for Polly.

Neither her mother nor father had turned up, which was peculiar, as Mr. Kane had always had an affinity for ceremonies, often cheering animatedly at the betrayer's pain. My eyes raked the crowd for a glimpse of her raven ponytail, her feral eyes. I rubbed at my wrist, gnawed at the inside of my cheek. Worry churned in the pit of my stomach, made my throat burn with the pain of it. The agony in my back reminded me that many things went unknown in this world, and the thought of something even worse happening to Polly made my head spin.

"Everything alright?" Chrys asked.

I nodded without thought. I couldn't let him see my worry, couldn't drag him into whatever trouble Polly had involved me in, couldn't risk his life like I was risking my own. My eyes were drawn by movement, and I watched as someone walked over to us. It was a boy I didn't recognise; a blond haired, pale boy with high cheek bones and a sharp jaw. He was attractive in a feminine way, all pink lipped and dark lashed, and as he approached his eyes darted from Chrys to me nervously. Chrys shifted uncomfortably before he put on a nervous smile.

"Hey Darwin," Chrys said as he ran a hand through his hair.

I frowned at the two. Darwin looked worried, his hands buried in his pockets, but Chrys looked terrified. His eyes darted around the room as if he were looking for something, or someone. Darwin looked back to me, his eyes raked me up and down before he turned back to Chrys.

"Can we talk? Outside?" Darwin asked.

Chrys waivered momentarily before he looked to me. He opened his mouth to say something, but I rubbed his arm reassuringly.

"I'll be fine. Just go," I gave them both a smile.

Chrys nodded, his cheeks red, before he gestured for Darwin to lead the way. I watched them walk away, both their shoulders tense, close enough to touch but making sure they didn't. I wringed my hands, tried not to worry as I turned back to see Doctor Lynn move to the centre of the stage.

He was a plump man, violet pupiled and red faced. In one hand he held a silver projector, in the other a flute of champagne. Waitresses with trays of champagne floated from doorways, distributed the glasses with grace. Doctor Lynn grinned out at the crowd as he positioned the projector on the edge of the stage. As he stood, he raised his champagne glass to the crowd.

"Ladies and gentlemen. Today is a joyous occasion, let us be seated." He grinned as a young waitress handed me a glass.

I combed the crowd in search for Darwin and Chrys as I sat, swirled the champagne in my glass. Alfie gripped his champagne flute so hard I worried the stem might snap, swallowed thickly as he looked at Doctor Lynn. The room fell silent within seconds. I sat in the silence, my unease growing with every second those three golden chairs remained empty.

95

"We are afforded the great luxury tonight of being blessed," Doctor Lynn began, his low voice commanding and compelling.

"We have been blessed by a great son of Perfection, Arthur Clarke. A young man with such an affinity for the eradication of Imperfection that he has climbed the ranks of our protector's way beyond his years. He has done us all proud, and today we are here to celebrate his achievements," Doctor Lynn gestured for Arthur to join him on stage.

Mrs Clarke kissed Arthur on the cheek, her eyes filled with tears. Mr Clarke had a proud smile on his face, his shoulders straight and head held high as if he were the one being awarded. Alfie looked up at his brother with the wonder and admiration of a child, and my stomach lurched at the longing on his face. Arthur beamed as he marched on stage, and the crowd clapped politely. Doctor Lynn shook his hand.

"We are so very proud of you, my son," Doctor Lynn said.

Arthur nodded. He looked genuinely touched to hear those words, and it was the first time I'd seen anything on his face apart from sadistic joy and superiority.

"As a reward for your hard work, we have granted you the privilege of venturing to Slum Nine. We believe your tenacity and your dedication to our Emperor will prevail in one of our most challenging Imperfection holdings," Doctor Lynn said as he patted Arthur on the back.

Arthur was breathless, looked at his mother, who was now crying. He touched his chest in disbelief. To be trusted with such a mission was a sure way to end up in the Inner Ring, or could even carve a path for him to end up as one of the Emperor's personal guard. It was an honour, and also a death sentence. If he failed, if he couldn't quell the unrest that had been brewing there for decades, then he would never return.

"I cannot thank you enough, Doctor Lynn," Arthur breathed.

Doctor Lynn shook his head, before he gestured to the projector.

"Don't thank me, Mr Clarke. Thank the Emperor himself." With that the projector flicked on, and Emperor Emercius beamed down at us.

Everyone in the room gasped. My mouth hung open wide at the sight of his youthful, ethereal face, the glinting silver of his hair. His large white eyes seemed to stare into my very soul, and I flinched as his smile intensified.

"My children." The two words sent an adoring chill through the room that made heat roll down my back in waves.

"Today is a glorious day. A day of celebration. A day to show the rewards of Perfection. Each and every one of you possess the ability to achieve similar Perfection, and to receive similar rewards. I encourage you to take this day as motivation, and as a warning." His face darkened as he said the last word.

The door at the back of the stage opened, and two Pioneers emerged holding golden chains. My stomach lurched as I saw what was attached to those chains; three captives. They were led to their respective chairs and forced to sit. Each of the three were tied to their chairs, but none of them resisted. They were motionless as dolls, pliable and subservient as the guards stepped back.

Doctor Lynn whispered something into Arthur's ear, before he exited the stage to join his tight faced wife. Arthur stood alone, but he did not seem afraid. No, he looked ecstatic.

I rubbed my arms as a chill rose in the room.

"There are those who deserve our adoration, and those who have forsaken perfection. Mr. Clarke has done us a great service in capturing each of these deviants. Today, it is his privilege to bring justice for us all," the Emperor nodded to Arthur, who smiled out at the crowd with bright, eager eyes.

There was polite clapping as he stepped aside, let us focus solely on those who were deemed imperfect.

"Shall we begin?" Arthur gestured to the first chair, theatrical in his passion.

As an attendant passed a rolled scroll to Arthur, I finally looked at the first person tied to the chair. He was a young man with thick black hair slicked back from his face. He would have been beautiful, if it weren't for the two jagged holes where his eyes used to be. He hung his head, turned it from side to side as Arthur unrolled the scroll. His clothes were pristine, not a spot of blood on them, as if he'd been dressed for the occasion. Arthur cleared his throat before he looked back out to the crowds.

"Lennie Porter, you stand accused of infidelity of the mind and eyes, of gazing upon a woman who is not your life mate. Lusting over another is a crime and an insult to the Emperor's good will. Do you deny this?" Arthur asked.

Lennie went to open his mouth, but the crowd roared up around me, their faces creased in anger. They shouted a million insults, words I couldn't even pick out from the chaos, all I could feel was their fury, their betrayal. I looked to the Emperor, who watched over the angry crowd with a triumphant smile. We were his pawns, bred and born to follow and to submit, and he had raised us into indoctrination successfully. We did not care how Lennie had lived his life, what lived in his heart, only that he had broken a rule the Emperor had made, and that was enough for us to turn on him. To revel in his pain.

Arthur couldn't keep his pleasure contained, he beamed back at his mother, who shed a proud tear. Alfie frowned, shook his head at Lennie, as taken in by it all as everyone.

"The people have spoken. Lennie Porter, I sentence you to purification by fire," Arthur held his hand out to the nearby assistant, who passed a burning white torch.

Arthur gripped the torch and gestured to the crowd, the shine in his eyes almost blinding. Everyone stood, their voices rose, spit flew, faces contorted in anger. I was compelled to stand too, but I couldn't make any words leave my mouth. The torch lowered to the stones below Lennie and set the chair ablaze, and all I could do was stare. Usually, I would have made a show of mouthing the words, of being one with the crowd, but I couldn't force them out.

Lennie screamed as the flames consumed him. There were children in the audience, they cheered as he thrashed sightlessly away from the fire. I kept my eyes on Lennie, on his agony. I forced myself to watch, to acknowledge what happened when you stepped out of line. The smell of burnt flesh mingled with the scent of sugar and icing, and my stomach rolled. His screams fell to silence as his flesh sizzled to blackened char. The Emperor nodded his approval.

Arthur moved to the second; an elder woman with thick grey peppered hair and a soft, beautifully aged face. Her mouth was sewn shut with a white thread. Her lips strained against the stitches as her eyes went around the room. Our eyes met, and pain speared through my stomach.

I looked away, and then hated myself for it. She didn't deserve my squeamishness, my weakness. I took a deep breath before I looked back up. Arthur held his torch up high. He looked as if he were going to set her alight without addressing her crimes, the flames reflected in his eyes as much as his sadistic joy. The Emperor raised his head just slightly, and with that subtle nod, Arthur lowered the torch, his face sobered.

"Mrs. Freya Calloway, you stand accused of besmirching the Emperor's name. Of spreading blasphemy, of using the voice he gave you to mar his name. How do you plead?" Arthur asked.

She strained against the thread that bound her mouth. A drop of blood dripped down her chin. Mrs Clarke shook her head, wept heavily now, her hand outstretched to the Emperor, who himself looked upset. Many of the crowd had fallen to their knees in sadness at the thought of anyone speaking ill of our Emperor. My legs gave out and I sat with a thump on the bench, no longer able to bear it. My eyes burnt with tears I couldn't explain. They fell down my cheeks and I pushed them away in confusion.

"The people have spoken. Freya Calloway, I sentence you to purification by fire." The torch came down with a ferocity that made my head spin.

"Burn! Burn!" Mr Clarke cheered.

I forced myself to mouth the words, aware that there were eyes searching the crowd now, looking for deviants. I didn't know how much longer I could sit here. That same burning need that had refused to let Carolynn fail, that raged to protect Lavender, rose up again at the sight of her burning body. I could feel the word burnt into my back searing as the woman died. A few of the strings that restrained her voice broke as she thrashed, spilt blood down her perfectly white clothes. Soon, though, she fell limp.

Arthur moved to the last man. The youngest of the three, he looked only a year older than I. His head was shaved, but only to show off his mutilated ears. Both his ears had been cut off, along with his fingers. The stubs had been cauterised, and they moved aimlessly as he looked at Arthur. There was a disgust on Arthur's face I had never seen before; his lips were pulled back from his teeth as he snarled, his nose turned up at the boy before him. The Emperor shifted uncomfortably; his eyes averted from the boy as Arthur looked at the last crime on the scroll.

"Michael Narrow, you stand accused of homosexuality and rape, of engaging in non-consensual sex with another man. How do you plead?" Arthur snarled.

There was a thump as Mrs Clarke fainted. Alfie rushed to scoop her into his arms, fanned her desperately as he managed to stand her up. She blinked hazily; her eyes rolled as she stumbled towards the door. The crowd hissed, a low, vile hiss that made my head buzz. Michael shook his head, muttered to himself.

"I'm guilty. I'm guilty. Emperor forgive me. I listened to the imperfect voices that whispered to me. Please, forgive me," he begged as a tear ran down his face.

"It's disgusting,"

"It's unnatural,"

"Burn him!"

The crowd kept shouting, and the Emperor nodded.

"I cannot forgive you, my child. Let the fire purify the imperfection from your soul,"

I stood before the torch could touch the stones. I turned and pushed my way through the crowd, unable to watch the burning of a boy who'd done nothing more than love someone.

"Now, my children. Revel in the cleansing of Imperfection. I must leave but let there be enjoyment. Eat, my children, and fear not the darkness, for Perfection is the light that guides us." The Emperor's words ushered me out of the grand hall as a small child climbed upon the stage and smeared icing on the dead's still smouldering faces.

I walked down the hallway, peered into each room in search of Alfie and his mother, desperate for a purpose to distract my unsettled mind. The voices faded as I pushed my way into the dark, cold night. I looked up at the sky and took a deep breath. I let myself breathe. I let the faded voices crash around me like waves against the shore, let them spray me with their harsh clarity. I heard a mumble, and a sigh, and I turned, followed the noise in hope of aiding Alfie. I walked around the side of the building and stopped dead.

Chrys was pinned against the wall, and Darwin, as angelic and beautiful as the first Pioneers, was kissing him.

I stood and watched, unable to move. Chrys pressed his hands into Darwin's back, pulled him closer, but all I could see was burning flesh and ash. I stumbled backwards, scared of what I'd seen, of what I knew it could mean for them both. My heel caught on the edge of a tile, and I fell, scraped my knees as I went. The pair sprang apart, their eyes zeroed in on me. Chrys swore under his breath as Darwin covered his face, shook his head woefully. I got to my feet, mumbled apologies, unsure what else to do.

Chrys whispered something to him, pressed his fingers to Darwin's face affectionately. The pair exchanged hissed words; Darwin was practically hysterical, his cheeks flushed red, his eyes frantic as they kept straying to mine. My heart thrashed behind my ears as I tried to think of what I could do, of what I could do for him, for both of them. I blinked and tried to burn the memory from my mind; knew that the image was dangerous there, that anyone could find it, use it. Chrys took Darwin's face in his hands, pressed his lips to his forehead, before he looked at me again. I turned, face hot with embarrassment at my lingering.

"Calluna." He ran to me, seized my wrist in his hand.

He was scared, his tousled hair fell over his eyes, made him seem younger than he was. His lips were swollen and bruised, his cheeks red. He opened his mouth, then hesitated. He searched my face for hatred, for anger, for disgust, but all I felt was fear.

"Calluna, I can explain," he spluttered, but I shook my head.

"Chrys. Someone was just burnt in there. Someone just died in there! Because…" I didn't know what to say, or how to put it.

The words were like ash in my mouth. All I could imagine was Chrys screaming, and Brielle, his life mate, watching from the side-lines, already picking out a new mate. Chrys bit his lip, his eyes filled with tears.

"I love him, Callie," he whispered.

My heart ached as I met his eyes. I pulled him into my arms and hugged him tightly as he shuddered. I closed my eyes and held him. All I could think about was the smell of his hair, the feel of his shoulders, the beating of his heart. How alive he was. How much I would do to keep him that way.

"I won't let them hurt you. I promise,"

Chapter VII

"Did you hear?" Alfie asked.

I looked up. I hadn't been listening. The whole walk home had been possessed by my thoughts of Chrys. I had stared at his back, at the curve of his shoulders and the way he dug his fists into his pockets and wondered how he'd known. Wondered what it was like to love someone so deeply that you would risk death. Yet as he talked to Darwin, that same protective desperation filled my veins, and I thought maybe I was starting to understand.

"Hear what?" I asked, out of it.

Alfie tucked a strand of my hair behind my ear, the corners of his mouth turned down as he took a breath. I narrowed my eyes, pulled myself from my distraction and looked at him then, really looked. His brow was creased, his eyes dark with sorrow.

"Polly… she was taken last night. Her parents are so upset, they can't even leave the house. The Emperor is looking into it, but they think the Mai-Coh came and took her. That poor family," Alfie said.

I shook my head, which had begun to spin. My eyes blurred as my feet carried me forward. Alfie was still talking, but his words were far off.

I couldn't make sense of it. Why would the Mai-Coh target their family like that? If the Mai-Coh had invaded, wouldn't we know? Wouldn't more people have seen them? With every question, the answer became more clear.

Polly hadn't been taken. Polly had known too much, and now Polly was gone.

I focused on Chrys' back once more, knew that everything Polly had said, everything she had warned me

104

against, was true. If they had taken her, and if she told them about me, then they would come for me too, and my mind guarded more than some dead girl's diary. My feet stopped moving, and Alfie looked back at me, eyebrow raised.

"Calluna? What's wrong?" He asked, but I couldn't risk him too.

"I... I have to go to Polly's house. I- I need to pay my respects."

I turned and walked away. They called after me, but I ignored them. I had to confirm my suspicions. My eyes roamed over the dimly lit houses as I passed, but they bought me no comfort. The empty windows, once inviting and warm, seemed now lonely and daunting. My hands shook as I turned a corner. A Hovear buzzed passed, two white suited Pioneers prowled the streets with eyes of silver and gold. The passenger looked at me, his strong nose crinkled as he passed.

I could see Polly's house at the end of the street. The curtains were drawn shut, the windows sealed tightly against the outside world. A thin line of white tape was secured to the front gate, with the golden word 'INVESTIGATION' embossed on its surface. I pushed past it, unlocked the gate and walked up the overgrown front lawn. I reached up my fist, a giddy fearlessness running through my body.

Before I could knock, the door opened.

Mrs. Kane looked down at me with disinterest, but not surprise. No, she looked as if she had been entirely expecting me, and her calm face sent a shiver down my spine. She wore a large white hat with a translucent veil that fell to her jaw, playing the part of a mourning mother. Around her neck hung a necklace of large diamonds, a piece so extravagant that for a moment I forgot why I was there. She looked vibrant.

"Calluna. What are you doing here? Didn't you hear the news?" She asked, but there was no intrigue behind her words, no real thirst for answers.

"I came to give my condolences. Polly was my closest friend," my voice caught as I said the words.

Mrs. Kane hummed, nodded as she looked past me at the garden.

"Yes. Tragedy seems to stalk this house." She fanned herself lazily as she looked at the porch, as if the house itself was to blame.

Her eyes flitted to the front gate, to the tape that hung off the fence, and she tutted.

"I'll have to get a gardener out tomorrow. The grass is growing terribly," she clucked as she adjusted her necklace, a faint smile on her lips.

That terrible, uneasy feeling in my stomach and head intensified. I tried to look past her, into the house. There was no sign of forced entry, no sign of a struggle. Polly hadn't left the house for days; if she'd been taken it would have been from here. Wouldn't there be more signs of a struggle? And why just Polly? Why not the whole family? Wouldn't her mother and father have fought for her, received an injury in the process? Mrs. Kane caught me looking and creaked the door further shut.

"Anything else, dear?" She asked.

"Yes. I would like to see her room. She… she borrowed a book from me, I would like it back." The words left my mouth in an unconvincing rush.

Mrs. Kane hesitated, her eyes as hard as ice. The tightening of her jaw alerted me to the fact that she definitely didn't want me in her house, but then there was a flash of something across her face, as if she were remembering something important, before she opened the door.

"Alright, but don't touch anything else. The Pioneers are coming in the morning to look it over." She gestured up the stairs.

I stepped inside and was overwhelmed by the heat. The vents were pumping out copious amounts of hot air, sweat beaded on my forehead. I eyed the vents in confusion. Heat rations were not awarded to the Lower Ring for another three months.

Mrs. Kane walked slowly into the kitchen, fanned herself as she picked up a cool glass of orange juice and sipped at it luxuriously. Mr. Kane was nowhere to be seen, but I could hear him pacing above. I gave Mrs. Kane an uneasy smile as she reached for her Commniglass. She waved me up, a disinterested gesture.

"Go on. I'm going to call your mother, let her know you're here."

I walked up the stairs quickly. I got the sneaking feeling that I didn't have much time. Polly's door was propped open wide to display the destruction within. The room had been torn apart; the mattress had been flipped, and it lent up against the wall like a child's den. The desk had all its draws pulled out, the contents sprawled across the floor, as if someone had been looking for something. Her books were torn, pages ripped loose. Her closet door was smashed open, her clothes dotted around the room. My eyes stung, but I held in the tears. The words Polly had said to me in the graveyard came back to me:

Klio found out something she shouldn't have, and they killed her for it.

I looked at the destroyed desk, at the papers thrown onto the ground and I knew. What she'd read in Klio's diary had put her in danger.

107

I was about to turn when I remembered what Polly had told me. That Klio had hidden her diary within her mattress. Maybe if Polly had left me something, it would be in that same place. I turned and moved towards the mattress, felt along its underside until my fingers sunk into a tiny slash, only a few centimetres long, maybe only an inch wide. I felt along its length, my heart in my throat as hope filled my chest. My fingers brushed against something papery, and I pulled it out, my hands shaking. It was part of a page, ripped from a notebook in urgency, folded over twice to fit into the slash she'd made in her final moments.

They know, C.

The letters were rushed and fevered, as if a three-year-old had scrawled them, but it didn't matter.

I knew what it meant.

I bolted out of her room and down the stairs. Mrs. Kane was mumbling in the kitchen, but at the sound of my footsteps she quickly fell silent. Mr. Kane had stopped pacing. I pushed the piece of paper into my pocket.

"I couldn't see it. Thank you, Mrs. Kane. I'm sorry for your loss," I blurted, reached for the door handle.

"Calluna, wait." I closed my eyes, my fingers so close to the handle I could feel the coldness of the gold.

I turned, dread thick in my mouth as I pulled on a smile. Mrs. Kane walked towards me, glass of water in hand. She reached out and touched my shoulder, offered me the glass.

"You were a good friend to Polly. The kind of friend she could tell anything, wouldn't you say?" She asked, glass still extended to me.

I nodded, scared to do anything more.

Mrs. Kane smiled thinly, but the smile didn't reach her eyes. She had never been a caring woman; both her daughters had been studious and academic instead of

108

debutants, and she had always hated them for that. Even now I saw it etched into the lines of her face, the resentment, the rage.

"Won't you drink, you look parched."

I looked at the glass, at the crystal-clear water, the condensation on the surface. My mouth was dry, my throat ached for moisture, but the way Polly had dragged me away that morning, insisted I didn't drink, it stuck with me now, and I knew better than to give in.

"No, thank you. I should go," I gave her one last smile.

Mrs. Kane nodded, although her fingers gripped the glass with a strength that could have shattered it.

"Of course," she said as I opened the door.

I didn't turn to say goodbye again. The note was burning a hole in my pocket, and all I could think about was the diary hidden under my bed. How long would it be safe there? What secret could possibly put Polly in danger? How long did I have before they figured out she'd given it to me?

I walked down the street, head bent low. I shivered against the air, so much colder than in the Kane house. Lights swooped around the corner, and I looked over my shoulder. A Hovear buzzed down the street; the dark windshield glistened under the moonlight. I shoved my hands into my pockets. Polly's note rubbed against the pads of my fingers, and I traced the jagged letters as the Hovear slowed, prowled behind me. Its lights framed me, cast a long, distorted shadow onto the pavement in front of me.

I kept walking, waited for it to pass. It stayed behind me; its hum barely audible. I felt eyes on my back, the hair on the back of my neck stood on end as it trailed me, refused to pass.

I turned another corner, my house in view. The Hovear followed. When I reached my garden gate, I paused, looked back at the Pioneers. They stopped, pulled over, killed the lights. It sat there, waiting, watching. I opened the gate, my pulse raging in my fingertips, and walked up to my door. The Hovear sat silently.

I walked into the house, my heart in my throat. I raced up the stairs and looked out of the hallway window. The Hovear still sat, no sign of moving. I went into my room and sat down heavily on the bed, my legs shaking.

I could turn in the diary, the note. I could cast Polly's name in darkness and keep my mind unchecked. It would save my brother, my family. I fisted my hands into my sheets, squeezed my eyes shut.

I couldn't do that to Polly, I couldn't betray her. Plus, whose to say they'd even believe me? If I turned it in, they'd assume I'd read it, and check my mind anyway. They'd see what I'd seen, and they'd kill Chrys without question.

I stood quickly, my head spun as I reached under the bed and pulled out the diary. My hand shook violently, the pages trembled as I held them. I hesitantly flipped open the cover, and the air left my lungs in a rush as I recognised Klio's handwriting.

I had to know. I had to know what they wanted so desperately.

The first pages were diary entries; drivel about school, about her life mate, about how perfect her life was. I flicked through the neat writing, until I turned to a page scrawled with numbers, so many numbers they didn't make sense. Pages and pages were filled with calculations, scribblings, symbols and letters. I kept turning and turning, frowned at it all as I tried to make sense of it. I turned to the last page and found a similar scrawling writing to the note Polly had left me.

After further testing, I have proven the level of drugs in the water supply causes decreased aggression, dulled perception and increased complacency. Further analysis to be conc-

The last word was broken, the pen smudged and harsh. All I could think about was the glass Mrs. Kane had offered me, the water I had drank every day of my life. I let the diary fall from my hands and stared at the wall. I swallowed past my sore throat, desperate for a drink but no longer able to stomach the thought.

I got up and walked over to the window, peeked through the curtain. The Pioneers had rolled down the windows, and I could see the passenger more clearly. It was the same Pioneer with the strong nose, his silver eyes focused on the dash. As if my eyes had alerted him, he looked up. Our eyes locked, and for a terrifying moment I was completely paralysed.

He smiled and raised his hand in a wave.

~~~

My foot tapped restlessly on the marble floor, created a constant *tink-tink-tink* in an effort to drown out my thoughts. The corridors of the Palladium were filled with anxious eighteen-year-olds awaiting their Appraisal meetings. Alfie had gone in ten minutes ago; he'd been nervous, paced back and forth, tried to coax some sort of encouragement from me. I wasn't interested, it hardly seemed to matter anymore. I'd offered him distracted words and fake smiles that he saw right through.

We were placed fifth, there wasn't much chance of us moving to the Inner Ring now. I was thirsty, so thirsty that my head was light. I kept tapping my foot, my fingers twisted around each other as I thought about what I knew, what the knowledge Polly had given me could mean. It would only take one of the Emperor's trained guards to sit me down, to reach inside my mind and see everything. The sound of heels approaching made me look up, and to my surprise Olivia stood in front of me, smiling smugly.

She looked beautiful in a sleek, tight-fitting dress. It was rather provocative, obscene, but it didn't matter. She was first, and there wasn't much she could do that would leave her stuck in the Hollow with such little time left.

"We've played a good game, you and I. You've been a good competitor. I'll be sure to send you a letter from the Inner Ring. Maybe I'll even Comm you, show you my house," she gloated, but I didn't feel my usual loathing for her.

I couldn't muster the energy to argue with her. That felt like a lie too, a way to make us compete for Perfection that we didn't even desire. She wasn't my enemy, she wasn't anything but the Emperors way of making me try harder.

"Well done, Olivia. You deserve it," I replied.

Olivia rolled her eyes, inspected her nails.

"Yes, sure. Well, enjoy the rest of your sad life." She turned and trotted off, waved to other girls as she went.

I sighed, held my head in my hands. The Pioneers had never left my house. As I had walked to the Palladium, they had moved further up the road, but they were still there. I tugged at the ends of my hair, sick to my stomach. I wanted to scream.

"Calluna Morano," a shrill voice called.

I stood, quickly went over all my prepared answers. I owed that to Alfie, he deserved the Inner Ring, he deserved the chance to escape his family. I straightened my skirt, pulled on a smile, and walked to the open door that would seal my fate.

She held the door open for me, her brown pupiled eyes took in every detail. She was pretty, as all residents of Sadon were, but only in the basest of ways. Her features were right,

112

her black hair was sleek, but her expression was stern, her lips sour. There was a desk set against a large window, two chairs and a small filing cabinet. A box of tissues sat at the corner of the desk, and the bin was filled with the soiled, tear stained remnants of my classmate's woes. I sat down, and the officer made her way around the desk. She braced her hands against the back of her chair and stared me down.

"What can you tell me about Polly?" she asked.

I stared at her, lost for words, my first answer already poised on my tongue. Fear gripped my throat as I met her cold, unwavering gaze. I swallowed, brightened my smile. I couldn't let them have my secrets, or Chrys'.

"She was my best friend," I replied, the only suitable answer.

The officer smiled, sat down in the chair, folded her arms. She gave me a practiced smile, one that was supposed to comfort me, was supposed to make me relax, but it only made the skin on my arms prickle.

"You and your life mate Alfie have been on track for the Inner Ring for a long time. You're both prime candidates. I would love to admit you, despite your position in the tables. If you could just provide me with some information about your friend, I can make it happen," she reasoned.

I pressed my lips tight. The offer of the Inner Ring, of giving Alfie and I the best life, of getting out of here, getting Lavender out of that house, it hung in the air as heavy as iron. There was an ache in my chest at the impossible decision before me. Alfie deserved happiness, I deserved it too. I deserved to get away from my father, and who knows? Maybe I could help my mother, my sister, help Chrys. An image of redheaded children laughing on a sun-drenched porch, of Alfie and I watching them from the doorway as they played, taunted me with its closeness.

Yet telling her what Polly had given me, telling her what I knew... I couldn't betray her, couldn't betray everything I had come to know. She must have sensed my hesitation, because she leant forward, her eyes darkened, her smile no longer smooth and polished, but sharp and foreboding.

"We're looking for something. A... diary. We want to see if she wrote about being involved with the Mai-Coh. If there's any indication to why they would target her. We just want to help find her," she tried again.

My nails dug into my thighs. The word disappointment burnt my back, my bones, every fibre of my being. She reached across the table and took my hand in hers. She gripped it so tightly my fingers turned white.

"I would hate for the Emperor to launch an inquiry into your family. There are rumours of unseemly things. I'm sure what you have seen would be enough for punishment; it would be a simple operation to extract what we needed from your mind. When we do, well, if the rumours are true, then Chrys would be killed by the morning. You mother, for producing such a degenerate, would have her womb carved out. You, for keeping such a secret, would be taken to Slum 5 for disobedience and flogged to the Riven Den."

I stood and ripped my hands from her grip. She stared up at me, observed me as my breath came hard. In five minutes, she had ripped every choice, every decision, out of my brain and laid them bare on the desk for me to choose. They'd strap me down, tap into my memories, and harvest them for proof; rumour wasn't always enough, but what I'd seen would sign his death warrant. They'd crack Darwin within a minute, and maybe they would be lenient with him, maybe they would afford him the luxury of redemption, but Chrys would die.

"Please. I don't know anything. Polly was my best friend, and I miss her. I... I don't know anything," I spluttered.

The officer nodded, waved me away. I stood, unsure of what to do.

"Don't… Don't you want to ask me my questions?" I stuttered.

She shook her head, all traces of her uniform smile gone as she drew out her Commniglass, pulled up the calling interface.

"No. I have all I need,"

~~~

I gripped Klio's diary in my hands. I could feel the seconds ticking past, each one longer and louder than the last.

My Commniglass kept buzzing. It was Alfie, wanting to know how my interview had gone. I couldn't bear to tell him what had happened. How could I tell him the truth? How could I expect him to understand why I'd kept this secret?

I looked at the diary, at the perfect, porcelain pages. At the ink smeared on the seams. Was Polly alive? Was she being tortured for the information I held in my hand? Would she have told them? No, if she had, they wouldn't have asked me.

My chest hurt, my head hurt, my fingers, my stomach. I kept thinking of Chrys, of what would happen to him if they took my memories. He wasn't safe, not while I kept this secret, not while I lived, not while this diary stayed in my possession, its words etched into my very blood. I groaned, smacked the diary against my forehead.

My Commniglass gave two swift buzzes, then fell silent. I glared at it out of the corner of my eye, and then picked it up. I swiped through the multiple missed calls to the voice message Alfie had left me.

"Please call me. Or come and see me. I just want to make sure you're okay,"

I sighed and looked at the diary again. Alfie was my friend, he'd do anything for me. He could help me with this burden, with this secret. Selfishly, I didn't want to carry this alone. I needed him, I needed someone to bear this.

Maybe together we could work it out, he could help me destroy the diary, maybe even help me find someone to take my memories.

I grabbed the diary and one of my larger winter coats, pushed the book under its thick fabric. I fastened the pear buttons and pulled up the hood. The Hovear had disappeared by the time I had come home, but I was wary.

I paused at my door, hand outstretched, fingers trembling. I couldn't go to Alfie's house. If Arthur caught even a whiff of this secret, I would be on my way to Slum 5 before I could say a word.

I pulled out my Commniglass and typed a quick message to Alfie.

'Meet me at the Hollow tree,'

I left my room, moved down the stairs. As I reached the bottom step, my father emerged from his office. He was polishing his letter opener, and at the sight of it the pain of that night came back fresh. I rubbed at the wound subconsciously as he looked at me.

"Going somewhere?" He asked.

"I'm meeting Alfie, we're going to celebrate our Appraisals," I lied.

My father nodded, squinted up at the bulb that swung between us. He held the knife up to the light, twisted it from side to side, inspected it closely, a smile creasing his cheeks. I squirmed, took a step towards the door. My movement made his head snap down, his smile completely gone.

"Your mother was far too dotting on you children. Loving you, nurturing you. Look where that has got us.

Disappointments. At least Lavender is not beyond saving," he pressed his finger to the edge of the blade, and nodded, "she's still... redeemable."

Rage surged up into my throat and I stepped forward, mouth open and fists balled. Before I could say a word, my mother emerged from the kitchen.

She gripped the door frame, unable to hold herself up. There was no hiding the damage he had done. Her skin, once clear and flawless, was blue and black. There was a neat cut on her left cheek, and a jagged, frantic one on her right. Her lips were swollen, her eyes sunken.

I closed my eyes as a tear ran down my cheek. It didn't matter what he did to her, not when she didn't leave the house. To the outside world, she was still the radiant botanist, taking time from her work to dote on her loving husband. Whatever happened behind these closed doors was of no one else's concern.

"Just go, Calluna," she whispered.

I turned blindly and walked out of the house. I gripped onto the diary as I walked down the street, tried to ground myself in the feel of it. I sobbed, scared, alone.

The air was too cold, too harsh as I stumbled round corners and down cobblestones. I turned down Alligold Street and was blinded by two bright Hovear lights. I raised my hand, tried to shield my eyes as I blinked the spots from my vision. I heard the slam of the Hovear door, and two dark figures moved towards me.

"Calluna Morano, you are to come with us." A strong, harsh voice commanded.

I went to turn, but there were already hands on my shoulders. I opened my mouth to scream, but one of the Pioneers slammed a strange smelling cloth over my mouth. I kicked out, my feet connected with the legs of the Pioneers, but it didn't make much difference. My head swam through something thick as my limbs grew heavy. I struggled to keep my eyes open as they dragged me towards the Hovear, mumbling to each other.

The hand fell from my mouth, the cloth dropped to the ground. I groaned, tried to form words, but my lips were leaden. The Pioneers pushed me against the side of the Hovear, one moved around to the driver's seat, the other kept my hands behind my back. I blinked a slow, heavy blink, and when I opened my eyes, there was a third person by the bonnet.

Within another blink, the first Pioneer was on the ground, and the other figure was moving towards me. The Pioneer dropped my arms, and I slid to the ground. There, I stared blankly as the two figures struggled. There was grunting, and screaming, and then silence.

The Pioneer was on the ground, blood pooled around his head, shimmered like shattered rubies under the lamplight. The figure knelt in front of me, drew down my hood, inspected me. I couldn't make out their features, couldn't see much but blur. He was shaking me, but my body wouldn't comply.

"Can you hear me? Can you stand?" His voice was low, deep, soothing.

I mumbled and groaned, tried to raise my hands. My eyes were closing again, heavier than before. He looped his arms under my legs and shoulders, and as my eyes closed, my body rose into the air.

Chapter VIII

I woke up with a jolt, my head contacted with something hard and cold. I hissed, reached up and pressed my fingers against my temple. My eyes peeled open reluctantly, still groggy from whatever drugs the Pioneers had pressed into my mouth.

I looked up; squinted through the window at my surroundings. The world was rushing past outside the grimy window I had banged my head against at an alarming speed. I looked at the rolling fields and trees, frowned at the lack of houses, the lack of people.

I tried to sit up, but something pressed me back into the weathered leather seat. I looked down at the belt that restrained me, ran my finger along the worn fabric, tried to pull at it. So different from Hovears, which were pristine and sleek and clean, this vehicle was from the old world, a relic of rust and grime.

"Oh look, she's awake," a voice from the passenger seat called.

I looked up. A pair of eyes as blue and dark as the night-time sea stared back at me in the rear-view mirror. I was stunned by their natural, unmodified beauty. He gave me a wink, before he propped his feet up on the dash.

"Have a nice nap, Golden Girl?" He teased as he ran a hand through his black locks.

His jaw was sharp, his cheek bones pronounced. He was all angles and lines, there was no sign of Sadon's softness. Freckles dotted across his nose unevenly, and his smile was crooked, slightly lopsided. I drank in his imperfection with unbridled awe.

"Leave her be, Kellan." This voice came from the driver's seat.

119

I recognised his voice as the boy from the night before. His angular, sharp eyes stayed on the fields ahead. His golden, tawny skin made my breath catch. It had a mellow warmth that glowed as vibrantly as the morning sunshine. He was built with muscle, broad shouldered, triangular in his shape, unlike Kellan, who was slim and lean.

I opened my mouth, then closed it. I looked at their clothes, the shades of red, brown and grey; tattered, dusty, splattered with blood.

The colours of the Mai-Coh.

My nails dug into the soft padding of the seat as I looked between them. My lungs squeezed, threatened to give way. I looked wildly for the door handle, for an escape. The engine screamed as we went over a large bump, and as the vehicle jolted, I reached out and seized the handle.

"I wouldn't," Kellan warned.

I looked from him to the door and back again. We were going so fast the outside world had turned into one huge smudge. Maybe the fall would kill me, but even if it didn't, I had no idea where I was, and I couldn't go back. I tightened my fingers around the handle, convinced for a second that death would be better than whatever the Mai-Coh could do to me, before I let it go.

I stared at the back of their heads. Maybe the Emperor hadn't been lying. Maybe the Mai-Coh had taken Polly after all. At the thought of her I frantically patted my coat, searched for the diary. I exhaled a sigh of relief as my fingers grazed the bindings.

"Do you... take girls often?" I said, hated how stupid it sounded.

My mouth was dry, gammy, as if it had been glued shut. Kellan snorted, rolled down his window. The smell of ash, dirt and fuel burnt my throat, and I choked on the unfamiliar scent. The driver frowned, adjusted the mirror so he could look at me.

"You really believe that crap your precious Emperor feeds you?" Kellan asked.

"No. We don't." The driver said bluntly.

Kellan rolled his eyes, propped his feet on the dash and fiddled with his bootstraps. The driver swatted at his feet, but Kellan pushed him off, continued to pick dirt from the soles. The hope that had started to rise at the thought of finding Polly was slowly fading, but I grasped for it, shook my head.

"What about a girl called Polly? Or Klio? Dark hair, pale, slim," I pressed.

I needed them to be alive. I needed to know I hadn't lost Polly forever, that I hadn't failed her. The driver looked at Kellan, and they shared a long look that I didn't quite understand.

"No. Neither of them," The driver replied, no trace of a lie in his tone.

I looked down at my hands in my lap, stained with street muck and dust. Either he was a terribly good liar, or Polly had been taken by the Pioneers. She'd be dead by now if they had.

Just like I would have been.

"Where are we going?" I whispered past the tears that lodged in my throat.

Neither of them replied. Kellan smacked his hand against the buzzing radio, tried to get it to work. He pressed a button, and a small tape jutted out. He took it in his fingers and rubbed at it with his sleeve, before reinserting it. He turned a dial, and loud music blared out. I jumped; my heart pounded in my chest as Kellan nodded along to the

121

screaming voices. The driver tried to turn it down, but Kellan cranked it back up.

"Come on Theodore, live a little. Kamal is going to lose his shit when you turn up with that," he jerked his thumb back at me, as if I were no more than spare parts, before he turned the volume to full. "You might as well make the most of your last days."

"Don't you mean we?" Theodore corrected him.

Kellan scoffed, brushed his hair from his forehead, gazed out the windscreen. I couldn't help but drink him in, the freckles on his cheeks, the deep olive of his skin, the way his lips moved to the strange music. I thought about how I might sketch him, but then I pushed that thought down. There was no place for art, not anymore. The Emperor had demanded I painted, had assigned me the hobby, and now that I was free, I wasn't sure what to do with the skill I had honed.

"You picked the princess up, not me," he replied.

I scowled at the name. *Princess.* He spat it like an insult.

They kept talking, not about anything important, which I'm sure was because they didn't trust me. Their voices were strange, both affected by accents from distant corners of the earth that I had assumed were long dead. Certain words seemed tinged, watered down by passing of generations, but still persevering. They spoke with lilts and dips, with inflection, with passion, and it was more beautiful than any music produced in Sadon.

With every passing second my stomach turned. Why had they taken me? Saved me? Would it be short-lived, this life they have given me? Living on borrowed time, owing it to rebels who could chose to do anything with it they wanted.

I looked between the two; both physically fit, both clearly trained for battle. My throat clenched as I spotted the sword that lay at Kellan's feet.

"Are you going to kill me?" The words left my mouth in a rush.

I didn't think they heard me, and I was grateful, until Kellan turned in his chair and looked me straight in the eyes. He looked at me without restraint, in a way I had never been looked at. So intimate, so prying, taking time to observe every detail. I flinched as his eyes roamed my body, drew down to my silk shoes, and then rested on my face. My heart pounded in my chest as he smiled a wicked, devastating grin.

"We'll see. Depends how useful you are," he replied with a smirk.

Theodore gave Kellan's shoulder a shove.

"He's joking-"

"Well I'm not-"

"We're going to look after you," Theodore shot Kellan a look, to which Kellan rolled his eyes.

"Why?" I asked.

Kellan leant his chin on his hand, blinked up at Theodore mockingly.

"Yeah Teddy, why?" He asked with a pout.

Theodore gripped the steering wheel hard, his eyes narrowed at the road. There was anger in the set of his shoulders, anger that came from more than Kellan's teasing.

"She needed me- us. I wasn't going to let them kill her," he hissed.

Kellan gripped his chest, pretended to be touched, before he looked back out the window, weaved his hand through the air.

"Always saving the princesses from their dragons,"

~

123

We drove until the sun sunk below the horizon and the rolling fields turned to the scorched earth I had come to expect from the outside world. The war had ravaged the lands, and I saw it now in the desecrating buildings and lack of greenery.

Kellan was singing at the top of his lungs as he rapped his fingers against the dash, while Theodore squinted into the darkness. Only one of the head lights was working, and it flickered dangerously with every bump and turn. I played with the window roller, moved it up and down, up and down, stared out into the darkness.

I huffed.

At first, I had been afraid, exhilarated, anxious. I'd catalogued every knoll and river like the artist I had once been, traced the plains and the textures and saved the vibrant colours in the hopes that one day I would paint them.

Now I was bored.

I fidgeted uncomfortably, flexed my numb toes. I bought my knees up to my chest, leant my head on them, tried to entertain myself. I watched Kellan sing, his eyes scrunched closed as he clasped at the air, his mouth wide open as he yelled. I gripped my calves tightly, mesmerised by his freedom. His skin was olive dark, a shade of beige-brown that was beautiful. The roman slope of his nose and the set of his brows were almost godly, and again I itched for oil paints, for canvas and hours to lose myself.

The music stopped, and Kellan's eyes shot open. He gave Theodore an angry look.

"What the hell was that for?" Kellan asked, but Theodore held a finger up to silence him.

Kellan scoffed, and opened his mouth to complain when something in the rear view caught his attention. He swung round in his chair; his eyes squinted into the darkness behind me. His eyes widened a fraction, before he pushed on my head.

"Get down. Cut the lights." He reached over the steering wheel and turned off the lights.

We were plunged into momentary darkness, before light streamed through the rear window. I turned in my seat, peered through the dusty glass. My eyes adjusted, and fear settled in my stomach as hard as a lead ball.

Behind us were two white, hulking trucks. Much like the Hovears, they were sleek, glimmering vehicles, but these had huge, golden tires that churned up the earth in their wake. They were made for war, and with every passing second, they drew nearer.

"I said get down," Kellan hissed as he grabbed me by the shoulders, pushed down hard.

He unstrapped my belt and yanked me by the leg into the foot space. I crouched down low, heart beating frantically as Theodore ground the car up a gear.

"I can't see," Theodore whispered.

"Let me." Kellan was already clambering onto the divide.

Theodore swore as he unbuckled and fell into the passenger seat. The car rocked dangerously back and forth before Kellan settled into the driver's seat. I could only see a tiny sliver of his face from my position on the floor, but as his hands found the wheel he grinned.

"Buckle up buttercup," Kellan pushed his foot down onto the accelerator and the car screamed in response.

Theodore opened the glove box and pulled something out. He inspected it momentarily, turned it over in his large hands, before he turned and looked down at me.

"Here, take this." He held out the object to me.

He pressed it into my hand. It was cool, metallic, and as my fingers wrapped around it, I realised what it was.

A gun.

"Don't give her that! She'll shoot you in your stupid face," Kellan cursed, but Theo ignored him.

He wrapped his hand around mine, pulled my finger over the trigger. His hands were warm, soft, slightly lined and burnt. He tightened my grip and gave me a reassuring look. There was no trace of fear, no worry that I might turn the weapon on him. There was only trust, good and pure and, as Kellan had said, stupid, but also endearing.

"If they catch up, and they come for you, pull the trigger. Don't hesitate," he ordered.

He waited for me to nod, before he let my hand go. I looked at the gun in my hand, so primitive, so rough. The car swerved, veered to the left, then to the right, and Kellan grinned, exhilarated by the challenge.

"We should stop," Theodore reasoned as he looked back at the tailing Pioneers.

"Are you crazy? I've got this," Kellan shifted up again.

The engine whined in protests as the windows rattled, threatened to crack and shatter with every bump. Theodore pulled out another gun from the glove box, clicked off the safety.

"We stand a better chance if we stop. We can't afford to lead them to the Slum."

Kellan groaned, and through my small window of sight I saw the fight in his eyes. The belief that he could outrun them. The moon washed over his face and cast his eyes into dark shadows as he cursed. He switched the lights back on and turned on the music.

"If I die, I'm so haunting you," Kellan hissed as he slammed his foot on the break.

The tyres screeched as my head wacked against the seat. I blinked the spots from my vision, my temples throbbed as the car slowed, the headlights from the Pioneer trucks intensified. My heavy, frightened breathing was the only sound as the car stopped, and Kellan cut the engine.

Both boys sat ridged in their seats. Theodore gripped the gun tightly next to his thigh, hidden from view. Kellan had both hands on the wheel, his body relaxed, his face calm, but the white of his knuckles betrayed him. The Pioneer trucks slowed and pulled up behind us. The crack of boots on hard dirt was deafening.

Theodore tensed, his shoulders stiff as two smaller lights emitted from Commniglass' came towards the windows. I sunk lower in my hiding place; my fingers trembled against the grip of the gun. The Pioneers shone their lights into the car, peered through the grimy window.

"Here we go," Kellan hissed through gritted teeth as a Pioneer rapped on the window.

Kellan rolled it down and gave the Pioneer a dazzling smile.

"I'm sorry, was I speeding?" Kellan teased.

The Pioneer looked between Theodore and Kellan, his eyes analysing as he came to the same conclusion I had.

Mai-Coh.

"Step out of the vehicle," the Pioneer commanded.

Kellan made a slight tutting noise as the other Pioneer came to Theodores's window.

"You know… I don't think I will." Within a second, Kellan had his hands wrapped around the Pioneers neck.

Theodore let two shots smash through the passenger window and hit the other Pioneer square in the chest. Kellan bought the Pioneers head down once, twice, three times with a deafening crack against the door frame. Theo kicked open the door and leapt out of the car, more shots echoing in the dark night. I heard grunting and turned to see Kellan being dragged through the open window. He struggled to latch onto something, but his hands found no purchase, his feet scrambled against the steering wheel. He landed with a thump on the ground. A Pioneer brandished his electric baton, flicked it to life. It crackled like lightening, cast a blue glint over Kellan's body.

The door opposite me opened, and a Pioneer leant inside the vehicle. His silver eyes found mine, and there was a flicker of surprise, that was quickly overcome with rage.

"You treacherous bitch," he lunged forward and grabbed me by the ankle.

I let out a yelp as he dragged me towards the door. I fumbled for the gun, my fingers slick with sweat, but it slipped from my grasp, tumbled under the seat. The Pioneer pulled out his whip, raised it above his head, and I held up my arm, ready for the blow. Theo wrapped his arm around the Pioneers neck, pulled him back away from me. The Pioneer let my ankle go, and I scooted back, reached under the chair for the gun. The Pioneer and Theodore struggled, all limbs and fists. The Pioneer managed to wrestle Theodore to the ground, pinned him by the throat with his foot. My fingers clasped the gun, and I pointed it at the Pioneer as he towered over Theo. I wanted to squeeze the trigger, I wanted to help. My fingers trembled against the metal, unrelenting.

A shot resounded through the night air, and the Pioneer crumpled on top of Theo with a gasp. Kellan lowered his gun, swiped blood from his nose. He walked over to Theo, who was struggling to pull himself from underneath the dead Pioneer. Kellan raised his foot and kicked the Pioneer onto the ground with a disgusted grunt. Theo scrambled to his feet, looked back at the trucks.

"Is that it?" He said breathlessly.

Kellan nodded, toed the dead Pioneer in the ribs. I lowered my gun, felt simultaneously disappointed and relieved. The bodies on the ground made my stomach roll, and bile rose in my throat as blood seeped into the earth. I crawled to the open door and the contents of my stomach flowed up out of my mouth. My body seized, and I choked as hot tears slipped down my cheeks.

This was real.

This was happening.

I was a traitor, and there was no going home.

"You better not be getting that in the car," Kellan called.

"Cut it out," Theodore said as he walked towards me.

He took my hair and pulled it behind my head with one hand, patted my back with the other as the last remnants of my stomach spilled onto the floor. I gulped down a breath of air, the taste of sick burnt my throat. I wiped at my mouth; my head pulsed as I sat up. He gave me a soft smile, let my hair drop. Kellan walked over to the Pioneer trucks, clambered up into the driver's seat.

"Don't baby her," Kellan shouted as he rifled through the glove box, checked the back seats.

Theo rolled his eyes as he reached forward and took the gun from my hand.

"Probably a bit too soon to give you one of these," he pushed the gun back into his waist band, revealed a strip of toned beige skin that made my heart thump.

He reached out his hand, and as I looked up at him, at the kindness in his eyes, something familiar and reassuring

129

washed away my fear. I took it, and he helped haul me back up onto the seat. Kellan gave a whoop from the Pioneers truck, jumped down and ran towards the car.

"Look what I found," Kellan chucked something at Theo, and he caught it with ease.

Theo looked at whatever was in his hand, inspected it closely, before he threw it back to Kellan.

"Keys? What for?" Theo asked.

Kellan looked at him, dumbfounded, as if the solution was plainly simple. Kellan looked at me, raised his eyebrows, jerked his thumb at Theo.

"Can you believe this guy?" he asked, then walked over to the dead Pioneer.

He grabbed one by the head, lifted him up. The Pioneer's head flopped lifelessly; his features slack. Acid rose in my throat again, but I swallowed it down, desperate to appear as more than a damsel in distress.

"We take their uniforms, we drive their truck, we avoid having to sneak into the Slum," Kellan grinned as he shook the Pioneers head.

"This guy gets it," Kellan gestured to the Pioneer.

Theo hesitated. He looked between the barely held together Mai-Coh vehicle, and the sleek, Pioneer truck. Kellan grabbed the lips of the Pioneer, manipulated them as a ventriloquist manipulates a dummy, his voice low.

"Come on, you know he's right. And so very handsome," Kellan imitated.

Theo sighed, palmed his face as he nodded. Kellan whooped, let the Pioneer drop with a thud. Theo walked over to the other Pioneer, examined the uniform. There were two large bullet holes in the chest plate, blood oozing down the stomach.

"This one's a bust," he said, kicked the Pioneer over.

I watched as they examined the dead Pioneers and something like anger boiled in my stomach. Something I couldn't really explain. A rage that kept boiling as they turned the Pioneers over, stripped them of their armour, their shirts. I clenched my fists as Kellan stripped off his shirt, pulled on the tight-fitting Pioneers garment.

Was this to be my fate too? A careless death? A disrespect that felt worse than the act itself?

Theo came around from the other side of the car. The uniform he wore was ill-fitting, it stretched against his muscles, the buttons barely doing up. He tried to pull the chest plate closed, but it wouldn't click. He bent down, looked into the car.

I was trembling. My teeth were chattering uncontrollably with rage. He frowned, reached out to touch me. I flinched away from his hand.

"Are you okay?" He asked.

I stared at him, and for a second the rage peaked, and I wanted to lash out. Hit him, kick him, grab his gun and shoot him. Scream about the way they treated the dead, as if they weren't people too. The violent thought shook my breath from my lips, and the rage fell as quickly as it had risen. He waited, hand unwavering, his eyes narrowed just a fraction as I smoothed my face with practiced ease.

"Yes. I'm fine," I replied.

Theo nodded; his hand still outstretched. He waited patiently for me to take it, and after a moment of hesitation I did. It was so overwhelming how large and warm his hands were. They were twice the size of my own, and when his fingers wrapped around mine, pulled me from the seat, I couldn't help but feel like a child.

I stepped out of the car, avoided the puddle of vomit, and took in the darkness. The dark, dusty ground stretched on for miles. It rose and fell, dipped and peaked, a rolling cascade of Imperfection. I had never seen something so beautiful. I looked up at the sky in wonder as I took in the stars; specs of light in their millions in shades of white, blue and green. So different to the muted skies of Sadon, where I could count the stars as easily as breathing. I would never count these masses, not in a lifetime of nights.

"Do you see these? Back home?" Theo gestured up at the sky.

I shook my head. I had never seen so many stars in my life. They shone like diamonds against black satin, and I was reminded of the light display in the Palladium, the hum of the orbs. I sobered as I thought back on it. Thought of Alfie. I wondered if he'd waited for me under the tree. If they'd questions him, if he missed me. At the thought of him, my heart sunk, and I turned away from the stars.

"Hey, come on. You can flirt later," Kellan called as he dragged the naked Pioneers into the Mai-Coh vehicle.

Theo grabbed a Pioneer by the shoulders and hauled him towards the car. I watched in silence. I forced myself to watch, to swallow the disgust and anger that had been bred into me. Once they were done, Theo took me by the arm, a weirdly gentlemanly gesture that didn't suit his bulky size, and guided me towards the truck. He opened the door for me and leant me his arm to push myself up.

He reminded me vaguely of Alfie, his kindness, his warmth. This familiarity made me both comfortable and hurt. I met his eyes, looked into their depths. They were deep set, distinctly curved, angular in a way I had never seen. They were beautiful in their uniqueness, the colour of dark oak. I reached out, brushed the hair from his forehead out of instinct. He took a minute step back, his body ridged.

"Your hair… You wear the uniform, but you don't look Perfect," I rushed to say as blood pooled in my cheeks.

Kellan joined Theo, tilted his head at me with an amused smile.

"Oh really? I think I suit white," Kellan brushed off his shoulder, admired himself.

I shook my head, although I couldn't deny how shocking it looked against his skin.

"They'll be able to spot you as imposters. Easily."

Theo looked at Kellan out the corner of his eye before relenting. He stepped forward, nodded, gave me his permission. I reached forward, smoothed his thick, dark hair back. I rubbed the dirt from his cheeks, the blood from his neck. I straightened his collar, tilted my head from side to side.

It wouldn't matter what I did. They would take one look at his skin colour, at the features that the Emperor rooted out long ago, and know he was an imposter.

"Was there a helmet? A head covering?" I asked.

Kellan snorted.

"Nothing can be done to save your ugly mug," Kellan sneered.

My patience frayed at the jab. I turned to him, insulted despite the fact it wasn't aimed at me.

"It's his skin," I replied in an attempt to defend Theo, who was stony faced and not pleased.

Kellan raised a brow, before he shook his head.

"I forgot how against people of colour your people are. You hear that, Theo? You're a mutt,"

"I'm Korean, not a dog," Theo shot back in an effort to jest, but his face was dark.

I opened my mouth to apologise, but Theo had already walked back over to the dead, looked over the scraps of armour. I fixed Kellan with an angry glare, although his comment wasn't far from the truth. It was true, Sadon was awash with white, for the Emperor found purity and Perfection in the lack of colour. It had never made sense to me, no matter how many times the history teachers had preached about it. But I had never spoken up, spoken out, defended those who the Emperor deemed Imperfect out of fear of punishment, and that made me complicit.

There were so many things I had let slip, so many things I had left unspoken, and I knew that Kellan, vocal, loyal, fierce Kellan, wouldn't take my thoughts as proof of my difference. What were thoughts without action? It was not enough to be quietly in disagreement, not when that changed nothing.

I gestured Kellan forward sharply, ready to fix his hair, to show that I could be worthy. Kellan looked at my hand. He pulled on a smirk, but there was hesitation in his eyes.

"I think I look handsome enough," he reasoned.

I shook my head, leant forward in my seat. His hair, unruly and curled to below his ears, was a dead giveaway. I reached out my hand to flatten it, my fingertips a millimetre away. His hands rose up and caught my wrists. His eyes shone as bright as freshly lit fire, and his face seemed to absorb the darkness of the night.

"Don't," he said.

His fingers tightened, and I winced, tried to wiggle free. Kellan held on for an agonising second, before he threw my wrists away. I bought my arms to my chest, cradled my pulsing wrists. Kellan turned away, jumped up into the driver's seat. He turned on the engine, flicked on the lights, illuminated Theos shadow.

"Come on Theodora. Pick your favourite handbag and hurry up." Kellan flashed the lights incessantly until Theo flipped him off and ran to the passenger's seat.

In his hand he held a silken head scarf, only slightly blood stained on one of the corners. As he strapped himself in, he turned to me, held out the material. His eyes didn't meet mine, but when I didn't take the material, he jerked it at me again.

"Come on. Cover me up," he insisted.

I took the fabric in my hands, rubbed it between my thumb and forefinger. It was so fine, something I might have worn on my journey to the Inner Ring. It occurred to me that this may not have belonged to the dead soldier, but instead to his wife. A gift he had been saving for his return. She will never see his face again, never feel this silk against her skin.

I hadn't realised I had begun to cry until Theo reached forward and rubbed a thumb across my cheek. I shrugged away the tears, flattened the head piece in my hand. I reached forward, fastened it loosely over his head, his mouth and nose, until nothing but his eyes showed. I pinned it into place with a loose hair grip. I smiled at him, gave his shoulder a squeeze.

"I... I think your skin is beautiful," I whispered.

I couldn't see his face to know his reaction, but I thought I caught a shadow of a smile in his eyes. He turned and looked out the windshield, his eyes following the Mai-Coh vehicle as it disappeared.

Chapter IX

The sun rose as red and swollen as an overripe tomato, illuminating the vast, endless sand in shades of ruby and amethyst. In the distance, to the west, there was a glimpse of something white, something shimmering and vibrant, but it rose and fell as fickly as the dunes. More concrete, more substantial, was the glistening silver fence, creeping closer with every second, that sectioned off the Slums.

The fence stretched on for miles in either direction, it disappeared up into the cloudless sky as far as the eye could see. It stretched to the east, followed the curve of Sadon's walls, far behind but still dictating every aspect of life. A large, wire number was strung up dead ahead against the fence; the number nine. In the distance, if I squinted hard enough, I could see the number ten, and the partition that separated the slums crimes.

The entrance gate was flanked with two guard towers. Once white, they were now weathered, yellowed from dust and sun exposure, smeared red at the base with spilt blood. Kellan slowed the truck as we drew closer. There were many other trucks just like ours, waiting to enter. It was orderly, patient, a remnant of Perfection in a land plagued by the Imperfect.

I could feel my heart rising, fluttering as the vehicle pulled to a stop. I drew down my hood, braided my hair with deft fingers. I unzipped my coat, careful to keep the diary concealed under its folds. Theo turned at the sound of movement, watched me preen. I sat up, fastened my multiple braids into place. I pinched my cheeks as we edged forward. A heavily armoured soldier was standing at the gate, holding a scanner. I leant forward, put my hand on Theo's shoulder.

"Switch with me," I whispered.

My heart was pounding against my ribs. I was jittery, my hands were shaking as Kellan frowned.

"What?" He hissed, kept his eyes on the truck in front.

"They might scan the passenger. If you don't have an ID chip, they'll know. I have one," I gestured to my wrist.

Kellan looked at the skin of my wrist, the blue and green veins that forked down my arms, as if he could see the technology that marked me as one of them. He nodded once, jerked his chin to the back seat. Theo lunged with a swiftness that didn't suit his size, ducked into the back. I moved into the passenger seat, smoothed my hair into place. Kellan looked me up and down, gave a tut of disgust.

"Perfect," he hissed.

I ignored his insult as I settle into the seat, practiced smiling. I folded my hands in my lap, pressed my thumb against my wrist, wondered if letting the guard scan me was a good idea. Would my identity be marked? Would it send an alert to the Emperor? He would know where I was.

He would know where to follow.

"So, are you my prisoner?" Kellan asked.

I shook my head. Slum 9 was not for the likes of me. No, if I had been captured, it would have been Slum 5 and the Riven Den. At the thought of Riven, I snapped my fingers.

"No." I undid the buttons of my dress, pushed it down until it pooled around my hips.

Kellan stared at my bra with a raised brow. I tried not to squirm under his gaze. This was the most exposed I had been to anyone outside of my family, and the caress of the humid air was almost luxurious against my skin.

"I thought your kind were frigid prudes?"

"Tell them I'm your Riven. That you're loaning me for the trip," I said as I leant forward, arranged my skirts around my legs.

Kellan reached over, his hand rested on my back. I jumped as his fingers traced the letters of the word that would forever mark me. I sat up, pressed myself flat against the seat. Kellan looked over at me, his mouth set into a line.

"Who did that to you?" He gripped the steering wheel tighter as the last truck in front of us edge through the gate.

I pressed my lips tight, not wanting to talk about it. I didn't want to think about that night, about the smell of ink and blood, about the pain that had threatened to splinter me in two. Luckily, the truck in front entered, and we were ushered forward. The soldier came up to the passengers' window, and rapped on it twice, swift and authoritative. I wound down the window and gave the guard a brilliant smile.

"State your business," he ordered, scrolled through the holographic scanner with unnerving pace.

"Supplies. Restock transport," Kellan said gruffly, adjusted his voice.

The guard looked up from his holograph. Surprisingly, his eyes were not modified. They were pure and green, on the small side, but simple. He looked at me, observed my bare body and intricate hair.

"She looks pretty fresh. Lucky guy," the guard mumbled, before he swiped a few controls on the hologram.

"Enter. Clear out before lunch. We have a raid party coming in. Don't want to risk any of our own caught in the crossfire," he gave me another once over, and smiled that horrid, knowing smile that belonged to men who kept Riven.

"Fuck her good for me. You're lucky your mate isn't crazy." He spoke over me as if I didn't exist.

Kellan pulled on a thin smile, placed his hand on my thigh, gave it a squeeze. My heart jumped into my throat, and I had to force myself not to flinch away from his touch.

"Oh, I will," Kellan reassured the guard as the gate crept open.

The Pioneers in their guard towers trained their guns on the fence line, eyes sharp and fingers forever hovering over the trigger. As we crawled through the gate, what lied beyond came into focus. There were huts upon huts, made from metal, fabric, wood, any scraps that could be salvaged. They were built on top of one another, their walls intermingling until it became impossible to distinguish where one started and the other ended. Waste ran through the uneven streets; it poured around people's bare feet, collected in dips and ran through open doorways, swept away what little possessions lingered within.

The people were just as desolate and broken as their homes. Children with skin pulled taut against bones ran under foot, their ill-fitting rags exposing skin and limbs burnt brown by the sun. There weren't many elders, but the ones who looked over thirty or forty were haggard, bent double, with limbs missing or wasted away. Their cheeks were hollow, and their eyes were devoid of life.

They marched onwards towards nothing but death, a welcome release from the hell they existed in. I watched it all, my hand pressed against the glass like a child at a zoo. I had never thought of the Slums like this, it had always been some far-off reality. Something to avoid, a place that had never seemed truly real.

No one deserved this.

Kellan pulled the truck to a stop, took his hand off my thigh. He checked the gun he had stored in his belt, flipped open the barrel, counted the bullets.

"We have an hour or so before the crew get here. We should collect supplies," Kellan said as he looked back at Theo, who nodded his approval.

"You know the rendezvous point? You think we'll get out of here before the raid?" Theo asked.

Kellan shrugged, opened the door. Neither of them took much mind of me, or bothered to involve me in their plans. I was their prisoner after all, even if they didn't admit it. I had no right to their information, no right to be included.

"Let's hope. Take the girl, gather food. I'll go look for weapons," Kellan didn't wait for a response, suddenly all business.

He jumped down from the truck and slammed the door behind him. Theo leant forward and passed me my coat.

"Zip up," he said, his eyes graciously not landing on my bare skin.

When I picked up the coat, its lightness made me panic. I opened it up, but the diary was missing. I turned in my seat, looked back at Theo with wide, alarmed eyes. The diary sat next to him, unopened. He followed my eyes and looked down at the diary. He took it in his hands, balanced it carefully in one palm, ran his finger across its cover. My palms were sweating as he fingered the pages, traced their edges as if he'd never felt something so fine, and maybe he hadn't. He held it out to me, and I snatched it back.

"A prized possession?" He asked, his eyes narrowed as I gripped the book between my fingers.

I nodded as I yanked on my coat, pushed the diary back into safety.

"Something like that," I replied as I zipped up the coat.

Theo's lips were pursed, as if he wanted to ask further questions, but he said nothing more. He jumped from the truck, held the door open for me to hop down. The stench of the Slum smacked me in the face as my feet touched the ground. Blood, dirt, death; the stench of Imperfection.

I pulled my sleeve over my nose, my eyes watered as I walked through the filth. Children stared up at us with eyes as large as saucers, mouths agape at our pristine clothes. A small child, a girl barely four or five, stared at me in awe. She had a large scar that ran from her left temple down to the right corner of her lip, carved her face in two. It was an old scar, once deep and red, now white and softened. She reached out a grubby finger to touch my white coat, and I instinctively shied away from her touch. Hurt flashed across her eyes, and she retracted her hand, slunk back into the shadows with her head bent low. I turned away from her, tried to ignore the guilt I felt about hurting her and followed closely behind Theo.

He towered over everyone else, a mountain amongst hills. I moved in his shadow, used him as a shield against the tide of watching Slum dwellers. They glared at us with resentment, with clenched jaws and tensed fists. I averted my eyes, scared I would see someone I recognised.

Slum 9 was a secret seller's prison, filled to the brim with Sadon's traitors. Those who allied themselves with Mai-Coh, those who sent letters in the dead of night. Those who whispered and colluded. It made sense why Kellan and Theo had bought me here.

Theo pushed aside a draped rug, a weathered but finely embroidered piece that didn't seem to belong, and pulled me through the gap it concealed. Behind the rug was a set of dark steps, shielded from the sun by huts that were stacked high up into the sky.

The steps were steep, slick with assorted liquids that I didn't dare to think about. I steadied myself against the walls, hands pressed against the sticky, uneven stones, took

141

each step slowly. Theo marched down sure footedly, as if he had descended these steps a million times.

We were descending into the depths of the earth, each step took me further into darkness, until I could barely see Theo's broad shoulders. I was about to pause, about to tell Theo I could go no further, when a metal clunk and the creak of a door opening bathed the stairs in light.

I blinked into the glare, peered through the door frame at the grand hall that waited for me. Its ceiling rose in a dome miles above my head, hollowed out of the rock by hands that had long since fallen still. The walls were uneven and jagged, as if carved in a rush. It was lit by wooden torches that burnt red and green, flames so unrestrained and uncontrolled it looked as if the place could go up in flames at any moment.

Inside there were stalls; wooden tables laid with items to sell. The aroma of burnt bread and braised meat hung temptingly in the close air, and my stomach whined in response. The din of chattering was deafening, a thousand voices and languages all in competition. Theo looked back at me, took in my coat.

"You should change. Kamal doesn't take to..." he trailed off.

He didn't have to say it, I knew what he meant. I ducked my head, stepped down into the chaos. Theo edged through the crowd with grace; he glided past traders with a gentleness that was endearing. People glared at him, at the uniform. They stared out of the corner of their eyes, pulled items subtly from their stalls and hid them under shawls. They felt his presence as tangibly as a knife against their throats, a loose cannon that could kill them all. I hated to think what my people had done here to instil such fear.

I moved through the crowd, almost invisible within their midst. They paid less attention to me; my hair style signified my status. They wouldn't turn their gazes upon a Riven, a fallen woman who still belonged to Perfection in the worst of ways. A whore to be whelped and drugged and broken until another could take its place. I slipped between elbows without any trouble, moved towards a stall stacked with clothes.

The lady behind the stall watched me curiously as I approached. Her eyes, rimmed in blue, followed my hands as I stroked the strange fabrics. I had never seen clothes in such wonderful colours; shorts as red as blood, shoes the colour of sunshine. It was clear this underground market was for the Mai-Coh; none of the slum dwellers wore clothes as bold. I picked up a shining emerald cape, its hood edged in gold and embroidered with autumnal leaves. Its fastening was a simple golden clasp, and its buttons carved from oak tied with green thread. I looked at the woman, gave her an experimental smile, unsure how trading worked. Sadon didn't work with money, only status, and I'd never had to buy anything in my life.

"Can I take this?" I asked.

She snorted at my nativity, took in my hair, my clothes. I could see her calculating how wealthy I looked, how well my master kept me.

"I'll take the coat," she stroked a finger over my sleeve.

I hesitated. I clung to it, pushed my hands deep into the pockets. My fingers brushed against my Commniglass, as cool and smooth as a sea washed stone, and I drew it out. I peered into its milky depths hesitantly, afraid I'd see eyes looking back. Something called me from within, a desperate plea that was both voiceless, and yet held within the voices of all those I held dear; Chrys, Lavender, Alfie. I placed it on the desk, shook my head to clear it of the temptation.

"Okay. Throw in the head scarf," I agreed as I snatched the lilac satin from the table.

She grabbed the Commniglass, twisted it in her gnarled hands. She looked into its foggy surface; its shine reflected in her empty eyes. She looked back up at me with mild intrigue as she rubbed her thumb across its surface. It pulsed, its light rose and fell as quickly as a heartbeat. She let it go with a gasp, and it landed with a heavy thump on the table.

I shucked off the coat, grasped Klio's diary in one hand, shoved the coat into her arms with the other. Startled, she balled the coat into her greedy hands, pushed it under her table. With frantic and unstable hands, I tucked the diary into the belt of my dress, refastened it so tight it hurt to breathe. I tried not to think about what that small pulse of light meant as I pulled the cape around my shoulders, fastened the clasp around my neck.

Before I could tie the scarf around my hair and properly convince myself everything was going to be fine, there was a shout, and the sound of gun shots.

I turned to look at the doorway we had emerged from, hoped I wouldn't see what I almost knew for sure I would, that pulse of light as harrowing as a dying breath.

The air left my lungs in a rush of fear. The floor dropped from underneath me and the room teetered, as if the walls were about to crumble and bury me alive.

Arthur stood in the doorway; his hand hovered over the gun strapped to his hip. His eyes roamed over the stalls as people tried to run, grabbed valuables as they tried to flee. People pushed past me, their shoulders bumped mine, but I couldn't move. My eyes were fixed on Arthur as he descended into the market, flanked on either side by Pioneer guards. Arthur, who had pulled my hair as a child. Arthur, who had punched a boy so hard he'd put him in a coma. Arthur, who had burnt a man to death for loving another man.

His face was controlled, calm, focused, but he couldn't keep the sparkle of delight from his eyes. He pushed an elderly man to the ground, stepped over his writhing body as if he didn't exist with a grin that was terrifying. I could almost feel his hand around my throat, cold and hard, his eyes dancing as the last breath squeezed from my lungs…

Someone grabbed my hand, and I finally broke my gaze from Arthur. Theo looked shaken; his eyes darted around the market for escape. Smoke was rising in the room as a market stall caught fire, its bread crackled in the flames.

"Move."

He pulled me through the swelling crowd, darted between stalls, pushed skilfully through material partitions and terrified Slum dwellers. I tried to fasten the scarf around my head, but the fabric kept catching on stray elbows, snagging and falling back onto my shoulders. There was an agonised wail, and I risked a look over my shoulder. Arthur held the woman from the clothing stall by the throat, my traded Commniglass in his other hand.

"Where did you get this?" Arthur growled, his once calm and eager face contorted in rage.

The lady scratched at his hand, gasped for breath, her eyes bulged red, her lips moved soundlessly. Arthur let out a primal yell and threw her with a strength that seemed unworldly. She hit the ground with a crack and fell instantly still. A yelp escaped my lips at the sight of her unnaturally bent back. Arthur looked up, as if he sensed my presence, and our eyes met. The room fell to ruin around me as his face went from rage to confusion, and then to hatred.

"Calluna!" His cry was world shattering, and it lashed at my insides, tore me apart.

Theo looked between Arthur and I, and then yanked on my arm so hard my shoulder gave an agonising groan. He pulled me with renewed fever as Arthur came barrelling towards us. A hole carved from the caves wall loomed ahead, promising freedom. Theo pushed through the thickening crowd, shouldered his way through the people with a grunt. The stairway was crowded, people were clawing, crushing each other in an effort to reach safety.

"Stop them!" Arthur ordered through the fray.

We were slowing, the crowd so tight knit it was hard to see through the clambering bodies. Theo kept pushing, his hand tight on mine, sweat beaded on his neck. I looked back, watched as Arthur threw people this way and that, growing increasingly impatient and frustrated. His nose flared as he kicked someone in the back, crippled them to the stones. Theo cursed, drew out his stolen Pioneer gun and fired it twice into the air. People screamed, dropped to the ground, scattered to the walls and under what was left of stalls. Theo took the chaos and ran, pushed us finally to the stairwell. He fired a third shot up into the stairs wall, sent rock and dust scattering over people's heads. They parted, the threat of his uniform, of my people, more terrifying than the fire that was starting to fill the air with acrid smoke.

Theo took the steps two at a time, left me stumbling and falling over my own feet. The gap was closing behind us as quickly as it opened; arms pressed against mine, fingers clammy with fear snatched at my skin. Feet, both bare and booted, trampled my own. I gasped for breath, the heat in the stairwell rising, rising, until my skin was ready to boil.

We were in complete darkness, I couldn't see those who pressed around me, nor could I see Theo, but his hand was strong and unwavering against my own. I closed my eyes and fumbled on, swallowed the terror that threatened to rip from my throat, bit my tongue until the taste of blood filled my mouth. I could no longer hear Arthur, I could hear nothing but the panting, whimpering breaths of the Slum dwellers around me, who too thought that this turmoil would never end.

146

When I was sure the darkness had consumed me whole, that I had fallen into the very depths of the world, a circle of light penetrated through the smoky darkness, lit my closed eyelids red. I opened my eyes greedily, drank in the single ray of light despite the stinging of my retinas. Theo's form glowed in front of me as pearlescent and glorious as the Emperor himself. His hand loosened on mine as we became awash with light.

The two of us stumbled gasping into the side street, the crowd filtered out around us. We both stood, bent double, sucked mouthfuls of cleaner air into our lungs. Theo looked up at me, his forehead shone with sweat. He leant over, grabbed the scarf and tied it roughly around my head, fastened the knot below my chin. His knuckles rested a little longer on my jaw as his eyes raked over me, took in the ash and soot that stained my exposed skin, but when he saw no sign of injury his brow relaxed.

He smoothed the headscarf down, his eyes distant as he followed the curve of my cheek. I wondered if he was as disgusted by my appearance as Kellan, if all he saw was the perfection that they had forged me into. I burned to know, but before I could even think about asking, he drew back, balled his fists at his sides.

"We need to get to the rendezvous point. This place is going to be crawling with Pioneers within minutes." Even as he said this, I heard the echo of Arthur's voice in the stairwell as he screamed for people to move.

I nodded despite the fact I was still breathless; my feet ached from the climb, my limbs weak with privilege, but I pushed on.

We wound through the back streets; every few streets or so I caught the glimpse of a Pioneer truck as it prowled the cobblestones, spat out Pioneers as it went. Theo kept changing our course, harshly turned at the sight of a soldier, hid behind waste bins and drew us into stairwells. His eyes scoured the landscape, forever darted over every possible

147

route, considered his every step as if one single foot wrong could be our downfall.

Maybe it would be.

He pulled me down a narrow alley, shuffled sidelong so his broad shoulders didn't scuff against the brick. He poked his head out tentatively, and as I went to follow, he grabbed me, pushed me flush against the wall. I opened my mouth to object, my back ached from the impact, but he clamped a sweaty hand over my lips. I struggled, but he fixed me with a daunting stare that made me stop. He shook his head only once, his eyes dark, his arms tense as I heard footsteps.

A Pioneer guard waltzed past, his Commniglass projecting the latest updates. I held my breath as he passed, stared up at Theo, who was unnaturally still. His body, pressed against mine, was solid and warm, coiled tight ready to pounce. My cheeks flushed red as we stared at each other, closer than I had ever been to another person. His breath fanned across my cheeks as we waited, the burnt oak scent of his skin enveloped us both. My fingers trembled, only partially from fear.

His eyes, like pools of bronze, met mine with an intensity that stripped me down to the bone. My chest heaved, and with every breath our bodies met. His hand softened against my mouth, as if just realising how hard he'd been gripping me. His thumb swiped apologetically over my chin, but he didn't let go.

"Mai-Coh spotted in the lower market quarter. All Pioneers please respond," a voice drifted from the Commniglass, and the guard made a disgusted noise as he broke into a run.

Once he was out of sight, Theo removed his hand, gave me as much space as he could given the width of the alley.

"That'll be Kellan. Always getting into damn trouble," Theo muttered as he moved out of the alley.

I followed behind, chewed at my lip as I kept my eyes trained on his back. I could still feel the heat of his body, the weight of his hand across my mouth, and my heart fluttered at the thought. I swallowed past the lump that had settled in my throat as he shook his head.

"He's going to get himself killed," he hissed, more to himself this time.

I wondered why the two had been paired together. Theo and Kellan, they seemed like two very different people. Theo was steady, he was warm, almost familiar. Kellan was entirely different; cold, sarcastic, reckless. They didn't seem like the likeliest of friends.

"How long have you been friends? You and Kellan?" I asked, unable to help myself.

I craved to know something, to feel like I belonged just a little. Maybe it was a remnant of who I used to be, the need to please, to be accepted, but the desperation to start making this all make sense outweighed my sense of self preservation. Theo looked back at me, his eyes narrowed. I thought maybe I'd overstepped a boundary, but he lifted a shoulder, looked back up to the sky.

"We grew up together. We went through training, became part of Kamal's guard at the same time. Can't seem to shake him, no matter how hard I try." He tried to seem hard done by, but his eyes shone with a concealed smile.

I nodded, and a hollowness replaced the unsteady beat of my heart. I thought of Polly, of the friend who I'd cared for as Theo cared for Kellan. I pressed my hand against the diary, and wished Polly had written in it too, just so I could feel close to her again.

The large fence loomed ahead, and beyond, tantalising and out of reach, stood the wilderness. It was rich, green, full of life. A bird dove out of one of the trees, swooped gracefully to the ground, and then veered up again, past the leaves and up into the sky. I watched it in wonder, jealous of its ease. I looked to Theo, and I wondered if maybe he could give me the same freedom as that bird. If he could unclip my wings and teach me to fly.

"Is that where we're going?" I asked, both exhilarated and anxious.

Theo stopped in front of a peculiar looking building. Although its windows were boarded up, the paint was as fresh and yellow as sunshine. The roof had been recently redone, holes fixed with wood and metal. It lingered here, the last house before the wildness of the untameable forest, as out of place as I was.

He turned, looked out at the wilderness, then back to me, as if he'd seen it a million times and was no longer impressed. I couldn't imagine ever growing bored of a place so terrifyingly beautiful. So real.

"You ever been anywhere with mud before?" He asked with a smile as he made his way to the bright yellow door, tactfully avoiding the question.

"My mum was a botanist," I said as I looked back out into that vast wilderness.

Once I stepped into those woods there was no coming back.

My feet faltered at the thought. I would never see Alfie again, or my brother or sister. I would never know what happened to them, if they were still alive after what I'd done. There was a finality to it that shocked me, that made my chest tighten. To never go home, to never turn back, it seemed so... definite.

I looked over my shoulder at the smoke that curled towards the greying sky. No doubt Arthur would be hot on our tail. If he caught me, would I see my family again? Would they praise my death like they had so many others? Would they mourn me?

"Are you coming, Calluna?" Theo called.

I looked up, dazed. My name in his voice was strange, but it bought clarity. He had his hand on the door, ready to push it open. He observed me curiously, his nose pinched. As I looked at him, it became clear why I had come to this point at all. My people wouldn't protect me, they'd tried to kill me. They would cheer at my execution and praise the Emperor for his blessings. They would vie for a chance at turning me in. They hated difference, individuality, and I couldn't ever go back, not even to check on my brother.

"That's what he called you, that's your name, right?" he asked.

I nodded despite the dangerous dizziness that threatened to drag me to the ground.

"Come on, we need to get inside." He pushed the door open a fraction, gestured me forward.

I gave one last glance back into the blazing Slum, one last glance at the life I was about to leave behind, before I moved forward. It didn't feel real, the movement of my feet, the journey ahead. Theo seemed a mere shadow as he held the door open for me, gestured me inside. As my mind clouded one thought pierced through it with alarming clarity.

"What about Kel-"

A hand wrapped around my neck; the words stolen from my lips. I gasped as I was yanked backward, my back connected with the flesh of another. Something sharp and cold pressed against my neck, and my eyes searched frantically for Theo. I didn't dare to struggle, the arm around my chest was slim but strong, and the teeth of the blade in the dark hand snagged my skin. The hot breath of my attacker fanned against the nape of my neck, measured and controlled. Theo stepped through the door, his mouth slack as he looked beyond me, at the person who had taken me captive.

"Ahzani, she's with us," he informed her calmly.

The arms relaxed hesitantly; the blade lowered from my neck. I stumbled forward, whirled around to look at who had released me. She was tall, not slim but not large, somewhere in between with strong legs and rough hands. Her skin was a deep coppery brown, reminiscent of cooling clay on a winters evening, mottled with small scars and tattoos. Her hair was pulled away from her face in twists as black as midnight. She raised a thick brow at me, twisted her knife round expertly, gave it a twirl before she sheathed it in her boot.

I was in awe of her effortless beauty. Her cheekbones were soft, but her jaw was sharp, her small dark eyes alight with mischief. She wore dark trousers, a billowing midnight blue shirt and dark vest overtop that gave a sharpness to her curves. She was masculine, and yet feminine; it was the way she held herself, the way her eyes danced, the way her red-brown lips quirked into a smile as she caught me staring.

"Could have given us a heads up. She stinks of Perfection," Ahzani turned up her nose.

With a finger she peeled back my cape, her nose crinkled as she examined my white dress. I balled my fists in the fabric of the cape to stop their shaking, but a quick flash of her smile showed she'd already seen. Her fingers moved upwards to toy with the golden clasp fastened around my neck. She was testing me; I sensed it in the smugness of her smile. She wanted to see if it was true, if Sadon really bred frigid, celibate prudes. I fidgeted despite my best efforts to stay still, and she had her answer.

Theo looked around the room, his eyes narrowed as they scanned the space. The inside was not as impressive as the out; plain wooden floor riddled with holes and damp, walls scribbled with drawings, words and symbols in varying colours. A single light fixture hung over head, its bulb lay in fragments on the ground below.

Theo strode to the back room, peered inside, his eyebrows knitted together in confusion. He walked back to us; his strides so large it took him barely three steps. He fixed Ahzani with darkened eyes; his lips pressed into a straight line. Ahzani tensed visibly, and I watched the fine lines of her neck as she looked at the boarded-up windows.

"Where are the others?" Theo asked measuredly, his voice flat.

Ahzani couldn't meet his eyes. She jerked her head towards the window, traced her long fingers along the edge of the table. Papers were strewn there, knives, guns, a sword, broken arrows. Blood mottled the scratched wood, faded into the fibres. She picked up an arrow, turned it on its side. She traced her finger along the blue feathers, her eyes so forcibly focused it was painful to watch. She let her gaze slip up to look at me, and in her eyes was a thinly veiled accusation, and in that one lingering glance I knew that my people had done something terrible.

"Priya's out back, burying Finn. They shot him and we managed to drag him back here before he died. Pepper and Jen were taken," she said it so casually, as if loss of this magnitude were normal, but underneath the calmness there was a stinging pain.

Her shoulders sagged as she wiped at the blood that stained her knuckles and the scratches that mottled her forearms. She stared at Theo, waited for him to share her pain. Theo sighed, rubbed a hand over his face. He looked at Ahzani, his eyes shone in the dim light. They shared a moment of silence that seemed to hold a million words I couldn't begin to understand. I waited for him to go to her, to hold her, but no such exchange happened. Ahzani fiddled with the arrow, her eyes slipped from Theo once more. She looked as if she were dying to ask something, her lips

153

pressed together to hold in the words she so desperately wanted to speak.

"Kellan?" Ahzani asked.

"Alive the last time I saw him," Theo replied.

Ahzani nodded, but her eyes were sad. She put down the arrow carefully, puffed out a long breath, before she straightened her shoulders, shook out her hands. Her gaze moved back to me; her eyes raked down my body, took in every detail. Her stare was as tangible as hands, and I pulled the cape more firmly around myself.

"Bringing Kamal a new sex toy?" Ahzani asked, her eyebrow raised.

I flinched at her words as my cheeks grew hot. She reached out and let her fingers graze where my hair fell against my neck. My skin sparked at her touch, and as her fingers plucked at my head scarf, revealing a lock of auburn hair, my heart stuttered, threatened to give out under her gaze.

She smirked as her fingers moved to my lips, pressed against my breath, and at the touch I could have sworn she took control of my lungs.

I jerked backwards; my bottom lip pulled between my teeth. I could taste ash and blood and something earthy. She gave me a pointed smile as she ran a hand through her braids in a gesture that could stop a thousand hearts and turned her mischievous gaze on Theo, who looked less than impressed.

"Well, after what happened with the last one..." she trailed off, examined her broken nails with a provoking side glance.

Theo rolled his eyes, clearly in no mood to entertain her mischief. He seemed in that moment much like a disgruntled father sick of herding his flock of unruly spawn. He rubbed

154

a thumb against his cheek, scratched at an itch that seemed more a subconscious tick than a skin irritation.

"Cut it out. She might have valuable information," Theo reasoned.

Ahzani tutted as the sound of a door banging open echoed through the house.

"Might might might," Ahzani teased, punctuating each word with the flick of her finger.

Before Theo could come to my defence, and before I could ask what happened to Kamal's last *toy,* a tall, brown skinned girl clambered into the room, dragged a shovel behind her. Sweat poured down her prominent brow and she swiped at it angrily, huffed through full, curved lips. Her ebony hair was pulled into a thick, oiled braid, and it swung over her shoulder and into her way, much to her annoyance. Her nose, a dominant feature that drew most of my attention, sucked in ragged breaths, and when her eyes, a shade of midnight coal, met mine, she blanched, dropped the shovel to the ground.

She reached for the bow slung over her back, but Theo raised a reassuring hand. Before a single word could be uttered, Kellan came bursting through the front door. He slammed it closed and pressed himself against it with a dramatic sigh. He was grinning, blood smeared across his face. He looked around the room like a wild animal chomping at the bit, took in our baffled faces, and slowly peeled himself away from the wood. He brushed the debris casually from his shoulders, pushed that wild, feral part of himself back down into his cool exterior as he took a step forward. He nodded with a dismissive shrug towards the door.

"Bring out the cake, this is about to become a party," he said as shouting echoed through the boarded windows.

Theo looked beyond annoyed. His nostrils flared as he shoved Kellan's shoulder hard, hard enough to leave a bruise. Kellan barely faltered, his feet inching a few millimetres in the dust.

"You idiot. You lead them back here," Theo hissed angrily.

He grabbed me by the elbow, not waiting for Kellan's witty retort. He pulled me rather unceremoniously towards the table. He held out his hand to me, clicked impatiently.

"Give it to me," he said shortly.

I blinked at him. He gestured to the diary under my belt. When I hesitated, he looked exasperated, his jaw taut and his eyes wide. For the first time, he was not the steady, kind and patient man I had come to know, he was something entirely different, something cold and harsh and forged from stronger metal. I pulled it free with trembling fingers as Priya hissed to Kellan.

"Are you crazy? She's going to get us killed,"

"Is not," Kellan retorted, as annoying and stubborn as a child.

As Theo took the diary, my chest lurched, desperate to snatch it back. I had promised Polly I would keep it safe, I owed it to her, and to Klio. Theo looked at me and his expression softened. He let go of my elbow, and he was once again that stoic, kind solider who had saved my life.

"Just until we get out of here, alright? I'm guessing its... important," he trailed off, insinuating he had sussed the subject matter of the diary.

"Yes," I managed to reply as Kellan reached over and snatched the diary from Theo's hands.

"What's this? A diary? Please do tell me I'm within these pages. Dark, handsome, a rugged hero."

As Kellan joked as a bullet flew through the brick, sent dust and moulding splattering across the floor.

Priya took the diary and slapped Kellan over the head with it, before she handed it back to Theo, who promptly pushed it in his bag. There was something in the way she looked at him, a momentary softness that peered through her prickly disposition, that shadowed her face in beauty. She caught me staring, and her hatred returned twofold.

"More like dim-witted and braindead," Ahzani muttered, leaned flush against the palm sized hole the bullet had caused, as if she were unafraid to die.

She peered through it as Priya loaded her bow, pulled the arrow taut against the string. Theo cocked his gun, counted the bullets into the barrel while Kellan pulled a long, square edged sword from the table, swished it experimentally through the air, let the tip caress the breath as it left my mouth. He smiled at me, squinted down the blade.

"Are you ready, pretty girl?" He asked with a cock of his brow.

I had no time to answer. A boot crashed through the door, knocked it clean off. Priya let her arrow fly, and it struck the Pioneer square in the jaw, jutted out the other side of his skull. He fell and was replaced by another. Bullets flurried through the walls like snow; through the boarded windows, through the roof, an endless storm.

I screamed as Theo lunged, tipped the table on its side. He took me by the shoulders and shoved me behind it. I put my hands over my ears as the shouting and the fighting erupted. I trembled as Theo peered over the table, let off one shot, before he ducked next to me.

"Priya to the left!" Ahzani called, and the quick strike of string on air alerted me to the firing of another arrow.

The sound of a leaden body hitting the ground assured me the arrow had hit its mark.

157

Theo moved, quick as a snake, fired once, twice, three times, before he ducked again. He looked at me as I whimpered, my hands knotted into my hair, my teeth chattering.

I was going to die here. They would kill me, or worse, take me home. Arthur never failed his missions, and now that I was one of them, my death was certain.

Theo touched my knee, a gentle reassurance that did nothing to quiet the terrified buzz of my thoughts, before he passed me a knife.

"Don't die," he stated plainly, before he disappeared.

"Az!" I heard Priya cry out as a wail echoed through the room.

I dared not look. I sat, back pressed against the underside of the table, the knife gripped tightly between my fingers, knowing almost certainly I wouldn't be able to use it.

There was a hiss and a thud, and I looked up to see Ahzani cradling her arm. She slumped next to me, removed her hand just enough to show the bullet wound.

"My favourite shirt as well," she grumbled as the dark shirt turned black with her blood.

The blood drained from my face as she dug the bullet out without so much as a noise, threw it to the ground. She squinted at me, as if assessing my damage, as if I were the wounded one, before she snatched the head scarf from my head. She wrapped it tightly around her arm, pulled the knot taut with her teeth. She spat blood onto the ground, her mouth stained with it.

"Another day, right?" Ahzani tried to breach normalcy.

The table was lurched from behind us to reveal two Pioneer guards. Theo, Kellan and Priya were outside, fighting the last of them in the street. I stumbled to my feet, backed myself up against the wall like a terrified animal as my breath came hard. Ahzani swore, before she launched herself at one of the two. The guard went down with a yelp akin to the sound of a hit puppy. The other, however, had his sights on me. My back met cool brick as he pursued me, his body twice the size of mine. His eyes were dark and magenta, his bloodied nose crooked and imperfect. He looked at me and knew instantly I did not belong here.

"Arthur reported a deserter. A stupid little girl who wants to be the Mai-Coh's new whore," his fist contacted with the wall beside my head.

I flinched, my chest tight, my fingers clammy against the handle of the blade. He smiled; his elbow pressed hard against my chest. In that moment I could smell parchment, I could feel the lazy heat of the summer sun streaming through the windows of my fathers' study. I could feel his pen knife scouring the letters into my skin, the oozing of blood down my skin.

"You'll fetch a lovely price, but I think I deserve a little fun first." His hand seized my thigh, and I lurched forward, dazed by the memory of ink and betrayal.

My breath left my body as his startled eyes widen. He looked at me, his enjoyment turned sour, his lips puckered in a half gasp, half gargle. Every beat of my heart was palpable as his blood poured over my hand. I looked down at the knife imbedded in his chest. I pulled it free in shock, and he stumbled, clasped at the weeping wound. He tripped over the table leg, fell with a thump onto the ground. Where before I could barely force myself to stare at Ahzani's wound, now I found myself fixated as the blood flushed as red as a schoolgirl's embarrassment on his shirt. He gasped, wordless and scared, as the blood wept from his lips, visceral tears that I found I could no longer shed. He gave one last breath, before his eyes fell dull and lightless.

Ahzani came to stand beside me. She looked down at the dead Pioneer, held her wounded arm as she sniffed. I could feel her watching me, but I couldn't tear my eyes away. I had taken his life; I had ripped it from him before his time. I wondered what the Emperor had planned for him. Children? Grandchildren? A house with a dog and a wife and roses in the front garden?

Ahzani's hand on mine was firm and reassuring as she unhooked my fingers from the knife, released it from my grip. She patted my shoulder before she moved towards the front door. I blinked, expecting tears, but my lashes were dry as dirt.

I tore my eyes from the Pioneer, looked down at where the knife had been in my hand. My fingers still remembered its weight, still curled as if the handle was there. Blood stained my skin as dark as the expensive wine my father had been gifted for his years of service. I wiped it down my dress, fiddled with the fastening of my cape. My fingers shook as I tried to unclasp it, to rip it from my body to throw over the Pioneer. He at least deserved that; he at least deserved a dignity in death. After a moment of fumbling I let my hands fall back to my side, broken by my failure.

Voices caught my attention, and I looked up towards the door. Ahzani was talking to Kellan, whose face was bathed in blood. I stared, my head heavy, my eyes barely focused. My body no longer felt like my own. Every breath felt like an intrusion, like it had been stolen from the man I had killed.

Kellan looked towards me, his eyes narrowed, his brow creased as Ahzani continued to talk. I could only imagine what she was saying. I wondered if she had told him I was weak, too affected by death, too perfect to kill without remorse.

Kellan gestured me forward, beckoned me with urgency. I took one last look at the Pioneer, at the limpness of his limbs, the blankness of his face.

Had he ever been alive? I couldn't imagine it.

I moved out of the house, flinched under the pale sunlight. I tongued my teeth, my mouth dry, my throat raw. My stomach was hollow, my legs empty, it was a wonder they could carry me any further. Ahzani gave me a nod, before she walked towards Priya. The smoke was thicker now, smothering the horizon, bleeding into the clouds. The world was burning, and we would too if we didn't leave. The hum of trucks winding through the streets was another reminder of the battle that was nearing; the shots of Pioneer guns, and the wails of the mourning a horrific backing track.

Kellan pulled his shirt from his trousers, exposing the too long stretch of the fabric, as if the shirt had been made for someone much bigger, much taller. He held it out to me, pushed it into my hands.

"Wipe it off before it dries. When the shock wears off you don't want to be smelling it all over you," he instructed, the nicest thing he'd said to me since we met.

I did as I was told, blindly and methodically. One finger at a time I wiped as much of the blood as I could onto his shirt. I swapped hands, scrubbed at the stains as deftly as washing a china plate. As I lifted the fabric, I caught sight of the flesh underneath. Skin pulled taut over lean muscles, dark hairs that trailed from his belly button down beneath his waist band. My stomach turned as I averted my gaze and let the fabric drop.

"Thank you," I managed to muster.

He eyed me, his brow tight, before he gave a satisfied nod.

"We need to disappear," Priya said as she pulled an arrow from a Pioneer's leg, wiped it off on her trousers before she replaced it in her quiver.

A rising concern twisted up my spine as I looked around the street. I couldn't see Theo anywhere, neither dead nor living. I dug my nails into my palms as Ahzani joined our

161

gathering, her eyes scanning the wilderness. There was an unspoken tension that surrounded Theo's absence, but no one said anything. Kellan cleared his throat and moved towards the fence, trailed his fingers along the shapes. He moved along it, paced methodically, counted under his breath. I followed behind without prompting. I felt Theo's absence as tangible as a flower feels the suns absence. Without him, I had no one, and I needed someone to survive.

Listen to yourself. I frowned at the ground, curled my hands into fists. I hated feeling so weak, like I *needed* someone other than myself.

Kellan came to an abrupt stop, and I caught myself before I smacked into his back. A wide grin spread across his face, and with a hoot he swung through a gap in the fence invisible to the naked eye, hidden in the geometric pattern of the fence.

"You son of a bitch," Kellan called into the treeline.

My chest softened as Theo emerged from the shadows, hidden there by stoic stillness. Kellan embraced him, and they grasped hands. Theo had a large wound over his chest, partially covered with a mix of leaves.

"Thought I'd try ward off infection straight away," he gestured to his injured chest as he looked over Kellan's shoulder at me.

He smiled at me, and I thought I saw genuine relief hidden in his eyes. I wanted so desperately to run at him, to wrap my arms around him. There was something about him, something about his warm kindness that reminded me so much of Alfie. I'd always had someone to care for me, I'd been promised to Alfie since birth. I didn't know how to exist alone, and Sadon had always taught us to latch to other. To need someone else.

Theo was that someone else.

Ahzani moved past me, threw an arm around his shoulder that made the both of them hiss, but neither seemed to care. Theo gave her shoulder a slap, and they shared an affection that I was too scared to show.

"Move," Priya hissed as she passed me, her shoulder connecting with mine.

I frowned at the back of her head, rubbed the spot her flesh had bumped against mine. If it weren't for the rising sound of advancing Pioneers, I might have ignored her. Yet they were coming, so I begrudgingly shuffled after them as they disappeared through the tree line.

Chapter X

I struggled to keep my eyes open as I leant forward, numb hands grasping for the heat of the fire. We had trekked through the wilderness until the sun had sunk below the horizon, and even then, we kept going, sightless eyes raking over the blurred undergrowth.

At first, the wilderness had been an array of wonder. The canopy above my head had sparkled with every shade of green, the pale blue sky a distant memory. The songs of birds had made my heart light with joy, and I had watched them in awe as they swooped from branch to branch, multi-coloured feathers smeared the humid air with beauty.

I had walked slowly, intimately with the creatures that moved around my feet. Rabbits of brown and grey scurried into concealed holes, insects of every size and shape buzzed like the hum of voices around my ears. Priya had snapped at me time and time again for falling behind, and I would scramble, feet snagging on flora and undergrowth to catch up.

Yet, as we delved deeper into the wilderness, my amazement turned sour. The trees grew closer, so close that Theo could barely squeeze between the trunks. The undergrowth grew thicker, vines and thorns tore at my dress and drew blood from my shins. The ground sloped upwards, bought us closer to the heat of the summer sun, and sweat coated my forehead as I huffed, forced myself up through the rocks.

When the forest turned dark, so did the animals

Deer's, thick flanked and quick legged, grazing with pricked ears. Boars, their blunt snouts dug into the earth, tusks rooting through the dead leaves. Priya gave Kellan a knowing smile, loaded her bow and shot one dead. She

164

carried it on her shoulders, unfazed by the blood that dripped down her back.

The animals that terrified me the most though were the wolves.

We only saw one, and when it came into view, strolling sure footed along a small ledge, Kellan stopped. The breath left my chest in a whoosh as it turned. Its grey fur rippled in the soft breeze, pointed ears twitched as it sniffed, snout pointed towards us. Kellan held up his hand, slowly lowered to his knees. The others followed, and as the wolf's lips pulled back from teeth as white as sharpened bone, my knees gave too. We waited there, watched the creature pad thoughtfully down the precarious ledge. It exuded a power and majesty that seized me by the stomach. When it opened its mouth and let out a solemn howl, my eyes pricked with tears. It waited, and listened, and when in the distance another howl echoed its cries, it leapt from the ledge and prowled into the wilderness.

I thought of the wolf now, its lonely call lodged somewhere deep inside my chest. The rhythmic cracking of the kindling managed to mask most of the hubbub of the wildlife. Still, the soft hissing of insects managed to set my hair on end.

I leant my elbows against my knees, tried to urge warmth back into my limbs. I stared into the flames, watched them flicker. Something about the way they swayed, so peaceful, so serene, made me want to reach out and touch them. A thud at my side bought me out of my own world, and I looked up, blinked the smoke from my vision. Kellan sat beside me, savoured a piece of charred bread. In his other hand he held a wooden bowl of dark soup made from the boar's carcass. He turned his gaze to the flames, as if they could tell him something. He tore a large bite from the roll, gave a slurp of the broth, before he held them both out to me.

I looked at the offering, my stomach pinched in hunger. He still didn't look at me, his eyes reflecting the flames, but he jostled the bowl of soup, it's contents threatening to spill onto the ground, conveying his impatience. I took them both, stared down into the brown liquid. The smell of rich meat, of salt and herbs made my teeth grind. I dipped the bread into the bowl, before I devoured it whole.

I moaned at the salty, almost earthy taste. It was so different to the richness of home, but with every chew I found myself falling more in love with it. I slurped the broth, barely chewed the tough chunks of meat. I caught Kellan watching me out the corner of his eye, his lips quirked up.

I straightened, wiped my hands down my dress out of habit. I stretched out my legs, folded one foot over the other at the fires edge, put the bowl down by my ankles in a rehearsed display of etiquette. My fingers were lost without the bowls warmth, and I tucked them into my armpits as I tried to correct my posture.

"Don't do that," Kellan said.

"What?" I asked.

Kellan stretched out his legs, toed the bowl at my feet, before he flicked it and the ash at my legs. I retracted my limbs almost instantly, avoided the debris by a hair's breadth. He pointed an accusing finger at my tucked-up legs.

"That. Don't bring that perfect bullshit here." He spoke the word 'perfect' with such venom I could almost feel its sting.

Priya puffed out a laugh as she moved into view, followed closely by Theo. She sat on the opposite side of the fire; her hands wrapped tightly around her bowl of soup.

"She can't help it," she hissed as her eyes raked down me with distaste, as if I were no more than a dead boar.

166

"It's programmed into them in the lab," she spat, her face framed in smoke.

Anger prickled under my skin like knife tips. I wanted to argue that what she said was untrue, but I had no such faith in what the truth even was.

"Come on Pri, cut her some slack," Theo urged, his voice gentle but firm.

Priya shot him a look. There was pain there, as if he'd betrayed her, and a softness to her lips that didn't quite make sense.

"Like she deserves slack," she retorted, her eyes focused on her broth.

Theo cast me a glance as I clenched my hands, nails biting into my palms. Kellan stayed silent as he toyed with the ash, dirtied his already ruined boots.

"She didn't do anything," Theo reminded her, his voice stronger now.

A warning.

Priya didn't seem to care. She shrugged; her knuckles white where she gripped her bowl. She was trying to act coy, like my presence didn't bother her, but I could see it in the curve of her brows. The discontent, the malice.

"You really believe that?" she questioned, and Theo shifted uncomfortably.

She looked up at me, a fierce hatred burnt brighter than the fire before us in her eyes. Theo seemed to shrink back from her, her words silenced him. I knew then that he didn't have as much faith in me as I thought, and why should he? I was the spawn of the Emperor's intentions, the product of perfection. To them, I was everything that was wrong in this world, everything they were fighting against.

"How many times did you sit idly by? How many people have you seen tortured? Have you seen killed?" she spat.

The urge to stand was as palpable as a pulse.

Say something. Defend yourself. Say anything.

Regardless of whether she was right, regardless of whether I had been submissive, I had been doing what I needed to do to survive. I'd pretended and lied and faked to win. The Mai-Coh, they wanted something real, something worthy, something I wasn't sure I could give. I bit my cheek, wondered what about me was real, wondered if anything about me was real.

"I haven't done anything to you." I whispered the only truth I had.

She laughed, an empty, hollow laugh. There were tears on her lashes, unshed and poisonous as acid. She fell silent, her gaze directed again at the bowl in her hands. Kellan shifted, averted his gaze as he pushed himself up. He seemed to know it was time for him to leave, and he walked away without a sound. Theo too looked into his broth as if it were the most interesting liquid in the world. I gnawed at the inside of my cheek as the silence stretched on. Priya let out a breath, sharp and uneven.

"When I was a kid, there were stories about Sadon," she began; her fingers slowly relaxed around the bowl.

"My mother used to take me to work in the washers when the power went out at home. They'd all sit there, her and the other women. They'd sit and trade gossip from faraway lands, dreams of something more, snippets of other lives. One of them got word about the New World, about a place of perfection where no one went hungry," she turned the bowl, watched the liquid move.

"We were from a poor part of Bihar. My dad and brother worked for these... terrible men. Killers, mercenaries. The thought of something good, of never having to work for bad

168

people again… they sold everything, the house, the clothes off our backs, my father's gold fillings. There was this boat taking people from India to the New World. We went, and the captain said we only had enough money for four," she seemed so lost in it, so lost in this memory.

So lost in her pain.

"My mother, my two sisters and I watched my father and brother fade to nothing on the shore. They had nothing. I…" she cut herself off.

Theo reached out and took Priya's hand. She looked up at him with shining, childlike eyes, laced her fingers through his. She rubbed her cheek with her shoulder, turned her gaze back to me. The memory seemed rehearsed, as if she had gone over it a million times. Committed it to scripture.

"My sister died halfway through the trip. She caught hypothermia. My mother wept over her for three days before the captain threw her body overboard. It was the smell. The stench of death, it made the other passengers nauseous." A tear rolled down her cheek.

She didn't brush it away this time.

"When we finally arrived, we walked across that glowing marble bridge. I remember the river, the water lapping at the columns. The Pioneers took one look at our skin and turned us away. 'Dirty blooded whores' they called us. We'd come all this way, lost everything… my mother lost it, she started screaming, begging. They took her, and my sister. I managed to run. Some Slum dweller found me in his basement, took pity on me, an eight-year-old immigrant, sold me to the Mai-Coh." She let go of Theo's hand, brushed her cheeks clean.

She sat up straighter, took a swig of her broth.

"A few years later we raided a Riven den, and I found my sister. Half dead in the Riven Dens with a Pioneer three times her age. She didn't even recognise me. She couldn't

169

even talk, I guess they never taught her how," she finished her soup, her eyes filled with anger.

I knew that as she looked at me, she saw them all. The Pioneer who rejected her and her family, the one who raped her sister.

"Your people. All you do is destroy," she hissed.

I looked at Theo, but he offered me no comfort. He met my gaze with a hard stoniness that hurt more than Priya's words. I stood instinctively. I didn't know where I was going to go, but I couldn't sit there, amongst the pain of the past.

I turned from the flames, but not before Theo put his arm around Priya's shoulders. I headed up the small path Kellan had carved through the underbrush, away from the horrors of my people.

Away from the fire the wilderness was plunged into darkness. My teeth chattered as I walked, the cape barely protected me against the nights breeze. Through the fog of my breath I could see Ahzani's torch, stuck in the ground. I rubbed my arms swiftly as she came into view.

My heart surged up into my throat as I realised that Kellan was with her, arm around her shoulders, a possessive gesture that made my heart thump. When they saw me he grinned, raised a brow. I stopped short in the clearing; afraid I had intruded on something. He nodded at me, gave me a winning smile as he stood up.

"My turn to babysit then," Ahzani said.

Kellan shrugged, walked towards me. He pulled a shabbily rolled cigarette made from thick leaves and musty tobacco from his shirt and popped it into his mouth. He stopped in front of me, looked over my face. He saw in it the words Priya had spoken, the guilt and pain I felt for her. He lit the cigarette, pursed it between his lips with a sly smile. He sucked a deep breath and exhaled a puff of smoke over his shoulder. I wrinkled my nose, disgusted by the smell.

"Be good," he teased, gave me a condescending pat on the head.

He winked at me, before he walked past. I turned, a bubble of words ached to burst in my throat. I watched him walk down the path, puffing away. I grunted, turned back to Ahzani, who leant back against the trunk they had been sat on. She raised a brow, inclined her head to me.

"Ignore the bastard," she trailed off; her eyes smug as she grinned at me.

"Unless you don't want to," she drawled, a world of suggestion hidden in that smug smile.

I chose to ignore that as I sat next to her. Up close I could see the details of her face more clearly. Her dark skin shone as if dusted by gold, her thick brows cut in a way that lent a sharpness to her otherwise soft face.

"Do you ignore him?" I asked as I rubbed my hands down my thighs, tried to coax warmth back into my limbs.

She snorted, threw her head back and laughed so brightly that it almost dimmed the stars. I couldn't help notice the tattoo that twisted over her collar bones, the lines and curves etched into her dark skin. My cheeks flushed as she looked at me. She grinned, pursed her lips.

"Do I look like a woman who's into men?" she asked, gestured to the tight cut vest and the black rings on her fingers.

Despite her jest, worry flashed in her eyes. It wasn't a hidden fact that the residents of Sadon didn't think same sex relationships were natural. That they caused terrible pain. That they were the mark of the Imperfect. I nodded, thought about Chrys, about if he was okay, wondered what he would think of Ahzani. Something told me he'd like her, look up to her even for being so bold, so unapologetic.

"So Priya?" I asked.

Ahzani gave a soft smile, satisfied I hadn't called her a degenerate whore destined for hell. She looked up at the sky thoughtfully, touched her lips.

"Priya isn't that way inclined, plus I don't think she's one for intimacy, although Kellan has tried and tried. Not that that is a testament or anything, he'll go for just about anyone," she looked back at me, her eyes alight with mischief.

"I gathered," I replied

She laughed through her nose, tilted her head back and took in the night stars. She looked so at peace, so beautiful. The moon cascaded silver over her dark hair, lit her in a way I had never seen anyone light up. I flushed, realised that I enjoyed looking at her, that her smile, her eyes, they made my heart sputter.

"I'm surprised he hasn't tried you yet," she said offhandedly, looked at me out the corner of her eye.

I scoffed, my hands shook as I pretended not to be affected by her words. The thought of kissing someone, being with someone, in any way at all, made my stomach turn on end.

"I don't think I'm his type," I replied

"Come off it. You were literally made to be gorgeous. Plus Kellan doesn't have a type; the only thing he cares about is whether your heart is beating." She tapped between my breasts, let her fingers linger against the neckline of my dress.

My cheeks were hot, my hands were hot, every part of me was hot, even the space between my legs. I sucked in a breath as she looked up at me through her lashes; damn, she

172

was a well-versed charmer. In Sadon, I had never had the chance to think about who I might love, really love, and whether that person would be a man or a woman. It had never seemed like a possibility, the threat of death too great to even give it thought. Yet now, in this clearing, with her fingers against my collarbone, the thought spread through my veins like fire.

"Have you ever kissed anyone before?" she whispered, inched closer until all I could see was her face.

I stood, flustered, my cheeks burnt red. I remembered Alfie's lips, the unyielding of my stomach, the lack of butterflies. I had never felt for Alfie even a fraction of what I felt now. I stuttered while Ahzani watched in amusement.

"I... I have, I mean, I did, it just-" I struggled for words, my hands flapped around in the air aimlessly.

Ahzani gave a loud howl of a laugh, her head thrown back, her mouth wide open.

"Been there. The first person I kissed was this guy, I can't even remember his name now. I just had to be sure, you know? It was the worst kiss," she gagged at the memory, shuddered.

"But then my first kiss with a girl... it was electric," she said, her eyes never left mine as she licked her bottom lip.

"Isn't kissing punishable by death or something anyway?" she asked.

"Something like that," I replied as I tried to steady the racing of my heart.

Ahzani stood, moved towards me, all smiles and hooded eyes and hips. I took a stumbling step back, choked on words that never would have made sense anyway. She reached out, touched my shoulder, let her fingers trace down my arm.

173

"Seems wrong, doesn't it? Taking that away from someone," her nails raked down to my hand, where she traced the line of my thumb, the indent of my palm.

I couldn't even breathe. My cheeks burnt, my fingers tingled. There was a lump in my throat the size of an orange.

"I could… give it to you, in both senses of the words," she smirked, her fingers flitted to my waist.

"Please, Ahzani. Give her more than a day." I turned to see Theo, and my breath left my lungs in a gush of relief.

Ahzani clucked her tongue as she moved towards Theo. She shrugged as if she'd done nothing wrong, but I could see the sympathy in Theo's eyes as he looked at me. My pulse slowed as Ahzani looked over her shoulder and gave me a wink.

"I don't think that one needs much convincing," she threw the words into the air for us both to process before she slapped him on the back.

"Tag, you're it," she said as she walked away.

Theo looked up to the heavens for strength, before he turned his gaze back to me. He looked at me funny, the way I imagined I looked when I saw the wolf earlier. He gestured to the stump, and without hesitation I moved and sat. My legs were weak.

I was weak.

"Sorry about her. She's… insufferable sometimes," Theo sounded genuinely apologetic, but there was amusement in his eyes.

"She'll leave you be. You're just new and pretty."

Pretty. A vapid, meaningless comment tossed between school mates. A pale insult, something Olivia might have sniped at me in the hallways. Back in Sadon, the word might have offended me. Yet here, now, coming from him; it was nice. I smiled to myself.

"I'm sorry if what Priya said hurt your feelings. She's had it tough," Theo said, almost reluctantly.

I could sense the pain in his voice. He rubbed his chin, his cheek muscles clenched as he looked down at the dwindling torch. There was a burning in my chest, an ache at the mention of her again. Of what my people did to her. Would I have helped her? If I saw her? I wanted to believe I would. I had to.

"What happened to her sister?" the words slipped.

A careless question.

Theo tensed; his eyes slipped back to me. There was darkness within that went deeper than just the colour of his eyes. He observed me, as if trying to figure out whether I could handle the truth. It was that look that made me regret the question.

"Priya's sister couldn't be saved. There was nothing we could have done. So... Priya took the shot," Theo said it so calmly, as if he weren't talking about murder.

I nodded, stared at my palms. Her sister was dead, and Priya had killed her. A pity kill, a mercy kill. Theo saw my fingers shake, and he reached out, took them in his. He wrapped my hands firmly in his, forced my gaze up. He fixed me with a stare so strong I could feel it as tangibly as his hands.

"You are not them. That's why you're here," he pointed to the ground, pointed to himself.

"That's why I saved you. They were going to kill you, but I knew," he looked at me, really looked at me, and it dawned on me that I owed him more than just a thank you.

I owed him my life.

His hands were warm, strong, and he was kind. So kind. Familiar in that steady, easy kind of way. I was attached to him, the same way I had been attached to Alfie. I needed someone. Someone to look after me. Someone to keep me safe. I knew he sensed that. I could see it in his face, this need to be needed.

Selfishly, I wanted to be needed.

Selfishly, I wanted to use that need.

I averted my eyes from his glance. It wasn't right for me to think that way. It wasn't right for me to see his need as a weakness for me to exploit. It wasn't right for me to think like *they* had taught me to think.

Theo took my chin in his hand, bought my face back to his. He didn't smile. He just looked at me in that stony, all-consuming way that I had grown to find comfort in.

"You *are* different. We can show you that," he said.

I wanted to believe him, but when I met his eyes, all I saw was opportunity.

Chapter XI

Sweat slicked my dress against my legs, pasted my hair to my face. My lungs wheezed with every breath as I struggled onwards. My legs were filled with acid and my arms were numb. Every part of me ached, but I pressed on.

The high summer sun was unlike anything I had experience before. The weather in Sadon always fell within a certain temperature; never too hot, never too cold. Yet here, with the foliage trapping heat like insulation, all I could do was pray I didn't faint.

I could see Theo ahead through my pulsing vision, lugging our portable campsite on his back as if it weighed nothing. Priya and Ahzani were chatting as they ambled up the steep incline without barely breaking a sweat. Kellan was whistling, the sweet tones echoed through the branches like gloating butterflies. They were getting away; Theo was already at the crest of the incline, his back retreating out of view. I wanted to catch up to them, I willed my feet to move faster.

The breath rattled out of my mouth as I took another agonising step. My feet slid on the damp ground; my knees contacted with the dirt. I let out a yelp as pain shot up my thighs, my hands grasped onto the shrubbery around me, thorns ripped at my palms. I landed with a thump on my back; my shoulders cracked at the impact. I took a deep breath, rolled onto my front, tried to push myself up. My hands slipped on the mud, stones dug into my palms until blood slipped down my wrists. My elbows were raw as I tried to hoist myself up. I let out a frustrated, primal growl, a scream of frustration, of hunger and anger and pain.

"Need some help there?" Kellan's voice came from above me.

I looked up at his outstretched hand and resisted the urge to bat it away in frustration. I shook my head; I didn't want to admit I needed his help. I got to my knees, took another ragged breath, planted my hands on the ground. My arms trembled as I forced myself upwards. My calves ached as I pulled one foot forward, and then pushed myself up. I wobbled; the forest teetered as I struggled to find my balance. Kellan's hand on the small of my back was strong; he steadied me as my eyes focused, my hands flailed for something to hold onto. My fingers wrapped around his wrist as I gained my footing. I looked up at him, defeated and irritated by his smile. He removed his hand from my back and shook mine from his wrist.

"Try not to fall down again, okay?" he said as he walked off, clearly not amused by my inadequacy.

Anger boiled in my throat like tar. All I wanted was to be out of here. All I wanted was to be as fast as them, as surefooted as them, as strong as them. Couldn't he see I was trying? Couldn't he see I wasn't made for this kind of journey?

"I'm not trying to fall," I hissed as my hem caught on a thorn branch.

My patience worn, I ripped the material free, tore it clean up the side of my leg. I gave an exasperated scream. I stomped like an impetuous child, no longer cared about the mud or the sweat. I was so angry; angry that he was strong, angry that he was fast, angry that I wasn't what they needed me to be, angry at him, at myself, at everyone.

"Well maybe try to catch up," he threw the words over his shoulder.

I broke into as quick of a run as my legs would allow. A boost of anger and frustration reared its head as I gained on Kellan, a searing heat that threatened to drown me with its rage. Without thought or reason I slammed my hands into his back. He stumbled, caught off guard by my assault. For a moment I was awash with triumph, a moment of brilliance and destruction that made me feel less bad about everything else that had happened so far.

I *could* be strong. I *could* be fast.

I smirked, proud of myself. Yet when Kellan whirled to look at me, my smile faltered. He cocked his brow, a smile pulled at the corner of his lips. My attack was not liberating or enlightening to him. It was foolish and childish. He gestured me forward, stretched out his arms, dared me to do it again.

"Come on, you must have more than that," he goaded me.

I hesitated. My confidence had slipped as quickly as it had risen. He waited, arms open wide, for me to act. I licked my lips, unsure of myself. I moved forward to push him again, slower this time, sensing a trap. His hands rose to meet mine, he latched onto my wrists and spun me so my arms were pinned against my back. He pulled me against his chest, his mouth close to my ear. He chuckled as I wriggled, desperate to free myself, my cheeks flustered. He gripped my chin between his thumb and finger, held my head steady as his breath fanned my cheek.

"You want to learn? I'll teach you, sweetheart. First lesson," he paused, his body pressed against mine.

I could feel his chest, his hips, the warmth of his stomach. My heart beat a mile a minute, my blood pulsed through my legs. The feel of his calloused fingers against my jaw stirred something raw deep inside me; my skin burnt at his touch.

"Never take the bait," he whispered, his lips against my ear.

I yanked forward with all the strength I could muster, almost sent myself tumbling down the hill in the process. I

179

wiped my ear furiously on my shoulder, unable to catch my breath. Kellan smiled as he straightened his collar.

"Never fight on someone else's terms, that's how you die," he said as he straightened his shirt.

"But I think you have some fight in you," he conceded, before he turned and sprinted up the hill, left me alone with the ache in my stomach and the feel of his lips on my skin.

~

It took us five days of travelling to break from the wilderness, where we were greeted harshly by a wasteland of sand. At the sight of its sprawling yellow mass I almost dropped to my knees and wept.

I was thirsty, constantly thirsty. My mouth was as parched as the desert before my eyes after days of dehydration in Sadon. The rations of water I was allowed never quenched my thirst, barely scratched the surface.

Yet, after a moment of staring with glazed eyes at the horizon, dust billowed into the air, and a black vehicle split across the sand. Theo hissed as Ahzani peered under the leaves on his chest. Sweat covered his forehead as he pressed his eyes shut, infection taking hold despite all his efforts. Ahzani shook her head, examined the wound.

"You'll have to see Farron straight away," she pasted the leaves back onto his chest with a careful hand.

Theo opened his eyes and nodded tightly. It was terrible watching his pain, the flinch of his cheek, the grit of his jaw. Guilt nagged at my stomach; they'd put their lives on the line protecting me, and now he was hurt.

Theo caught me staring and gave me a smile. He reached out and gripped my shoulder despite the obvious pain it caused him.

"It'll be fine, I've had worse," he gestured to his chest as if it were no big deal.

I nodded, although I didn't quite believe him. Priya looked between the two of us and gave a disgusted groan. Kellan was whispering something to Ahzani; by the smile on his face I could tell it was something sordid. Ahzani seemed less than interested. Her eyes were trained on the truck as it neared, her fingers flexed nervously as it slowed. Kellan reached out to touch her on the hip, but she caught his hand with a pointed stare.

"I'm still a lesbian, remember?" she threw his hand away.

Kellan rolled his eyes as the truck came to a stop, and the doors opened.

"I wonder what Meredith will think about what you told me..." he trailed off with a smirk as Ahzani went bright red.

A tall, thick thighed girl hopped down from the passenger seat. Her hair sprung around her head in a tightly coiled afro, a thick, voluptuous halo that shone in the high afternoon sun. She beamed with a happiness that took me by surprise. Her dark chestnut skin was mottled with black freckles, her coal eyes flecked with gold. She was tall with big curves and a well fed stomach, every bit the woman I wasn't. I looked down at my own small curves and my heart dropped.

"Theo! Az!" she called, her smile intoxicating.

Ahzani tensed as the girl threw an arm around each of their necks. Theo winced but managed to smile through the pain.

"Meredith. You're awfully perky," he acknowledged her with a pat on the back.

She pulled back, her smile never wavering. A second person moved from the driver's seat; a slight boy with fair hair, a few years younger than I, who looked way too young to drive. He moved towards Kellan, and they nodded to each other, mumbled a few words with stern faces. I had never seen Kellan look so serious. His mouth was hard and his eyes were dark as he told the young boy something. The boy looked towards me, gave me a quick up and down, before he turned back to Kellan, his face paler than before.

"Well, I had such a great driving partner," she jerked her thumb at the young boy, who scowled.

"She's been like this all day. It's driving me insane." The boy's voice was juvenile, it still held the highness of youth.

"Well, it's a beautiful day, Roscoe. What isn't there to be happy about?" she asked, but her attention was no longer on him.

Priya, who had been silent during the whole exchange, gave a snort, before she stormed towards the truck. She yanked open the back door and clambered in, gave the door a good slam behind her. Meredith winced; her smile faltered.

"Not everyone sees it that way," Ahzani said, a tightness to her voice that made Theo chuckle under his breath.

Ahzani elbowed him in the ribs, but Theo didn't relent with his grin. Meredith moved between the two and approached me. I expected disgust, I expected anger, but instead I was met with the calmness and worriedness of a mother. She reached out and touched my cheek softly, her brows drawn in pity as she chewed on the inside of her cheek. She had such a round, soft face, so full of joy and kindness.

"You've been through a lot, haven't you," she said as her eyes strayed to the blood that marked my dress.

Something broke inside me then, shattered as easily as glass. Her kindness was foreign, so pure and unmasking, that I couldn't understand it.

Couldn't deserve it.

Her skin colour, her size, it would have her killed by *my* people, and yet she looked at me like I was a long lost

182

friend. I shied away from her as guilt swelled my throat. She gave a sigh as she looked over her shoulder at Theo.

"Kamal won't be happy," she said.

"Yeah, I know. I'm ready," Theo replied with a smile that softened the acrid taste of shame in my mouth.

Meredith smiled, before she took my hand in hers.

"Come. You must be tired,"

~

I woke with a jolt, my breath caught in my throat as I snorted. I blinked bleary eyed, something warm pressed against my side. I looked around, confused. It was dark, and I was sat in the truck bed, Kellan opposite me. He smirked at me, closed his eyes and opened his mouth wide to snore in mockery of me.

I shivered as the truck moved onwards. The wind whipped the hood of my cape against my face violently, howled like wolves calling to each other in the darkness. The person beside me shifted, their arm draped over my shoulders. I looked up to see Theo squirming uncomfortably. He smiled down at me, shifted to pull me closer. I fisted my hands into my cape and tried to absorb some of his warmth as my teeth chattered.

We were in the hills, the peaks stretched for miles in either direction. The truck was ambling up the cavern between two sheer rocky faces, struggled against the incline with a groan. As we climbed upwards, a soft light illuminated the horizon in hues of saffron and gold. I squinted from under my hood, tried to get a better look. As we reached the peak, Kellan let out a series of howls that made my stomach plummet.

"We're home, baby!" He cried as he threw his fist in the air, smacked the side of the truck as if spurring it on.

Below the peaks, shrouded in the cover of a ring of mountains and forests was a sprawling camp. Fires flickered in clearings between tents, and people were dancing, swaying, their laughter echoed through the air. There was a large bonfire set off to the left, where a twisted wooden throne and a bunch of tables were set to the back, allowing space for dancing. It seemed most of the camp were there, dancing, eating, with someone sat in the throne presiding over the ordeal. A chill ran down my spine at the sight of the shrouded figure, and as we descended into the camp, Theo tightened. I looked up to see him frown, his face suddenly paler. He pulled Klio's diary from his backpack and held it out to me.

"You should take this. If you offer it to Kamal, he's more likely to... not kill you," he said.

I took the diary in my hand, surprised how comforting its familiar weight was. I held it to my chest, chewed on my lip as the truck slowed. Mai-Coh walked around us, covered in smeared ash and paint. Dark skinned women in garments of every colour with gold bands around their arms whispered as they stared at me. Men with scars and buzzed hair brandishing swords and guns exited tents with trousers half done up from their latest conquest.

I squirmed uncomfortably as the truck rolled to a stop. The engine cut, and Roscoe jumped from the driver's seat, instantly greeted by a small, dark-haired woman wearing nothing but a loin cloth and strategically placed red paint. She gave him a kiss on the cheek, before she took his hand and lead him in the direction of the rising smoke. Kellan stood and vaulted over the truck bed. He landed gracefully, stretched his arms out wide, clearly happy to be home. Far off to the right two girls giggled as they looked at him, their smiles painted red and black.

Theo kicked open the truck beds door, clambered down and held out his hand to me. I took it, stretched my aching legs as I stepped from the truck. The two girls approached

Kellan, and he threw his arms over them both. I looked away as he planted a kiss on the shorter of the two, his hands travelled below her skirt.

Theo kept a hold of my hand as we weaved through the chaos. There was laughing, talking, moaning. The sway of bodies was lit against the canvas of tents, tangled and tantalising and so sexually distracting I could barely breathe.

Theo was talking, but I couldn't register his words. A thousand eyes stared at me out of the darkness, lips pulled back from teeth as they took in my stained white clothes. I was in their home now. I was their enemy.

I focused on the clearing instead of the burning hatred that pushed against my skin, on the fire that flickered twice the size of Theo. Bodies swayed in the smoke, hips sensuous and tantalising. Music, rhythmic drumming and whining instruments swelled like waves against the mountains. Smiles and laughter flashed through the flames, teeth gleaming akin to the wolves. Whispers of fabric floated as thin as trailing clouds, exposed skin and body parts I had never seen exposed on another person. My cheeks grew hot both from the fire and the embarrassment.

One of the dancers met my eyes, her face half shrouded behind a hijab. She was covered from head to toe in worn silk the colour of blood, and she moved with the grace of a trained dancer, merely a whisper on the wind. Her blue rimmed eyes bore down below my skin, deep into a place only the Emperor had seen before. Her eyes widened, started by the realisation of who I was. She moved away from the dancing circle and towards the looming wooden throne.

My throat swelled as she moved to the figure, and I quickened my steps, desperate to get there before she did. Through the flames I could make out the man who sat above the rest more clearly. He didn't look anything extraordinary. His skin was a golden brown. He had dopey, deep-set eyes the colour of caramel, and jet-black hair slicked back off his forehead. He had a short, well-kept beard not quite connected to his moustache, which was merely a whisper under his nose. His body was not built like Theo, but he wasn't as slight as Kellan. All his features individually seemed harmless, ordinary. Yet together, they created something dark and foreboding.

It was the way he held himself; poised, controlled, every movement calculated. It was the way his eyes surveyed the scene in front of him, every detail accounted for, every person counted and watched. He reminded me of the Emperor in that sense, his ever-knowing gaze, his poise.

He perched his elbow on the arm of the throne, his eyes drawn to the approaching dancer. She sat on the arm of throne; his hand moved up her back to rest between her shoulder blades; a possessive gesture. She bent down to his ear, and he listened intently, his eyes never straying from the party. His face darkened as she pulled her mouth from his ear. She went to stand, but he grabbed her by the wrist, fingers pressed hard into the flesh. She turned back to him; her eyes wide.

She looked terrified.

Theo came to a stop. His hand tightened on mine as the figure turned his gaze on the two of us. There was a depthless anger there, a betrayal that seemed almost tearful. He stood slowly, let the dancer go. She scampered off, sunk back into the dancing circle. Theo straightened his shoulders, turned to look down at me. Framed in the star light he was as beautiful as anyone the Emperor could have fathomed.

"Give Kamal this," he tapped the diary, "Be strong."

I had no time to argue. Kamal stood, raised a hand. The music stopped. People turned, the laughter, the chatter, they all ceased into agonising silence. Kamal kept his eyes steady on Theo, his hands poised by his side.

"Bring her," his voice carried miles.

It held a weight and authority that could not be denied. It was not loud; it held no emotion. It was steady. It was daunting.

Theo gave my hand a squeeze, before he moved us through the crowd. Everyone parted before us, as if they were afraid to touch me. Afraid Perfection was contagious. Kamal did not move from his throne. He stood in front of it, framed by its wooden mass like a deer before a giant oak. He seemed evermore, everlasting, eternal.

We came before him, and I shifted uncomfortably, the weight of hundreds of eyes heavy on my back. It dawned on me then that this may all be for nothing. That Kamal may take the diary and kill me without a second thought. That this journey would be over as quickly as it had begun.

Kamal looked down at me, his eyes as dark as the night sky. I retreated into Theo's shadow; my hand clammy in his.

"What have you bought me."

Theo let go of my hand, stepped forward. He bowed his head to Kamal, a sign of respect that was given freely, not submissively.

"They were going to kill her-" Kamal laughed, shook his head.

"And you stopped them?" he asked, incredulous.

Theo paused, cleared his throat. A bead of sweat rolled down his neck, his shoulders tensed.

"She needed our help," he paused, as if considering something, before he continued. "She has something for us," he looked back at me, jerked his head towards Kamal.

I hesitated. My fingers were white where they gripped the diary. Kamal looked at me, his eyes narrowed. Theo cleared his throat, gestured me forward again, more vigorously this time.

"Take down the hood. Let me see you," Kamal said.

My fingers shook as I reached up and tugged down my hood. I swallowed past the dryness in my throat as I moved past Theo. Coming out of his shadow was like a loss, like a wall crumbling and leaving me exposed. I straightened, reminded myself to be fearless. The Mai-Coh didn't respect meekness.

If I had to pretend the rest of my life, I would.

Kamal leant back in his throne; his lips pressed tight. He shook his head, his fingers tight against the arm of the throne. He looked like he couldn't bear to look at me, his eyes flashed with disgust. Yet he kept them on me nonetheless as I came to a stop at the foot of his throne. I gazed up at him, dwarfed in his presence. He rubbed his chin, gave a humourless smile.

"They couldn't have made you any better," he hissed.

I tried not to shrivel. I brandished the diary, a peace offering that I hoped would save my life. His eyes zeroed in on the binding; his eyebrows twitched as he leant forward once more. He held out his hand. I could see the head of a wolf peaking from under the sleeve of his shirt, its mouth snarling, its eyes black and heartless. I placed the dairy in his hand, and he snatched it quickly. He peeled open the cover, browsed through the pages. A light behind his eyes ignited as he read onwards. After a moment, he looked up from the pages. His eyes did not land on me, but went to Theo, who looked relieved.

"Interesting," his voice was barely above a whisper, but the hint of a smile graced the corner of his lips.

He turned his head and whistled. Seemingly out of thin air, a woman appeared out of the shadows. Her appearance was shocking as she emerged, as if she were mist cresting a mountain. She was covered head to toe in thick blue and gold brocade fabric, a dress that concealed her figure and limbs completely. Her face was both light and dark; her skin was mainly dark brown, but there were patches that lacked pigment, veined with blue tattoos that disappeared down below her hijab. She looked so young, she couldn't have been more than fifteen, with an aquiline nose and shocking white brows. Her eyes were as colourless as the Emperor's, and at the sight my stomach lurched.

Her hand shot out; a dark wisp too quick for me to focus on. She took the diary, and it disappeared beneath her shroud. The pair did not exchange words, but she seemed to understand. She did not seem to fear Kamal, like everyone else did. She met him with the grace of an equal, maybe, dare I say, a superior. Her eyes fanned over me briefly, only slightly interested, before she sunk back into the shadows as quickly as she came.

I wanted to call to her, but Klio's diary was already gone. I bit the side of my tongue as Kamal turned his attention back to me. He itched his beard, smoothed the hairs as he considered me.

"Do you want to be here?" he asked.

"Yes," I answered without hesitation.

I needed to be here. Without question, there was no turning back. I had left everything behind, my family, my friends, my whole life. There was nothing else for me now. If I went back, I would be putting Chrys, my mother, even my father, at risk. Kamal seemed doubtful despite the conviction in my voice.

"She killed someone." It was Kellan's voice that rose from the crowd.

I turned to see him stagger through the crowd, shirt half on, one shoe missing. His cheeks were red, his hair tousled as he pushed himself breathlessly in front of Kamal, who looked less than impressed.

"She killed a Pioneer. Ask her. Stabbed him right in the chest," he imitated stabbing someone, a pantomime that only served to make Kamal's eyebrows draw down.

Kamal looked up to the sky as if for strength, before he turned his now irritated gaze on me.

"Is that so?" he asked.

I nodded as I rubbed at my hands, as if the blood still stuck there. Kamal shrugged.

"She can face the Square. If I like what I see, then I'll think about it," he relented.

Theo stepped forward, shook his head.

"No. Not the Square. She won't make it," Theo put his arm out, held it in front of me, a protective move that made the corner of Kamal's mouth twitch.

"It's the Square or I shoot her right here," he stated plainly as he beckoned a dancer forward.

Theo opened his mouth to protest, his forehead lined with worry, but Kellan stepped forward, touched Theo's arm softly. They exchanged a moment of unspoken conversation before Theo lowered his arm.

"If she faces the Square and doesn't forfeit or die after three minutes, she stays," Kellan reasoned.

Kamal debated as the dark-skinned woman danced in front of him, steps that didn't seem sexual, but ancient and meaningful. He seemed to barely notice our presence as she twirled, powerful in her movements.

"Ten minutes. If she does last, then she has to share all of Sadon's secrets. And... Theo, you're not to train her. I see you've already grown soft on her," he said dismissively.

190

Theo's jaw tighten, but he made no move to refute the claim. Anger flared in my chest, my fate being bargained before me without my say. Kellan wavered; his lips pursed.

"Five minutes and I'll train her, and if she's not fighting fit by our next raid, I'll kill her myself," he replied.

My hands shook at his words, at the thought of death, at whatever the Square was. I glared at Kellan, at the promises, the bargains, he was making with my life. His face did not waver, his eyes showed nothing but truth, and the weight of the agreement settled like a stone in my chest. Kamal waved a dismissive hand.

"Done. The Square will be prepared by the morning, and if she loses…" it was now he turned his attention on me again as he pushed the dancer out of the way, already bored.

His eyes blazed as he took in my face, the features that marked me as perfect. He wanted me to fail, he wanted to execute me in front of his people, to make a point of me. I tried not to flinch, but I couldn't help it.

"She dies,"

Chapter XII

The sun had begun to rise, a dim yellow spot on the horizon; clouds striped red and pink across the sky. The fading smell of smoke subsided to the fresh morning dew, the air thick with moisture. The sweet sound of birds waking and calling to each other echoed through the dripping branches.

In the dim morning light, Kellan lead me through a densely wooded pathway, his sleeves rolled up past his elbows. Theo had been sent to the infirmary despite his protests, leaving me alone with Kellan, who had said nothing to me. We walked in silence despite everything I wanted to say to him.

I wanted to shout at him about what he'd negotiated on my behalf. I wanted to ask him if he was serious about killing me, but I had a feeling I already knew the answer. I scowled at his back as he pushed his way past an errant branch. He cast a look over his shoulder, grinned at me.

"Keep up," he winked.

I scowled harder. Through the break in the trees I could see a small clearing. There were four weathered wooden posts stuck into the ground in the shape of a square, and white paint provided an outline. Even from here, I could see the blood soaked into the hardpacked dirt. Kellan bound into the Square without a care, his eyes turned up to the sky as he spun. I moved out of the treeline but made no attempt to follow. I lingered in the shadows as he kicked at the dirt, dust rising around him as if he were some holy saint. He cast his gaze towards me, rolled his eyes.

"Don't piss about. Come here," he beckoned me forward.

I scowled, folded my arms and fixed him with a challenging gaze.

Insufferable idiot.

He waited; his face unfazed by my dissention. Behind us, a branch snapped, followed by a low growl, and I belted up the hill to join him, terrified of what might come for me. He seized me by the wrist, but I pulled myself free, my teeth bared.

"Don't grab me like that. I'm not a child," I hissed.

Kellan raised a brow but said nothing. He drew the toe of his boot through the dirt, created a line between the two of us. He rolled up his sleeves further, stretched his arms. My eyes followed the tightening of his skin, the shift of muscles, and my legs went soft.

"Stand here then," he gestured to the line.

I did as I was told. He stretched his arms above his head, winced as he cracked his shoulder, a remnant of an old injury. I shook my hands out, knew I should be doing something, doing anything but stand there like an idiot. The soft warble of voices echoed somewhere far off, and my heart rose into my throat.

Kellan shook his body out, his hair bounced as he opened his eyes. He held his fists up to his face, his elbows tucked into his ribs. He smirked behind his fists as he bounced on the balls of his feet. He was made for this, for fighting, for rebellion, for anarchy. It was clear in the lines of his body, in the shining of his eyes. He was born to be a solider.

"The key to a fight is to keep on your toes. Always keep moving. Come on, try," he bounced back and forth, his feet light and soundless.

I held my hands up. I felt stupid as I edge from foot to foot, every limb fatigued from travel and hunger. Kellan

193

dropped his arms; his face fell as he moved towards me. He jabbed me in the ribs, and I whined, scowled at him again.

"Tighter. Right now, you're vulnerable," he moved my elbows closer to my body, moved my fists up.

His fingers against my skin were warm and rough, his touch informative but lingering. I held my arms tight, my shoulders strained.

"Now tip toe. Back and forth," he demonstrated.

I tried to copy, but my movements were slow, clumsy. He nodded thoughtfully; his lip caught between his teeth as he observed me, tried not to laugh at my hopelessness.

"Try throwing a punch. Aim for the body first, break their defences, then go for the neck, the jaw, the side," he tapped each of my body parts in turn.

He held up his fists again, his smile unbridled.

"Come on. Punch me."

I didn't hesitate. My fist flew towards his chest with an anger that I dredged from the depths of hell itself. It was a slow, weak attempt, and he deflected it the way a horse swats at a fly. While my arm was loose, his own fist gave a tap to my ribs; gentle, as if I were a helpless toddler.

"Winded. Easy to break down. You'll be done within the minute. Again," he gestured me forward.

I tried again, this time with my left, and aimed straight for his smug grin. He grabbed me by the wrist and gave me a harder punch to the gut. My breath rushed out of my mouth as I took a step back. He pursued me; his fist swung for my cheek. I ducked, stumbled back again, my feet unsure on the dusty earth. He pressed at me, as eager and sly as a mountain cat, his jabs calculated; one to my shoulder, one to my chest, until my feet stumbled over the white line.

"And now you're disqualified. Don't give up your ground," he straightened up, his eyes turned to the treeline.

The voices were louder now. Kellan tutted, before he looked me in the eyes. I could see the lack of hope there, the shift of uncertainty, and I tightened my jaw, tried to muster some confidence.

"Try to move around. Most likely Kamal has chosen someone strong, someone he thinks will knock you out quickly. They'll be big, but slow, and hopefully will wear out sooner than you. Keep light, get up if you fall. You only need to stay conscious for five minutes." The voices rose and I could see people approaching.

Kellan grabbed my cape and ripped it from my shoulders. I reached out to take it back, but before I could he had already ripped a strip clean from it.

"Let them see you. See what you were, and who you are now," he said as he took me by the shoulders and spun me around.

With one hand he gathered my hair, tied the strip of fabric around to secure it. He spun me back just as quickly, and my head whirled as people emerged into the clearing. Kamal, clad in a sleeveless black tunic and tight trousers, led the charge. A large, bald man followed in his wake. He lumbered forward, his muscles taut and large from years of heavy lifting, his face covered in scars. There was battle in his deep-set black eyes, the kind of battle one should never walk away from, and yet here he stood, a behemoth ready to knock me down. My stomach ached as he met my eyes and sneered. Kellan put his hands on my shoulders, forced my attention back to him.

"It's five minutes," he reassured me.

I nodded despite the clawing inadequacy that ripped at my insides. He hesitated, his mouth hung open as if there were more he could add. He seemed to think better of it.

He joined Kamal, who had positioned himself at the edge of the Square. There was a small crowd, mostly men chomping at the bit to see a perfect girl get killed. There was one small girl, maybe ten, with cropped black hair and wide, saucer like eyes. She was petite, her arms short and thin. She lingered beside Kamal, dwarfed by his presence. Kamal didn't acknowledge Kellan as he came to stand beside him. The large man sneered at me as he spat on the ground, revealed a multitude of missing teeth. I recoiled, my fingers shook as Kamal took a step into the Square.

"You are here today to shed your perfect skin, and stand trial for the crimes of your people," he called in a theatrical voice.

It was utterly dramatic, the way he talked, but no one seemed to share my view. He raised his hands to the heaven, his eyes upturned.

"May the gods have mercy on your soul," he said, his smile undeniably sadistic.

The large man howled, a deep, spine shuddering noise that echoed through the morning sky. In the distance, a chorus of howls responded.

"Step forward, challenger," Kamal boomed, and I braced myself for the earth-shattering stomp of the large man.

He didn't move.

Instead, the small girl, almost half my height, moved silently into the ring. I blanched, my eyes frantically moved to Kellan, who looked equally surprised. He reached out to touch Kamal's arm, maybe to plead he reconsider, but Kamal brushed him off without thought. His grin was unbearable, his eyes dark and depthless with enjoyment.

The small girl rolled her neck, the arms I once thought as small seemed instead toned, slim but strong. I tried to breath evenly, tried not to let my fear show, but I knew it was all over my face.

"Five minutes. Begin." At his words, the small crowd thinned.

The observers moved around the edges of the Square, surrounded us, allowed no escape. When they were in positioned, they began to stomp; a slow, ominous thumping that was louder than my own heart. The small girl lifted her fists, her delicate hands already swollen from a recent fight. She took a step towards me, and it was as if all Kellan's tutelage went out of my head.

I instinctively took a step back, my legs weak. She advanced, unfazed. Her eyes were flat, her face blank. I lifted my own arms as the stamping quickened. A few of the watchers started to hum, their eager faces awaiting the first punch. It only took a second of my distraction for her fist to connect with the side of my head. A roar exploded from the audience and I tried not to stumble despite the spinning of my head. I blinked through the haze in my vision, forced my feet to move back and forth, side to side. I threw my arms towards her stomach, but she was quick. She moved like a flash; her rebuttal landed hard on my chest. I tightened my elbows, forced myself to focus.

Think, just think.

"Stop teasing her, Enrana. Finish it," Kamal shouted, already bored by the ordeal.

Enrana stepped forward, so close I could hear her steady breathing. She landed three quick punches to my stomach, and as I keeled over, another to my eye. I fell, my knees hit the ground with a jolt, keeled onto my side as pain splintered through my body. My eyes spotted black, threatened to fade as the roar of the crowd joined the roar of blood in my ears. Blood dripped from my nose as her foot contacted with my ribs. The air was knocked from my lungs as I gasped, unable to catch my breath, unable to breath at all as her foot came down again. My ribs splintered, gave against her force, but I refused to scream, refused to let them have that satisfaction. Distantly, Kellan was yelling for me to get up.

I laid there as her foot came again, and again, my bones cracked, my lungs empty. Something rose in me, something hot and angry, something primal that had been born on my father's desk among paper, blood and ink. It bubbled into my mouth and I shouted a wordless cry as I reach out and grabbed her ankle. I yanked, and she fell onto her back with a gasp.

I scrambled to my knees, spat blood as I struggled to choke down a breath or two. Enrana rolled onto her front and pushed herself up, unfazed by the fall. I too managed to stand, my chin slick with blood. There was a light in her eyes now, an embarrassment, a vengefulness.

I didn't let her get the first punch.

I threw both my fists towards her wildly, my arms ached, my ribs groaned at the movement. One fist blew right past her, but the second managed to land at her shoulder. I let myself feel some sort of triumph as she returned my punches, a swift jab to my already aching ribs.

The crowd was screaming, a cacophony of voices that made this feel like a simulation, a weird dream I wouldn't fully remember. I swallowed my mouthful of blood, consumed by frenzy. I lashed out again and again; uncalculated, lazy punches that couldn't have contained much power. Some of them landed, most of them didn't, and each time Enrana replied with power and precision.

It felt like hours, days even. I knew the time was almost over when I looked at Kamal, whose teeth were bared. His face was shadowed with rage, spit flying from his mouth as he yelled.

"Finish it Enrana!"

She looked at me as I swayed, my arms loose, my body barely able to carry itself. There was a flash of hesitance in her young eyes, as if she might like to see me succeed. Yet it ebbed as quickly as it rose, and she strode forward, her arms

198

lowered. She grabbed me by the hair, yanked my head back. I yelled, the pull of each hair like the prick of a needle. She threw her own head forward, her forehead contacted with mine with a crack. My vision dulled to a red rush as I fell. The pain was so hard that the fall to the ground was like nothing in comparison. For a moment there was nothing but darkness, an all-consuming, agony filled darkness. Then, the world returned, and I rolled onto my side as the counting began.

"Ten. Nine. Eight,"

Through my lashes I saw Enrana take a step backwards. She turned away from me, satisfied I was done for. I fought against the darkness that tried to pull me under. I knew if I let it take me, I would be killed. I knew if I fell into that comfortable, painless place, there would be no awakening. I fought every instinct bred into me; be quiet, be comfortable, be subservient. I fought the crippling need to give in, and searched for that fire that had been stoked.

My hands roved along the slick ground for purchase, for strength. I tried to push myself up. My aching arms refused to cooperate, sluggish, soft. I groaned; my swollen eyes struggled to open.

"Seven. Six. Five," the numbers were harder than any punch.

I planted my palms on the ground, rolled onto my front. The yelling subsided, fell to a hush that was somehow worse. Enrana turned slowly, her eyes on me as I pushed myself to my knees. My ragged breaths were the only sound, despite the countdown, as I bought one leg from underneath me.

"Four,"

I stood, and the movement sent my vision back into turmoil.

"Three,"

I swayed, almost lost my balance again.

Stay awake. Stay alive. Let them see you. Let them see your strength.

"Two,"

I straightened, swiped the blood from my face. I looked over at Kamal, saw the disbelief there, and gave him a bloody grin.

"One,"

The crowd exploded into applause. They rushed past Enrana, who looked both disappointed and pleased. They surrounded me; hands reached out to grab me, to welcome me. I allowed them to lift me up towards the sky. I closed my eyes, took a deep breath of fresh air as I hovered there, floated in the crowd of hands like a spirit.

My face was slick and swollen, each breath hurt my ribs beyond comprehension, but I was whole. I was home.

Kellan was yelling, his happiness unparalleled. Kamal stood alone, his face blank. He stared at me, eyes cast into darkness, lips pressed thin, and I knew then he'd been looking forward to killing me. The crowd cheered, then let me down, hands and bodies pressed against mine like a familiar embrace. I struggled to find my balance, and within a second of my feet touching the ground Kellan's arm was under my shoulders. His mouth pressed to the side of my head in an ecstatic kiss before his lips moved to my ear.

"I didn't think you had it in you," he whispered.

The crowd parted as Kamal moved through, his fists balled at his sides. His jaw was tight as he stood before me. He stared at me a moment, before he held out his hand. I took it without hesitation; an adrenaline ran through my veins that triumphed my fear of him. He shook my hand once, before he let me go.

"Welcome to the Mai-Coh. I'll arrange a meeting once you've..." he looked me up and down, a slight smile on his lips.

"Recovered. We'll see what you have to say about Sadon." With that, he turned on his heels and walked away.

As he passed Enrana, she shrunk, her shoulders sagged, her arms wrapped around herself. He looked down at her with a sternness that could make any man tremble. He shook his head at her, before he departed. Kellan blew a breath through his lips as he shook his head.

"I really thought you weren't going to make it," he said as the rest of the crowd filtered off, the entertainment and newness of me already faded.

I leant heavily against him, the adrenaline slowly subsided to unflinching pain. My legs buckled, no longer able to support my weight. Kellan caught me, turned up his nose as my blood stained his shirt.

"Okay, I get it. No need to be dramatic." He scooped me up into his arms as if I weighed nothing.

The darkness beckoned to me as Kellan walked, and I allowed myself to sink into it, desperate for release.

~

I awoke to the hum of hushed voices. I tried to force my eyes open, but only one complied, the other swollen shut. Pain bolted down my spine as I tried to sit up, and I winced, fell back against the pillows with a grunt.

There were other beds lined up on either side, plain iron cots with the same rough sheets. Most were empty, but there were some Mai-Coh lying in recovery. One had a bandage wrapped around his head and right eye, his other eye bruised black and purple. Another was pale and slicked with sweat, hooked to a bag filled with thick black liquid, their mouth lolled open and eyes empty with fever. There was a small child with their arm and shoulder bandaged and no mother in sight.

"Calluna," Theo's voice startled me, and I looked to my right.

He was sat at my bedside, his chest bandaged under his shirt. He looked better, his skin had gained some of its colour back, and his eyes no longer looked fevered. I was surprised he'd waited here for me, and the thought of him sat there, caring for me, set my heart racing.

He reached across the bed and rested his hand atop mine as if he could hear the swooning thoughts racing through my mind. I blushed under all the bruises; my fingers interlaced with his despite the pain in my arms.

"Kellan said you did well," He continued as he gave my hand a soft squeeze.

I tried to shrug nonchalantly to offset the nervousness that had settled in my stomach, but even the slightest movement made me hiss in pain. Theo put his other hand to my shoulder, his face lined with worry.

"Don't move. Farron will be back soon. You just need to rest," he reassured as his hand moved from my shoulder to brush the hair from my face.

His nails caught on the shred of the cape still lodged in my hair, and he took it between his fingers. His smile dropped as he rubbed his thumb against the fabric's length, before he let it go, his eyes blank.

"I tried to convince Kamal to let me train you, but when he has something in his mind…" he trailed off, his lips pulled taut as he shook his head.

My stomach sunk as I remembered the words that seemed so far away. Was it really such a bad thing to care for someone? Was it that Kamal hated the idea of one of his own liking the enemy? The thought of being trained by

Kellan, with his quips and his impatience, made my stomach lurch.

I didn't attempt to say anything in response, the silence was soothing. It was nice to relax, to breathe, to not have to think what was coming next, even if it was for a moment or two. As I looked at Theo, at the curve of his nose and the crook of his neck, I found myself missing Alfie. It was not the first time I had drawn comparison between them, yet Theo's hand on mine, his soft voice and his still presence, it was undeniable.

I withdrew my hand from his, all too aware how close we had grown in such a short time. If Theo was offended by my retraction, he did not show it. Instead, he looked towards the tents entrance, where a tall, broad-shouldered girl was bustling towards us. Her skin was as dark as the midnight sky, a raven's feather could not have compared to its cool onyx shade.

"You should be resting," she shot at Theo as she neared my bedside.

She balanced a roll of bandages under one arm, and a wooden box under the other. She let both items fall onto the foot of my bed, narrowly missed my toes as she fastened a red head scarf around her bald head. Her eyes trailed up and down my injuries with a scrutiny that could only come from years of practice, that simply could never be learnt from books or tutelage. She lifted my arm carefully, her hands soft against the bandages, and when I winced, a light flashed in her eyes, as if documenting the reaction somewhere deep in her memory. She continued to examine, her fingers prodded and poked, her eyes forever twitching. She finally came to my face, and she tutted as she stroked a finger over my swollen eye.

I took her in as she worked, transfixed by her calmness. Her face was masculine, her nose strong, her jaw square. She wasn't necessarily pretty; she had a hardness that I had expected I would find in the Mai-Coh. Her lips were pressed thin as she examined my jaw, turned my head this way and that. When she was satisfied, she pulled back and turned her attention to Theo, her eyes narrowed.

"I told you to rest," she scolded.

He shook his head as he patted his chest firmly.

"I'm all healed. Fit as I've ever been," he retorted.

She didn't look convinced, but instead of arguing she turned to her wooden box. She opened it, rattled through its contents, pushed aside vials and syringes, as well as one well used hand saw, before she came across a glass pot of brown cream.

"Here. Rub this in twice a day to fight off the infection. Change your bandages just as often," she advised as she pushed the cream into my hand.

I unscrewed the lid, curious as to what she'd given me. It smelt raw and sweet, a mixture of honey and ginger and something earthy. I wrinkled my nose, but screwed the lid closed and kept it gripped between my fingers. The girl looked at my clothes, her eyes drawn to the stains and rips.

"You should probably bathe too," she said plainly, too matter of fact to be an insult.

She picked up her wooden box, left the bandages on the bed for me to take. She turned to leave; her attention caught by the fevered man's coughing.

"Farron," Theo called.

She turned, her arms crossed, her face almost impatient. Theo cleared his throat; his head ducked under her perilous gaze.

"Thank you," he muttered, as if the words hurt to say.

She nodded, barely acknowledged his words, before she strode over to her other patients. It was a matter of seconds

204

before Kellan pushed through the tent's doors, his unruly hair sprung around his forehead like a nest. He was grinning. I wondered if he ever stopped smiling, if he ever stopped feeling smug. As he swaggered over to us, his face bright as the morning sun, I thought the answer to that question was no.

"I see you're awake." He nodded at me, turned his attention to Theo, "and look who's by your bedside. Prince Charming himself," Kellan teased.

Kellan laughed at his own joke; Theo rolled his eyes. Farron shot Kellan a sharp look over her shoulder, her lingering eyes as burning as her patients' fever. He raised a hand to wave, unfazed by her seething rage. Farron narrowed her eyes until they were barely slits, before she turned back to her patient, her shoulders clenched.

Kellan shrugged, before he clapped his hands, rubbed them together like he was hatching a devious plan.

"So, who's ready for some training?" he looked at me eagerly, desperate to do something.

I blinked at him. I looked down at myself, at the layers upon layers of bandages, at the swell of my wrist and the blood that drenched my dress, then looked back up at him.

He wasn't serious. There was no way he was serious. When I didn't say anything, he raised a brow expectantly, gestured to the door.

"Farron said she needs to bathe, then she needs to rest," Theo replied, harsher than I expected him to.

"Brilliant. I've been needing to bathe for about a week now. I'll take her," Kellan seized me by the wrist, pulled me up, and I hissed at the pain in my chest.

Theo's hand shot out to grip Kellan's forearm, his face thunderous.

"I don't think that would be wise," Theo said through clenched teeth.

Kellan snorted, clearly wanting to rise to the challenge. The thought of being naked with either of them made my heart stutter. Didn't I get a say? Didn't I get a choice? Wasn't this new life suppose to be *mine*?

"Come on, Theo. Since when have I been wise?" Kellan retorted.

"I said no,"

"And I said yes, so it seems we're at an impasse,"

Kellan's grin only served to anger Theo further. They stared at each other, unwavering. I cleared my throat, wiggled my arm from under both their hands. The pair continued to stare for a moment or two more, before Theo broke the exchange, his eyes drawn to my face.

"I'll go with Kellan," I decided.

Theo's face fell, and he withdrew into his chair, his jaw tense. Kellan looked both surprised and triumphant. I didn't particularly want to go with either of them, but he'd said it himself; Kamal didn't want us to spend time together. I didn't want to test Kamal's limited patience, not with the memory of his disappointment burning a permanent place in the back of my mind.

"Alright then. It's settled," Kellan smirked.

I frowned at him as I pushed my legs over the side of the bed. My feet were bare, and when they touched the cold earth a shiver wormed its way up my spine. I stood, and found my legs were much more stable than I had thought. I attempted to stretch my stiff shoulders, but the slightest movement made my ribs prickle with pain. I let out a breath, and risked a look back at Theo.

He had stood from his chair and was watching me with caution, his hand half outstretched, ready to intervene at a

206

moment's notice. Guilt burnt my throat at the concern in his eyes, and I wanted to sink into his chest. I wanted to cry, I wanted to let him take care of me, I wanted him to swaddle me and never let me go… but I couldn't. I couldn't be selfish, not here. So I moved away from the safety net of his shadow, gave Kellan a withering smile.

"Let's go get you undressed," Kellan gestured me towards the exit.

I shot him a venomous look.

"Stop it," I warned as I walked towards the tents exit.

Kellan tried to play innocent as he held the divide open. The camp was so different in the sunlight. The tents shone in a multitude of colours, a tapestry of freedom. People were busy making weapons, cooking food, everyone had a purpose. There was no milling about, no relaxing, no boredom. I thought back to Sadon and how frivolous the free time we had was.

"Stop what?" Kellan asked innocently.

I narrowed my eyes at the back of his head as he led the way.

"You know what. Teasing Theo like that," I replied.

Kellan scoffed, brushed off my words.

"It's all in good fun. It's how we show our love," Kellan mocked, made a kissy face in the direction of the infirmary tent.

I chose not to challenge him further; it was a waste of my limited energy. I followed him as we wound through the tents. I caught glimpses of training; children practising choke holds, archery, hands gripped around the hilts of swords almost as big as them. It was strange to see their discipline, their focus. It fascinated me to watch a small girl, maybe five, throw a much larger boy over her shoulder.

The mountains loomed ahead of us, dusty peaks of grey and white that stretched to hide the Mai-Coh's existence, and as we moved onwards their shadows shielded us from the morning sun. Kellan took a sharp left, and we were faced with a cluster of boulders. He picked his way through them, an invisible trail only he seemed to know. I stubbed my toe and let out a curse, which made him splutter.

I muttered to myself, grew impatient as we were confronted by the gaping mouth of the cave. I squinted, tried to peer past the darkness, but the cave seemed nothing more than shadows. Kellan walked blindly into its depths without so much as a word. I bunched my fists into my skirt, bit down my fear as I followed.

Once inside the cave, there was a moment of darkness, before wall mounted torches illuminated our way. It was strangely warm; the walls tinted a blue grey under the flickering flames. Condensation dripped hot as boiling water onto my skin as we walked. There was a soft blue light towards the end of the tunnel, and as sweat beaded on my forehead, we emerged into a large opening.

The belly of the cave was vast, its walls rippled from years of running water and speckled with luminous blue algae. There were several steaming pools at different levels; water cascaded in through a crack in the wall. The bottom pool overflowed into a narrow trough that bent under the caves walls and dropped off somewhere deep beneath the earth. I stared in awe at the natural wonder nature had created.

"There used to be a volcano around here somewhere, millions of years ago. Hence the heat," Kellan said as he swiped at his forehead, his hair pasted against his skin.

I nodded, still stricken by the algae that cast a light blue glow across the entire cave. There was a shuffling, and I turned to see Kellan shift out of his shirt. I averted my eyes, my heart sucked into my throat.

"What are you doing?" my voice was high and shrill even to my own ears.

Kellan turned, unashamed by his naked torso. I held my hands up to shield my eyes, but he moved further into my eyeline, desperate to push me. I huffed, squeezed my eyes shut as blood rushed to my face.

"It's not a big deal," he said, and this time, there was no humour to his tone.

My fingers were trembling. The thought of his nakedness, the shame of it, it filled my veins with acid. Celibacy, modesty, purity, they were the pillars of Sadon, and they were hard to turn away from.

"It is to me," I replied.

There was no way to explain how Sadon had made me feel about exposed flesh. I still remember the sessions they taught in school when I was five or six, the shaming of our bodies, the punishments for exposure, the sins linked to sex and sexuality.

"This place isn't always so empty." With that, he shed the rest of his clothes.

I heard him lower himself into the water. I opened my eyes a fraction to see him submerged up to his neck. I let out a sigh of relief, then wrapped my arms around myself. Kellan cocked his head expectantly, gestured to the water.

"In you get," he urged.

I fidgeted, nervous. I didn't want him to see me, to judge me. He sighed, rolled his eyes.

"So I can't see you either? This is no fun." Despite his words, he covered his eyes.

I rushed to take off my clothes. I went as fast as I could despite the pain it caused, terrified he'd see. I didn't trust him not to peak. My skin was black and blue, deep grazes on

209

my knees and ankles, scabs on my knuckles. I tiptoed over to the pool, lowered one foot experimentally into the water. It was hot, not just warm, but almost scolding. I lowered myself in, relaxed into its shining depths. I leant my head against the wall of the pool, let out a long sigh, felt as if I were bathing in the summer sky. Kellan peaked through his fingers, then let his hands drop.

"See? It's not so bad," he reasoned as he flicked water at me.

I didn't have the energy to retort. I sunk deeper into the water until it lapped up to my ears. I folded my arms over my chest just in case, but Kellan didn't seem very bothered. I absently wondered how many women he'd bought down here, how many women he'd seen bare. I cringed at the thought; the number seemed infinite.

For a minute or two, I let myself relax, I let the water burn away the stress that had built up over the last few days. A smile tugged at my lips, and I allowed myself to feel happy.

Kellan threw something rough and spongy at me, and I opened my eyes, not best pleased he'd disturbed me. He held up a hand in surrender, before he passed me a brown oval of soap. He'd thrown a loofa, frayed around the edges and worn from multiple owners. I picked it up from where it bobbed and scrubbed at my skin. The soap was gritty and smelt like pine, but it washed the dried blood from my body all the same. I lathered it into my hands and tried to tackle my knotted hair. I tugged at the lumps of dirt and grime, almost gagged as fragments fell into the water. My fingers caught in the mess and pain prickled along my scalp. I hissed, yanked my hands free with an angry huff.

"Let me," Kellan said.

I'd almost forgot he was here. I narrowed my eyes, dropped my hands back into the water. He waded until he stood before me, hand outstretched for the soap.

I couldn't breathe. I couldn't feel my fingers.

"What?" I asked.

He quirked an eyebrow, took the soap from my hand and motioned for me to turn.

"Watching you struggle is painful," he said plainly.

I turned, unsure if I was capable of doing anything else. Goosebumps rose on my shoulders at the brush of his fingers. I resisted the urge to shiver, bit down the anxiety that threatened to make my knees give out. His fingers in my hair were gentle as they worked at the knots. I tried to remain still, but I couldn't help fidget; every pull, every brush, every passing second set my skin on fire.

His hands fell to my shoulders, rubbed soap into the places I couldn't reach. I squeezed my eyes shut against the raging nerves in my stomach. The scrap of his nails between my shoulder blades made me tense; my back arched out of instinct.

Kellan let out a laugh through his nose, his breath fanned against my neck. His hands moved lower still, brushed against my waist. His thumb pressed against my scar, and I flinched out of habit.

"Tell me," he demanded.

I swallowed, tried to think past the roughness of his callouses. I didn't want to think of my dad, not now, not with his hands on me and my stomach in knots and my heart beating a mile a minute. I didn't want to think about how wrong this would be in Sadon, how I would be killed for it.

"My father," I said plainly.

I didn't want to explain. The memory flashed as dangerously as the blade that had marred me. His fingers moved to my stomach, pulled me back until his skin touched mine. Every line of his body pressed against every

211

line of my own. His fingers fug into the v of my hips as his lips crested my ear.

I couldn't feel.

For a second, a beautiful, terrifying, burning second, I didn't even exist. Fire and fear splintered through my chest, flamed through my veins from the tips of his fingers.

I was alight.

I was alive.

"Tell me how." His voice was low in my ear.

I pulled away, turned back to face him, folded my arms over my chest. My skin prickled with goosebumps, my nerves frayed to fragility.

"Don't touch me like that." I spat, managed to keep the tremble out of my words.

"Or what?" he asked.

A good question. *Or what?* What would I do?

I met his dark eyes across the water, his face cast blue and black, his smile as deadly as any weapon. Something about that grin, that gorgeous, breath-taking, devastating grin, turned the shaking in my limbs to steel. I stood sharply, my fists balled at my sides, hair stuck to my back. My chest rose and fell, bare for us both to see. His eyes drifted down to what I had exposed to him, a part of me I had never expected to expose to anyone but Alfie. I let him look, took that power from him.

He would not make me feel ashamed, he would not make me nervous of my own body.

This was my body now, and no one could lay claim to it without my permission.

"Or I'll end you," I said, my voice barely above a whisper.

I climbed from the pool, didn't wait for him to shoot some stupid quip my way. My dirty clothes lay in a damp, bloody pile at my feet, and despite how the thought of putting them back on made me want to groan, I picked up my dress and went to pull it on.

"Take mine," Kellan was beside me, but there was a respectful distance now.

"I don't want your pity," I spat as I eyed the shirt he held out to me.

It was relatively fresh, the one he'd been wearing this morning. A red button up with long sleeves and an even longer hem. I kept my eyes on it, tried not to let my gaze wander down his stomach to the part of a man I had never seen.

"Just take it," he said, pushed it into my arms.

I snatched it from him without a thank you. I pulled it on as he walked over to his trousers. I couldn't help but watch him. I committed every line of him to memory; the expanse of his back, the lines of his shoulder blades as he pulled on his underwear, the way his hair curled around the nape of his neck. My fingers fumbled on the buttons as he turned, his stomach cut with muscle, his hips sharp. I wondered how many fingers had traced those lines, how many nails had raked down those arms.

"If you're a spy, I'll kill you. You understand?" he said as he buttoned his trousers.

"You don't understand. Even if I wanted to go back, they'd kill me," I replied.

"And do you?" All his bravado, all his charm, melted away to the seriousness of a warrior.

It was terrifying, how different he looked without that smile. How in a second, he could morph into the killer I had been afraid to find here. I swallowed, unable to meet his eyes.

"No."

He was in front of me then, his hand on my wrist, his fingers pressed so tight I had to fight the urge to yelp.

"There's nothing I wouldn't do to keep my people safe. If I had to choose, between protecting you and protecting them, I will always choose them. I will not hesitate." He looked down at me, looked me over as if taking that bath had revealed exactly who I was.

Now that I was clean, I knew he would see me fully. See the full scale of perfection I had been moulded into. I grit my teeth, met his gaze head on.

"Then I won't give you reason to choose," I replied.

His fingers relaxed on my wrist and he pulled away. He walked towards where we had entered, and I assumed I was to follow. I scooped up my old clothes, smoothed a thumb over the marred white fabric. A pang of sadness made my eyes sting. My home was dead to me now. I would never wear white again.

"Good. I'd hate to waste a pretty face,"

Chapter XIII

"You're doing it wrong," the child next to me gloated.

I grit my teeth, tried not to ball my hands around the delicate fishing thread. I'd already knotted it too many times to count, and I didn't want to have to sit and unpick my mess yet again.

"Shut it Ren, no one likes a showoff," Ahzani said from my other side.

The young girl, Ren, puffed out an annoyed breath, muttered to herself as she went back to her section of the net. Ahzani leant over to look at the mess I was creating, narrowed her eyes at the too large holes and the crooked lines.

"She's right though," she whispered so the other children didn't hear.

I groaned, let the net fall from my fingers. We'd been at it for what felt like hours. I'd barely had time to change before Ahzani had come and found me, pulled me to my first training session. I had expected swords, bows, arrows, daggers, but instead I was met with children barely past ten and a tangle of fishing thread that needed turning into a net.

"I don't get why I have to do this," I complained.

All the other children were adept, their nimble fingers making light work of the large net we were weaving as a whole. I couldn't get the hang of it; my fingers were cut and bleeding, almost numb from the constant repetition.

"It's about building patience, teamwork, attention to detail... plus it's easier to get the kids to do the slave work," she said with a lopsided grin.

I rolled my eyes, picked up the threads I had been working on. My holes were always too big, or the wrong shape, or just plain wonky. I fiddled with the knot, tried to tighten it further.

"So you're wearing Kellan's shirt," Ahzani observed, her eyes alight with mischief.

I shot her an irritated look as my knot slipped and came undone. Ren snickered, pulled her knot effortlessly. I pulled a face at her, swore under my breath.

"I have to give him credit, he worked fast," she continued, inspected a young boy's handiwork, adjusted his knot before passing it back to him to finish.

"Nothing happened." I replied, tried to untangle my fingers from the net.

"Sure sure," Ahzani said dismissively.

"I thought you people were sexless prudes," one of the children said, their head cocked as they stared at me.

I blanched, looked back at the ten-year-old with my mouth hung open. Ahzani cackled, a laugh that made my cheeks burn red.

"Great. I'm getting bullied by children now," I hissed as I yanked my fingers free.

The thread cut into my thumb and I cursed, bought the bleeding wound to my mouth.

"Alright kids, get lost. Go on," Ahzani shooed the group off.

As they went, Ren stuck her tongue out at me, a smug smile plastered on her dark brown face. I stuck my tongue out back, glared at the back of her head until she disappeared from view.

Ahzani stood, held her hand out to pull me up. I took it, my knees groaned as I stood, stiff from sitting for so long. I stretched my cramped arms over my head, breathed in the clear afternoon air. Everything smelt different here, smelt real. There was no artifice, no overpowering stench of flowers. Ahzani gathered the net, inspected my horrible section with a raised brow. I offered her an apologetic smile.

"I think you need to practice," she said as she chucked the net into the box of supplies.

"No kidding," I muttered.

"You'll get it eventually. Give me a hand with these," she gestured to the other box, and despite how badly my hands hurt, I stooped and picked it up.

We walked down the path back to camp; we'd trekked up into the forest and found a secluded clearing to work on our nets. It was peaceful, calm, and I found myself relaxing into the sounds of the woods and distant training.

"So when do I get to practice properly?" I asked.

I hadn't been eager at first, but the interaction with Kellan in the baths had made me realise I was weak. I couldn't defend myself, not against the warriors around me, especially not against Sadon. I needed to be strong, I needed to be able to fend for myself.

"Pfft, you can't tie knots and now you want me to hand you a sharp blade? No shot," she replied.

"I might be good at it," I reasoned.

"And I might be good at sucking dick, but you don't see me rushing to subject myself to that," she said with disgust.

"How did you know? That you liked women?" I asked, then almost regretted it.

217

It wasn't my place to ask questions like that, like we were friends. Ahzani cast me a look out the corner of her eye, a smile pulled at her lips.

"I knew pretty earlier on. I just always thought girls were interesting, powerful, intoxicating, and boys were... plain stupid," she said, and it wasn't like I could argue with her.

I nodded thoughtfully, shifted the box in my arms as the weight pressed into my wrists. We emerged from the woodlands and into camp, where people were racing around with decorations; wreaths of flowers, candles and armfuls of firewood. They rushed towards the clearing I had seen the night of my arrival.

"What's going on?" I asked.

Ahzani looked towards the clearing, and something like pain flashed behind her eyes. She opened her mouth to speak, but then there was someone running towards us, and her attention was elsewhere.

"Hey, how did you get on?" Theo asked, took the box from my arms.

"Pretty useless. And I'm fine, by the way," Ahzani said as she balanced the box in her arms.

Theo rolled his eyes, didn't give her the reaction she was griping for.

"I tried to talk to Kamal today but he's stubborn. He doesn't want me to train you," he said, his face tight.

I squeezed his arm, gave him a kind smile. At least he'd tried for me, asked for me.

"It's fine, really. I have Ahzani,"

"And Ahzani could really do with a hand," she said again, looked pointedly at the box in her arms.

Theo shot her an irritated look, but took the box anyway. She grinned, triumphant.

"I suppose you got her clothes for the ceremony?" Ahzani asked.

"The ceremony?" I asked.

Theo looked hesitant, his lip caught between his teeth. I looked between the two of them, apprehensive for the answer.

"It's a... full moon thing," Theo jerked his head at the clearing, which now had a large bonfire ready to be lit at the centre.

"What kind of full moon thing?" I asked warily.

Something about the way they both looked, like they were scared to tell me, scared of what my reaction might be, told me it couldn't be anything good.

"I'll explain later. Let's set you up a tent first," Theo artfully dodged the question, shoved the boxes back into Ahzani's arms.

"Such a gentleman," she grumbled.

His hand on my back was warm and steady as he led me away from the clearing, but the thought of tonight, the thought of seeing Kamal and whatever the ceremony entailed, it churned in my stomach until all I could think about was those three citizens burning for their crimes.

~

I sat on the floor of my newly allocated tent, pulled my hair into two French braids. Theo had helped me erect a tent, despite instructions that I had to do it alone. I'd tried, snapped at Theo to leave me be when he'd tried to point out that the waterproof sheet went on the outside. After an hour of sweat and cursing, however, I'd slunk back to him with

219

my tail between my legs and begged him to help, to which he grinned and gave me a friendly mocking.

It was a modest space; a pallet arranged with furs on the floor, an oil lamp hung from the cross section above my head, a hand carved chest filled with clothes that had been borrowed from various people. Theo assured me I'd get some of my own clothes at some point, but not until the next trip to the Slums. He'd also assured me the place would feel like home soon enough, not that I believe that. I felt more alone than I had in days, sat in the empty circle that would be my life from now on.

I finished my braid and swung around to look at the dress on the bed. Ahzani had come in later in the afternoon, and like a tornado had strewn clothing all around the room in search of an outfit for tonight. She'd explained that on every full moon, a ceremony was held for fertility, both for the crops and for the Mai-Coh women. A handful of virgins who had turned sixteen would be selected, and Ahzani joked that some months there would only be one or two, because the Mai-Coh loved to mess around, but the humour had been laced with anger. The Priestess who had taken my diary, Akari, would perform a ceremony which would end in... well, she'd only insinuated, but it wasn't hard to guess.

I stared at the outfit she had picked for me. A low cut, sheer yellow dress with bell sleeves and a slit up both sides of the legs. It was embroidered with golden stars that sparkled in the dim lamp light, glittered almost like powdered diamonds.

I rubbed the material between my fingers experimentally. It was soft, silky, but it lacked the refinement of richer fabric. Its thinness gave it away, and yet compared to everything else I owned, it was a crowning glory. Ahzani had given me that grin of hers as she'd held it up, and I'd shivered as she'd explained in detail how it would complement my figure.

220

I sighed and stood. I could already hear the drumming in the distance and the laughter of passing Mai-Coh. I shuffled out of my borrowed clothes and pulled on the dress. It hugged my waist and showed off way more of my breasts than I would have liked. The sound of the drums warbled and rose like calling voices, and I knew it was time to leave, but I couldn't bring myself to go.

I didn't want to go out there, to have all their eyes on me. I was so different to the rest of the girls, who were all so strong. My arms were weak, my thighs still held some of the softness of wealth. I felt, for the first time in life, like I was ugly.

I startled as someone barged their way into my tent. I turned; my heart thrashed in my chest at the intrusion. Roscoe blinked in confusion, his head turned from side to side, eyes narrowed as he took in the tent. His eyes landed on me, and I raised a hand in a half wave, unsure why he was here or what I was supposed to say to him. He blanched, stumbled a step or two to the right. He was drunk, I could smell it on him. He hiccupped, laughed at himself, and then seemed to realise I was still there.

"Hey," I tried to broach a conversation to ease the awkwardness.

He took a step towards me, and then another, until he reached out and took the hem of my dress in his hand. I slapped his hand away, my blood pounding in my ears, but he didn't relent.

"You know," he drawled, gave another hiccup.

"Kamal will probably put you in the next one. The ceremony," he slurred, tugged at the hem of my dress.

I gave him a push, a very light one, but he wheeled back like he'd been hit by a truck. I straightened myself, balled my hands at my sides as he steadied himself.

"Over my dead body," I stated.

221

Roscoe was younger than me, he was practically a child, not more than fourteen, a few years away from being a man. He could not talk to me like that. Roscoe laughed in that way only drunk people can laugh, shrill and unencumbered.

"Oh really?" he spluttered.

I chewed my cheek, unable to answer. The door to my tent flew open, and Kellan stood, wineskin in hand, eyes narrowed at the scene in front of him. He seized Roscoe by the shoulder, pulled him back a step.

"Come on, kiddo. Who let you drink the adult stuff?" he asked as he dragged Roscoe away.

"I'm old enough," Roscoe tried to reason through a pout.

Kellan blew out a disbelieving breath.

"Yeah right. You're like... two," Kellan gave him a shove, and Roscoe tumbled from my tent without another word.

Kellan turned, attempted to smooth his hair down as he came towards me, but it stuck up regardless. He met my tense stance with a sceptical look, handed me the wineskin. I eyed it suspiciously, before I took a sip.

I choked as the wine slipped down my throat. It was fruity, almost like blackberries, but so sour it burnt. I pursed my lips, gave the wine back to him. He smiled; a wide, relaxed grin that seemed truly genuine. He ignored the shake of my fingers, and for that I was grateful.

"Sorry about him," he jerked his head towards where Roscoe had exited.

I shrugged it off, determined not to let it phase me. Kellan eyed me as he sipped at his wine, as if studying me, his lips tinged purple. I did not shy from his gaze, he'd already seen way more of me than I cared to admit, and there was no point being bashful.

"Shall we?" I gestured to the outside world.

Kellan gave a short nod, held open the tent's door for me. I stepped into the surprisingly warm night. The air was thick with the smell of smoke and alcohol, bitter and cloying. The sky hummed orange, lit by the bonfire that blazed in the distance. People walked past in good spirits; they drank and sang songs I had never heard.

"I didn't think you'd be so eager," Kellan said offhandedly as we followed the procession of tipsy soldiers.

I shook my head, pretended that the whole ordeal didn't make me sick to my stomach. A stone heavier than I could bare settled in my stomach; it turned and churned every time I thought about the naked bodies I would witness later.

"Like you said, I have to get used to it." The words were sharp as they left my lips, harsher than I meant them to be.

Whether I was getting better at deception or Kellan simply didn't care, he seemed to accept my answer. He drank again from the wineskin, unbothered by its sourness. He looked beautiful under the darkness, as if he were designed to live within it. The lack of sun leant his skin a burnished glow, his hair as pitch as the sky. His lashes fell across his cheeks like feathers, gentle and almost feminine.

I forced my eyes to the dirt below my feet, ashamed by the tingling of my fingers and the jump in my chest. I traced the footsteps that trailed before me, the indents people had left in the dirt. Some were bare, some booted, some so haphazard and smudged they didn't seem to be human at all. It was fun, almost. To see those who had walked before me, to know my footsteps were merging with theirs.

"You know... I wouldn't let him put you in the ceremony. If that's what's on your mind," Kellan said almost hesitantly.

I looked up at him, but there was no emotion on his face. His eyes focused straight ahead, reflected the shifting light.

223

He kept drinking, as if the words had never left his lips. I internalised my smile, returned my gaze to the people before us.

"I'm not worried," I replied.

"Of course not," Kellan confirmed, a smirk on his face as if he didn't believe me.

"I'm not," I said, firmer this time.

Kellan held up both his hands in mock surrender.

"Okay. You're not," he said, still smirking.

I gave him a nudge with my elbow. He looked at me out the corner of my eye as we approached the bonfire.

"I could knock you on your ass right now," he reminded me.

I shrugged as confidence blossomed in my chest. The wine I'd sipped had settled like lightening in my veins, had filled me with an impatience to breathe and live and exist.

"I don't think so," I tried, to which he burst out laughing.

"You wait until training. You'll see," he warned as someone approached us.

A young girl, all dressed in red. Her face was hidden behind a thick veil that I was sure she couldn't see out of. Every inch of her skin was covered, right down to her ankles. All I could see were her hands, slight, childlike, pale and fragile. In one hand she held a bowl of red paste. She dug her fingers into the paste, held them up.

Kellan crouched, allowed the girl to smudge the paste in two thick lines spanning from his right temple down to the left side of his jaw, over his closed eyes. She turned to me; fingers coated. I bent, as she was so slight; her head barely reached my shoulders. She placed her fingers on my forehead, pressed two dots above my eyebrows, then

224

another two below my eyes, and a final pair on my chin, before she brushed her thumb down the bridge of my nose. The process was special, sacred, and when she was done, I felt cleansed.

I pulled back to see four other red shrouded women doing the same to other newcomers and realised that these were the offerings for tonight's ceremony. My smile faltered as I watched her retreat, and I resisted the urge to wipe the paste from my face.

"Calluna!" Theo's voice boomed above the crowd.

He ran towards us, red swirls painted on both his cheeks. He embraced me, his hands warm on my waist, his elevated breath fanning my cheek. When he pulled back, he looked as if he wanted to say something, but his eyes slipped from me to Kellan, who opened his arms wide.

"What, no hug for me?" Kellan asked through a pout.

Theo gave Kellan a playful push on the shoulder, and Kellan smiled. He went to take another swig from his wineskin, but only the tiniest drop fell into his mouth. Kellan frowned and threw the skin over his shoulder, where it narrowly missed a stumbling man.

"I'm gunna go find another one of those." With that he disappeared into the swaying crowd, his eyes drawn to where a pair of girls were giggling.

Theo moved his weight from one foot to the other. He seemed nervous, his smile shy, and I wondered how much blood changing wine he'd had to drink.

"It's going to start soon," Theo stated plainly, as if he had nothing else to say.

Why was he so nervous? Maybe he didn't like the ceremony either. Maybe he was more like me than he was like Kellan.

In the distance, a girlish shriek echoed, and I looked up to see Kellan grab the ass of a small Hispanic girl as he

225

chugged from a large wine skin. Theo tutted, shook his head, only further emphasising their differences.

"He's going to cause a lot of trouble tonight," Theo hissed under his breath like a scolding mother.

I snorted, which drew Theo's attention with a grin. He cocked a brow, the lines around his eyes crinkled as he gave my shoulder a bump.

"What?" He asked.

I shrugged, my head light and airy. I craved the sour taste of the wine, craved the tartness, and I looked around for more to no avail.

"You love him," I teased.

Theo pulled a face, made a disgusted noise as he walked towards the fire. I chased after him, no longer concerned by Kellan's antics.

"It's true, you love him," I teased, elongated my words.

Theo didn't seem offended, no matter how many times he pretended to blanch. He smiled down at me with something so light and brilliant it could have lifted me into the sky.

"You're already so... different." The word different was such a wonderful compliment, and my giddiness steadied as I met his eyes.

I blushed, found myself clawing at my braids. My hands felt so empty, and so did my mouth. I struggled to find the words I wanted to say.

I wanted to tell him I was grateful, that if it weren't for him, I would be in a prison, or dead, or worse; a Riven. Luckily, the drums swelled to challenge the mountains, drowned out any opportunity for conversation. Kellan gave a loud whoop, but I didn't turn to look at him.

226

Theo ushered me towards the ring forming around the fire. The crowd thickened, drawn to the ceremony like moths, and fellow Mai-Coh jostled and pushed their way to the front. Theo wrapped his fingers around my upper arm, pulled me back as a pair of younger men muscled their way in front of us. I was glad of the obscured view as the five red shrouded women made their way towards the fire.

They kept their heads bent down; their hands folded before them. The drums thumped twice more, then fell silent. I held my breath as the silence settled over the procession. It held a tenseness that made the hair on my arms stand. Theo's fingers on my arm were the only things that grounded me as I leant forward, strained onto my tiptoes. The haunting trill of a violin filled the smoky air, played a sorrowful tune. Its notes struck something inside me that made my eyes water, something lost and bleak. It somehow remined me of my mother, singing to me as a child. It reminded me of dark nights afraid in her warm arms.

The girls raised their arms, fingertips stretched to the stars. The violin was joined by another, and the girls swayed, their moves fluid, soft, like spirits caught in a storms wind. A flute joined the chorus and their feet moved, a tangle of delicate steps unseen beneath their dresses. As cellos and violas swelled, they span around the fire, twirled as effervescent as the flames. They danced on and on, span and span until I was sure they were dizzy. The music came to a crescendo, and at its hight, Akari emerged, her hands throw high into the sky. The five young girls flung themselves to the floor, bodies pressed to the dirt in a bow. The instruments fell away as the flames turned blue; lavender smoke rose to curl around the priestess's feet. She moved towards the girls as if she floated amongst the clouds.

Within the smoke there were animals, wolves that prowled with eyes of red, stags that strutted with hooves of steel, rabbits that pranced unruly above my head. I couldn't help but marvel at their smoky beauty.

"Rise," Akari's voice was melodic, so beautiful and ethereal it could make a mountain tremble.

The five girls rose, stood side by side as sturdy as sentinels. Kamal emerged from the crowd; his chest bared for all to see. His skin was intricately decorated with tattoos, almost every space inked. Just below his collar bones were the outline of two hands, sinewy and angelic, their index fingers pointed towards each other, almost touching. The words *divided utterly* were inscribed just above the knuckles in curving, slanted letters. Swallows swooped down in a v to his belly button, feathers of every colour spread wide across his waist. The contours of his sides were decorated with men in battle uniform, entire armies with shields and spears. As he turned, his arms outspread, I saw the wolf that prowled across his back, tail twisted, ears pointed. Amongst it all, delicate and out of place, was a small heart, almost invisible, hidden between the paws of the wolf, with the letter J drawn messily within.

A remnant of another life.

"Friends," Kamal called.

His voice carried as if it were contained within the wind. It echoed above our heads as if it came from the heavens, but it did not tremble or waver.

"Brothers and sisters, we come before the gods to ask for fertility in our time of need. Let us begin." Kamal took a knee before Akari, who pulled from the folds of her dress an iron dagger, its twisted handle encrusted with blue jewels that glittered under the firelight.

Those around me pressed forward, tightly knit, arms linked. Theo's arm threaded through mine, and the stranger on my other side did the same. I winced against their sweaty flesh, wriggled uncomfortably. Akari's blue veined eyes were upturned to the sky, her childlike hands clasped around the hilt of the knife. Her lips parted, snow pale to reveal teeth as perfect and white as the stars.

"Come." Her single word made the earth beneath my feet quiver.

Akari approached them, and each held out their hands. With a movement so fluid I barely caught it, Akari drew the sparkling blade over the palm of the first girl. The girl quickly clamped her hand shut to prevent the blood from dripping onto the ground, fingers clenched. Akari moved down the line, each girl sliced. When she had nicked the last, she pricked her own finger, and held her hand to the fire. When her blood hit the flames, they jumped green and purple, thin tendrils snaked into the sky.

"With the blood of these virgins, we offer the gods our sacrifice."

Each girl extended their hands, some trembling, some steady, and allowed their fingers to relax. Blood sizzled amongst the kindling, and the fire rose still, its flames as raw and red as the wounds on their hands. Akari mumbled, words I couldn't hear, but doubt I would understand even if I could. Her lips moved unnaturally, her skin trembled, vibrated with every word. The five girls fanned out around the fire, took up the same mumbling. The firewood popped and crackled, sparks spat and hit the earth before our feet. I wanted to flinch, but the arms that bound me had tightened to the point of constriction. There was no escape.

"Look," Theo whispered.

I couldn't look away even if I tried. I was transfixed, my eyes glued to the flames as they churned. Akari's eyes glowed from deep within, a bright and undeniable light. She truly was a vessel for the Gods, a being more pure and powerful than the Emperor could ever be. Akari yelled out then, a scream that had no words or identifiable meaning, but struck me so deeply my heart stuttered and stumbled. She fell silent, the light within her eyes died to nothing, and her shoulders slumped forward as her chest heaved. There was complete silence, no one even breathed as Akari looked up at the sky.

At first, there was nothing. Then, a drop of rain. A spec that fell upon my cheek so cool and sweet I wanted to touch it. Then, another, and another, until the rain flowed freely. It did not extinguish the fire, which still raged in hues of blue and green. Kamal stood, turned his head to the sky and opened his mouth to drink the sweet water from the Gods. Akari gestured to the girls, and slowly, they undressed.

"Now that the Gods have blessed our lands, let them bless our people. May those who have been named come forth."

Kamal rubbed his hand across his mouth, blinked through the rain as the girls stripped naked. My stomach constricted at their naked curves. Water ran through their hair, trailed down the lines of their bodies. I tried to yank free from those who held me, but Theo's arm only tightened. I looked up expecting the squeamishness I had seen earlier, instead I saw excitement. I saw revelry.

"Theo," I attempted, but he hushed me as Kamal claimed the first, a short, busty, pale skinned girl with deep ashy hair.

He pulled her to him, and she quivered, whether from the rain or fear there was no telling. I expected to see excitement on his face, or at least lust, but there was a tightness to his jaw and a blankness to his eyes that I didn't understand.

"Come forth," Akari bellowed.

Four men came forward, and the last I sadly recognised. Roscoe stumbled towards the fire like a toddler, all elbows and knees. His hand fell upon the tallest of the offerings, a dark haired, homely girl almost twice his height, russet skinned and long limbed. She tried not to flinch, but I saw in the way her shoulders sagged the awkwardness she felt.

"Let the God's bless our people with fertility. Let those we offer bare the strongest of us all," Akari called.

As the men undressed, I forced my eyes closed, my lips pressed tight. I shook my head, tried to ignore the grunting and whimpering as the ceremony continued. My fingers clenched tight as the moaning grew louder and louder, rattled my head. Was this any better than Sadon? Was this any better than forced life mates? Where was the freedom, where was the choice?

As a scream bubbled in my throat, the arms that constricted me relaxed, and I opened my eyes. The young women were being ushered to a tent by Akari as they pulled the remnants of their dresses haphazardly over their shoulders. Kamal stood, his trousers hung loosely around his hips.

"My brothers and sisters! We are blessed by the Gods. Let us celebrate!" He bellowed, and the crowd roared.

The circle disbanded as the final girl disappear into the tent. Akari stood, hand perched on the fabric, as if something had distracted her. She turned; her eyes caught mine. I saw something in her face then, a foreboding that made my blood run cold. She pulled her hijab closer and let the tent flap close behind her as she disappeared.

Mumbling drew my attention away from the eerie tent and to Roscoe, who still sat on the ground struggling to stand up. Kellan emerged from the crowd, looking barely better than Roscoe, but he helped the young boy stand nonetheless. I shivered, soaked through from the rain. I turned to Theo, who was busy chatting to a friend I didn't recognise. I watched them talk, as if what had just happened were some sort of game. Theo even laughed as the unnamed man imitated a sex position gone wrong. I turned from him, something sour settled in my stomach. I joined Kellan as he tried to calm a frantic Roscoe.

"I love her! I lo... I love her!" Roscoe yelled as he tried to take a step towards the tent.

Kellan laughed as he restrained the young boy.

231

"There will be others, come on kiddo," Kellan urged, but Roscoe was having none of it.

"No! I love her!" Roscoe yelled, eyes glazed and sightless.

I reached Kellan, who looked at me with a smirk.

"Enjoy the show?" He asked as he wrapped his arms around Roscoe's neck.

I cringed, shivered as I looked back at the fire that was finally burning more naturally. Roscoe struggled, arms flailing, his lips pouted. He clawed at Kellan without much success. He mumbled, tearful as he tried to move.

"I love her," he whined.

"Do you even know her name?" Kellan asked, which made Roscoe slump backwards.

Kellan relaxed his grip, and Roscoe stumbled, his arms crossed. His eyes were watery as he looked towards the tent. Kellan gave him a pat on the back, and I felt sorry for the young boy.

"Don't worry, in nine months you'll see her again," Kellan said.

I blanched, my eyes wide. Kellan looked back at me, confused by my reaction.

"I didn't think she meant that," I whispered, unable to raise my voice out of sheer shock.

Hadn't that just been a line? A throw away sentence in an outdated script? Kellan let out a puff, shrugged, as if child mothers were a normal occurrence.

"It wouldn't be much of a fertility ritual if it didn't work," Kellan said simply.

It didn't matter that he was right. It didn't matter how normal this seemed to them. Those girls, their lives would be forever changed. Barely women, robbed of choice, robbed of something they would never get back. Kellan sensed my anger, and he sighed, put a hand on my shoulder.

"They tried stopping it once. Back when my mother was a child. For a year and a half they refused. And for a year and a half no crops grew. No animals grazed. No fish lived. No babies were born. Famine raged through the camp, we lost half our people. We don't... we don't have a choice." He said, his eyes fixed on the tent as it pulsed with light.

Had his mother grown sick? Had she suffered in those years? I bit the inside of my cheek; despite his explanation, despite how essential it clearly was, I couldn't come to terms with it. Would never enjoy it.

"She won't have to raise the baby. She'll have a normal life," he tried to reassure me, but the idea of her child being ripped away from her only made my stomach tighten.

"I'm going to go back to my tent," I grit out.

I turned, but Kellan caught my wrist, pulled me towards him.

"Come on, stay," he tried.

I hesitated, my eyes drawn back to the tent over and over. I hated to think what was happening in there; the spells, the rituals, the pain those girls must be enduring. I wanted to turn my back, I wanted to walk away, to ignore it. I was reminded of Sadon, of the Palladium ceremonies where I had thought those same things. My head pulsed at the thought.

"I don't know," I looked back over my shoulder at the path towards my tent.

Kellan sighed as Roscoe thumped back onto the ground, gangly legs askew, hands hung in the dirt in defeat. Kellan looked at the boy, gave another, more exasperated sigh, and then turned back to me.

233

"Callie please. At least help me put him to bed," he negotiated.

The nickname took me by surprise. It was warm, affectionate, familiar, and the way he looked, hazy eyed, flushed cheeks, softened my resolve. I nodded, and Kellan smiled. He let my wrist go, scooped Roscoe over his shoulder like a small infant, and strode off with all the confidence that existed in the world. I followed behind, eyes frantically scanning those around me.

In Kellan's shadow, I was moderately safe, but still with every leering look and slanted word fear prickled the nape of my neck. I had conquered the Square, I wore their clothes, I had endured their ceremony, but I was not one of them. As Kellan shouted to friends, bumped shoulders, jostled a dozing Roscoe, I found solace in the details of the party.

Kamal had taken up residence on his throne; on either side stood a beautiful woman. Both were tall, statuesque, creatures of daunting strength. They wore bronze breast plates and copper shoulder guards, coiled metal skirts that clanked against their knees. Neither drank, but held a wine skin in one hand, a spear in the other. Kamal leant back, physically relaxed, but his eyes saw as much as mine, more so. He was waiting, ready for a fight that was not coming. He met my stare, and I realised I was the reason he was waiting. He expected them to come for me, he expected them to follow.

I looked down at my wrist, at where the identity chip nestled just below the skin. I traced a nail across the faded scar.

"Kellan," I looked up, and he whirled around, Roscoe's head narrowly missing a tent pole.

He waited expectantly for my next words; head cocked to the side. Roscoe mumbled nonsensically, wriggled, but Kellan smacked the young boy on the ass and shushed him.

"We need to do something tonight," I said.

Kellan raised an eyebrow, gave me a lopsided smile as he raised a coy shoulder.

"Oh yeah? Let's drop the kid off and get to it then," he replied, his voice low and seductive.

Before I could refute his advances, Kellan had turned and was striding away from the crowd with renewed vigour. I jogged to keep up, and soon the noise of the party faded to the hum of the come down; drunken whispers uttered between friends, limbs against limbs to seize the fertility rituals advantages. I tried to concentrate on Roscoe, on his sleeping face.

He was so small, so soft, so delicate. As Kellan walked towards the hills, Roscoe's eyes fluttered, his lashes pale and light against his cheeks. My chest filled with sweetness as his lips parted, the whisper of words lost in dreams caught on his tongue like a fly in a crystal web. As the earth slanted upwards, my eyes were drawn from Roscoe, and instead fell upon a large tent carved into the side of the hill, high above the rest. It was a mix of hard wooden beams and thick purple sheets, sheltered partially by a tight knit grove of trees. Light shone from within, and even from here I saw the shadows of gathered people.

"Who lives up there?" I asked as Kellan shouldered his way inside a tent.

I stooped in after him, glad for the relative warmth the animal hide provided. Kellan dumped Roscoe unceremoniously onto his pallet, but the young boy barely stirred. Kellan braced his hands on his waist, stretched himself out as his face scrunched up.

"You mean Kamal's place?" Kellan asked, not even having to see where I pointed to.

A grand tent for a grand man. I wondered who was in there, if Kamal of their presence. The hair on my arms stood

235

at the thought of Kamal finding them, uninvited. The idea of his wrath twisted as sharp as a blade inside my throat.

Kellan stretched his arms above his head. His shoulders clicked, and he made a triumphant hum as he straightened himself out. He fixed me with a smile and nodded at the floor.

"So, you want to do it here? I don't think the kid will wake up," Kellan said as he scratched the back of his head, looked down at Roscoe.

I narrowed my eyes at him, folded my arms over my chest. It was a testament to his arrogance that he thought everyone wanted to sleep with him. I pushed down the butterflies in my stomach, told myself to concentrate on the annoyance instead of the queasy excitement.

"No," I replied, to which Kellan shrugged.

"No really, I don't think he'll wake up," Kellan prodded Roscoe in the ribs with the toe of his boot.

Roscoe mumbled, swatted at the air as he turned over. Kellan raised a brow, as if that explained it all. I took a step back, fisted my hand into the skirt of my dress.

"No. I need to cut something out of me," I held my wrist out.

Kellan made a disgusted face but took my wrist in his hand none the less. He turned it over, then side to side, held it up to eye level, really squinted, before he let it drop.

"Right, and you trust me to do that because I'm... sober?" he mused.

He posed a great question, of course, but all I could think about was Kamal and his searching eyes, and the Pioneers who could be tracking me. I eyed him, the slow blink of his eyes, the drunken tilt of his smile.

On the one hand, he could seriously disfigure me; I could lose a hand or bleed out and die.

Yet, on the other hand, I could be endangering everyone here, everyone whose helped me.

I sighed, massaged the bridge of my nose to ease the headache that was beginning to form.

"I don't have much choice do I," I replied begrudgingly.

Kellan scoffed, gave a dramatic bow as he pretended to be touched.

"I'm flattered, really," Kellan wept.

Regardless, he pulled back the flap of the tent and gestured me out. I took one last look at Roscoe where he had curled into a ball. I leant down and pulled the furs around him firmly, stroked his forehead tenderly. He settled more comfortably, the ghost of a smile on his lips. It pained me to think how much he looked like Lavender then, the softness of his face, and I thought of her, thought about whether she missed me. I smiled as I stood, tried to imagine her happy, imagine her softly dozing as my mother read her a story.

I waited for Kellan to mock me, but he said nothing, his eyes moved from Roscoe to me. He stood patiently, waited for me to move, and I saw the tenderness he held for Roscoe barely concealed behind his drunken eyes.

The party raged on in the distance, the cries of drunken idiots echoed through the darkening night sky, but we moved towards the infirmary tent soundlessly. Kellan pulled me inside and guided me by the shoulders to a bed. I sat cross-legged while he rooted through the many wooden boxes littered on the table. He produced a small knife, barely the size of his thumb. He made a triumphant cry, stumbled as he made his way over to me. As I began to second guess my choice, he balanced the blade between his teeth, one hand grasped bandages, the other a small bottle of clear alcohol.

"You're sure?" he asked around the knife as he opened the bottle.

"Honestly, I wouldn't," he finished as he spat the knife out, doused it with the alcohol.

He rubbed it into his hands, then took a sip. His face screwed up at the taste, his lips pouted as he made a noise low in his throat. He shook his head vehemently, then offered the bottle to me. I took it without hesitation, took a large gulp. The liquid was more like bleach that alcohol, different from the lightening sourness of the blackberry wine, so strong I was sure it stripped my throat of all its cells. I choked, gasped for the sweet release of air. Kellan looked at me expectantly, awaited my answer. My teeth clamped together as I rubbed my thumb over the skin of my wrist, the faint line of the chip barely feelable under my flesh.

I held out my wrist without hesitation. My hand shook uncontrollably, but Kellan didn't take much notice. I gnawed on the inside of my cheek as he took my wrist in his hand, squinted at the skin. He held up the blade, his hands surprisingly steady. As the tip came to rest against my skin, I flinched, drew back my arm out of instinct. I cursed myself as Kellan fixed me with an impatient look.

"Can you... I don't know, talk to me?" I asked.

Kellan drew back, lowered his blade. Beyond his bravado and sarcasm, there was something closed and guarded. I saw it in the way his eyes shuttered, the way the lightness faded behind them at the request of intimacy. He opened his mouth to object, but I rushed to interrupt him.

"Please. I won't be able to if you don't." I was on the verge of begging, and his shoulders sagged as he let out a breath.

238

"Fine." He said shortly as he snatched my wrist.

He hesitated, looked up to the peak of the tent as if deliberating over something before he waded up some bandages and gave them to me.

"For your mouth. Don't want you biting your tongue off."

I took the fabric and pushed it between my teeth. It was rough, lukewarm against my tongue, tasted faintly of alcohol. I squeezed my eyes closed as he bought the blade close to my skin. A faint whimper left my lips as the knife barely scratched the surface.

"I remember my mother," he said as he pressed the knife deeper.

I clamped my teeth down hard against the fabric as blood slipped down my arm. The blade was cold, and the pain was blinding. It shot up my arm like a thousand burning needles, and as he pressed deeper, my vision blurred, tinged black around the edges as my pulse thumped in my ears.

"Most of us don't even get to see them, but I remember her. Little glimpses," his tone was soft, as if the memory was precious, and I listened despite the cold sweat that plastered my dress to my back.

"She had this red hair, nothing like yours, though. It was paler, more orange blonde I guess." I yelled out as the knife went deeper, and a wave of heat threatened to drag me into unconsciousness.

My cheeks were wet from sweat and tears as the blade clicked against the chip.

"I remember her laugh, too. It was so ugly, this snorting, cackling mess that made everyone look at her." I could hear the smile in his voice, and even as he pried the chip from my flesh and a scream tore from my throat, I was glad.

He retracted the blade from my flesh, and I let out a choked cry of relief. My wrist throbbed, my fingers were stiff and sticky with blood. I went to open my eyes, but Kellan forced them closed with blood-soaked fingers.

"I'm going to stitch it closed," he said as he pulled the bandage from my mouth.

I took in a deep breath, my mouth dry. I kept my eyes squeezed shut as he snapped the surgical thread.

"So, what happened to her?" I asked, my voice hoarse.

There was silence as he jabbed the needle through my skin. I hissed; teeth dug deep into the flesh of my cheek. I curled my toes until the nails dug in, strained against the soles of the too small shoes. Every stroke of the needle and pull of the thread was inescapable.

"We went to Slum Four once, that one with all the thieves. It was only supposed to be recon. Supplies and things. Turns out, one of the Slum dwellers betrayed us." His voice, once soft and familiar, was now sharp with hatred.

He finished the stitching, and I peeked through my lashes at his handywork. My arm was drenched with blood, but the stitching was relatively even. He opened the bottle of alcohol and upturned it over the wound. I winced at the burning; hot tears spilled down my cheek as pain consumed me whole, threatened to cleave me in two. My lips wobbled like a child as I shivered. Kellan unravelled the bandages. His face was cast in shadow as he turned the fabric round my wrist once, twice.

"What happened to her," I repeated, softer this time.

Kellan wrapped the bandage around my wrist with careful hands. The chip lay by his knee. It dripped with blood, but still shone silver and magnificent against the rough sheets. He radiated an energy that was ugly and dark. There was pain etched into the lines around his eyes, the crease between his brows. Whatever the answer was, it was going to be horrible, and yet I had to know. I needed to know what my people had done to him to make him hate them the way he did.

"They were waiting for us. She tried to protect me, and they shot her. Kamal saved my life." He tied a knot in my bandage, let my wrist drop.

I cradled the throbbing skin to my chest, probed the injury experimentally. He wiped his hands on a cloth, his movements carful and controlled as he methodically moved from one finger to the other. The clench of his shoulders told me the conversation was over. I reached out instinctively to rest my hand on his knee out of pity. He looked down; his eyes narrowed. There was a flash of something behind the composure he tried so hard to keep up at all times; a light as wicked and dangerous as lightening that I could almost mistake for pain. In that glimpse I thought I saw something more than sarcasm, something more than quips and drunken sex, something broken, shattered beyond repair.

"I'm sorry," I whispered, almost afraid to say the words.

He jerked his knee as if I'd burnt him, and my hand fell limply onto the bed. He stood, suddenly itching to move. He tidied what he had used, his arms twitched as if he had too much energy, as if he'd been shocked by a thousand volts of electricity. I pushed myself from the bed; my legs wobbled as my feet touched the ground. My limbs were heavy now, drained by pain. I yawned, rubbed my arms to try to warm myself up. The sweltering summer sun had dissipated to a bitter chill, encouraged by the rain that still pattered all around us.

I took a step, stubbed my toe, hissed at the blinding pain. Kellan looked at me over his shoulder, as if he had forgotten I was there. His face was cast in shadow, and I thought in the waning light of the torch I saw the shimmer of tears on his lashes. He turned from me, too quickly for me to be sure.

"Come on then. Bedtime," He nodded towards the exit.

"What about enjoying the party?" I asked, although I didn't much feel like partying anymore.

His story had sobered me, along with the pain, and the question was more for his benefit. I hated to think I'd ruined his night. Kellan shrugged at my words.

"I plan to get wildly drunk and find someone to have sex with. Can't have much fun if I'm minding you, can I?" he said it in a way that cut something deep inside me, so dismissive and blunt.

I hated how those words hurt. I hated the sting in my chest, the rejection that threatened to send tears down my cheeks. I tried to reason with myself; he'd exposed such pain, such trauma, was it not natural to want to drown that out with mindless fun?

I smoothed my face; I wouldn't let him see that he'd hurt me. I followed him, kept my eyes on the ground. It took us less time than I thought to reach my tent. Kellan held open the flap for me, and I stood still, arms crossed, mouth pressed tight as I tried to figure out what I wanted to say. He gave an exasperated sigh, let the tent flap drop.

"Come on now. I don't have all night," he encouraged, gestured impatiently for me to come out and say it.

I wasn't sure what I wanted to say, but there was this burning need to let words spill between us. I wanted to apologise for what happened to his mother, I wanted to beg him to trust me, I wanted to scream at him for dismissing me so quickly. I was both tired and exhilarated, charged and yet drained by pain. He tapped his foot, folded his arms, let out another long, exaggerated sigh. My anger dissipated as my words died in my throat. Anything I said would sound stupid and immature, and I hadn't the energy to challenge him. I walked past him and lifted the flap.

"Good night," I said simply.

I didn't wait for his reply. I let the tent fall closed behind me and slumped down onto the pallet. I rested my arms by my side, stared up at the ceiling as I listened to Kellan's retreating footsteps. I had half expected him to come in after me, to prompt me to talk. I was foolish for thinking that way, for being so self-centred. I wasn't in Sadon anymore, no one was forced to care about me. Kellan wasn't Alfie, but Theo almost was.

I thought about Theo then. Sweet, steady Theo. Safe and kind, someone who had saved me, cared for me, risked his life here for someone he barely knew. I had been repulsed by his remiss attitude towards the ceremony, but this was commonplace. This was their way of living, and he had no reason to find it repulsive.

I had half the mind to get up, to go and seek him out, to apologise for leaving him, and to propose some sort of relationship, but my limbs had grown heavy. My eyelids slid closed as I thought about him. It would be nice, to have someone protect me as Alfie had. To have someone to rely on, to confide in, to grow to love. As sleep tugged at the corners of my mind, a small voice somewhere deep inside told me that it wasn't fair, that using his affection, being with him would never be fair, as it hadn't been with Alfie. That no matter how steady Theo was, I would not feel the rush I felt with Kellan, or Ahzani.

I pushed the voice away and fell into ignorant sleep.

Chapter XIV

"Calluna."

I jolted awake struggling for breath, gasped against the heavy air. The tent was hot, and my skin was sticky with sweat. I blinked as I took in my surroundings, momentarily forgetting where I was. Dawn light filtered through the tent in hues of red and brown, made the small space feel bloody and close. As my eyes found Theo in the dim light, my heart slowed to its regular pace. I forced a weak smile, pushed my hair from my forehead, winced at the pain in my wrist. Theo stooped down, touched the back of his hand to my forehead. He frowned before he stood.

"Did you drink last night? I couldn't find you," he stated, his voice flat.

His eyes were narrowed, his brows drawn down, and the pull of shame nagged at my throat. I stood; my knees cracked as I stretched. I held out my wrist to offer some sort of explanation, bandage blood soaked and slightly sweat damp. Theo kept his hands tucked under his arms pits, but his eyes flashed with worry.

"I asked Kellan to cut my identity chip out." My voice was hoarse, and I cleared my throat past the dryness.

Theo nodded as if this was a perfect explanation, but he was chewing the inside of his cheek. He rolled back onto the balls of his feet, bounced up and down.

"Breakfast?" he finally said, but the flush of his cheeks and the set of his shoulders made me think he wanted to say much more.

"Okay. I'll change," I replied in a measured tone.

Something was off about him today. He was distant, distracted. His eyes skirted mine, and with every mounting second, a clawing dread rose in my stomach.

"Okay. I'll wait outside." He didn't wait for my reply.

He left, nothing but a breeze in his wake. I fought the urge to call after him and put my mind to changing. As I pulled off last night's dress, I processed everything I had thought last night. Was I wrong to want familiarity? Was I wrong to want comfort? As I pulled on a shirt, I tried to reason with myself.

I liked Theo, he was nice, he cared about me. I could make him happy, and he could make me happy too. I wriggled into a pair of too big trousers and slipped on my shoes as I talked myself up.

"Just ask him. Suggest it. Don't be a baby," I chided myself as I pushed out of the tent.

It was early morning, and the smell of smouldered fires still lingered in the air. There were many sickly faces and black rimmed eyes from the night before. A shirtless man was passed out mere feet from my tent, and a half naked girl was in the process of slipping from a tent. Theo stood among it all, towering over the sordid remnants of last night as pure as a saint. He squinted into the morning sun, thick hair slightly askew. He turned at the sound of my footsteps and gave me a tight smile. He gestured for me to walk, and I did so.

A nervous smile tugged at my lips. I clenched my clammy fingers open and closed, open and closed. Unease had settled in my throat, and my heart was fluttering as desperately as a wounded bird. I glanced at him, and he seemed equally unsettled.

"Did you have fun last night?" I asked to break the ice.

It sounded silly and pathetic, but it was all I could muster. He shrugged, played with the edge of his sleeve.

245

"It was fine. I left not long after you did. I wasn't feeling it." He itched the back of his neck, finally looked at me.

He looked so awkward, put out almost. His nose was scrunched up tight, as if he smelt something bad.

"You know, if you want to sleep with Kellan, I get it." The words left his mouth in a babbling rush, and my cheeks burnt at the insinuation.

"Theo," I said softly, but he interrupted me.

"I get it. I do. Most girls want to," he continued, growing pinker and pinker as he picked the edge of his nail.

"Theo," I said louder to try and make him stop.

The thought of Kellan was making my stomach contract. I could feel the blood pumping under my skin, each beat a terrifying thump that made my throat burn.

"I mean, he's a great guy and all." I took him by the shoulder, forced him to stop in his tracks.

I kissed him. I pushed my lips hard against his to stop the words spilling any further. I squeezed my eyes tight and waited for him to react. He resisted at first, his lips unyielding, but then he softened, his hands found my waist, and I was falling into something dark and endless. There was no jump in my pulse, no dizziness in my head. As his lips moved against mine, gentle, caring, not pushing too hard despite the tense of his shoulders and the firmness of his hands, there was nothing but emptiness and sorrow.

I pulled back, let out a breath. I had hoped that the contact would stir something, that I would feel something rise and jump and scream in my chest. I only felt sad and silly. Theo opened his eyes, a smile so surprised and sweet it almost broke my heart. He ran a hand through his hair, stumbled over his words. I put a hand on his shoulder, smiled at him.

"I don't want Kellan," I replied.

Theo laughed; a sweet, unbound laugh that made my smile more genuine. He looked so happy, his eyes creased with laughter, and warmth rushed up to chase away the darkness in my chest. Looking at him, at his smile, it made me hopeful. I could do this for him, I could do this for us. I could be happy as long as he was happy, because I needed his support. I needed to make him happy, like I'd needed to make Alfie happy. Maybe after time I would grow to love Theo as I had loved Alfie. Loved him as a friend, loved him as a confidant. I had to believe we could have that.

"We should…" he jerked his head in the direction of the dining tents, and I nodded.

He hesitated for a second, and then held out his arm, as if he weren't too sure of the conventions of a relationship. It occurred to me then that I might be his first crush, that he was just as inexperienced as I was, and the thought softened the awkwardness that had settle in my chest.

I took his arm and let him lead me onwards, well versed in the art of appearances. Theo walked with strength in his stride, his head held high, a soft smile pulled at the corners of his lips, his cheeks pink. As we neared the dining tents, I caught Priya chatting idly to a tall, armoured girl brandishing a spear. As we neared, she looked up, and her face fell. Her lips pursed sourly, and as we walked past, her eyes followed me, two dark slits of never-ending hatred. I didn't shy from her gaze. I had nothing to be ashamed of.

The deafening clatter of the dining tent was a welcome distraction. Voices fought to rise above each other in the vast expanse, chairs clattered, tables scraped as Mai-Coh charged for breakfast. Ahzani sat next to Meredith, head tilted back in a howling laugh. She caught my eye as I passed and cocked a brow at the two of us. There was no time to feel embarrassed by her knowing eyes; before I could even sit, I was being accosted by an Amazonian-esque armoured servant of Kamal.

247

"He wishes to speak with you." She didn't need to specify who *he* was.

I swallowed thickly, went to remove my arm from Theo's, but he tightened his grip. I looked up at him, at the set of his shoulders and the protective look in his eyes. He met her stony stare with an equally unmovable expression, his hand hard on my arm.

"Can't she eat first?" he asked, his voice unwavering.

The girl, who looked like the last person you'd want to mess with, didn't even blink at Theo, her gaze trained on me. She waited; her face set as solid as stone. Two mountains that refused to bend to the wind.

"Come." It wasn't a question.

I gave Theo a reassuring smile and wiggled my arm free. People were already beginning to stare, eyes pulled from mounds of overbaked bread and dark brown meat. Theo opened his mouth to object, but I didn't give him the chance. I took the first step away from him, and the armoured girl took the lead. Her strides were long, and I stumbled to keep up at we departed the tent. My stomach rumbled lowly as the tangy smell of overripe fruit faded to dust and dirt.

The air was already thick with heat, the sun unhindered by clouds. It was strange, to feel such an affect from the changing seasons. Sadon had been a place of perpetual spring, of sweet breezes and comfortable heat and flowers always in bloom. Yet the sky was a startling blue, washed pale in comparison to the suns blinding light. I pulled at the collar of my shirt as sweat trickled down my neck. The armoured girl barely broke a sweat. Her hair, cropped close to her head, was wiry and dark. Her skin glowed as dark as the night sky, flecked with scars and stretch marks.

Someone threw their arm over my shoulder, and I wheeled around, my shoulders tensed at the unsolicited contact. Kellan looked down at me, a grin plastered on his face. He was brimming with energy, his face bright, his hair gently tousled, curls falling over his forehead. He looked fresh, as if he'd had a full night's sleep, but the bruises on his neck betrayed his appearance. He gave a nonchalant shrug as the armoured girl turned. At his appearance, the corner of her mouth turned down ever so slightly.

"She comes alone," she said bluntly.

"Who says I'm coming for her? Maybe I'm here for a completely unrelated reason," Kellan speculated, pulled on an innocent face, his smile intensified as her right eye twitched.

"Don't play games with me," she said, her hand tightened on her spear.

I shrugged Kellan off, shot him a dirty look.

"I'm fine," I hissed.

Kellan rolled his eyes, a gesture so dramatic and emphasised I thought his eyes might fall out of his head.

"This," he said, pointing at the ground at his feet, "is a free country, last time I checked. I can do whatever I please," he said with a smug nod, his arms crossed defiantly across his chest.

The girl slammed the heel of the spear into the dirt with a crack, and I was surprised that the earth didn't cleave in two. She looked plucked from the land of the gods, a hero and a warrior blessed with strength and severity beyond measure. Her scarred face was firm under the sun, unswayable by Kellan's charm.

"If this was a free country, there wouldn't be a need for Mai-Coh, would there." She hissed.

Kellan waved her off, not taking no for an answer. He stared up at her without fear, his smile provoking.

"Alright, alright, let's not keep Kamal waiting now," he said as he folded his arms.

He tried to act serious, his brows pulled down, but his lips were pulled into a mischievous grin, and his eyes shone brighter than the sun itself. I looked between the two. The girl was at least an inch or two taller than Kellan, and her arms were toned, her thighs carved with muscles that could have crushed his head. I thought she might take that spear and stab him, and who could have blamed her? She relaxed her grip on the handle, a sign of retreat. The corner of Kellan's mouth quirked up, and he clapped his hands.

"That's the spirit," Kellan said as he took the lead.

"You're lucky you're annoying," the girl muttered, but nonetheless she fell back, allowed him to continue.

I marvelled at the back of his head. It was a surprise he'd survived this long without being killed. I risked a look at the girl who walked behind me, and there was the faintest ghost of a smile on her lips.

I looked back at Kellan with renewed wonder. He may be an idiot, but he was a lucky idiot.

We walked the rest of the way in silence. Kellan bounced along, smiled and waved like a hero in his glory. He looked nothing short of godly, his skin glistened like polished honey maple wood, lovingly kissed to tanned by the sun. Freckles mottled with scars, trophies of his triumphs in combat, a road map to his victories. His hair fell around his head like a crown of onyx, curls that trailed over his forehead that surely would have been a line in a bard about his Kingly conquests. He was magnificent, there were no other words for him. I itched to write him into immortality, although I had never written anything so grand in my life. It seemed unquestionable, the need to immortalise him in grand tales, so those that come after may know of his fineness. I considered asking for paint, so I could put him down, so that people may see him when we were long gone, but I pushed down the foolish thought. This was a place of war, not a place of creativity.

I found myself staring and averted my eyes, my cheeks burnt red. He'd rejected me last night, and threatened to kill me more times that I could count. He was nothing but misery, but misery that beautiful…

Kamal's tent loomed much larger than I had thought the other night; as daunting as a fortress it hung over the camp. Two more armoured soldiers stood at the doorway, their eyes as dark as ink. The girl who had escorted us here positioned herself far to the left, marked her place with her spear. She gave us no instruction, instead went still, melted back into routine. Kellan pushed his way into the tent without invitation, and I had no choice but to follow.

Kamal sat on his bed; furs spread around his legs, leather vest unlaced and open. He was reading Klio's diary, deep in thought. He looked much less daunting, a pencil between his lips instead of a sword in his hand. He had trimmed his beard, parts still gruff and uneven, and it alluded to the youth that still coursed through his veins. There was a smallness about him, swallowed beneath the high rise of the tent and the mounds of blankets. My breath caught at the sight of him, as if I'd seen the secret behind the curtain.

He looked up at the sound of our footsteps, and the child retreated back within the warrior. His gaze skirted me, fell on Kellan with a frown that could have crumbled kingdoms.

"You're inescapable," he mumbled, but gave Kellan no instruction to leave.

Kamal rose, kicked the furs off to reveal bare feet. He moved to a table, slumped down into the chair. He pushed back the mountains of books, laid Klio's diary open for us all to see. He gestured me over as he pulled out a sheet of thick paper, rolled it out next to the diary.

"This, here. Your friend talks about a water treatment unit," he pointed to a sketch of pipes surrounded by calculations.

It all looked foreign to me; I'd never seen such a thing. Kellan came to stand beside me, peered over my shoulder. He took in the numbers greedily; his fingers traced the pages with the intimacy of a lover. His shoulder pressed against mine as he edged closer, and I could smell him; smoky, sweet, almost musky.

I concentrated on the page instead of on him.

"Do you know where something like this might be?" Kamal asked.

I shook my head. Sadon's water came from Slum One, but the Slum was dense with filtration and fishing buildings, overcrowded from a time before where there had only been one prison for those that defected. It was a maze of wooden buildings perched on stilts, rising out of the water like defiant weeds, with no course or reason. There was no telling which one could hold something like this. Kamal pressed his lips together, flipped through the pages as he thought.

"Where did she get this information from?" he gestured to the pages of statistics and research.

"She worked at the Palladium. She was a doctors assistant, training in infectious disease," I chewed the information over as it left my mouth.

"Maybe she found something there?" Kellan voiced the thought that had been forming in my mind.

Kamal nodded, rubbed his eyes as he turned another page, and then another. His eyes were dark, as if he'd been reading all night, but he still had a focus about him that I understood. The diary had a kind of power, an all-consuming pull that had threatened to swallow me whole too. His fingers traced Klio's writing with a familiarity that made me think maybe he'd already fallen too deep.

"Is that where they'd keep records of this kind of thing?" Kamal asked, and he sounded hopeful.

"I guess so. Every sector has one, it's like an information centre," I tried to explain, annoyed I hadn't paid much attention when we'd toured as children.

Kamal produced a pencil, held it out to me.

"Can you draw a map?" he asked, softer than I had ever heard him speak.

I swallowed, apprehensive. What Kamal was suggesting was an invasion, a recovery of information that could end up in the people I loved dying. I looked at the outstretch pencil and saw nothing but blood and ash. Despite my thirst for art, despite how badly I wanted to smell the lead and smear my hands as I drew, I couldn't. I thought of Chrys, of Lavender and Alfie, of their lives being forfeit because of my decisions. Kellan gave me a nudge as Kamal's patience wore thin.

"You're not second guessing this now, are you." Kamal asked, his voice stern.

My fingers shook, but I took the pencil. I sketched the Palladium first at the centre of the page, then the surrounding streets, roads I had taken my first steps on, roads I had trodden every day, roads I was about to bathe in blood. I sketched my house and a pang of longing for my mother sobered my enjoyment for art. I wondered if she was okay, wondered if Chrys had been discovered.

I pushed the thoughts away as I drew the boundary between the Hollow and its surrounding sectors, Ira and Lum. I etched the farmlands, all that I knew about them, and the image came to life with a vibrancy I had missed.

I missed my bedroom, I missed the acrylic paints in the art studio at school, and I missed those days my art teacher had pushed me, pushed me to better myself, pushed me to a position in the Emperor's gallery. When I finished, Kamal snatched up the roll, and Kellan shouldered me out of the way for a better look. I let them as memories filled my eyes with tears.

"Are you thinking what I'm thinking?" Kamal asked.

Kellan pointed to the Palladium, then traced his fingers along the roads slowly.

"We take this route, and-" I interrupted, blocked the route of his finger with the pencil.

They both swivelled their heads towards me, equally unimpressed. I elbowed my way between them, turned the map towards myself as I blinked the mist from my vision. Power surged through my veins fuelled by their stares.

I was important. I was needed. I was useful.

"You can't approach from this street. Doctor Lynn and the high officials live here," I marked their houses with curving X's.

"They patrol every night, more so just before I left." I moved to the second approach to the Palladium, crossed that one off too.

"These roads all lead to the Inner Ring," I sketched the wall that divided the Outer ring and Inner ring, thought about how badly I had wanted to cross it only weeks before.

"They have a lot of Pioneers here, guard gates, check points. There's usually a team there, to stop any Lower Ring kids sneaking over the wall." I drew them too.

Their eyes were both surprised and eager, as if they were hurt and healed by the information I reeled off. Maybe it had become easy to forget where I had come from, maybe it had slipped their minds what a wealth of knowledge I was. That I had been one of them.

Kamal looked at me with tight lips and clenched hands. He did remember, and it hurt him to see me now, a product of the people who had done nothing but ruin his life. I turned my eyes back to the paper as my eyes blurred.

"What about this one?" Kellan pointed to the west entrance after a long pause.

I rubbed at my eyes as I thought about it, thought about the street that would lead them there and realised that my house would be on the impact path. I had half a mind to say no, that there were cameras, or guards, or anything to put them off. I chewed on the inside of my cheek before I nodded. This was bigger than me, and I could no longer afford to be selfish.

"Mostly residential."

Kellan took the pencil from me, started to mark out a plan. I flinched at his harsh lines as they marred my rendering, wished I'd snatched it back from him.

"If we take these streets," he marked off four, including mine, "then we have a clear entrance and exit plan. If the majority of their Pioneers are in the East, it'll take them some time to come to defence," Kellan said excitedly.

Kamal nodded as he flicked through a few more pages of Klio's diary. He looked up at me through his lashes, as if he wasn't quite sure he wanted to look at me head on. He gave me a sharp nod, before he rolled up the map.

"We'll call a meeting in a day or two. Discuss our options. For now, she needs to be trained. She'll be useful when we raid," he directed these comments to Kellan, as if I wasn't there.

I frowned at his dismissal. If it weren't for me, he wouldn't know a thing. Kellan went to take my arm, but I shrugged him off.

"What do you need the plans for? Why do you need to know where it is?" I asked, my words hot and angry.

Kamal glared at me, clearly not used to being treated with such disrespect. He took a measured step towards me, and I didn't feel so brave anymore. His eyes were dark, his face cast into shadow. He was so close I could smell him; the scent of blood and iron that marked a warrior.

"The Emperor and the Pioneers have been pumping your water full of drugs to keep them complacent. To keep them docile as sheep for the slaughter. If we take out the system, then the people will rise," Kamal said, as if it were all so simple.

The water that had made my head blur every day, that had made me soft and weak, would taking that away be enough? Maybe Kamal was right. Maybe if the people didn't drink the water, the affect would ware off, and there would be a revolt, but the drugs were only a small fraction of the hold the Emperor had over us all. The people of Sadon loved the Emperor, loved his safety, and feared his wrath. That fear of rejection, of squalor, the same fear that turned classmates to informants, and neighbours to foes, kept us all under his eyes, under his spell. I wasn't sure the drugs were going to be enough to sway those so deep in the lies. Kellan seized me by the arm before I could voice my thoughts.

"Don't worry Kamal. I'll train her up," he said as he dragged me out.

I stumbled as Kamal sat back down on his bed, nestled back within the furs. Kellan's hand was hard as iron against my arm. He yanked me all the way out of the tent, where I finally wrestled myself free.

He spun on me, finger pointed accusingly, lips peeled back from his teeth in a snarl. He looked as if he wanted to shout, to scream even, the flash of frustration deadly behind his eyes. My heart battered against my ribs as he wavered, something ticked over behind his eyes. He lowered his hand, let his face fall, and I let out the breath I had been holding.

"I've stuck my neck out for you. Remember that." he said sharply before he turned on his heel.

"Eat. Be at training in an hour," he shot over his shoulder.

~

I'd seethed over breakfast, tore into half stale bread with the teeth of a monster. Theo had eyed me with apprehension as I'd ripped the flesh off a turkey leg, eyes narrowed at the table. Once I'd eaten, I'd pushed myself up from the table with a bang, muttered a goodbye at those I sat with, and stormed off.

Something about Kellan riled me up, stirred such irritation and anger in me that I didn't even understand. I stomped through the woodlands to the Square, too angry to take in the beauty of the trees in the morning sun.

I could see Kellan, forest green shirt rolled up at the sleeves. He'd managed to drag a crate up with him; he was rifling through it now, examining swords, rubbing his fingers across dirty guns. I burst into the clearing with more oomph than I intended. Kellan looked up lazily, gave me a cold stare.

"You're late," he stated simply.

I moved over to him without retorting, despite the fact I wanted to do nothing more than bark angry words at him until my throat grew soar. I bent over the chest to look at its contents, intrigued by the days lesson. A pair of long, thin daggers lay carefully polished to one side, silver and daunting, they were as delicate as needles. There were guns too, some were small, almost dainty, carved with symbols and letters, others were thick and dark. I went to reach out, to pick one up and turn it over for inspection, but Kellan smacked away my hand.

"Not that one," he said, as if talking to a child.

I straightened and pouted like one, crossed my arms as I looked down into the chest. Despite the fact I knew I probably wouldn't be able to wield any of the weapons confidently, his insistence to treat me as lesser made me all the more determined to use them.

"Well which one then?" I replied insolently.

Kellan chose to ignore my impatience as he sifted through the weapons. His fingers were thin, calloused, almost artistic as he turned each over as if they were as delicate as jewels. He picked up a handgun; black, old, the handle scuffed, warn from the sweat of a thousand hands. He held it out to me flippantly, as if it were nothing more than a pencil or cup of water. I flinched as the mouth of the barrel gaped at me, an endless void of nothing that contained unimaginable horror.

"It's just a gun, Callie," Kellan said, as if that would make me feel any better.

It didn't, though, as all I could think about was the damage I'd seen them do. I thought about Polly and Klio, if they had met their fate staring down the nose of a gun much like this, only whiter. I thought of the Pioneers who had died at Kellan and Theo's hands, of the families they had left to mourn.

I hesitated, before I took it. There was no more time for reluctancy or delicacy, whimpering or cowering. I held it loosely in my hand; it was surprisingly heavy. Kellan picked up another gun, this one was larger, silver, less worn. He opened up the chamber and loaded the bullets as if he'd done it countless times. He clicked the chamber back into place, held it up experimentally, looked down its length, then dropped it down to his side.

He moved with practiced grace; the mannerisms of a warrior trained from birth. He looked at me, at the way I held it as if it might bite me, and the corner of his lip turned up. I wondered what he thought of my inability, if it confused him that someone could grow to my age and not be able to wield a weapon.

"If you hold it like that, you'll end up shooting yourself in the foot," he gestured to my feet, the shoes that were miles too big.

I pressed my fingers more firmly around the grip, but Kellan still tutted. He reached out, wrapped his fingers around mine, pushed my finger over the trigger. I ignored the feel of his skin on mine, tried to concentrate as he steadied my grip.

"You have to keep a good hold on it, or when you fire the recoil will break your wrist. Trust me, it hurts," he gestured to his own wrist, the small spattering of scars that resided there.

I nodded, held the grip tightly even though it hurt the flesh of my palm.

"Alright. Good. Now, find a comfortable stance. Feet shoulder width apart, knees slightly bent," he prodded my knee with the butt of his gun, and I bent them accordingly.

"Lean forward into the fire. That's important for recoil. Don't break your spine," he pushed his palm against my spine, bent my back.

Blood rushed to my cheeks as the warmth of his palm seeped through my too thin shirt. My mind buzzed with a thousand thoughts and feelings as my skin hummed under his hand. I tried to ignore how his voice and commanding tone made my stomach roil, pushed those feelings down deep.

259

"Focus." He said as if he could hear my thoughts.

I shifted, tried to get some distance between us, tried to keep all his advice in mind. I looked out towards the woodlands, imagined pulling the trigger. I shivered at the thought.

"So what am I shooting?" I asked, my voice thick.

Kellan pointed to the closest of the four posts. It was littered with bullet holes, some so low they looked as if they'd been shot by a child.

"Take the gun with both hands. Put your finger firmly around the trigger." He stood behind me, moved my hands into position.

All I could think about was him. The warmth of his chest, the strength of his arms, the feel of his breath on the nape of my neck. We stood there and I knew he'd be smirking, delighting in taking such an advantage. He moved closer, until I was consumed by him. The outside world faded, the sky, the ground, the breeze, it paled to the scent of him.

"Now size up the target. Its only 30 feet, it's not too far. Try to aim higher than you want to, just to start." His breath fanned my ear as I squinted at the post, my heart thudded against my ribs.

"Press your finger down."

I squeezed my finger down, and the bullet fired. The gun kicked back, and if it weren't for his hands on mine, I was sure I would have dropped it. The sound was deafening, and for a moment there was nothing but ringing. The bullet grazed the post, left a scuff mark on its side.

"Again," Kellan ordered, his voice low in my ear.

I shot again, missed again. Then a third time. Then a fourth. Kellan held me steady, as unwavering as the post I couldn't quite hit. The rise and fall of his chest acted as an anchor, and I focused myself on it, pulled myself into his rhythm. We stood and existed as one.

"Take a breath. Keep yourself centred." He shifted slightly as he said it, nudged my feet further apart.

My stomach lurched as my legs widened, and all I could think about was the tangle of limbs, the way he'd touched those girls, and how stupid it felt to be so taken with my thoughts. My hands stilled as I took a deep breath. I closed my eyes, tried to force the doubt from my body. I squeezed the trigger and the bullet slammed into the wooden post with a crack.

I should have been happy with the triumph, but as I looked at the hole in the wood, all I could think about was the Pioneer I couldn't shoot. Of the family I would have taken him from.

I felt nothing but revulsion.

"I don't want to shoot someone." The words fell from my mouth without warning.

Kellan let me go, turned me to look at him. I shivered at the absence of his warmth even though it wasn't cold. He looked confused, annoyed even by my statement, his hands hard on my shoulders.

"You can't be serious," he said, and when I showed no signs of changing my statement, he gave a short laugh.

"Alright, perfect little princess," he said as he moved forward.

He was so close now that I had to look up to meet his eyes. My body thrummed at the feel of him, unwarranted and unwanted. I took a step back, my cheeks red and my breath caught in my lungs, but he pursued me.

"What happens when we go to Sadon and a Pioneer pushes you?" he asked as he gave me a shove.

I stumbled back, struggled to keep my footing. The gun was slick and heavy in my hand, a weight instead of a weapon. His hand wrapped around my neck, held me steady, his face near centimetres from my own. The pressure of his fingers made my breath come hard, and both fear and something hot and itching coursed through my veins. His face was thunderous, his eyes dark and wide and all-consuming as he looked at where his fingers pressed into my skin.

"What happens when one of them knocks you down?" he pressed on, pushed me down to my knees

I tried to shift backwards, away from the fingers against my throat that made me feel so hot. His grip intensified, and I fought the whimper that begged to escape.

"Kellan stop," I begged, but he shook his head, his shoulder taut.

"Sorry, can't hear you, I'm a scary Pioneer about to kill you. What are you going to do, Calluna?" he asked, dared me to shoot him.

I blinked up at him, chest heaving, gun still limp in my hand. He waited all of two seconds, before he pulled the gun from his waist band, clicked off the safety. He pointed it down at me with a precision I knew I would never possess.

"Now what? My guns drawn; your life is seconds away from ending. Do something," he shouted.

No, he *begged*.

I shook my head, let the gun fall from my hand.

I couldn't. I wouldn't.

He kept his finger over the trigger, and for a terrifying second, I thought he might pull it. The ground was unsteady below me, as if I might plummet all the way to the centre of the earth. I met his eyes and tried to convey that I was sorry. His chest rose and fell with anger, his eyes wild as he stared down at me. I wondered if he saw nothing more than a Golden blooded Pioneer, an enemy. The wind stirred around us, whistled between us, tousled his curls.

He lowered the gun, threw it back into the chest as if it were nothing more than a toy. He snatched the gun up from beside me and turned his back, but not before I caught the flash of disappointment in his eyes.

"I can't help you. You'll have to find someone else," Kellan said, suddenly all too serious.

I wished he would insult me, make a joke, shoot something sarcastic my way. Anything but the disappointment that radiated from his body; the tight, clipped, almost pained tone of his voice. I rushed to my feet; my blood thumped behind my ears.

"Teach me how to fight. How to defend myself. Please Kellan," I begged.

He shook his head. A movement that I swear shook the earth.

"You don't have what it takes. I'll talk to Priya, get you enrolled in some kid's classes," he said as he slammed the chest closed.

"Priya hates me," I shot as desperation gripped my throat.

I didn't want to lose him, I didn't want to learn from someone who would rather see me dead. He didn't reply to that. He lifted the chest with ease, dragged it down the path. I followed, jogged to catch up.

"You said you'd train me," I pointed out.

"I didn't think you'd be such a coward," he shot back.

I balled my fists. I wanted to hit him, as hard as I could, but all I could do was stare at him with childlike anger. I hated that he was right, I hated that I was still holding on,

263

still hesitating, still trying to be perfect. I hated myself, but more so I hated him for pointing it out, for making it so evidently clear.

"You said-" I shouted, but he slammed the case down and turned to me.

"What makes you think we're friends?" he said, and I stared at him blankly, mouth hung open.

His eyes flashed with real anger; his face lined with it. He was as frightening as thunder, a true force to be trifled with. My heart thudded in my chest as I returned his gaze. My mouth moved soundlessly; no words formed.

"Theo picked you up that night, not me. I said I'd train you because if I didn't, you'd already be dead, and I felt sorry for you. Nothing more than that," Kellan spat.

He let the words hang between us before he picked the chest up again and continued his journey. My eyes stung, but I didn't let myself cry. I wouldn't allow him to see how much pain his words twisted in my stomach; I wouldn't allow him the satisfaction.

"You'll never be worth as much as Theo" I shot at his back, wanting to hurt him as much as he'd hurt me.

Pain clawed at my chest as he walked away. I wanted so badly to believe he was simply angry, but there was truth to his words that I couldn't escape.

"Why don't you ask why he was there that night. See how worthy he is," he replied, before he disappeared into the tree line.

~

The days began to bleed together. Although Kamal had said he would call a meeting, he hadn't. Tension hung in the air as close as the sky before a storm. Everyone could feel a shift, even if they didn't know why. People brawled more frequently, easily piqued into fights by the hostile atmosphere. I found myself around Ahzani most of the time in an attempt to escape the anger that hung like death in the air. She was fun and easy to get along with. She taught me how to make arrows and took me to some medical classes led by Farron.

I hadn't asked Theo about why he'd been at the Hollow that night. Although a part of me itched to know, I knew better than to pull on loose threads. What use would it be, creating an argument and losing another valuable ally?

I turned my head up to the sky, squinted into its blueness. The weather had grown increasingly hot, and my skin had burnt under the sun's rays. I was waiting for my new trainer, as I had been for at least ten minutes. After waiting a few days without being approached by Priya, Theo had promised he'd sort something out for me.

I wished he could train me, but Kamal had stuck to his word. Any time he saw the two of us together, he'd come and drag Theo off, or throw something at the two of us, or shout words of abuse until Theo retreated. I was lonely despite Ahzani's company, and I longed for stolen moments caught between guard changes with Theo.

Even if time wasn't proving affective at encouraging feelings.

The sound of angry footsteps turned my attention to the edge of the clearing. Priya emerged, face cast in fury. She wore salwar trousers the colour of jade, threadbare and worn around the ankles as if they'd been turned up too many times. Her tank top, a shade of amber speckled with flecks of copper, clung to her broad shoulders and revealed her abdomen. She looked beautiful, and yet wicked and wrathful, like some vengeful spirit. My mouth fell open in surprise, my brows furrowed as I went to stand.

"Up. I don't have all day," she hissed as she rolled up her sleeves.

I bit the inside of my cheek as I pushed myself up. I wanted to point out that she was the one who was late, but I had limited options as it was. Priya pushed a stray curl out of her face as she seized me up. I stood, expecting some sort of instruction, a barked order.

Kellan had always begun physical training with stretches, but Priya didn't seem to have that same patience. Within a flash, her fist had contacted with my stomach.

My breath left my throat in a whoosh as I keeled over. Sick rose in my throat, but I forced it down, sucked down as much stifling air as I could bare. As I tried to stand, her fist landed another calculated hit on my still healing rib, and then another on my left arm, which instantly went numb.

"Stop," I choked as I stumbled backwards.

"First lesson," she said as she knocked my legs from underneath me.

I landed harshly on my ass, with no choice but to stare up at her as I cradled my aching abdomen. Her eyes were as dangerous as a wild animal, filled with a frenzied rage that rivalled even Kamal's ferocity.

"There are no breaks in war. There is no mercy, there is no 'going easy'," she said.

She clenched her fists, and I thought she was about to beat me to death. Maybe she thought so too. She took a step back, let her shoulders relax. She gestured me up with a curt nod. My breath wheezed as I stood. Pain hummed across every inch of my skin. I missed Kellan and his, all be it limited, patience.

"Again." She took her stance.

Her skin glowed acorn brown, her hair, twisted around her head in a large braid, glinted like a raven's crown. I tried to remember what Kellan taught me, bounced from foot to foot, held my fists close to my face. The corner of her mouth turned up slightly, as if amused by my effort. She was blazingly fast, almost too quick to see. I threw a fist at her face, a lazy, angry throw that she bent away from with ease. I threw another, and another, but she weaved as easily as if we were dancing. Sweat dripped down my back as my lungs burnt. I was tired, and hurt, and weak.

I threw my fist out one last time, more of a slap than a punch, but Priya stepped back with ease. I dropped my arms, bent over to catch my breath.

"You will never fight," she said, the words more hurtful than any attack.

I stared at the ground as it blurred, watched my sweat drip into the dust. My limbs burnt acid hot. Her words lit a fire in my stomach, and as I looked up at her through my hair, her smile all too smug, something snapped. Her words, Kellan's, Kamal's, the scornful stare of every Mai-Coh who thought me lesser than, they rose and churned until red exploded across my vision.

I let out an exasperate cry and charged at her. I was tired of everyone saying I was too weak, that I was a coward, that they knew my worth. She let out a surprised squeak as my shoulder collided with her stomach. I wrapped my arms around her waist, dug my nails into her skin as we toppled over.

Her back hit the ground with a thump, her breath forced from her chest. I clambered on top of her, didn't allow her the opportunity to get her bearings. She squirmed blindly, but I didn't relent. I grabbed both of her arms, forced them into the dirt and stared down at her with ferocious triumph. She twisted, but I locked my knees around her waist, refused to let her rise.

Weeks of eating the Mai-Coh's food, of walking and training and running, had slimmed down the fat of Sadon, replaced it with a different kind of strength. My arms, my legs, they were strong, not slim or delicate or plump. Her lips peeled back from her mouth in a disgusted snarl, her teeth bared.

"Get off me you gold blooded bitch," she hissed as she thrashed.

I didn't let up. I was shaking with adrenaline, high off the pain. I couldn't stop myself from smiling as she writhed. She let out a grunt as she kicked out.

"Why do you hate me?" I shouted, louder than I intended.

She stared up at me with ice cold detest. She pressed her lips so thin I could barely see them.

"You stupid-" I interrupted her by raising her arms and then slamming them back into the ground.

She winced, and at the sight of her pain there a spark of joy.

I *was* strong. I *would* fight.

"Why do you hate *me*?" I asked again.

She stopped struggling then. Her stillness was almost more frightening than her resistance.

"You don't deserve him." The words made me relax my grip.

In that second of confusion, she turned her head and bit down on my injured wrist. Pain split across the skin as blood soaked the bandages anew, and I let out a howl so loud it sent birds screeching from their nests. I retracted my wrists on instinct, and she pushed me off. I tumbled to the ground, rolled over onto my back and jumped up to face her.

She stood very still as she rubbed where I'd been gripping her arms. I held my wrist close to my chest as the pain ebbed away.

"This is about Theo?" I asked, dumbfounded.

She gave me a cutting sideways look as she flattened her hair. Her fingers pulled apart her braid, and her hair fell around her like a midnight wave. I saw it then, in the way her fingers faltered as they pulled her hair back into plaits, in the slant of her brows.

"You love him." It was an accusation more than a realisation.

In a breath she was in front of me, her face inches from my own. She expected me to fear her, to flinch or to cower, but I no longer did. She was as human as I was.

"Don't say another word," she hissed.

"That's a stupid reason to hate someone," I retorted all too confidently.

Anger flashed across her face, but there was pain behind her eyes. I felt almost sorry for her, for what she'd lost, and what I'd taken from her, whether I intended to or not. She opened her mouth to say something, a string of insults a mile long, but after a pause she seemed to reconsider. She turned from me, walked away with her fists clenched at her sides.

"Find someone else to train you. I'm done,"

Chapter XV

"Do you miss your family?" Theo asked as he ran his fingers through my hair.

We sat alone in a secluded clearing that the trees were trying to reclaim. They leant in on us, thick branches obscuring the star-studded sky. The night had managed to ward off some of the heat, replacing it with a sweet breeze that smelt like sun burnt clay and ash. I sat between Theo's legs; head leant against his chest. He was warm and slightly dewy with sweat, and for the first time in a while I was at peace.

I mulled over his words, sleepy from such a large dinner. His other hand rested on mine, and I played with his fingers absently. They were large, only marginally scarred, his knuckles hardened from years of training. I traced the pale scar that forked up his thumb and wondered how he'd gotten it, if he'd been young, if he'd been scared.

"I miss my brother and sister. My mum too," I replied simply.

I tried not to think about my family, but every night I saw their faces. I worried for Chrys, for the secret that could kill him. I worried about my mother too, about whether he was hurting her. I chewed my bottom lip, gnawed at the dry skin until it bled.

"Are they good people?" Theo asked, almost hesitantly.

I tilted my head to look up at him. His face was relaxed, his eyes heavy, his lips parted as he met my gaze. He didn't look like he thought otherwise, like he thought they couldn't possibly be good. Instead, he looked curious, as if I could change his mind. His chest rose and fell behind my head, and I could feel the thrum of his heart, steady and strong.

I continued to trace my fingers up his arms, joined the bruises into a pattern. It was natural with him, out here alone and away from the world. It was easy to imagine we were love struck teenagers from a distant land, far from the quarrels of our world. That we were normal, and that there was nothing we needed to worry about apart from the dawn.

I liked to entertain those fantasies, it was better than the alternative; that he loved me, and I didn't love him back.

"Chrys cared more about my sister and I more than anyone. He... he likes other guys so... that's why I was out that night. I was going to suggest to Alfie that we leave. The Pioneers were already after me because of Klio's diary and if they would have looked into my mind..."

The words hung between us for a few minutes, before Theo shifted. I scooted forward as he stood and held out his hand.

"Come with me," he said, hand still outstretched.

I took it, allowed him to yank me to my feet. He didn't let go of my hand as he tugged me onwards. The sky had darkened beyond sight, the campfires extinguished, most tents dark and undisturbed. I stumbled anxiously through the darkness, unsure of where we were going.

We walked along the rim of the mountains; their sheer faces cast silver in the moonlight. We trailed along the outskirts of the camp until the tents stopped and were replaced with trees. On our right stood rows upon rows of Mai-Coh vehicles in many stages of repair and a large steel workshop, its windows still lit. The sound of drilling and sawing was faint but audible, and it followed us as Theo kept moving. We walked through a grove of thin trees, their needles sharp and sappy against my bare arms, before we were met by a vast expanse of fields. Theo stopped, turned to me with a grin, and when I opened my mouth to say something, he hushed me.

"You'll scare them," he whispered, barely audible.

He turned and walked towards a collection of wooden stables that sat perched on the hill before I could ask him who he meant by *them*. I hesitated to follow him, hopped from foot to foot as I looked around at where we were. A howl echoed through the woodlands, followed by the crack of branches underfoot. I ran to catch up with Theo as he pulled open one of the large wooden doors.

"What are you doing?" I hissed as he disappeared inside the stable.

A dark chestnut mare lay nested in the hay, legs tucked underneath her body. My breath caught as she raised her head, her eyes as black as the endlessness of space. Theo stooped down in front of the majestic creature, brushed the hay from her side to reveal a foal, white and brown spotted and as small as a dog. It slept soundly by its mothers' side; head nuzzled into her stomach. Theo beckoned me forward, and I knelt by his side as if I had no control over my own body.

I held my breath, scared my existence would break the trance. Theo took my hand in his, guided it to the mother's neck. He pushed my hand into her mane, and there was warmth there, the dull beat of life beneath her skin. I let my hand linger, savoured the thud of her heart.

She didn't seem to mind as I ran my hand down her shoulder, across her back. Theo guided my hand to the foal, and I was surprised how soft its coat was. The foal stirred, lifted its head to look at us. I sat very still as it got clumsily to its feet, teetered as it took a few sleepy steps. The mother didn't stir but kept her eyes on her child as it came towards us, protective and wary of the guests. Theo was watching me as the baby sniffed, as curious as I was. I reached out tentatively and trailed my fingers across its nose.

"They're beautiful," I breathed.

All too soon, Theo stood and guided me out into the night. I stood in the cool air; head tilted to the sky as he locked up. I closed my eyes and breathed it in, breathed in this life that was utterly mine now. A life I had control over, a life I could do anything with, and joy filled my chest with warmth and light as I took another long, cooling breath.

Theo's fingers clasped my chin, and before I could open my eyes and thank him for what he'd shown me, he'd tilted my head to the side and pressed his lips against my own. My heart dropped into my stomach, all joy and brightness fled into the night as he embraced me, his arms strong against my back, my chest pressed into his so hard I could barely breathe. His lips were desperate, seeking, almost impatient. My fingers trembled as I tried to push back, pull out of the grip that was more like a cage that an embrace. He pulled me to him harder, took from me the freedom I had been admiring seconds before.

This kiss was no measure of love; it was a staked claim, a reward for his hard work, and how he took it, without permission, without empathy, made my blood boil.

I yanked back, turned away so I could scrub the heat from my lips. I was shaking, I couldn't stop it. I couldn't dig out the confusing anger that had settled deep in my stomach. Isn't this what I had wanted? To be loved? To be wanted and needed? Yet this, how that had felt, was too close to the performance of Sadon. Where I had felt safe in clearing, I now realised that I was nothing but a prize to be claimed.

"Calluna," he said, his hand on my shoulder.

I ignored the pull of his fingers, concentrated on slowing my breathing. Maybe he hadn't meant for it to come across that way, maybe he'd just been too lost in his feelings to notice my stillness. He cared for me, I owed him my life, my love, my affection...

He turned me softly, his eyes as bright as the midnight moon, his brows turned down in concern. He traced his fingers along the back of my hand in an effort to comfort me, but all it did was intensify my nausea.

"I'm sorry," I said.

It was the only thing I could say. I didn't want him to hate me, to leave me with nothing and no one. I needed so badly to love him in the way he deserved to be loved. To give him what he had given me; a life worth living.

"I understand. It can't be easy, getting over what they put in your head," he whispered as he took my face in his hand.

My cheeks reddened as he pushed my hair from my face, and I struggled against the urge to cringe. I allowed his words to swim around my head, to find a place to take root.

Maybe he was right. Maybe this was all I was destined for, this was all I would ever feel, this sense of wrongness attached to physical connection. I wanted to believe that the celibacy, the fear of love and pureness, was the reason I couldn't look at him and feel butterflies. That it wasn't him, just how it hadn't been Alfie. It was me.

I was the problem.

"I can't promise you anything," I said, but he shook his head, unbothered by my weakness.

"From the moment I saw you, I knew you were mine. It doesn't matter how long it takes," he said, smoothed the hair from my face.

Mine. The word was so harsh, so primal. I *belonged* to him, like I had belonged to Alfie, like I had belonged to my father, to the Emperor. Had I traded one leash for another? Had his kindness, his sacrifice, been under the impression that he would get back what he put in, and more so? Had he always expected this? Would he have taken it if I were unwilling?

My jaw tensed as I fought the tears that threatened to give me away.

No.

I would not mess this up. It didn't matter, none of it mattered. He had given me a life, a chance to start new, and I owed him my effort.

He pressed his lips to my forehead before he put his arm around my shoulder. I allowed the gesture, because what other choice did I have?

"You have me now. I'll protect you," he said as he guided me back to camp.

~

I bounced from foot to foot, shook my hands out as I tried to think what to say. I'd been stood outside Kellan's tent for a while now, debating whether or not to enter.

"Ask him, just ask him," I whispered, tried to force myself into action.

I took a step forward, then stopped, pushed myself back.

Coward.

Despite Theo's pushing, I didn't want to beg for Kellan to train me again. I didn't want to see that smug smile of his, or have him reject me out of spite.

Yet here I was, outside his tent like an idiot, because Kellan was all I had. The other soldiers capable of training never even glanced my way, still wary I was some kind of spy. Theo had offered to ask on my behalf, but I didn't want to owe him any more than I already did. If I was going to survive, I had to do this myself. I had to earn some sort of independence.

The sound of giggling within alerted me to the fact he was not alone, and I groaned, smoothed a hand down my face. Of course he was with someone, he always was.

I sighed, pushed down the anxiety that threatened to eat me alive, and forced my way into unimaginable embarrassment.

His tent was smaller than I expected, overcrowded with a multitude of things. There were red hilted swords crafted from obsidian plunged into the ground, lined up as uniform as soldiers. There were guns too, pulled apart to wreckage in the process of being fixed or cleaned. On the far side of the tent was a large pallet, stacked with furs, and atop it was Kellan, his arms wrapped around a dark-haired girl. His back was to me, and I watched the muscles there tense as his arms tightened around her.

Blood rushed to my face as I cleared my throat, my mouth dry. He turned his head almost lazily, seemingly unbothered by my presence. His eyes raked over me with the intimacy of a lover, and when they again rested on my face my heart thrashed harder. His hair was stuck up at all angles as the girl ran her fingers through it, coaxing him back to the activity at hand. He turned back to her with a smirk.

"What brings you here, Callie?" He asked, clearly delighting in my discomfort.

I looked up at the roof of the tent, where clothes hung drying. I focused on counting the buttons on one of his shirts instead of the wet noise of their kissing.

"I came to ask you to train me," I said through gritted teeth.

He made a mildly surprised noise but didn't turn. I huffed, crossed my arms as my cheeks burnt.

Prick.

"I seem to recall you're a terrible student," His voice was muffled where he buried his dark head in the nape of her neck.

Insufferable, stupid prick.

My nails dug into the flesh of my arms as I averted my eyes. I bit my tongue to hold back the anger that was begging to spill from my lips.

"Please, Kellan," I hissed, the words hard to get out.

He turned, fixed me with that smug smile I had been dreading. He gave the girl a slap on the shoulder, and finally she poked her head up. Her skin was a golden brown, her hair fell over her naked chest in dense ringlets. She had a pinched face, a curved nose and bitten red lips. She narrowed her liquid bronze eyes at me with a hiss.

"Are you kidding?" she said.

Kellan pushed himself up from the pallet, and I averted my eyes as the furs fell from his naked body. He jumped, tugged down a shirt from the makeshift drying lines he'd put up.

"The Gold blood? Seriously?" she spat the insult at my feet as Kellan pulled on his shirt.

"Are you going to pick up a gun?" Kellan asked, ignoring the girl still in his bed.

"No. I can't," I replied.

Kellan shook his head as he pulled on his trousers, fastened the tie at his waist.

"Then I can't help you," he said simply.

The girl pulled the sheets around her firmly, sat up straight so she could get a real look at me. Her eyes were as searching as torch light, illuminating all my flaws. I didn't fidget, I let her look all she wanted. I'd grown accustomed to

277

the hateful stares of the Mai-Coh, and hers was nothing special.

"Priya won't teach me, Ahzani says she has her hands full with the kids, Theo isn't allowed, and everyone else..." I let my eyes fall purposely back on the girl who looked at me with such disdain.

Kellan didn't need to follow my gaze to know what I meant. He crossed his arms and gave me an unbreakable stare. Eyebrow cocked, head slightly slanted, lips just shy of a smile. He knew I had no one else, he knew he was my only shot. The girl huffed, threw herself back into the pile of furs.

"Like anyone else would help you," she muttered just loud enough for me to hear.

Kellan rubbed his forehead harshly, before he kicked up a shirt from the floor and threw it at the girl.

"Out," he commanded.

She seized the shirt as if it were a weapon, shuffled into it before she stood. She stomped towards the exit, stopped just short of me. Her face was sour, scrunched up tight as she examined every inch of me. I matched her, rose to her challenge. Whether she found what she was looking for or not, she made a disgusted noise and shook her head.

"Gilded snake," she hissed as she departed.

Kellan stifled a chuckle, and I shot him a dangerous stare.

"So, when do we start?" I asked.

He scooped something up off the floor and threw it at me. I stumbled to get a hold of it, my hands faltered on its surprising weight. I brushed my fingers over the coarse material. It was a thick winters jacket, but inside the lining was something heavy and soft, pliable like wet sand.

"Put it on, we need to improve your cardio first,"

~

"Run. Run. Run, Calluna!" Kellan boomed at me from where he jogged a few paces ahead.

I could barely breath. My breath surged out of my chest in wheezes as my legs stumbled forward. Sweat ran off me like rain, drenched my clothes and pooled in my shoes. Kellan ran backwards effortlessly, his forehead dewy, his hair slightly damp. He cocked a brow at me, and I pushed myself onwards, spurred on only by my anger at him.

The weighted coat bumped against my ribs, threatened to drag me to the ground. Our venture up what Kellan called the 'Children's play hill' was harder than I thought. I had no stamina, two minutes into the incline the back of my legs burnt, and my mouth was dry. Kellan held the waterskin in his hand, shook it teasingly at me.

"Come on, you're almost done," he encouraged as he turned and continued onwards.

The peak was close, I could see the hill tapering to a stop, but it felt a thousand miles away. I concentrated on Kellan, on the pump of his legs, on the sweat on his back, on how easy it was for him. I convinced myself that one day, it would be easy for me too.

Blood rushed in my ears as I crested the hill, blinded by the wash of yellow as the desert came into view. I gasped, half in relief, half because I could barely breathe. My knees gave, and I fell gladly towards the sweet release of the dirt.

I landed with a thump; everything ached, but I was glad of the rest. My legs twitched from the exertion; my fingers almost numb from clenching. I yanked off the weighted jacket, desperate to feel the cool breeze on my skin. Kellan dropped the water skin on my chest, and I seized it greedily. I fumbled with the clip, let out a growl as my fingers slipped against the cork. With a huff I yanked it out with my teeth, water escaping down my face.

I moaned at the sweet coolness of the water, drunk so desperately I choked. When it was empty, I threw it on the ground with a grunt, sucked in air like a desperate pig. I squinted at the sky, tried to imagine a time when my body didn't feel so shit.

Kellan nudged my ribs with his foot.

"I can't really be bothered to dig a hole for you, so I hope you're not dead," he said as he continued to push the toe of his boot into the flesh of my side.

I pushed his leg away, forced myself to sit up. The world spun around me as I stood, my heart still barely keeping up. Kellan stood facing the horizon, his hands on his hips as if he ruled everything before him. I moved to join him, to look out at what he saw. Beyond the desert stood the wilderness, a break of green that split from the burnt ground and rose like a mirage. I couldn't see anything past that, not the Slums or Sadon, but I found myself squinting nonetheless.

"I can't wait to get back out there." I turned at his words.

There was an eager smile on his face, his eyes alight with anticipation. He looked ready to run all the way back to the Slums on foot if he had to. I thought about what Kamal had said, about calling a meeting, and wondered if Kellan knew something I didn't.

"And are we? Going back out there?" I asked.

His smile faltered as he looked at me out the corner of his eye. I waited, folded my arms despite how much effort it took.

"Kamal will tell us when to act. Until then, I wouldn't go around asking questions," Kellan warned, but I wouldn't accept that.

"What's he waiting for? I drew him the map, he said he'd call a meeting, so what's he waiting for?" I pushed.

Kellan narrowed his eyes at me, turned his back on the desert and wilderness like it pained him to do so. He faced the camp again, his eyes trailed the pathways, the clearings. He looked upon it all with the disinterest of years of monotony. There was longing in his eyes, a longing for something more, for adventure. It was strange, how he could look at all this freedom and still yearn for more.

"What did I just say about asking questions?" He gave me a pointed look.

I frowned at him, but there was no real feeling behind it. His tensed shoulders and restless fingers gave him away, and I let out a laugh through my nose. For all his effort, I still saw straight through him. He inclined his head, pulled a face at my amusement. His eyes moved up and down the clothes that barely fit me, the shoes that threatened to slip from my feet, and suddenly his smile was all too wicked.

"You know, I suppose your past due some new clothes. I guess I could schedule a visit to one of our suppliers," he mused, his eyes bright with the idea.

"I thought we weren't friends," I reminded him, although the prospect of getting clothes that were solely my own was exciting.

He brushed the comment off, threw an arm around my shoulders, then pulled a face at how sweaty I was. He wiped his skin down with the edge of his shirt.

"Now what on earth gave you that idea?" he said with a wink.

Before I could argue about the conversation we'd had the other day, he'd taken off. He ripped down the side of the hill so fast he looked beyond human. I sighed, wiped the sweat from my forehead and went after him.

I suppose I couldn't complain about him helping me, whether it was merely for his own good or not. Yet as I watched him disappear into the labyrinth of tents, hair as dark as a storm cloud, I reminded myself that his help was merely conditional. He was temporary, and I couldn't trust that. Not when my life depended on it.

I tried to keep up despite the wheeze of my lungs, but he'd disappeared into Kamal's tent way before I could catch up. I rambled up the slight hill, too tired to care about whether I missed the conversation or not. When I finally reached Kamal's tent, their voices hummed soft as rain. Well, more Kellan's voice, too fast and animated to interrupt.

I slumped onto the ground, hung my head as I caught my breath yet again. After what felt like an endless tirade from Kellan, there was a momentary pause, before Kamal muttered something, and Kellan whirled out, his smile unchallengeable.

"Let's get out of here," he beamed as he seized me by the arm and dragged me up.

"Just me and you?" I asked.

I didn't know how I felt about that. Kellan and I, alone wherever we were going, no buffer or protection. No guarantee he wouldn't get bored and leave me there. I crossed my arms, frowned as he quirked a brow.

"Scared I'll have my way with you?" he teased with a wink.

"Not a chance," I said even as my cheeks burnt with the idea.

"Oh there's a chance," he shot back.

I opened my mouth to object, my stomach churning at the thought of that *chance*, but he spun around before I could say a word.

"Come on!" He yelled as he barrelled through a pair of children, almost sent them flying.

I rubbed my forehead; the beginning of a headache speared its way through my temples. I broke into the fasted jog I could muster, groaned at the pain in my calves. Kellan ran carelessly through groups of people, didn't seem to notice their angry stares and balled fists. He pushed and shoved, jumped over boxes, slid round corners like an excited toddler. I panted as I followed, tried to convince myself this would all be worth it.

We arrived at the vehicle grounds I had seen with Theo, the smell of petrol and electric heavy in the air. Kellan walked down the lines of vehicles, eyes squinted, head tilted from side to side as he tried to choose. He worked his way towards the workshop, swung inside one of the garages, where a red and green vehicle was hoisted above head height. Someone was working underneath it, welding something next to the front wheels. Sparks framed their rough helmet, sprayed onto the ground where they bounced, threatened to catch light. Kellan tapped the person on the shoulder, and they turned off the tool, placed it on a rough wooden bench.

"This one ready to go?" Kellan asked, and the engineer removed their helmet.

I was surprised to see Ahzani, her hair pulled into a tight knot, grease smeared across her cheeks. She gave Kellan a pointed look, balanced the helmet under her arm.

"What for?" she asked suspiciously, her eyes narrowed.

Kellan's smile faded, and a flash of panic momentarily clouded his eyes, before he let out a loud breath. She wasn't supposed to know, that much was clear.

"I'm taking Callie here to get some clothes, but you can't come," he rushed to say before she could ask.

Ahzani let out a laugh as she shucked off her thick work jacket and gloves, revealed the tattered clothes below. She wore no shirt under her overalls, exposed scarred chestnut skin and an assortment of tattoos. Wildflowers and thickets arched down her spine and over her collar bones, coy fish leapt around her wasit. She was a work of art, beautiful and unique.

"Like you could stop me. I'm bored as hell," Ahzani said as she grabbed a set of keys from the side.

"I said no," Kellan warned even as his eyes devoured the bare patches of skin.

I pushed past him to stand next to Ahzani, a fire setting in the pit of my stomach. I didn't like the way he looked at her, the way he treated her. He raised a brow to feign amusement, but he looked less than impressed by my dissent.

"I want Ahzani to come," I said firmly.

Ahzani snickered as she twirled the keys around her fingers, proud of herself. Kellan palmed his face, dragged his fingers down his eyes, before he turned on his heel, threw up his arms.

"You'll be the death of me," he said rather dramatically as he stomped off.

"Wrong way jackass," Ahzani called after him as she gave me a pat on the back.

"Nice job," she whispered, planted a kiss on my cheek.

I jumped, blood rushed to my cheeks and neck. She gave me a wicked smile, before she slammed a button on the jack. The car sunk to the ground, the hissing air so loud I had to cover my ears. Kellan returned and swung into the driver's seat without missing a beat, hands braced against the steering wheel in anticipation. Ahzani held up the keys, nodded for him to move over. His mouth dropped open in a mock gasp, before he flipped her off. He shuffled over into the passenger's seat, muttered to himself in exaggerated anger.

"Let's hit the road." Ahzani patted me on the back, before she made her way to the driver's seat.

~

Night fell differently in the Slums. Where the camp was all open sky and glittering stars, the Slum was shrouded in smoke. Kellan and Ahzani slunk through the alleys still preforming their offkey rendition of a long lost song. I followed behind, pulled my borrowed coat firmly around my shoulders. The hair on my arms stood on end despite the extra covering, and I couldn't help but feed the unease that had settled inside me.

Every corner seemed to unfold a new layer of confusion and anxiety. Half dressed women with sunken cheeks and painted smiles darted through the haze, bare feet nimble on the icy cobblestones as they whispered from house to house. Children peeked head outs of glassless windows, saucer eyes shining back at me through the darkness. A short, almost plump man nestled in a doorway gave me a sordid smile, upper lip curled back from teeth made of metal. His hair, thick and dark, was slicked back from his forehead, almost wet from grease. He shifted to look at me more directly, pushed his hands deep into the pockets of his coat.

"Want some Peelers?" he asked as he rattled something in his pocket.

His eyes strayed down my body, and I shivered as I tried to pull the coat tighter. He withdrew his hand from his pocket and nestled within the podgy flesh were three triangle purple tablets. They glittered in the lamp light of his doorway, shimmered like powdered jewels. Ahzani took me by the arm, gave the man a cutting glance.

"Ignore him," she said as she tugged me onwards.

His eyes followed me even as we rounded the corner, a putrid stain on my back I was sure I'd have to wash off.

"What were those?" I asked.

285

Ahzani kept her stare ahead, but there was hesitancy in her eyes. Kellan drifted too far ahead to hear our words, but still she looked anxiously in his direction, as if to double check he wouldn't hear. My hands clenched in my pockets as I thought about what she didn't want Kellan to know, what kind of secret wasn't safe for him to overhear. I didn't think many things got past Kellan, but the look on Ahzani's face told me otherwise.

"Drugs, the same kind of stuff they give to Riven's, but its unrefined," Her voice was hushed, as if the words were some terrible secret.

I shivered again at the thought of Riven's. Daughters of families the Emperor cast out, serving a sentence as punishment for their parent's actions. Ahzani swallowed thickly; her eyes almost luminescent in the darkness as she looked at me.

"We used to come down and take them sometimes, just to relax," she whispered, her voice barely audible, and I found myself leaning into her, desperate for a lick of trust.

"They make you forget, just a little bit, you know?" she said, her eyes seeking.

I didn't know, but I wanted to. She waited, as if needing my recognition, so I nodded mindlessly. Ahzani let out a breath, puffed her cheeks up as she itched at her wrist.

"I never thought they could kill you. I thought it was just harmless fun." I sensed then what she was building to, and I no longer craved the information, no longer wanted to be confided in.

"Anyway, that's how she died. Kamal's girl, Jin. She was really... sad. She used to come here a lot, and then one day she didn't come back." Her eyes shone bright with the painful memory.

I let the words take me. I thought about Kamal's tattoo, the J inside a heart, and wondered what she was like. I wanted to imagine her with the ink, laughing as he squirmed, tongue stuck from her mouth as she tried to concentrate on making it neat. I tried to picture her, to bring her to life in my mind, but all I saw was a blank face, purple tablets and rippled skin bruised black as it decayed.

"Trading secrets?" Kellan's voice made both of us jump.

He loomed in front of us, face cast in shadow, eyes alight with mischief. Ahzani lifted her eyes to the sky, tried to act aloof as she adjusted the shoulder of her overalls.

"I don't remember inviting you to the conversation," she quipped, elbowed past him.

"I don't need inviting," he retorted as she disappeared down a side street.

The street was narrow, and it petered to a triangular dead end. The buildings were dark, almost black, and made of real bricks, unlike the rest of the slum. They lent in on us like bent women whispering, heads tilted so low I thought the slates might fall on our heads. A large, red door nestled where the streets walls joined, a door that seemed to belong to no house. Ahzani walked up to it, knocked on it three times, paused, and then knocked twice more.

We waited, silence settled over the three of us, the only sound that of distant chatter. The sound of locks sliding and keys turning replaced the hum of Slum life, and the door slid open. A tall, skeletal woman looked back at us, dressed in the finest pink silk gown. The fabric hung from her slim shoulders, exposed her bony limbs. Her face, pinched and wrinkled, was neither surprised nor concerned by our presence. Her pale owl eyes settled on Kellan, and she broke into a smile that threatened to shatter her fragile face.

"Kell *tesoro!* My sweet boy." She reached out and touched his cheek affectionately.

Kellan grinned at her, gave her hand a squeeze. There was an accent to her voice, floating and foreign in a way that reminded me only vaguely of Kellan. Although it was easy to imagine he had been birthed to this place, that his ancestors had belonged to this country before Sadon and before the war, there were moments, rare words, that alluded to the fact that his lineage spread further than the broken bones of America. Her voice conveyed that same accent, although hers was still thick and raw, as if she'd only moved yesterday.

"Agnes *cara*. Mind if we pop in?" He asked, as if venturing to a friend for afternoon tea.

Her eyes strayed to Ahzani and I, and her smile faltered.

"Why have you bought me this?" she asked, gestured to me.

Her lips pursed as she took in my ill-fitting clothes and dust-stained face. Ahzani shifted in the evening breeze, her lack of clothing doing her no good in the falling temperatures.

"Come on Agnes I'm freezing my tits off," Ahzani whined as she hopped from foot to foot.

Agnes hesitated only a second or two, before she stepped back from the door, gestured us inside. Ahzani eagerly bustled in, rubbed her arms as she disappeared down the corridor. I looked to Kellan, waited for him to lead the way, but he lingered on the threshold, his eyes darted back where we came from.

"Go on in, I'll be back soon," he said.

As he turned, the glint of a gun pushed under his waist band caught my eye, and I realised then that this wasn't just about clothes, that Kamal had given him a task in exchange for this frivolous excursion. I'm unsure what made me do it, but my hand shot out, caught him by the wrist. He turned, eyes narrowed, arm tense under my fingers. I met his eyes, tried to find the answers behind his guarded face.

288

"Don't... Don't die." The words came from my mouth unexpectantly, but I meant them all the same.

Surprise split his face before he took a step back, shook off my hand. He pulled on a smile, but his eyes were changed.

"No one could ever kill me." He gave me a salute before he jogged off.

"You're letting the draft in," Agnes complained as she inched further behind the door.

I moved past the doorway, and as Agnes locked the door behind me, I took in my surroundings. There was a hallway, long and narrow and twisting, that sloped down like the markets Theo had first taken me to. Ahzani had disappeared into its depths, but I heard her humming. Agnes moved past me, dress trailing behind her as she floated downwards. I was left no choice but to follow.

The walls glowed under dim iron framed lights, red textured wallpaper a remnant of a time long ago, reminiscent of royal palace homes and brocade gowns. The floor was solid and wooden, my shoes clicked against it as I walked. The hallway tapered out to reveal a plush lounge, a picture-perfect replication of an old-fashioned speakeasy. Green armchairs were arranged in a semicircle around an elevated dark wooden platform illuminated under a bright pink light. There were two changing rooms separated by thick velvet curtains, and a door to the right that led off out of sight.

Ahzani flopped down in one of the armchairs, propped her legs up on the arm, stretched out like a lazy cat in the sun. Agnes took me by the elbow, her fingers thin but strong. She tugged me to the platform, forced me to stand. Ahzani framed me between her fingers, pulled a smile.

"I'm thinking orange," Ahzani mused as Agnes moved around me.

Agnes tutted, shook her head. Her brows pulled down as she examined me, moved my hair away from my face. There was life still behind her weathered eyes, a youthfulness that warmed her wrinkles.

"With her hair colour? Bah." She waved Ahzani's comment off as she seized me up.

Her eyes were all seeing, and they made me uncomfortable. My shoulders slumped; arms crossed over my stomach in an effort to protect myself from her critique. She was having none of it. She pushed my shoulders back, forced my arms by my side.

"Green, dark blue, purple," she corrected as Ahzani huffed.

"At least let her show a little skin," she retorted with a sultry smile.

My cheeks darkened at her words, at the thought that she wanted to see more of my body, but Agnes took no mind. She pulled a measuring tape from deep inside the recesses of her dress, measured my arms.

"I make art, not sordid sex costumes," Agnes frowned as she wrapped the tape around my waist, then my hips.

Ahzani pretended to be hurt by the comment, but soon she settled down, sprawled more freely across the chair. Agnes worked, measured every inch of my body, muttered to herself every once in a while in a language I didn't understand. The measuring tape snapped shut, and Agnes took a step back, rubbed her pointed chin thoughtfully. Behind her eyes her mind ticked over, ideas forming and changing, swirling and building. An artist's mind, a mind I could understand.

"I suppose I have a few things I can alter," she mused, before she turned on her heels, disappeared behind the door on the far side of the room.

There was rustling, banging, a hiss of anger. Ahzani pulled a face as she inspected her hair, picked at the split ends of her braids. I stood awkwardly, looked around the room as I waited. There were pictures on the walls, grainy, barely pigmented, some of them were black and white even. They had all been taken here, in this room, with the subject stood on this very platform. I looked at each one in turn, wondered how old the photos were. As I trailed the lines of photos, my eyes were drawn to one of Kellan. He was younger, his hair longer, but his smile was the same. I found myself smiling at the gangly youthfulness of his body, the awkward tilt of his head.

"*Cazzo!*" Agnes interrupted my staring with a curse, and I turned to see her carrying an armful of fabric.

She dumped the pile onto an armchair, sifted through the garments, then pulled one out. A pair of baggy red trousers made of something like canvas, and a cropped shirt the colour of damp sand. She held them out to me, positioned them against my body as she tilted her head.

"Try these," she said after a brief pause.

I took the clothes, turned and moved towards one of the changing rooms. I drew the curtain closed behind me, adjusted to the small space. The walls were covered in graffiti, names of previous clients etched onto the wall forever. I traced the scratched letters with my fingers, mouthed the names; Dana, Kimi, Obadiah, Freddie.

A pale blue light flickered overhead, reflected in the full-length mirror. Its surface was slightly marred, black mottled at the corners, hairline fractures forked along the edges, but the picture was clear enough. At first, I didn't even recognise myself. All I saw was a stranger. Skin that had once been milk pale was now sun kissed and slightly burnt. Hair that had always been silky and controlled sprung in untidy curls around my face. I found myself fascinated by my own reflection. I tugged off my clothes, desperate to see more.

My borrowed clothes dropped to the ground, and I stared at myself. Where there had been softness before, there was no longer. The slight plumpness of wealth had ebbed to the well fed strength of hard work. My thighs seemed harder; my legs looked stronger. There were bruises too, cuts and scrapes and pain, but I marvelled at what I saw. I traced the lines of my body, unafraid to do so, and gauged how each movement felt. I closed my eyes and revelled in the feel of fingertips against my skin.

"Hurry up!" Ahzani's voice made me jump, and my eyes snapped open.

I took the trousers in my hands, pulled them on. The waist was loose, but they were the right length. The shirt fit well, if slightly too short for my liking. I pushed back the curtains and walked to the platform. Ahzani took me in with teasing eyes, her chin propped on the arm of the chair.

"Strike a pose then," she instructed.

I awkwardly stuck out my arms, feeling less confident by the second. Ahzani burst out laughing, while Agnes simply massaged the bridge of her nose. Agnes came towards me, sewing box in hand. She pushed two of her fingers down the waist band of my trousers, and I yelped, almost fell off the platform. Her other hand shot out to steady me as she probed the space between my skin and the trousers. She knelt, laid her sewing box on the ground, popped it open and fished out a needle and thread.

"Hold still," she instructed as she threaded the needle with ease.

I looked over her at Ahzani, who was still snickering.

"I think she looks great." Ahzani gave a thumbs up, then winked.

I pulled at the hem of the shirt, made uncomfortable by the exposure of my stomach. I still felt unsure about the flaunting of my skin despite the new body I was learning to grow into.

"The tops too short," I interjected as Agnes took in the waist of the trousers.

"That's how it's supposed to be," Ahzani said, as if it were obvious.

I sighed as I waited, shifted my weight from one leg to the other. Agnes worked in silence, each pull of the needle precise and delicate. It only took her a minute or two to complete her work, and when she pulled back, I found the waist hugged my body. I turned, kicked out my legs to test their durability.

"Yes. I like it," Ahzani confirmed, as if the clothes would belong to her, and I were simply the model.

Agnes didn't wait for my opinion, she moved to the pile and picked up a new garment. A square necked lilac dress embroidered with deep plum flowers. She handed it to me, waved me back to the dressing room.

I couldn't help but feel like one of Lavender's dolls, being dressed up for the entertainment of others. I drew the curtain closed behind me rather aggressively, changed out of the first set, and into the dress. It hugged my chest too tight, the gauzy material emphasising the breasts I barely had. It hugged my figure all the way to the hem, which fell just above the knee. In this dress, I was no longer a girl. I was a woman.

The sound of bustling and laugher alerted me to Kellan's arrival. Agnes cooed over him, and Ahzani greeted him warily. I heard caution in her voice, and I knew she too had wondered where he had disappeared to.

I met my eyes in the mirror once more, and for the first time in a while, maybe ever, I was strong and beautiful. Not beautiful in relation to others, not beautiful because I had to be, but beautiful in a way that made me feel... whole. I hadn't realised my hands were shaking until I reached up to take the curtain between my fingers. I tugged the curtain back, and walked out into the lounge, feet catching slightly out of nervousness. I stopped in the centre of the room, held my arms out for inspection. Ahzani looked me up and down, taken aback.

"Wow. They really do make them well," She breathed.

Kellan tore his eyes from the notepad he was scribbling in, his hair windswept. He looked at me, and for the briefest second I thought I saw a flash of appreciation, before he looked back to his notepad, pencil gripped between his teeth.

"It would look better off," he replied, his knuckles white where he gripped his notebook.

Ahzani threw up her hands, tilted her head back so she could fix him with a scowl.

"You're so horny, it's disgusting. I bet you'd even bang the bone woman," Ahzani nodded towards where Agnes had disappeared into her storage room.

"Would and could, Azzie darling. She has a special soft spot for me, don't you Agnes?" He raised his voice so Agnes could hear him.

She emerged, trailed sheets of fabric whispering around her feet. She had a pencil tucked behind her ear, and in one hand she grasped papers marked with lead.

"Yes *amore?*" She asked as she neared him, a sweet smile on her lips that she seemed to reserve only for him.

"I was just telling the girls how much you beg me to fuck you," he said it so plainly I choked on my breath.

I snorted and gurgled as I tried to compose myself, cheeks burnt red as Agnes leant against Kellan's armchair. She didn't seem the least bit bothered that both Ahzani and Kellan had hoisted their legs over the arms of the chairs, lounging around like listless toddlers, muddy boots marring the upholstery.

"Oh yes, *piccolino*. Countless times. I ask and ask and ask," she teased as she placed the papers in his lap.

Kellan looked up and gave her a lopsided smile that made him look much softer than the man I'd grown to know.

"I'll say yes one of these times, Agnes," he replied as she ran a finger down his arm.

Ahzani pretended to throw up as Agnes gave a dismissive wave of her hand. She bent and kissed him on the forehead.

"Like I haven't heard that before. Half the time I think you're just leading me on so I'll help with that mission of yours," she said as she came over to me, bony fingers tracing the seams of the too tight neck.

Ahzani swivelled so she laid on her belly, her chin propped on the arm of the chair as she looked at Kellan, who seemed very interested in a loose thread.

"You're on a mission without me," she pointed an accusing finger at him.

Agnes tutted, fiddled with the straps. Kellan looked through the papers Agnes handed him, eyes narrowed, brow slightly creased. He circled something, referenced his notebook. I half thought he wasn't going to acknowledge her, his eyes focused intently. Ahzani looked ready to burst, her face reddening with every second.

"It's top secret," Kellan replied.

"Secret! What a load of shit, Kamal told you not to tell me, didn't he?" Ahzani accused as she sat up straight, her arms folded.

Agnes bustled around my feet, adjusted the hem as she went. I watched the two of them, their back and forth like siblings. It made me long for my own siblings, for the comfort of family.

"That's what secret means, Az," he replied.

Ahzani frowned. She chewed on her thumb as she churned over this new information. I saw how it bothered her, to be left out. It had never occurred to me that she too lived by the rules of the girls in Sadon despite the masculinity she presented, the rules of gossip and secrets and popularity. That Ahzani, much like myself, felt the sting of betrayal at the slightest word. As Agnes picked a thread out of the back of my dress, made the neckline looser, I found myself asking:

"So what's the mission?"

Kellan looked up, gave me a really good look this time. His eyes traced the curves the dress had given me, the body he'd helped me grow into. He lingered not on my breasts as I had expected, but on the curve of my hips, the slope of my ass. His fingers tapped almost restlessly on his pencil as his eyes narrowed. I refused to fidget as Agnes moved to stand before me, a welcome shield from his prying eyes. Ahzani looked at Kellan expectantly, amused by my dissent.

Kellan sighed, put his pencil in the middle of his notebook, slammed it closed. He stood, moved towards me. Agnes slunk back to the pile of clothes as if she sensed his intentions. He reached out, took a lock of my hair between his fingers.

"I never knew it was so curly," he mused as he gave a tug.

I snatched my hair back, frowned at him as my heart thudded dangerously against my ribs. I would not let him intimidate me into changing the subject. His fingers lingered at the nape of my neck; his thumb pressed tightly to where my pulse jumped. I tried to control my breathing, my nostrils flared as I tried to breathe through my nose.

"Don't change the subject," I replied, stronger than I thought possible.

Something about the clothes, or maybe the observation that my body was stronger now, made me fear retaliation less. I had a voice, and a mind, and I had the right to use them. Ahzani snorted, then snatched up the papers that Kellan had left in his seat. He turned at the sound of crinkled paper, all traces of humour gone, his eyes wild with panic. He lunged at her, but she slipped free. She was smaller but faster, and as Kellan scrambled after her, she began to read.

"Give it back, Ahzani," Kellan warned as he leapt at her hands.

Ahzani ducked, jumped over an armchair, sent clothes flying. Agnes sighed, jabbed a needle between her teeth as she sunk into a chair and started working. I watched the carnage unfold as the pair chased around the room. All of a sudden, Ahzani came to a stop, her eyes lifted from the paper, her mouth hung open.

"We're taking the slum?" she asked, her voice barely above a whisper.

Kellan snatched the papers, his face red. He smacked her over the head with the rolled-up documents, but she barely flinched. She gawked at him, awaiting answers. He looked back at me, as if trying to figure out if I could be trusted with whatever Ahzani had read. Finally, though, he let out a breath and threw himself back down in a chair.

I sat on the platform, a heavy thump of anticipation, and Ahzani joined me, her arm pressed against mine. Kellan looked at the two of us, his fingers tight against the paper that now seemed so precious and important. Even Agnes, who was docking the hem of a navy skirt, looked mildly interested, her eyes strayed from time to time to where Kellan sat.

"Kamal asked me to find the names of those who'll fight. We put out the word when you drew up the map. I met with Kade tonight to finalise the details," he said.

"Whose Kade?" I asked

Adrenaline pulsed in my veins at the thought of attack. It hummed below my skin as reckless as fire, flames threatened to devour me whole.

"He runs this place." It was Agnes who talked, her eyes cast down on the thread she wove.

"The Pioneers like to think they have a hold on this place, but nothing happens here without Kade knowing. The outer Slums, they all have a Kade somewhere. Eight, nine, ten," Agnes continued, snapped the thread with her teeth.

Ahzani and I both leant forward, soaked in her every word. Agnes smoothed her hand over the new hem, placed the garment on the arm of the chair as she looked up. Her eyes shone with history, years of suffering and hiding. I knew then why Kamal wanted to take this place, a place the Emperor had been struggling to keep a hold on for years. The people here had nothing left to live for, nothing but their fight, and if the Mai-Coh could take it, it would make him look weak.

"The people I named are good people. People who want a better life. Kade's people..." she trailed off.

"Kade has an army, an army we can use," Kellan countered gently.

He cared for this woman, that much was obvious. His eyes were soft as he looked at her, and a flicker of rejection flashed across his face as Agnes shook her head.

"Kade and his people want nothing but power and destruction. They will turn on you the minute they see fit," she countered as she stood.

"What does Kamal think?" Ahzani asked as Agnes walked towards us.

She dropped a few clothes into my lap, fixed me with a tired smile.

"I shall make some custom pieces. Send them with a scout," she said.

Before I could thank her, she disappeared into the back room, closed the door.

"Kamal wanted an alliance. One I sealed tonight," Kellan answered as he stood, pushed the documents into his pocket.

Ahzani jumped to her feet, a ball of energy more blinding than the sun.

"But what about what Agnes said? Can we trust him?" she asked.

"We need them to take this place, to get a more substantial foothold. We cannot take Sadon without first taking this vantage point," Kellan tried to reason, but Ahzani seemed more affected by Agnes' words than him.

"We should listen to her. What if he turns on us?" She asked.

"We have to take the chance," Kellan countered, but there was doubt behind his eyes too.

Ahzani shook her head vehemently, her jaw tight. She turned to me, her eyes hard.

"You think this is stupid, right? Tell him this is stupid."

She had something to lose, that much was clear. I'd seen the way she'd looked at Meredith, the longing in her eyes. Her life was good, it was fun and easy and I realised with a shock that she didn't care about the war. I wondered how many Mai-Coh would feel the same, that it wasn't worth the easy life they currently had.

I stared back at them, unsure how to respond. I knew nothing of tactics, or of who Kade was or what he might do. Ahzani waited, her face growing more irritated by the second. I sighed, braced my elbows against my knees, pushed my hair off my face. We couldn't sit idly by as the people of Sadon suffered, as the Mai-Coh fell further and further into the past.

Something needed to be done.

"I don't know. I think... I think this slum is our best bet. If we wait too long, the Emperor will send more Pioneers to take it. He already is. Maybe... Maybe Kellan is right," I replied.

Ahzani stared at me open mouthed, then snapped her jaw shut. She turned and stormed off, unimpressed by my statement. I watched after her, my words sour in my mouth. I hadn't meant to hurt her, to alienate one of the true friends I had.

I rose, gathered my clothes in my arms as Kellan went to thank Agnes. They exchanged very few words before Kellan handed her something silver and closed the door.

"Let's go home,"

Chapter XVI

Alfie's POV

My mother fussed over my tie, preened at my jacket as we waited on the porch. I shrugged her off as sweat dampened my back. The afternoon was bright and pleasant, clouds chased across the sky, wisps of cotton framed against stunning azure. The day had been quiet, as if the whole world was sighing in unison. I eyed the road, awaited the Emperor's car, no such relaxation for me. It had been two days since we had received the holo asking for my attendance at the Keep, and since then I had barely slept.

"Stand straight. Speak clearly. This is the upmost honour," she whispered as she brushed a lock of my hair one way, and then the other.

She frowned at me, her lip caught between her teeth as she examined my appearance. She looked so proud, her cheeks flushed, her eyes bright. I couldn't help but think she had the wrong idea about this summons. Ever since Calluna had been taken, I'd felt them watching me. I'd felt everyone watching me, waiting for me to crack. Every day I felt her absence like a weight on my back, I never knew it was possible to miss someone's presence as tangible as you might miss air. That her being here, being around, had such an effect on me. Mother took my hands in hers and gave them a gentle squeeze as she smiled.

"You're going to do this family so proud," she breathed as a Hovear hummed around the corner.

I stepped away from her, pulled at my collar as the Hovear came to a stop outside our gate. A Pioneer in white robes embellished with golden flames rose from the passenger seat and moved to open the back door for me. I swallowed thickly, smiled at him as I ducked into the back seat. The driver met my eyes in the mirror, gave me a curt nod. I nodded back out of respect as the passenger climbed back into the car.

I felt the need to introduce myself, to thank them, to say anything to break the silence. I resisted the urge as the Hovear came to life and pulled away from my house. I watched my mother, who waved as she clasped at her chest in pure joy. I turned my focus on my hands, which sat limply in my lap. I clasped them together, then let them rest, and then turned them over. I was useless, completely lost. Usually, I was in control during social interactions, maybe even on the better foot, but something about the leather interior and the smell of jasmine made me feel like a child.

I turned my attention to the window to occupy my racing mind. The Hollow whizzed past, the glamour of the Palladium blended with the grandeur of the city officials' spacious houses. As we wound through the streets, the houses became larger and further apart, until the sun was shadowed by the large wall that separated the Outer Ring from the Inner Ring.

The car slowed as we pulled to the gate. I waited patiently as words were exchanged between the driver and the guard. I strained to listen to what they said, but their voices were too low. The gate slid open, and the Hovear moved onwards.

The District of Sarrar was more beautiful than any picture could have depicted. I gaped at a future that had seemed so close only weeks before. Houses that were more like mansions, crystal swimming pools that reflected the early afternoon sun, sports courts that sprawled bigger than the houses themselves. I pressed my nose against the glass, tried to soak it all in. This was what I was destined for, this was what I deserved, and yet there would be no chance for me anymore.

I sank back in my seat, my teeth clamped tight. What would happen to me now? Calluna was gone, the searches had turned up nothing. If they didn't find her, I'd be alone, and there would be a permanent stain on my name.

My eyes stung at the thought of her never coming home. It stung that I might never see her face again. That never again would I take in my fingers a lock of her fire washed hair. I closed my eyes, and I could see her eyes, green and bright and framed with lashes so thick they cast shadows across her cheeks. The corners of my mouth turned up as I pictured her smile, the pale pink of her lips, the carelessness of her laugh. I leant my head back against the headrest, no longer wanting to gaze upon what I could never have as a tear slipped down my cheek.

"Mr. Clarke."

I startled awake, unsure of when I dozed off. I looked around, momentarily confused by my surroundings. A golden eyed man stared at me through the rear window, identity chip scanner held out. I looked out the windows, head still fuzzy with sleep. The sandy bricked walls of the Emperor's keep loomed above us, and the sound of rushing water alerted me to our position on the bridge. I'd never seen the palace before, and I found myself lost.

Painted on the walls were white and gold illustrations, the story of our Emperors arrival. The Emperor's ship landing in the woods, the original Mai-Coh, pretending to welcome them and then attacking them in the night. There was the Great War too, the Emperor's silver tears as he lost brothers and sisters. The illustrations that framed the ruby encrusted gateway was the victory, the Emperor on one side, the adoring public worshipping him on the other.

"Mr. Clarke," the guard spoke again, and this time I held out my wrist.

Light poured over the skin, and as it did so I looked out the rear window. The bridge stretched for miles, a marble masterpiece bathed in sunlight. The water shone turquoise and teal as it rushed past the pillars that kept us afloat.

Beyond the bridge I could just see the glimmer of Slum One's fence, the water shacks teetering on stilts.

The scanner's light turned green, and the Pioneer stepped back. The man sunk back towards the glistening walls, and I sobered as I saw past the beauty and marvel. Pioneers lined every inch of the wall, stood on ledges barely a foot wide with guns half the size of them. Atop the walls were guard towers, white and blue tipped roofs and glassless windows. Pioneers stared down from those too, sights marked on the bridge. There would be no attack from behind the keep, the Inner and Outer rings served as a semicircle of protection, and the bridge alone would force any invader towards a watery death.

I swallowed thickly at the thought of invasion, refocused my eyes on the gate as it swung open to reveal the paradise within. My breath caught in my throat as I gazed upon something so many never would. The circular walls that enclosed the Keep were a mosaic of the jungles of the old world. Powerful lions roared at the sun, rainbow fish glided through lakes, trees rose high and bore fruit encrusted with emeralds. However, none of that compared to the sprawling grasslands that surrounded the palace, containing the very animals that the mosaic depicted. Animals that had long been dead, animals poached and slaughtered before the Emperor's time; white leopards, big black stags, rhinos and tigers and zebras. They roamed peacefully outside my window, each seemingly unbothered by the rest.

I caught the eyes of a jaguar and saw not the feline eyes of a cat, but the white eyes of the Emperor. Experiments, genetic resurgence generated in the lab. These were not the same animals that our ancestors hunted; they were better, more brilliant. Perfect.

A refraction of light blinded me as we moved onwards, and I rubbed my eyes, confused by the brightness. I looked down below the vehicle, where spots of light danced across the Hovears underbelly. What I had assumed was plain gravel I realised were instead millions of grey moonstones, jewels mined from the deepest recesses used as driveway decoration. I yearned to reach out, to pick one up and take it home to my mother, but I dared not take something from the Emperor.

I pulled my eyes from the sprawling land and to the Keep, desperate to indulge in its decadence. The large building was a feat of architectural beauty, a palace plucked from a history book. Its ivory towers were topped with golden statues of daunting knights, mounted on rearing horses with diamond eyes. They reached up to the heavens with their swords as if they were ready to jump down into the realms of men.

The grand estate was made of the finest white stones veined with silver; bought from the Emperor's homeland they sparkled as if laced with stardust. Large glass windows reflected the outside world, provided small glimpses through gossamer curtains at the treasures inside. The front doors were made from the sacred oak of the original Mai-Coh, trees that legend says held the spirts of Gods. Now they stood embossed with vines and leaves, bronze handled and forever belonging to the Emperor.

At the centre of the palace stood a large tower made from gold, its spiralling rooftop edged in platinum. Flowers of every colour climbed in vines up its walls, the top of the tower surrounded by a large balcony filled with greenery, the only way to see inside, as the walls were absent of windows. It seemed strange to me, that all this finery lay within the grounds, but there were no windows to behold it.

I squinted up at the balcony, tried to catch a glimpse of the Emperor within. All I saw was shrubbery, and the faintest wisp of white trailing curtains.

The Hovear came to a stop, and I wasted no time jumping out. My feet crunched on the precious stones, shoes shattering the gems to shards, and I hissed in guilt.

How could anyone feel comfortable standing on something worth more than they would ever earn?

Neither the driver nor the passenger got out, maybe for that exact reason. I waited, shifted uncomfortably as I stared up the steps. The doors remained closed, and I thought maybe this had been a terrible joke, that the driver would order me back inside and I would be taken home immediately.

The door fell open at last, and a girl emerged. She was dressed in the clothing of the Riven, a sheer golden dress that left nothing to the imagination. My pulse jumped as she swayed down the steps, bare feet dainty against the stone. Her ankles and wrists were encircled with golden bands, cuffs that could be electrocuted from forty paces away. Her hair fell down her back in waves of gold, a rich blond so vibrant it challenged the tower for beauty.

She stopped on the bottom step, hands crossed over her stomach. She smiled, a perfect taupe smile that caused dimples to prick her cheeks. Her eyes were large, as blue and endless as the river we just crossed. I found myself breathless as I looked at her, unable to tear my eyes away.

"Mr. Clarke, it is my pleasure to welcome you." She bowed her head, curtsied low.

I rushed to speak, my cheeks hot and red.

"Alfie, please," I replied.

My voice cracked, and I kicked myself mentally at how stupid I sounded. She raised her head, the corners of her lips turned up just slightly.

"Alfie." She tested the name in her mouth, and I melted.

I forced myself to stop staring at her. She was beautiful, but she was not mine. She was downcast, a servant serving her parents sentence, and she was not Calluna.

My stomach sunk at the realisation of my betrayal. How could I think of this girl this way, when Calluna was out there, in pain, scared, begging to come home? When I lifted my eyes to her once more they were empty of lust. She did a good job of hiding her disappointment, but I caught the dimness in her own eyes as she turned.

"Please follow me Alfie. The Emperor is most excited to meet with you," she said as she walked back up the steps.

I followed, my eyes focused beyond her, into the Keep itself. A grand entryway met me, all sweeping walls and polished floors. A variety of servants scuttled before us; men in trailing silver robes carrying thick tombs, books bound in leather and half crumbled to dust. Riven in their shining gold, heads bent, arms filled with plates, food and clothing. White suited Pioneers stood guard outside large golden doors, arms folded, eyes cast towards anyone who moved. My Riven guide walked slowly, allowed me to take in the sights.

I gawped, mouth hung open as I took in the high arched ceilings and twisting corridors. We walked for maybe five minutes until we were met by a large, round room; the base of the tower. Stairs jutted out from the walls, spiralled up into the heavens. Tapestries of every thinkable colour hung along the staircase, depicting a world long forgotten.

"You must find this all very intriguing as a Historian," she said as started the climb up the stairs.

I opened my mouth to agree, to spill my admiration for the beauty of the old tapestries, the depictions of Gods and heroes, damsels and dragons, then I frowned.

"How do you know that?" I asked as I climbed further up the stairs, started to get out of breath.

She paused, her hand trailed up the banister as she continued seamlessly. She looked over her shoulder coyly, brushed her hair behind her ear. She had this look about her, the same look the virginial damsels had in the tapestries. She seemed shy, her eyes so wide and bright they reminded me of a small puppy.

"The Emperor has told me many things," she said simply.

"Like what?" I asked, breathless.

I couldn't help it, I wanted to know what the Emperor had told her. What she thought of me. She untucked her hair from behind her ear, but not before I caught her blush, her smile containing a girlish giggle.

"Of your perfection. Of how you've lost your life mate," she replied.

I almost stumbled at her words. She turned, reached out to steady me, but I shied away from her. My heart ached as I remembered the reason I was here, that this splendour, this experience, was about to be tainted with questions about her. The Riven stepped back, smoothed her dress as she began to climb again.

"I'm sorry that she's gone." She didn't sound convincing.

We climbed the rest of the stairs in silence. I tried not to fret, but every step was like another nail in my chest. I couldn't help but assume the worst. Had they found her dead? Was she injured? Would I ever see her again? By the time we reached the large doors that would admit me to the Emperor's private chambers, I had almost picked a hole through the pocket of my trousers. The Riven turned, hand rested on the door.

"Please, take off your shoes," she said, all flirt replaced with professionalism.

I slipped off my shoes, and she bent to pick them up. My heart fluttered in my chest as she put her delicate hand on the door. I straightened my tie, flattened my hair, tried to straighten my socks with my toe. She pushed the door open, and for a second, I was blinded by the brightness. I blinked, squinted past the spots in my vision.

The room was different to what I expected. Where the rest of the palace was steeped in glamour, this place was homely. There were bookcases filled to the brim with books, armchairs and coffee tables arranged as if ready for friends, rugs and matching cushions that looked as staged as they would in the store they came from. There were no walls, instead large balcony doors that stretched the circumference of the room, flung open and framed in gossamer curtains. Everything was white, of course, but there was no sense of grandeur here, only a close comforting feeling that made my eyes feel heavy.

"Alfie, my son, come before me," the Emperor's voice seemed to pierce my softening mind, and I looked up, dopey eyed and fuzzy headed.

He sat in a white throne build out from the wall, stone carved to smoothness by relentless hands. He glowed from within, his alabaster skin shone as bright as the stars he'd come from. He was taller than the average man, an indicator that this was not his true form. His limbs were just shy of human, too long, too willowy. His features were also not quite right, an attempt at mimicking human's mundaneness. His nose was long, his cheek bones delicate, his jaw sharp. His silver hair was pulled into a knot atop his head, a delicate golden head piece fastened to keep it in place. He looked ageless, maybe only a few years older than I, but his eyes gave him away. Even though completely white, without pupil or iris, they held a wisdom that almost took my breath away. Within their endless depths were the secrets of the cosmos, of time and life itself.

I moved forward and stood before him, dropped onto one knee, bent my head.

"Your eminence, I am eternally grateful for this opportunity," I said as I kept my eyes focused on his golden shoes.

He reached out and touched the back of my head, and every nerve in my body sung at the raw power that vibrated from his fingertips.

"Rise, my son," he ordered, and I did as I was told.

I stood before him, unsure of what I could possibly offer a man such as this. He stared at me, his eyes seeing beyond the beauty he had bestowed upon me to something I would never understand. His fingers traced something atop the arm of the throne, a pattern or sequence or numbers that surely meant something.

"I need to ask you some questions, my son. About your life mate, Calluna," he stated without emotion, folded his hands across his lap.

"Of course. Anything I can do to bring her home," I replied.

He nodded, looked thoughtfully to where the curtains pushed against their poles, desperate to fly off into the world. I wondered if he liked it here, if he felt trapped, if he ever longed to go back into the stars. I wondered if he was lonely. Many of his brothers and sisters were killed in the Great War, the ones that survived were few and far between. The Pioneers were mere descendants of his original people, watered down cross breeds that couldn't hold a candle to his species.

"It has come to my attention," he paused, as if unsure.

I found myself leaning in, desperate for even a lick of information about the girl I loved.

"That Calluna went of her own free will with the Mai-Coh, and that she is working with them." The words drowned me.

They buried me. They squeezed any breath out of my lungs, and I stood there, breathless and confused. I shook

310

my head, a deft movement that only served to rattle my screaming brain.

"No. She would never," I responded.

Calluna would never leave me, never leave her sister or brother. She would never go with them. She loved this place, and loved me, and she would never be so selfish as to put me here, in this situation. The Emperor's lips thinned, and there was empathy in his face then.

"I thought you might react this way. That is why I bought someone here who could convince you." At his words, the door opened, and Arthur emerged.

I wanted to run to him, to throw my arms around him and be told this was all a lie. A misunderstanding. However, the shadows under Arthur's eyes and the steel set of his shoulders only made my heart sink deeper into my stomach.

"Please Arthur, my child, explain what you saw in Slum 9," the Emperor pushed Arthur to talk.

Arthur looked at me, and there was hesitancy in his eyes. There were scratches and bruises all over his face, and there were deep bruises encircling his wrists. He did not look like the fearless warrior he had that night at the Palladium, excited for the promotion.

He looked broken.

"Please, Arthur. Your brother needs to know," he urged, his tone sharper now.

Arthur looked away from me, focused on a point on the wall, took himself to that place soldiers were trained to go when confronted with hard decisions.

"I caught her in the black markets of Slum 9. She was with a Mai-Coh boy, and they fled together. She did not resist him, and she was wearing a Mai-Coh robe. We recovered her Commniglass and her coat. It seems she gave them up willingly." I shook my head at his words, unable to accept them.

"She wouldn't." My voice sounded small and pathetic even to my own ears.

Arthur's arm twitched, as if he were about to reach out, but he seemed to think better of it. The Emperor nodded Arthur his thanks.

"You may leave," he instructed.

Arthur opened his mouth, as if to object, but the Emperor fixed him with a sharp gaze that silenced any words he wished to speak. He turned, but not before I caught the flash of fear in his eyes. I caught his wrist in my hand, and before either him or the Emperor could interject, I pulled him into a hug.

I could feel the bones in his back more clearly than I ever had before. His clothes seemed loose across his shoulders as I pulled him against me, and when his arms finally closed across my back they were almost bony. I pressed my face into his shoulder and breathed him in. Beneath the smell of ash and blood, I could faintly smell the detergent our mother uses. I could faintly smell that bitter, burnt orange scent that belonged to his skin alone. I breathed in the familiarity and wished with every fibre of my being that he would be okay, that I would go home tonight and so would he, that he wouldn't have to go back out there and keep doing this to himself. I let him go much sooner than I would have liked, and Arthur instantly moved towards the door without a word.

"Alfie," the Emperor's voice was measured, controlled.

I turned to face him once more, misty tears still caught on my lashes. I nodded, ready for whatever he needed me to say.

"Did she mention anything to you? Did she voice any discomfort?" he asked.

I tried to cast my mind back to those days that seemed so far away. A thread tugged at the back of my brain, and I thought, and thought, knew there was something to be found there. The Emperor leant forward, as if he sensed the struggle inside, his nostrils flared.

"She... she was a little distant after she was put on the Register. I think she was upset that she'd disappointed everyone, disappointed you," I said.

"And when Polly vanished?" The Emperor pressed, and the thread tugged harder.

"She was distraught. She visited her house, to pay her parents-"

"She visited Polly's home?" he interjected, his fingers turned white from where they gripped the thrones arms.

"Yes. To pay her respects. Polly was her closest friend. Then the night she went missing she wanted to meet me. She'd missed a lot of my calls, but she wanted to see me," I replied as I thought about the hours I had waited below the Hollow tree, the numbness of my fingers as I'd called her again and again, the terror that had settled in my bones and had never truly gone away.

The Emperor reached for me, took my hands in his, and that same buzz of power flooded through my veins.

"I have to see. Let me see her." He didn't wait for me to answer before he reached inside me.

I stood in the expanses of my brain, a floating consciousness, and watched the Emperor materialise. Here, in the limitless possibility of my mind, he was something beyond himself. A spectral being with silver blue luminous skin that seemed almost transparent. He towered much taller than in real life; his hair flowed freely in silver sheets down to his knees. His body was no longer human, it was different to anything I had ever seen. It was thin yet strong and littered across his skin were the scars of the wars he had won.

We both stood perfectly still, his back to me, as he seemed to think, to jumble through all that was necessary. Then, the floor swooped from below us, and I was falling. My arms grappled for something to hold onto, to stop the fall before I hit the ground. Things rose around me, buildings, houses, my street. The whiteness turned to cobblestones and darkened night sky, and I could smell icing and burning.

The memory surrounded me, and just as I was about to hit the floor, I stopped. I floated, weightless and unhurt above the ground as the Emperor watched. There was Calluna, walking beside me, and my heart caught in my throat as I tried to reach for her. I opened my mouth to speak, but no words formed. My hands came up empty, and she kept walking away. I saw on her face what I hadn't that night, the lines that puckered her forehead, the worry in her eyes, her teeth sunk into her lips. I wanted to ask her what was wrong, I wanted to shout at myself for blabbering, for ignoring what was so plainly in front of me. I looked at my past self with hatred as I watched myself talk away, oblivious.

The Emperor watched too, his eyes narrowed at her as she stumbled and stopped, startled by the news of Polly's disappearance. Worry was replaced with panic as she turned and fled, and I reached out my arms to hold her, to catch her, but she passed through me with ease.

The Emperor flicked his hand, and the memory slid away, replaced by another. We stood in her bedroom, and I kissed her, and I watched that small moment of happiness and wished I could repeat it again and again. When she pulled away, I felt her loss as tangibly as I had that day. When she turned back to me, the next words were so loud I flinched.

"Do you ever…. ever think that maybe we don't know something… that something isn't right here?"

The memory fell, and she stood there, suspended, mouth open, as if attached to strings. The Emperor reached out, put his hands on either side of her head, and the whiteness trembled. My feet dropped to the ground, and when I looked down, it really was ground. Dirt, mud, dust. I looked back up and saw Calluna screaming, her mouth open wide as the space before us tried to shift into focus. It was blurry, but there were shapes, objects, the smell of firewood. I tried to reach for her, to pull him away from her as she screamed. Everything shook violently, and there was a piercing behind my eyes. My knees quivered, and as I fell Calluna fell too.

I opened my eyes and I was back in the Emperor's keep. I was on my knees, my cheeks damp with tears. My mind was tattered, flimsy and pricked with holes. I could barely focus, my forehead seared with pain. The Emperor sat before me, his hands back in his lap, his eyes far off. I tried to stand, but my legs were too weak.

"They're coming…" the Emperor whispered, before his eyes snapped down to me once more.

"Your family will receive a transfer soon. You are to move to the Inner Ring by fall. Good day to you, my child," he gestured into the air, and my Riven guide appeared again, red cheeked and half undressed.

"Help him, Winnie, he'll be quite weak on his feet," he instructed.

Winnie linked her arms under my shoulders, helped me to my feet with surprising strength. She kept my arm over her shoulder, her hands on my waist as she guided me towards the door.

"He might be too weak for your services, but try anyway," the Emperor said as the door shut.

Winnie guided me down the stairs, although I wasn't much help. My feet dragged on every step as I thought of her, of what I'd seen. Had she really been there, or had she been a memory? I tried to pick through the soupy remains of what the Emperor had left me as she ushered me out of the palace, and back to the waiting car.

The driver and passenger were absent, and the heat had doubled since moving inside. She leant me against the searing hood of the car as she struggled to open the back door, and I saw on her shoulder a fresh bite mark. I reached out and traced the indents, and she flinched, covered the mark with the shoulder of her dress. She pulled open the door, and rather roughly shoved me into the back.

I fell back, my head hit the handle of the opposite door as she climbed in after me, straddled my lap. I tried to swat at her as she bent and kissed me, but my arms didn't seem connected to my brain. Her lips were hard and hot, her legs soft against my waist. Her small hands drifted down my stomach to the fasten of my trousers and skilfully opened them without struggle. I pushed her off, harder than I intended, and she toppled backwards, almost fell out the car.

"Stop. I don't want this," I said as well as I could.

She looked down at me with a hatred that I had never experienced before. Her eyes flashed as she fisted her hands in my top.

"This is my job. He won't be happy if I don't," she said, her voice wobbled slightly.

I pushed her again, lighter this time, so that her hands dropped from my shirt. I propped myself up on my elbows, looked her in the eyes. I felt sorry for her then, for the life she had to lead, but I would be faithful to Calluna until the end, and nothing could change that.

"I don't want this," I said, firmer than before.

Her shoulders drooped as her eyes dropped from mine. She shuffled backwards, got out of the car. I sat up fully, felt the need to apologise, or say something. She straightened her clothes, folded her hands in front of her neatly. The golden bands that shackled her clinked as she took another step away.

"I shall call the driver. Goodbye, Mr. Clarke,"

Chapter XVII

I saw Alfie. I stood somewhere only half formed, but somehow I knew I was at the Mai-Coh camp. It was something in the air, the smell of firewood, the shifting blue of the sky, the shaking objects that kept coming in and out of focus. I saw him, stood as plain as day a few meters away. Joy that could have cracked my ribs in two spread through my chest, and I smiled, tried to reach for him. Then, pain exploded across my temples. A blinding, piercing pain that made my muscles spasm uncontrollably. A scream tore from my throat as what felt like knives were driven deep inside my skull. I screamed and screamed until my throat ran dry and the taste of blood filled my mouth.

I tried to move, to fight away from whatever held me, but I stood there frozen. Distantly, I heard Alfie crying, and as I managed to open my eyes, I saw the Emperor, his face cast in fury, his eyes glowing as they saw deep into my soul...

"Calluna," Theo's voice woke me, and I thrashed, fought against his arms in confusion.

He held me still, pulled me between his legs and into his arms. My chest rose and fell raggedly as I struggled out of sleep and into consciousness. I stilled as he embraced me, his arms strong against my own, and I leant into him, relaxed into the safety of his embrace. As I stilled, he let my arms go, wiped the sweat from my forehead gently as I cried. I squeezed my eyes shut against the world, terrified of what I'd seen. Weeks of training, of running, of swimming and climbing had made me feel strong, but in that moment I was as weak as I had been that day in my father's office. Theo held me, pressed his lips into the top of my head, shushed me gently.

"Is she alright?" Kellan's voice made me look up.

He stood by the door, arms folded, barely visible in the shadows. I sat up, rubbed my hands across my face, dug the heels of my palms into my eyes.

317

"I'm fine," I lied.

Kellan stepped forward; dark circles hung under his eyes. He looked troubled, as if he hadn't slept in days. I wondered what could possibly be keeping him up.

"Can you tell me what the hell that was about?" Kellan asked.

Theo stood, moved in between Kellan and I. It was then I remembered that all I wore were the tan bindings Agnes had made for me; rolls of fabric wrapped around my breasts, hips and thighs. I stood regardless of how naked I felt. My hair spilled down my back in thick curls, and in a spinning moment of head hurting nostalgia, I could remember being young, and sitting on the kitchen table while my mother snipped at my unruly locks. I stumbled through the memory, so sharp and clear I was unsure where I really was. Theo steadied me, careful hands on my elbows.

"He wants to find me. He knows I'm here-"

"Does he know where *here* is?" Kellan interrupted, suddenly all too awake.

I shook my head, swallowed thickly against the pain of the memories than kept surging up.

"No, not exactly," I replied as my head spun.

"I'm taking her to Akari," Kellan seized me by the arm, but Theo stepped in between us.

"She needs to rest. She can barely walk," Theo put an arm over my shoulder, tried to coax me back to bed.

Kellan refused to let go of my wrist, gave me a tug that was surprisingly gentle.

"That man can't have free access to her brain. Akari can help," Kellan reasoned, and I watched Theo waver.

He let me go reluctantly, his forehead lined with worry. He gestured for Kellan to lead the way with a clenched jaw. Kellan nodded, a stiff agreement between friends.

The late evening was muggy, the air close and humid. The night sky was only just turning from mottled grey to deep navy, the stars pricked through thick clouds. The low rumble of thunder made the hair on my arms stand. I couldn't help but feel like the Emperor was watching. Every corner, every shadow was heavy with his presence. My head ached, my limbs were brittle and tired. A gust of wind cut through the heaviness of the air, and I shivered.

Akari's tent loomed ahead, lit blue and green in a flash of lightening. Another clap of thunder opened the skies, and the roiling clouds began to weep. The rain fell in sheets, soaked me down to the bone, stuck my hair to my neck. My teeth chattered as I wrapped my arms around myself. Theo turned, hair dripped into his face, shirt stuck to his shoulders. He reached for me, pulled me into his side. He was barely warmer than I was, but I revelled in the comfort. Kellan made a disgusted noise before he jogged to her tent, left us alone.

"What did you see?" He whispered, barely audible above the crashing thunder.

I shivered, but this time not from the cold. As Kellan drew back the entrance of Akari's tent, I felt a thousand memories, a thousand versions of Alfie, stare back at me with betrayal and sadness. I bit back the guilt as I moved from out of Theo's arms. It suddenly felt wrong to be comforted by him, wrong to indulge in a relationship that only served to betray Alfie further.

"My life mate," I answered through chattering teeth as I went to enter Akari's tent.

Theo went to follow, but Kellan's hand shot out, stopped him in his path. I turned with a frown, confused at Kellan's averted gaze and taut shoulders.

319

"You shouldn't. Out of respect," Kellan said in a low voice to Theo, who shook his head.

"Screw respect, she's not going alone." He shoved Kellan off, stepped into the tent after me.

A fire roared at the heart of a deep pit in the centre of the tent, its silver blue flames flickered elegantly in the storms breeze. The air in the tent was unusually cool, and my damp limbs shook violently. Akari stood at the far end of the tent, hands poised over a large metal bowl, assorted herbs and liquids spread across the wooden stand.

Here, in the comfort of her own home, she was not concealed. Gone were the thick, figure distorting dresses and cloaks; now I could really see her. She was not like the Emperor, as I had once thought. Her hair was white instead of silver, and it fell in loose ringlets to her waist. She wore a light blue slip, and as she turned, it shimmered in the firelight. Her eyes were not white, but instead icy blue, and as they landed on me her face pinched.

"Get. Out." She hissed at Theo as she moved into the shadows, drew them around her so thick that she couldn't be seen.

Kellan still stood at the entrance, eyes turned up to the sky, adamant not to encroach on Akari's privacy. Theo reached out, took my face in his hands and planted a kiss on my lips. I didn't move, but the feel of his lips was poisonous. He'd pushed in here knowing Akari couldn't be seen uncovered, without care or respect for her; what kind of person does such a thing?

When he pulled back, he met my eyes, a burning gaze that was more possessive that protective. I shivered at the darkness there, and for the first time I realised that there was so much I didn't know about him.

"Come on. Now," Kellan seized Theo by the collar and yanked him towards the door, which was an impressive feat considering his eyes were closed.

"Sit," Akari instructed once they were gone, materialised from the shadows.

I did as I was told, looked at her over the fire. She looked so young, so different here, where no one would see her. She was not only a powerful priestess, but an ordinary girl, a girl who could easily have been from the Inner ring. Yet, as she pushed her hair behind her ear, I thought maybe I was wrong. She was beautiful, there was no denying that, but there was something else too. The prominence of her cheekbones, the wideness of her face, that indicated she was more than one of the Emperor's brethren. She caught me staring, met my eyes steadily.

Her eyes burnt as brightly as the flames reflected within them, and I found myself unable to look away. There was a tingling, like a feather running down my spine, at the base of my neck. It wasn't uncomfortable, like the painful intrusion of the Emperor or Mrs. Leath. It was light, gentle, careful. I welcomed the caress, closed my eyes, before the feeling fell away, and my eyes snapped open.

"I see," she mused as her fingers toyed with the flames.

Her fingers did not burn but glided through the fire like ice. She looked into the flames, tilted her head as if they were whispering something to her. I wondered what it would be like to have that sort of power, to be at one with the world. If this power stemmed from her relation to the Emperor, or the gods that the Mai-Coh worshipped.

She looked back up at me as if she'd heard every thought.

"It is both. My father was one of the original Pioneers, and my mother was one in a long legacy of Muslim women gifted with natural power. The powers I have been blessed with come from them both," she replied to my thought, and I gawped at her, sure I had heard her wrong.

"But the original Pioneers came to earth over a hundred years ago…" I trailed off, looked at her anew.

She continued to smile; her fingers trailed through the ash that gathered around the fires rim. She drew something there, symbols, ancient and beautiful. She looked barely a day over fifteen, her face ageless and soft with youth. I shook my head deftly, my head burnt at the thought, and yet the origin of her birth was beautifully sorrowful.

Two single souls from opposing worlds, fallen for each other despite all that tore them apart. A love born from death and destruction, a love that was always bound to end in tragedy. It was beautifully poetic, and I wondered what had happened to them. Akari lifted her stained fingers, stood gracefully. She moved towards me, took my chin between her fingers.

"You have to let go of him," she said, her voice not childlike, but the voice of someone who has lived several lifetimes.

I didn't have to ask who she meant. My eyes pricked as she pressed her ash-stained fingers against my forehead.

"I can't," I replied, my voice barely above a whisper.

She showed no emotion as she continued to draw symbols across my forehead. Her face was blank, her eyes empty. There was no tolerance there for weakness, for love. Over her long life, she must have seen what love did to people, what it caused, what it left in its wake. I trembled under her delicate hands; unsure I could do what she asked of me.

"He's the bridge between you and the Emperor. As long as you hold onto the past, you'll be vulnerable. I can perform a short-term remedy but…" she trailed off as she dropped her hands from my face.

322

A tear fell down my cheek as she walked over to her herbs. Alfie had been a part of my life for as long as I could remember, an extension of myself. I had spent my time here in guilt, missing him, craving him so deeply I had found him in Theo. When I closed my eyes, I saw his smile, and the thought of never seeing it again, of purposely blocking it out, made me choke on my tears. She sifted through the vials, picked up one filled with pink and green star shaped leaves.

"He's my best friend." These were the only words I could muster.

Akari faced me once more as she tipped a few leaves into her palm. Something flashed across her face then, something sharp that I didn't quite understand. She moved back to the fire, held her closed fist over the flames.

"To be one of us, you cannot have sympathy for them," she said as she opened her hand.

The leaves fell into the fire and the flames jumped pink and green. The letters on my forehead burned, the ash seared into my skin. I resisted the urge to rub it off as Akari muttered; an ancient language that hummed through my blood like honey. She closed her eyes, pressed her hands deep into the fire until she was engulfed in flames. She stood, a terrifying contrast of icy blue and brilliant flames, and I thought in that moment that there didn't need to be a Mai-Coh army. This girl, no, this *woman*, could take the Emperor all by herself.

The searing on my forehead intensified, before Akari pulled back, and the pain faded. She sat with a thump, her breath coming raggedly. I touched my forehead; it was warm, the ash dried into my skin. I picked at it with my nails, but the marks didn't budge. Akari took a deep breath, before she looked back at me, this time gently, as if looking at a wounded child.

"Theo had sympathy for me," I said.

323

I couldn't forget about Alfie, couldn't push him to the back of my mind, pretend he never existed. I would never be able to purge him from my heart. She met my words with a blank stare and a shake of her head.

"You're more naïve than I thought if you truly believe Theo was there by coincidence," she said flatly.

My nails dug into the seat below me as I thought about Kellan's words, and now Akari's confirmation. I stood, arms locked at my sides, lips pressed into a thin line.

"Thank you," I said as I turned.

I didn't know who I was angrier at; Akari and Kellan for teasing me with knowledge, or Theo for withholding it, or me for being so weak and naïve. I stormed out of the tent; the rain smacked into my face so hard it took my breath away. Both Kellan and Theo stood in the rain, waiting. When he saw me, Theo moved towards me, his face lined with concern, but my anger forked through my chest as dangerously as the lightening above us. He tried to reach for me, but I snapped back.

"Why were you at the Hollow that night?" I asked.

Theo looked taken aback, his hands fell back to his sides. He looked over my shoulder at Akari's tent, then closed his eyes as he sighed. He looked back at Kellan, who stood with arms folded, hair plastered to his neck, an impartial expression on his face.

"What did you tell her?" he asked.

Kellan shrugged, but I didn't wait for him to retort with something witty or sarcastic. My chest rose and fell hard as my limbs shook. I knew I wasn't only angry at Theo, but I couldn't help it. I needed to let it out, to allow myself to explode.

"This isn't about Kellan. Tell me, Theo. Tell me why you were there," I demanded.

Theo looked down at me, his eyes shone, his eyebrows drawn down low as he gnawed at his lip. There was regret in his eyes, a sadness that made my anger soften just slightly, but it was too late to turn back. I needed to know, I needed to know the truth. I was sick of lies, of pretending and faking and preforming.

"Kamal sent me to kill a soldier, the soldier from the market. To send a message." He saw the rising shock in my face and rushed to continue.

"But when I saw you Calluna, when I saw them take you, I couldn't leave you there," he touched my cheek, traced the lines of my tears.

I scrunched my nose tight against the tears that threatened to spill. Arthur had never been my friend, I'd never been fond of him, but the thought of Alfie losing him made my chest ache. I pushed past Theo and broke into a run.

The thunder clapped above me; the wind howled against my body as I fled. My eyes blurred and I fumbled for my tent door, fingers numb, arms aching, brain racing. I fell through the door, shaking relentlessly as I tried to rub warmth back into my arms.

Why hadn't he told me? Why had he kept such a secret? What else was he keeping from me? If I hadn't been pretty, if he hadn't felt sorry for me, would he have killed me too? He'd taken me that day, but was that really for my benefit? I was *his*. His prize. His conquest. A golden trophy to flaunt.

My head ached as I fell onto my palette, face buried in the pillows. My head throbbed; was that all I was? My father had been a possessive man, my mother had been his property, was that the life I was destined for? I'd been so desperate for protection, for someone like Alfie, had I willing looked past his flaws? He'd walked into Akari's tent without care or respect for her wishes, her modesty. He'd claimed me without my willingness.

325

He saved your life.

I screamed into the pillow as the two parts of myself warred. The part that demanded submission and the part that craved freedom.

"That's a tad dramatic." I sat up at the sound of Kellan's voice.

I glared at him through the clumps of my wet hair, nails sunk deep into the furs below my stomach.

"Get out," I hissed.

He'd been there that night too after all. Kellan rolled his eyes, rung the water out of his shirt.

"How does that work by the way?" He gestured to his own forehead.

I sat up dramatically, slammed my hands into the palette so hard pain shot up my arms.

"Akari said it's a short-term fix, alright? You can go now," I said, gestured back out towards the storm.

Kellan cocked his head one way, then the other. He squatted down, his eyes level with mine, hands gripped tightly between his knees.

"Then it sounds like we need to bring the raid forward, before he can, you know." He made a bizarre gesture around his head meant to symbolise mind reading.

I couldn't help the smile that pulled at the corner of my mouth, and Kellan clocked it, his eyes brightening. He reached over and brushed the hair back off my forehead with a force that drew my eyebrows up. My smile grew, and Kellan gave a chuckle.

We stared at eachother, and for a moment there was nothing but us. His smile was genuine, it warmed his eyes like the sun warms a lake. My stomach lurched at the creases

326

around his eyes, and I blushed, gripped my knees hard. His eyes strayed to my lips, and his smile fell. It was like watching a great feat of architecture, the way he composed his face. The way he smoothed his brow, set his lips, forced his eyes to darken. I watched him lock himself away and my heart sunk.

"We all have to do bad things to survive. Theo included," he said, his eyes now far away.

I frowned at him, but there wasn't the same anger or sadness behind it. Why was he defending him? Was I wrong to judge Theo so harshly?

"Early tomorrow, alright?" he said as he turned.

He didn't give me the opportunity to reply. He disappeared back into the night, and I found myself watching where he stood for a while, a smile on my face.

Chapter XVIII

Sweat dripped down my legs, turned my socks into a soggy mess where I stood. Kellan had really meant early and roused me only two or three hours after I'd fallen asleep. He'd taken me for another weighted run, before he taught me basic self-defence; blocks, holds, evasion. It had made me feel empowered, strong, but now, stood in Kamal's tent, I felt as small as a mouse.

Kamal stood centre, no longer the young boy wrapped in furs I had seen those weeks ago, but a hardened battle general. He wore a shirt made of oil slickened leather as dark as oak, its laces tipped and looped through bronze. His hair was fixed behind his head with a wooden clip, and a sword was slung low over his hips. He commanded the attention of the tent without a word, his eyes transfixing.

Kellan, Theo, Priya, and Roscoe were among the crowd, all stood as silent and serious as Kamal. There were others too, those whose names I didn't yet know. An elder man, maybe thirty, with dark russet skin and short clipped hair, a petite blonde-haired girl with dark, almost black eyes.

We stood in silence; the tension so thick I thought it might suffocate me. I wasn't sure what we were waiting for until Meredith burst into the tent, slightly out of breath, a short, stern girl in tow. She had the same beige skin as Theo, if a few shades darker, and when she took Meredith's had I realised she was Meredith's girlfriend. She wasn't what I imagined; not pretty or vibrant, but instead strong and angular. Her eyes were as sharp as daggers, but when they turned on Meredith they filled with warmth.

They both nodded their apologies to Kamal and joined the crowd. Ahzani shifted uncomfortably next to me, her eyes drawn to the pair. It had come to my attention in the last few weeks that Ahzani was desperate in love with

Meredith. Even now, Meredith's presence in the tent seemed to brighten it somehow, her smile even softening Kamal's steely resolve. Yet Meredith seemed oblivious to Ahzani's adoration, her eyes only for her girlfriend.

Ahzani didn't tear her eyes away from them as the pair whispered something to each other. I elbowed her in the stomach, and she finally turned, her cheeks dark. Kamal observed the crowd he had assembled before him, barely thirty or so people, his eyes narrowed as he took in each face. When his eyes landed on me, he took in the ashy marks on my forehead, still present but fading fast. I didn't flinch under the hardness of his eyes. I had a right to be here, I'd proved that time and time again.

"You have been chosen." His beginning words sent a shiver down my spine, adrenalin sparked in the pit of my stomach.

"The people in this room have been trusted with a mission of upmost importance. A recovery mission that requires stealth." When he said this part, he looked pointedly at Kellan, who pretended to be preoccupied with something in the rafters.

"Tonight, we may celebrate, but before daybreak, we shall join Kade's army in Slum Nine, and take it forever." There was a murmur of excitement, but Kamal raised his hand, bought the room back to silence.

"Then, at the fall of night, we will travel to the Hollow and take what we need. We will burn and kill those who stand against us, and so will be the rising of the Mai-Coh, and the liberation of the people of Sadon will begin." He raised his fist, and the group roared.

I found myself silent. It was an honour to be here, to be trusted, but all I could think about was the safety of my family, of Alfie. I slipped from the crowd, walked into the light evening air.

The storm had come and gone, cut through the heat and left the air mild and grey. I breathed it in, looked out over the camp. It was unusually quiet despite the preparations being made for tonight's celebration. A hand landed on my shoulder, and I turned to Ahzani. There was sadness in her face as Meredith's laugh echoed through the night. I gave her fingers a squeeze, and she forced a smile.

"Get ready with me?" she asked.

"Yeah, of course," I replied.

She nodded, forced a tight smile, but her eyes still remained dark. I smiled at her and thought that maybe we understood each other better than anyone else. Theo emerged from the tent, along with Priya. They were talking animatedly, and Priya was smiling. A beautiful, carefree smile I had never seen her wear. However, as soon as her eyes landed on me, her face fell back to its usual sullenness. Theo looked too, and as Ahzani walked away, he moved to catch me.

"Can I talk to you?" he asked.

Ahzani stood waiting, arms folded over her chest, her face cool and collected, but her eyes still swam with hurt. I nodded her on and met Theo's eyes. He looked tired, dark circles hung under his eyes, lines pressed into his forehead, lips bitten dry.

"I know I didn't tell you, but I wanted you to trust me. I wanted to help you," he said.

I chewed the inside of my cheek as Priya hung behind us, eyes burnt into my forehead. He looked so sad, so sorry, and the sight made my stomach turn. I owed him, that was something I couldn't forget. He'd been there to kill Arthur, he'd lied to me about it, but hadn't he protected me? The thought made my head burn; he'd claimed to *own* me. He'd said I was *his*. Where was my choice in that? Sadon had

330

always been a place of debt and subservience, but wasn't this supposed to be different?

I met his eyes again and saw a flicker of impatience there, and I knew I had to say something.

I needed him.

My stomach sunk at the thought, and those same invisible bars that had kept me silent in Sadon closed around me once more.

"I get it. I understand," I replied.

He leant down and pressed his lips to mine. I leant into his chest, pressed my hands into the back of his neck, pulled him closer. I waited for something to rush inside me, for anything to happen. I waited for my heart to soar, but it plummeted, leaden with the price of my freedom. All I felt was dirty. I pulled away from him, took a step back. His eyes fluttered open, and he smiled, breathless.

"So, I'll see you later?" he asked.

I nodded but I didn't say anything. I gave him a final smile and turned, but not before I caught the anger and hatred on Priya's face.

~

Ahzani sat behind me, legs either side of my head as she braided my hair. I pulled at the straps of the lavender dress I'd tried on what felt like years ago, felt even more exposed now than I had then. She slapped at my fingers, tutted under her breath.

"You look hot, alright? Leave it be," she said in a tone that bordered on motherly.

I dropped my hands back into my lap and sat still. Ahzani worked silently, still a bit out of sorts from seeing Meredith with her girlfriend. I kept thinking back to Theo, about the kiss we'd shared, the life I was setting myself up for. I

331

resisted the urge to gnaw on my lips, as I didn't want to mess up what Ahzani had painted. She'd already whined when I'd smudged the dark kohl around my eyes, and I didn't want to be subjected to her annoyance again. I twiddled my thumbs as she pulled her fingers through my hair.

"How do you feel about Meredith?" I asked.

Her fingers falter in my hair.

"What do you mean?" she asked as she continued.

"Well... how does it feel when you... think about her? When you touch her?" I asked.

My cheeks burnt with embarrassment as she continued to work. She shifted her legs awkwardly, let out a long breath.

"I don't know. I guess... like my heart starts beating really hard and I feel like I can't breathe. It's like... I ache for her, you know?" she said as she finished the braid.

She gave me a pat on the shoulder, and I turned, hugged my knees. The problem was, I didn't know. I'd never felt like that, maybe I never would. Maybe she saw what I was thinking, because she leant forward and took my hands in hers.

"You'll feel like that one day. Maybe not with Theo, but it'll come," she reassured me.

I nodded, and as her thumb smoothed across the back of my hand, I did feel something. My heart fluttered as I looked at her, at the curve of her lips, the way her waist coat cut her waist. She was beautiful, extraordinarily so. Her hair was twisted into several Bantu knots, her suit a deep wine red that glittered against her skin. I didn't quite understand how I felt about her, but I knew it was something, knew that she stirred something in me that I didn't understand.

I dropped my eyes from hers, embarrassment hot in my throat. I pushed myself up, gave her a final twirl. She stuck

332

her thumbs up before she stood herself. She adjusted the collar of her shirt, and the gesture sent a bolt of heat through my stomach. She linked her arm with mine, gave me a broad smile that almost hid the sadness in her eyes.

"Let's go get super drunk," she said as she pulled me from the tent.

It seemed that was the goal tonight. Not a single Mai-Coh walked without a bottle in hand. As we neared the bonfire, both of us were handed wineskins. Ahzani took no time tearing hers open and drank half the thing in one. She looked to me, head cocked, wine dripping down her chin. I snapped off the top of my own and gave it an experimental swig. It was sweet and warm, but it didn't burn like the stuff Kellan had given me. I drank more, and Ahzani jeered.

"Now finish that one and I'll get you another," she said, before proceeding to finish her own.

I rushed to follow, drank the liquid down so fast I could barely breathe. It settled in my stomach, a ball of warmth that made me giggle. Ahzani snorted, took the wine skin from me and led me through the crowds. People were already drunk, swaying back and forth to music played on drums and guitars. I couldn't see Theo or Kellan, but Priya stood close to the fire. She wore a deep pink lehenga embroidered with swirls of silver, exposing her midriff. It was too fine, too beautiful to have been made here, and the slight ware to the hem, the faded yellowing sun stain on her shawl, told me it had been gifted to her. Maybe it had been her mothers, and the thought made me flinch as I remembered what she'd shared with me in the woods.

Her hair was loose, and it framed her face beautifully. A golden chain looped over her forehead, woven into the threads of her hair, along with a set of large pink earrings, equally ancient and regal. She looked breath-taking.

She looked up, met my eyes through the haze of the fire, and her smile dropped. The flames danced in her eyes,

333

dangerous and all consuming, so angry and hurt. I looked away, ashamed of myself. Ahzani ran towards me, wineskins in hand.

"Drink, I wanna see what perfection looks like drunk." She gave a devious smile, wiggled her eyebrows as she held the wineskin out to me.

I snatched it up, glad of the distraction. As long as I didn't have to think about tomorrow, I was up for anything.

We kept drinking until my fingers turned numb. Everything around me dulled into a different state of consciousness, like I was there, but watching from above. The weight that had been crushing me to death had lifted from my shoulders, and I was free of all the guilt and inadequacy that had hounded me.

I danced with Ahzani; my body swayed to the music, my arms above my head as I closed my eyes and breathed in the heady smell of smoke, lamb and wine. Ahzani's hands trailed down my sides, traced the curves of my waist. I swayed with her, oblivious to everything and anything around me. I sipped from my wineskin, revelled in the sweetness.

Her fingers were like lightening as they traced the lines of my shoulders, pressed between my shoulder blades and drew me closer. Her body against mine hummed, warm and solid and strong. I draped my arms around her shoulders, tilted my head back with a smile at the feel of her. Everything was on fire, and I would have gladly burned as long as I was in her arms.

There was another hand on my shoulder, and I turned, my head spinning. Kellan smirked back at me, his eyes hazy and unfocused.

"I wanna show you something." His breath was tainted with the sour smell of stronger alcohol.

Ahzani snorted from behind me, her hands still on my waist. His fingers tightened on my shoulder as she tried to pull me back to her.

"Yeah, don't fall for that one," she drawled.

Giggles surged from my throat, and I snorted despite my best efforts. It all felt so funny, so unreal, so distant. Her hands, his hands, I couldn't tell them apart, and I almost didn't want to. Kellan jerked his head away from the party.

"I. Want. To. Show. You. Some. Thing," he punctuated each word with a squeeze of my shoulder.

I looked around, my head heavy, my eyes blurred. The world spun, a dizzying display of flames and bodies. I stumbled, turned back to Kellan with narrowed eyes.

"Alright," I said despite my suspicions.

I took his arm, if only to steady myself, and moved out of Ahzani's grip.

"Don't get pregnant! You'll be no fun then," Ahzani called after me.

Kellan led me away from the throbbing crowd, and I followed him blindly. Hiccups bubbled from my stomach, and he rolled his eyes.

"Drink this," he held out his wineskin.

I took it without question, swigged. It burnt more than the wine had, and tasted more like chemicals than fruit, but I drank it regardless. Kellan led me to the treeline, pulled me through the branches, before he let me go and charged ahead.

My fingers trailed against the trees as I passed them, my feet dragged through the underbrush clumsily. The thrumming of music could be heard even here, in the recesses of the forest, but it was faint and slowly fading. I turned my face up to the star-studded sky, breathed in the

335

thick scent of pine and midnight dew. I closed my eyes and allowed my feet to take me onwards, felt a serenity that was almost weightless. I wondered absently what it would be like, up there amongst the stars. If it would be cold, if it would feel as beautiful as it looked.

Kellan's shouting turned my attention back to the earth, and I watched as he balanced precariously on a fallen tree, feet nimble but slowed by the copious amounts of alcohol in his system.

"Where are we going?" I called after him, unable to contain the smile that spread across my lips.

My balance faded as I rushed to catch up to him, my vision blurred at the edges. He held up his hands for the wineskin, and I threw it as hard as I could muster. He barely caught it, almost fell. He took a long gulp, jumped from the fallen tree, landed with as much grace as a three-legged cat. He stumbled, thrust his arms out dramatically.

I caught up to him, gave him a shove as I took the wine skin again and emptied the rest of its contents into my mouth. Kellan whined, snatched the wineskin back in anger.

"Never you mind," he replied, his eyes bright with mischief.

He pouted; his shoulders theatrically straight as he stomped off in some sort of act of defiance. I trailed after him, each step took us deeper into a seemingly endless void of foliage. My legs ached, and just as I grew impatient and bored, Kellan pushed through a veil of brush, and bought us to our end.

In front of us lay a rolling grassland so broad and inescapable I felt as if I were standing on the edge of the world. The moon, swollen and silver, rained its light down on the shivering grass, turned it into glimmering ice. The breath in my lungs faded as I looked outwards, momentarily sobered. It was remarkable, something so big, something so… all encompassing.

Kellan took my arm, pulled me towards him. My back pressed to his chest, he pointed to the horizon, his warm, alcohol tainted breath flush against my ear.

"You see that?" He gestured to something in the distance, something glimmering, something almost out of sight.

I nodded as I squinted, shifted from foot to foot as the warmth of his body against mine made blood rush in my ears.

"That's the sea. You know, I've heard stories about what's past there," he said, proud of himself.

He let me go, tumbled to the floor. I sat too, grateful for the rest. He laid down, his head rested on his hands as he stared up at the sky. His smile was brilliant in the quivering moonlight, so bright it challenged the sky with its beauty. He caught me staring, his eyebrow tilted as he patted the space next to him.

"Some really cool stories," he said enticingly.

I laid down, my head span as I stared upwards, awaiting his promised stories. When he didn't begin, I gave him a nudge with my elbow.

"Go on then," I prompted.

He chuckled, a laugh low and deep within his chest. He shifted, jiggled his legs as if making sure they were still there.

"I met a trader once in Slum One. The water one, you know?" he turned his head, double checked to make sure I was following on.

I gave a nod that made my head spin.

"Well, he told me that beyond the sea, there's a land full of gold, of snow and diamonds and a land where people aren't sectioned by perfection. He told me that he had seven beautiful daughters, and seven strong sons, and that the land was so prosperous that the people never stopped smiling," Kellan said, his voice childlike in its wonder.

"Wow," I breathed, tried to imagine such a world, but my drunken brain would not comply.

"He told me that one day, he's going to bring his daughters here, and he'll marry one off to the Emperor, and then he'll kill him and be the King," Kellan sounded so in awe of the man, his eyes hopeful and wide.

"Pfft, yeah right," I replied.

Kellan propped himself up on his elbow, stared down at me with a scowl.

"He could! I bet he could!" He replied, as adamant as a stubborn child.

I rolled my eyes, amused by his foolishness. A trader's words into the wind, a drunkard's promise, completely meaningless.

"The Emperor doesn't marry. He'll never marry. He has his… Riven's and things instead," I replied, waved my hand dismissively.

Kellan sat up straighter, leant over me so as to obscure my view of the sky. His brow was set, his eyebrows drawn down low.

"He said his daughters were super beautiful. More beautiful than any Mai-Coh or Slum dweller or Pioneer," he attempted, but I scoffed.

"Every father thinks their daughters are beautiful," I pointed out.

338

He paused, his mouth pouted, his brain ticked over and over. He chewed on his lip, his eyes thoughtful.

"I think you're wrong," he gave me a jab to the side, nodded at his proclamation.

I raised my brow, jabbed him back.

"So that makes you right?" I asked, delivered another jab to his ribs.

He barely flinched. He nodded, sure of his decision.

"Yes. Obviously," he jabbed me again, and I squirmed as his hands went to my waist.

"Not possible," I began, but I didn't get to finish my sentence.

He dug his fingers into my waist, a calculated jab that made me squirm, and I poked back. I thought back to our self-defence class, how to wrestle your opponent. I clasped his hands, tried to roll him off of me, pushed my legs between his to twist him away, but my limbs were heavy and slow with alcohol. He slipped free, continued to trace burning trails up my sides. We grappled, a tangle of limbs and squeals and grunts. He ruffled my hair, pinned my hands above me as the friction burnt my head. I went for his face, tried to push him away as I laughed.

"Kellan!" I cried through my giggles.

I went to try and bite his arm, teeth bared, fingers scratching. He steadied my face, and just as his hands left mine, he kissed me. His hands cradled either side of my head, no longer fighting but gentle. His lips were hot, sloppy, uncontrolled. The tension that had built between us through training exploded into something hot and volatile. Ahzani's words made sense, because I felt it.

God, I felt it.

339

That rushing, hot surge of blood that made my heart beat at twice its normal rate. That squirming in the stomach, the need to feel more and yet less and yet nothing at all. A confusing, horrible, wonderful tangle of lips upon lips that just didn't make sense.

I kissed him back, pushed against him, arched my back off the ground just to get a centimetre closer. I looped my arms behind his neck, pulled him to me. He let out a shuddering breath, his hands tightening on my jaw. My lips moved desperately, and when he opened his mouth, when his tongue brushed against my bottom lip, I let out a sigh.

His whole body tightened, a tenseness that sent a thrill down my spine, and just when I'd decided to throw any caution to the wind, just when I'd decided to let him strip me bare and take me under the moon, he yanked himself back.

He didn't open his eyes to look at me. He scrunched them closed, his lips pressed tight. He shook his head, a movement small but damning, before he rolled away.

He exhaled a large breath, resumed his relaxed position.

"Do you think he really will bring his daughters over here?" He asked, resumed where we left off.

I couldn't answer. I raised my hand, touched my lips. They were bruised, still wet. I stared up at the sky and tried not to think about what had just happened. I'd seen Kellan do a lot more after drinking a whole lot less. I shouldn't take it personally, and yet my stomach roiled.

"I think so, and hopefully I'll be there when it happens," he mused.

I hummed my agreement as I looked deep into the sky and realised that I was truly doomed.

Chapter XIX

I dreamt about Ahzani and Kellan. I dreamt about their hands, their lips, their bodies. I dreamt about kisses in the woods, fingers on my waist, dances by the firelight. I dreamt about them both, and my body burnt with want.

Pain lanced through my temples as I came to. I groaned, forced myself up despite the agony that clouded my vision.

The sun had not yet risen, but there was whispering outside my tent. With everything that had happened last night, I'd almost forgotten what awaited me at dawn.

I forced myself to stand, lurched as the tent spun and my stomach writhed. *Never again* I reassured myself as the taste of cherry wine came back all too strong. I still wore the dress from the night before, muddy from our trip through the forest. I winced at the memory of Kellan, of the kiss we'd shared under the moon.

As I pulled off the dress, yanked on a pair of trousers, I wondered if he'd say anything this morning. Would he tease me? Would he pull me aside? I don't know which would be worse.

As I pulled on a jumper Ahzani burst in, eyes barely open. She looked worse than I felt. Her hair sprung around her head in tight coils, exposed the bruises on her neck from whoever she had slept with last night. She blinked at me, rubbed a hand over her eyes.

"Where did you go last night?" she asked, her voice hoarse.

I concentrated on lacing up my boots instead of answering her. I didn't want to talk about what had happened with Kellan. If I thought about it too much, it would make my stomach turn in that way that didn't make a lot of sense.

"I walked around a bit, tried to clear my head," I replied as I straightened up.

Ahzani cocked a brow, leant back against my chest of drawers. She wore a pair of dark trousers and a fitted waist coat the colour of moss, her arms bare. She twisted the thick black ring on her index finger, round and round until all I could focus on were the callouses and scars, the way the tendons in her hands twitched. I swallowed hard past the lump in my throat, forced my eyes back to hers.

"And did Kellan... show you something?" she asked.

I gave her a shove as I moved out of the tent, desperate for air. The sky was grey, the sun barely peeked above the horizon. It was cool, and I was grateful for the lack of heat. Ahzani followed at my heels, desperate for all the dirty details.

"Come on Cal, you know you want to tell me," she said, her voice low.

I rolled my eyes, tried to massage the pain from my forehead.

"Nothing happened," I told her.

She gave a disbelieving huff but said nothing more. We moved to the vehicle compound, where the others were waiting for us. Theo was chatting idly with Roscoe, and it irritated me how good he looked. He looked well rested, as if he'd barely drank, and a part of me hated him for his effortlessness. He looked up at the sound of my approach and gave a smile.

"Hey. I couldn't find you last night, did you have fun?" he asked as he put an arm across my shoulder.

Ahzani opened her mouth to make a comment, her eyes mischievous, and I dug my elbow into her stomach. She whined, keeled over, hacked out a breath before she spat. She shot me a dirty look before she went to stand with

Roscoe, who was bouncing eagerly from foot to foot in anticipation.

"Yeah, me and Ahzani had fun," I replied.

He smiled, squeezed my shoulder, and as I looked up at him I realised I needed to tell him what when I met his eyes I felt the overwhelming urge to tell him everything. Not just about Kellan and I, but about how mad he made me, how disrespectful he'd been to Akari, how I didn't belong to him. The surge of defiance made my palms tingle, and as his eyes darkened, I opened my mouth.

"Look, Theo. Kellan-" The roar of an engine cut me off, and my head throbbed at the sound.

Kamal rolled down the window of the truck he steered and poked his head out.

"Today we conquer!" he cried, and the crowd roared, if a little more fragile than the night before.

"Tell me later?" Theo said as Priya approached.

I opened my mouth to continue, but I didn't get the chance to speak.

"Ride with me?" Priya interjected, her voice meeker than usual.

He nodded to her, bent down and pressed his lips to mine before I could say a word. I flinched against the bitterness of this kiss. The complete opposite to last night, it was trapping, damning.

Priya made a disgusted noise, grabbed Theo by the arm, dragged him away from me, and I was half grateful. As he retreated a step, the words surged in my throat. A part of me hoped he'd lose it. A part of me hoped he'd turn and never speak to me again. A part of me longed to be free of this debt he'd put on me.

"Kellan kissed me." The words left my mouth in a rush.

Theo stopped, his back tensed. Priya stared back at me, her lips parted in surprise. Theo turned, his eyes shining with betrayal, his mouth pressed into a thin line. His eyes misted with sadness, but his fists clenched in anger, and I saw that part of him I'd feared all along.

"What?" he said, his voice barely above a whisper.

People rushed around us, jumped into waiting cars, lugged trunks of weapons, but the chaos faded to nothing as we looked at each other. Priya put her hand on Theo's shoulder, whispered something to him I couldn't quite hear. With every word his eyes darkened further, and my heart thumped in my chest. Had I signed my own death warrant? Would this be what killed me? Theo had always been the one to vouch for me, and I'd betrayed him. My selfish need for freedom could cost me my life.

"We need to go," Priya said, loud enough for us both to hear.

Theo snapped his eyes from mine and turned. I watched him climb inside the roll cage, his hands on the wheel, eyes downcast as Priya whispered poisoned words to him. Something desperate and visceral clawed inside my chest, a nagging sense of loss and pain that I couldn't quite understand.

I stepped forward, about to go after him; who was I without him? Who was I alone? Was I anyone at all? I opened my mouth to call after him, but a hand on my arm stopped me.

"Don't chase what you don't want," he warned.

He had a cigarette balanced between his lips; smoke billowed from his nose as he looked down at me. He was pale, paler than usual, and his eyes were red and tired. I pulled my wrist from his grip, scowled at him.

"How would you know what I want?" I hissed.

344

He shrugged, his eyes trained on Theo as he disappeared into the line of vehicles. Did he know something I didn't? He'd known Theo a long time, maybe he'd seen the possessive and protective parts of him often enough to know when not to push him.

I took another step away from him as my hands trembled. Everything felt like it was crumpling; the security of affection I had always relied upon, the safety of others I had sought out my whole life. The thought of being alone, it terrified me.

I scowled at Kellan, at the dark shadows under his eyes. This was all his fault.

"You shouldn't have kissed me," I growled.

He didn't react, took another drag from his cigarette before he dropped the butt to the ground, squashed it with his boot.

"Now why would I do that?" he replied as he finally turned back to face me.

"You kissed me," I spat.

"Not that I recall," he said with a shrug as he squinted into the morning sun.

"I kissed a lot of people last night after all," he finished as he tugged at the collar of his shirt.

There, below the fabric, were the tell-tale purple marks of hickeys. My whole body shook. It had meant nothing. Losing Theo's protection, surrendering to that part of myself I had kept locked away for so long, it had all been trivial to him.

I balled my fists to hit him, but then there were fingers around my wrist, and I turned to meet Ahzani's eyes.

"Kamal is waiting." She gripped me by the shoulders and turned me forcefully.

345

My nostrils flared as she walked me to the car she'd pulled up. I climbed into the passenger seat, slammed the door so hard the window splintered at the edges.

"I hate him," I growled.

Ahzani started the car, put it into drive.

"Join the long line of girls he's wronged," she replied.

I glared at him as Ahzani drove forward. I wanted to jump from the seat, pummel his beautiful face into a mess of blood. I wanted to pin him to the ground and wrap my hands around his neck, trace the lines of his waist, feel his skin against mine-

I sucked in a breath and pulled my eyes away from him as I battled the conflict in my mind. I wasn't just angry at him; I was angry at myself. Angry that my body betrayed my mind, that I felt that way about him when I didn't want to. Angry that I'd pushed myself to mess everything up.

Ahzani flicked on the radio, and as the music filled the car I closed my eyes, desperate to forget.

~

The Slum was on fire.

The sun rose over the horizon and painted the early morning sky blood red, black plumes of smoke rising to smother the clouds.

"Shit," Ahzani breathed as she slowed the car down.

The fence lay forgotten in the wilderness, the Slum completely at the mercy of the wildness that chased us. Even through the closed windows I could hear screaming and gunfire. Ahzani pulled the car to a stop, and as she turned off the ignition, her fingers shook.

"Do you have a weapon?" she asked as she reached into the back seat.

346

I shook my head, my heart pounded in my ears. Last night this had all seemed so distant, so glamorous, so easy. Now, sat at the Slums edge, flames raging through the buildings, I was terrified.

"Here." She handed me a gun, but I shook my head.

"No. I can't," I managed to choke out.

Her eyes narrowed as I placed the gun in my lap, unable to even hold it. She pulled out a dagger, its blade jagged and as long as my forearm.

"Take both. Please," she said, and the fear in her voice was harrowing.

Despite the terror that had settled in my throat as hard as a rock, I took the dagger, pushed the gun into my waist band. The thought of using it made my stomach turn, but I didn't want to argue with Ahzani, not when she was all I had left.

The passenger door wrenched open, and we both startled. Ahzani pointed her gun at the intruder, her hands steady. I gripped the hilt of the dagger, my palms sweaty against the wood. A young boy looked back at us, blond hair drenched with blood, ash plastered across his face.

"Kade sent me to bring you," he said, his voice still high with youth.

Ahzani lowered her gun, let out a breath.

"Maybe knock next time," she muttered as she opened her own door.

I jumped down, my legs unsteady. The young boy gestured for us to follow. He led us down a narrow street where the houses seemed relatively untouched. There were a few smashed windows, a door pulled off its hinges, but no fire raged here. The smell of the smoke was unbearable even still. I pulled the collar of my shirt up over my nose, tried to breath evenly as the boy pushed open a door. Inside were most of the crew, as well as some of Kade's men, although Kellan and Roscoe were absent.

The room was small and close, the ceiling so low Meredith had to bend her head. Kamal stood at the far side of the room in deep conversation with a man I didn't recognise.

He was short and stocky, surprisingly plump for a Slum dweller. He had thick, grey smattered hair and a deep, ugly scar that ran from his temple to his jaw, forcing his right eye permanently closed.

"That's Kade," Ahzani breathed.

At the sound of our approach Kamal and Kade turned. Kade beamed at us, showcased his lack of teeth.

"My friends," he bellowed in an accent so thick and foreign it took me by surprise.

"I see you have a Golden Girl," Kade nodded to me, and my toes squirmed under his gaze.

I reached up to my forehead, where the ashy marks were fading fast. There was no telling how long they would last, and every second ticked away as visceral as the last. Kamal gave Kade a slap on the back, a hearty show of affection between old friends.

"Our friends in the Slum have done most of the work for us. The Pioneers are holed in their guard towers. We must take them before they can barricade themselves in," He addressed the group, and Kade sneered.

"We shall flush the rats from their holes, and this place will finally be ours for the taking," Kade shouted, and his men roared with pre-emptive triumph.

Greed flashed behind his eyes, and I was reminded of Agnes and her words of warning. Even now, I could see his ego soaring, his mind ticking over, plotting for what would come next. Kamal seemed not to notice the short man's ambition as he barked orders.

"Meredith, Keeks, Priya, Elios, Obadiah. You five take the east. Theo, Krenna, Forbs, the west. The rest of you, fan out, take down the stragglers. Ahzani, Calluna, you two come with me. I don't want to let you out my sight." He said the last words especially to me.

I clung to the dagger in my hand, reminded myself that the Pioneers weren't the only enemies. I saw it in the way Kade's men leered at me like I was a prize to take home and frame above the mantle. It was an honour to kill a gold-blood, even more so to take home a perfect woman to warm their beds and bare them children.

I shivered as Theo came towards me, representing another form of entrapment. He gave Ahzani a look that made her tense, and she gave my wrist a squeeze before she moved to Kamal's side. He pulled me into the corner of the room, his eyes dark and serious.

"Theo-," I began, unsure where the sentence would take me, but he didn't allow me to speak.

He pushed me against the wall, kissed me so hard I thought I might crack. I balled my hands against his chest as my stomach plummeted.

I couldn't breathe.

He pulled back, pressed his thumb to my lip to silence any words I might speak. His eyes traced every line of my face as I trembled; I should have told him I kissed Kellan. I should have told him I fucked him even, anything to break from this. I'd been stupid to think this was better than outcast. I was trapped behind bars I had pleaded for him to craft.

"I see how they all look at you," he whispered, inclined his head to the group of Kade's men who watched us intently.

349

"But I won't let them have you."

Protection. Defence. Security.

None of the things I craved anymore.

"You're mine," he whispered.

With that he pulled away and joined the others in his group. I watched his back, and wondered if that had been one last kiss, in case he died.

A part of me hoped he would.

I swallowed the bile in my throat and wiped away the tears that stained my cheeks.

I was going to be free of him. One way or another. I did not belong to him. I would belong to no one anymore.

"Are you alright?" Ahzani whispered when I joined her.

I nodded stiffly, turned my attention to Kamal, expected anger at mine and Theo's public display. Instead his face was soft, his eyes sad. He opened his mouth as if to say something, the words caught on his tongue, before he shook his head, held his hand out to me.

"You are one of us now. I will protect you if you need it," he said, and I saw in his eyes he meant not just tonight, but forever.

He gripped my forearm, and I copied the gesture. A sign of respect among warriors. Among equals. He let me go as quickly as he had taken hold and turned to Kade.

"Take us there,"

Kade nodded, no longer smiling. He wore armour, although it barely fastened over his rounded belly. He pushed open the backdoor and gestured for us to follow.

We moved as a unit, Kamal and Kade at the front, Kade's men in the middle, and Ahzani and I bringing up the rear. A deadly quiet had settled over the Slum, and by extension us. We complied with the silence, our mouths pressed closed and our eyes alert. I surveyed every window, every door.

We passed through two streets before we were met with civilians. They stood outside their doors; weapons made from furniture brandished. There were already some dead, chests gaped open from bullet holes, but there were dead Pioneer's too. Their white uniforms turned crimson in death, the slum dwellers pulled at their lifeless bodies, tore their limbs free and wielded them with cries of revolution. I averted my eyes as a young girl pried a tooth from the mouth of a Pioneer and held it up for her mother.

"Has everyone risen?" Kamal whispered as we moved through the rioting crowd.

"Almost all. Some are still scared, but we will flush them out once the Slum is taken," he replied, his voice low.

I thought of Agnes as I looked at Ahzani, who looked equally concerned. I wondered if she would kneel to him, but it didn't seem likely. Neither of us voiced our worries.

The sound of gunfire pierced the quiet, and the group stilled. Ahzani raised her gun, looked down its sight as she scanned the rooftops. Kamal gestured silently for us to move towards a building on the right. Kade nodded, then nodded three of his men onwards. They broke from the group as we moved to the building's doorway.

They turned the corner and started to shoot. One went down, speared through the neck. Another fell, shot in the leg.

"Move!" Kamal shouted as he ran to help the fallen soldier.

Watching him was otherworldly. He slid behind the dead soldier, hoisted him up as a shield as he let off five precise shots. Shouts echoed as his bullets met their marks, and Ahzani rushed to follow him.

"Behind me," she ordered, her voice sharp.

I ran low behind her as we joined Kamal. I looked around the corner and saw seven dead Pioneers. The wounded soldier whined as Ahzani pressed her fingers to the wound. She pried the bullet free before she tied a length of fabric around his thigh.

"Can you walk?" she asked, to which the soldier shook his head.

Kade muscled over, his gun drawn.

"Then you are no use to us." He shot him between the eyes before anyone could interject.

A cry slipped from my lips as I jerked my head away, but I had already seen the bullet pierce his brow, and the blood that had sprayed across the cobblestones. Kamal stood and pushed Kade, his face filled with fury.

"We could have helped him!" he shouted.

Ahzani stood, covered in the man's blood. Her eyes were empty, but she was shaking. Kade pushed Kamal off of him, pointed towards the towers, just visible through the pluming smoke.

"We have no time for the injured. If they lock themselves up there, they'll snipe us down one by one and you'll never get your precious information," Kade snapped.

Kamal looked as if he were about to explode, his hand gripped the hilt of his gun, his finger still over the trigger. There was a split second where I thought he might shoot him, but then he turned.

"Let's keep moving," he hissed.

I touched Ahzani's arm and she turned, a tear caught on her lashes. I wiped the blood from her face with the edge of my sleeve as we moved forward again. She smiled to me, but her eyes were as dead as any corpses.

We moved through the street, but there were no Pioneers to be seen. At least, not alive ones. We emerged into the courtyard, the tower flanked on all sides by battle. Meredith and her girlfriend flanked to the left, Priya provided overwatch from a nearby roof, arrow knocked and ready to fly.

I looked for Theo, raked the bodies that were scattered around the guard towers, but I didn't see him. Panic rose in my chest as a door at the base of the tower opened, and a flood of Pioneer emerged.

"Get down!" Ahzani dropped to her stomach, yanked me down with her.

I threw myself to the ground as bullets whistled past my ears. I breathed in the dust and the dirt; my heart rammed hard against my ribs. I gripped my dagger with both hands as the sound of boots and screaming came closer. Someone seized me by the shoulder, dragged me to my feet, and I wheeled around. A Pioneer brandished his baton, and it crackled with blue-white electricity. I ducked as he swung it towards me and I thrust my dagger into the flesh of his belly. It penetrated his skin with ease, and I dragged the blade down through his abdomen.

Blood and guts poured from the wound, and I clambered back, pulled the knife from his body. He fell spurting blood, his hands fumbled for a weapon, but it was too late. He ceased to live, and I barely had a second to process it before another solider came for me.

She barrelled towards me with bared teeth, weaponless but fearless all the same. Her hands closed around my throat, and the force of her weight toppled the both of us over. The dagger slipped from my hand as I hit the ground, and I gasped against her pressing fingers. I pushed at her face, clawed at her eyes, but she was relentless. I jammed my fist into her throat, and she choked, loosened her grip.

I rolled her off of me, choked down as much air as I could as I crawled away. I fumbled through the bodies, my hands slick with blood, the dagger nowhere to be seen.

Find it find it find it.

My lungs brunt as I searched the cobblestones, and the growl of the pioneer behind me told me I was running out of time.

Her fingers on my ankles were hard as stone, and she yanked me backwards, nails dug into my flesh. My chin smacked the ground, split the skin and rattled my jaw so hard my vision wavered. As I blinked the spots from my vision, I caught the glint of my weapon.

I seized it, kicked out at her chest until she let go. I twisted round and jumped on top of her, pinned her to the ground. I didn't hesitate this time; my blade sunk into her throat once, twice. I kept stabbing and stabbing as the light left her eyes, her blood spattered my face, ran down my legs. My hands shook as I stabbed her once more, her throat a mangle of flesh and bone. I sat back on my ankles, her blood everywhere, all over me. My skin was sticky with it, my soul drenched with it.

She was dead, and I was finally alive.

I stood, my head heavy, my arms tired. I looked up to see Kamal and Kade moving towards the open doorway. Ahzani lay on her belly a few feet away, her gun trained on the windows of the guard tower, one eye closed as she looked down the sight. She let off a shot, and a Pioneer fell from the tower without a sound. I heard my name, like a whisper on the wind, and I looked around. I was lost, swallowed whole by something dark, and when Kellan ran towards me, it didn't register.

"Don't just stand there!" he yelled as he snatched my elbow and dragged me towards the tower.

I pressed my back to the cool stone, came back to myself slowly. Kellan looked as bloody as I had expected. A large cut forked across his forehead, oozed blood into his eyebrow. His eyes darted across the large expanse, took in every detail, before he looked at me. He took in the blood that covered me from head to toe, his jaw clenched. His hand lingered against my arm, warm and sure, as his thumb smoothed across the inside of my wrist.

He leant forward, his mouth open, and I caught a glimpse of the boy he'd been last night, the boy who believed in sailors' stories and whose kisses made me want to *beg-*

Before he could say anything, and before I could lose my god damn mind, Roscoe barrelled towards us, looked as fresh as when we'd left the camp. I occurred to me that Kellan was the reason for that, and my anger towards him softened.

"I'm going to ask Lola to marry me," he exclaimed.

Kellan frowned, dumbfounded by the proclamation.

"Who?" He asked.

"Lola! The girl from the fertility ceremony. We started talking, and I'm going to ask her to marry me when this is done," he explained.

Kellan patted the young boy on the shoulder, gave a grin.

"Well, that's cause for celebration, but shall we deal with this first?" Kellan gestured inside the tower.

Roscoe nodded, his eyes bright and infatuated. A spark of hope kindled deep in my stomach, and that part of me that had started to awaken crackled stronger, urged something more than darkness into my limbs. Kellan headed into the tower, and I followed on his heel, dagger in hand.

The stairs were littered with the dead, Pioneers and Slum dwellers alike. There were two dead Mai-Coh too, and as we passed them, Kellan closed their eyes.

As we reached the top, there was a shot and a scream. Kellan shouldered open the door in time to see Kade shoot the remaining Pioneer. Kamal was slumped against the communication board, his hand clasped at his shoulder. Blood spilled down his shirt as he took out the bullet, held it between his finger and thumb. He examined at it as he spat blood.

"You good?" Kellan said as he came to his aid.

Kamal nodded, eyed Kade out the corner of his eye. Kade didn't seem to notice Kamal was wounded, his eyes were drawn to the window. He looked out across the burning Slum, his eye alight, his mouth open in a smile. He looked like a child who'd been given access to all the toys he could ever wish for. Kellan watched him, and the warning Agnes had given finally register. He stepped forward, cleared his throat. Kade turned, his smile diminished as he looked upon him.

"We have kept up our side of the bargain, time for you to play your part," Kellan said, his voice firm.

The corner of Kade's mouth turned up in a snarl, but he returned Kellan's words with a crocodile's smile.

"I know the deal. I'll hold this place in your name until you return," Kade said.

Until you return. Not forever, not in partnership. His alliance was fickle, fleeting, but we had a party fit for a raid, not a war. We were outnumbered for now; we had no other option but to nod and agree.

"Roscoe fetch the vehicles. We head to Sadon at nightfall," Kamal instructed as he pressed his hand hard against his wound.

He gave his shoulder an experimental roll, hissed at the pain. He looked to me, took in the state of my clothes, and let out a chuckle.

"I guess you're not Golden anymore,"

Chapter XX

The lights of the Hollow shone as bright as stars in the night sky, the wall a glistening arc of white that cut through the land. I gripped the door handle as Meredith slowed the vehicle. The Hollow was not far off now, and the vehicles would raise the alarm if we rode them any closer. She looked at me as she opened her door, her eyebrows drawn down in worry.

"Are you going to be alright?" she asked.

I looked at the walls I had once called home, the ones I had been so desperate to imprison myself behind and dread settled deep in my chest.

I was not a prisoner anymore. I would not go quietly. I would not let them win.

"Yes." I replied as I slipped from the car.

Theo waited up ahead, as large and daunting as a mountain. In the shadow of the walls, so close to the life I had played, I was reminded how much I really owed him. If it weren't for him, I would be rotting in a prison, or dead, or a Riven at the Emperor's beck and call.

When he turned, and his eyes met mine, I swallowed that debt and locked it away. Threw away the key and let it burn. Debt, blind loyalty, co-dependency, I'd left that behind.

I was no one's property.

He ran to me, reached out to touch me, but I stepped back, fists balled at my sides. He cocked his head, sobered. I took the confusion to note his lack of injuries; had he been playing it safe? I hadn't seen him on the battle ground, had he hidden? The thought made me frown.

"You don't have to come," he broached.

"I do." It wasn't something to debate.

He was taken aback by the strength in my voice; something flashed in his eyes akin to irritation. I smiled, glad I was getting to him. Good.

There was no time to continue the conversation though. Kamal gestured us over, and our diminished crowd gathered, stood as one. We looked to Kamal, awaited his orders. He stared at Sadon, its brightness reflected in his eyes, and I realised that he'd never imagined this day would come.

We let him take it in, let him savour the moment. He turned to us, his crew, his family, and laid his hand on his heart.

"Today is the day." He said, his voice cracked.

Kellan reached out and put his hand on Kamal's shoulder. There was love between these men that ran deeper than a life debt, a respect and familiarity that I wished I could understand. Kamal nodded to him, before he pulled the map I'd draw all those weeks ago out of his pocket. Everyone crowded round, took in the route. My heart jumped as my eyes skimmed over my house, over Alfie's. I wondered if I'd see them, and then wondered what would happen if I did.

"We take these streets, and we take them fast. We'll only have a short amount of time before the Pioneer army comes. We get into the Palladium, get the plans and go. Everyone know their part?" he asked.

Everyone nodded.

"Good. May the spirits guide us," he said, glanced up at the heavens.

The group scattered; Kamal, Kellan, Theo and others were to head to the palladium. Meredith lead a group for over watch, and Ahzani...

"Come on kiddos," she teased, gun slung over her back.

Roscoe scowled at her, arms folded over his chest.

"It's not fair," he said.

"Life's not fair," Ahzani countered as she walked away.

I followed; every step caused my heart to rise in my throat. We moved as one towards the edge of the wall, and hidden behind a growth of bramble was a hole. Small, almost too narrow for someone to pass through, rough from hands that had so desperately pulled the bricks free.

Ahzani passed through first, grunted as her gun caught on the cement. I stared down that dark tunnel, at the light on the other side, and took a breath.

I edged through sideways, held my breath as the bricks brushed my shoulders. There was darkness, and the smell of damp earth, but then I was through, and I was back home.

Under the light's nostalgia washed over me as dangerous as sea waves. I thought about the days I had spent wandering these streets, aimless and childish, playing my part in the charade of life. Ahzani beckoned against the wall, and I pressed myself against the brick. I knew who lived here, a young couple only just given housing rights, and the thought made my head spin.

"We need to take a building near the Palladium, one of the four streets Kamal wants to take. Any suggestions?" she asked.

I knew what I should say, that the best street would be the one I grew up on. It was only two streets away from the Palladium, and from a three story we'd get a good view, but I didn't want to risk my families lives. Wasn't that why I'd wanted to run in the first place, to protect them?

"I'll take us." I said, forced my fear down into my stomach.

I took the lead without waiting for Ahzani's permission. This was my home, these were my streets, and I knew them better than anyone.

The air smelt fresh and pleasant, and it was strange not to hear jeering and drunken laughter. I slipped through front gardens, tried to stick to the shadows, but the lights were so blinding I had to squint, no longer used to the glow of electricity. Ahzani followed behind, as silent as she always was, while Roscoe trailed, still sulking.

We reached my street, and I stopped at the edge. I looked at the cobblestones and remembered being ten and scraping my knee in a game of chase. I looked at Alfie's front garden, tidier than the last time I'd been here, and thought about the cuddly toy parties we'd had.

My eyes watered as my gaze moved to Alfie's window, its curtains drawn. I wanted to run to the front door, fling it open and go to him, hold him, apologise for all I'd put him through.

But apologies were ash compared to what I was bringing here today.

"That one?" Ahzani pointed to Alfie's house, and I shook my head.

"No. That one." I pointed to Mrs. Moore's house at the end of the street.

She was an elderly lady nearing her expiration whose husband had died a few years ago. She was allowed no children, allotted no pets. There would be no struggle there.

I moved across the street, kept my head down. No matter how much I wanted to look at my old home, I couldn't bring myself to do it. I ached for Lavender and Chrys and my mother, but I couldn't put them in danger.

Ahzani passed me, moved to the door. She gestured for us to come close before she knocked on the door once, twice. There was no answer of course. She tried the handle, and the door swung open. There was no need to lock doors here, there was trust in this community.

Guilt rose in my chest as we walked into her house. Ahzani gestured Roscoe up the stairs as she drew her gun. I didn't grip my dagger any tighter, I let it lie limp in my hand. She nodded her head at the living room before she went into the kitchen. My eyes strained through the darkness of the hallway as I looked at the closed living room door. My fingers shook as I reached out to take the golden handle in my fingers.

I hesitated.

Mrs. Moore had never done anything to me, had been nothing but kind. I shook my head, tried to dislodge the perfect way of thinking I'd been trained to generate since birth. It crawled back, gnawed at the corner of my brain. A shot echoed from up the stairs, and I ran up, charged into the bedroom, my heart thumping in my chest.

Roscoe stood over Mrs. Moore, his gun smoking, his eyes wide. She laid face down on the carpet, unmoving. Her silver hair spread around her head like a halo, her bright white nightdress creased from the struggle. Ahzani arrived behind me, stared at the scene before her.

"Put her in the bath," she whispered to me, her voice thick.

I pushed past Roscoe, who was shaking. I took Mrs. Moore by the shoulders, her skin still warm. I dragged her towards the bathroom, hauled her into the tub. Her head lolled back, mouth and eyes wide open. Ahzani and Roscoe were whispering, but I barely registered their words. I stared down at her, expecting disgust, or sadness, or grief.

I felt nothing.

362

Another shot echoed through the night, and the hair on my arms stood on end. Another person dead, another death on my conscience.

Ahzani came into the bathroom rubbing her temples, her eyes heavy.

"Roscoe's downstairs. Think the old lady spooked him a bit," she said.

Another shot and a scream. We both stared at Mrs. Moore's lifeless corpse as the reality of this night set in. She reached out and gave me a gently pat on the back.

"I'll set up in the bedroom, get me a snack?" she asked.

I nodded, headed down the stairs. Roscoe sat at the kitchen table, head in his hands. I moved around him; unsure I could say anything that would help.

The fridge was fully stocked, and my stomach growled at the familiar refinement of Sadon's food. I picked up a few peaches, their skin soft and juicy. I kicked the fridge closed, looked at the back of Roscoe's head. His shoulders were shaking as he tried to stifle his sobs. I walked over to him, put the peach down on the table. He looked up, tears caught on his lashes. There was no longer the need or want to be at the centre of the action, but the sadness and loss of innocence of a young child.

I brushed his knuckles with my fingers, gave him a half smile, before I headed back up the stairs. Ahzani stood by the bedroom window, gun ready, eyes focused on the street. She turned as I approached, grinned as I offered her a peach.

"Never seen one of these before," she said around a mouthful, ravaged the peach like it would be her last meal.

I crinkled my nose as the juices ran down her chin but did the same, revelled in the artificial sweetness. I leant into this bizarre moment of peace, ignored the blood on the carpet, ignored the sound of gunfire and relished the ease of her company.

We sat up there for hours, talking about everything and nothing and all the things in between. She told me about her childhood, how she'd met Meredith and all the stupid things she used to do, all the trouble she used to get in with Kamal. I listened mostly, told her small things about my sister, my brother. I laid back on the bed, turned the dagger over and over as we enjoyed a rare moment of silence. Blood had dried along the blade, turned the silver maroon. Ahzani shifted, squinted out the window.

"What the…" she trailed off.

I shot up, followed her gaze. The citizens of the Hollow were running down the street in their pyjamas, children wailing under their mother's arms. There was a fire raging a street over, and the Palladium was lit up brighter than any celebration. A Hovear cruised down the street, and I ducked, my heart hammering in my throat. Ahzani looked down the sight of her gun, kept it trained on the Hovear as it passed. When it had, she leant back, looked down at me where I crouched.

"You can't be scared," she whispered despite the wobble in her voice.

I forced myself to stand, to look out the window at the building I had been avoiding. My house lay quiet, dark, oblivious to the chaos outside. I felt its pull as hard as a hand around my throat. The faint smell of smoke wafted through the open window, and as the fire jumped from one window to the next, one of the Mai-Coh ran down the street. It was a girl I didn't know, a short girl with thick hair and deep-set eyes. She had a bow in her hand, but her quiver was empty. I watched her run, and I watched the Pioneers chase after her.

"Shit. Shit." Ahzani looked down the sight as the Pioneer aimed.

364

A shot rang out, and the Mai-Coh girl fell. Ahzani let off two shots, neither hit their mark. The sound of a chair hitting the ground made my heart jump, and Roscoe ran out into the street.

"Roscoe!" Ahzani yelled.

I took off, barrelled down the stairs without a second thought. More Mai-Coh were streaming down the cobblestones, weapons drawn and aimed at the Pioneer's who pursued them. People fell; innocent people, Pioneers, Mai-Coh.

The fire had engulfed a building on this street too, and it raged uncontained. I jerked around, tried to find Roscoe among the pulsing crowd. My fingers buzzed with adrenaline as I searched each face, pushed past the wailing masses to find the boy who was too young to be here.

"Roscoe!" I shouted.

My lungs burnt as the smoke grew heavy. I choked, pushed through those who fled.

"Roscoe!" I screamed as loud as I could.

I heard whimpering, and I turned towards it. People crushed around me, an endless sea of arms and legs and fear, but through the fray I saw Roscoe. He laid on the ground, his nose bloody, his eyes wide. A Pioneer stood above him, gun drawn. I launched forward, elbowed my way through the crowd, struggled against the wave of people as the Pioneer smiled.

He shot him. It was quick and soundless. Painless even. Roscoe didn't even cry. The bullet pierced through his forehead, lodged deep inside his skull. He fell limp on the ground, and I stopped short. The Pioneer fell shortly after, but it was too late.

Ahzani had been too late.

My eyes watered, but I knew there wasn't time to cry. I looked at my home, at the fire that raged only two houses away. I had to warn them, why weren't they fleeing? I turned to look back at Ahzani, whose eyes were on me alone. She was saying something, but the crackle of the fire and the screams around me drowned her out.

I should go to her. I should fight. I should do something, anything but what I want to.

My fingers shook around the hilt of my dagger as I looked back at the house that had imprisoned me, the house that had broken me, and with trembling fingers I let the dagger drop.

I had to save my family.

I ran to the gate, vaulted over it with a strength I didn't know I had. I charged up the garden I had spent so many days in as a child. The roses, once vibrant and beautiful, were shrunken and wilted. I reached for the handle of the door, and a bullet pierced the wood only a hairsbreadth from my shoulder. I looked back at Ahzani's window, but the smoke was so thick I couldn't distinguish her face.

A warning shot. A shot that begged me not to go back in there, not to betrayal her trust.

I shook my head, regardless of whether she could see.

It wasn't a choice. I couldn't let my family burn.

I flung the door open. The hallway was dark but unchanged from the day I left. My father's study door was shut, but I didn't let my eyes linger.

Let him turn to ash for all I care.

I charged up the stairs, thrust open my sister's door. She lay in bed, covers pulled up to her chin, her fluffy bunny tucked under one arm. Her eyes landed on me, and her mouth dropped open.

"Callie!" she cried.

She vaulted out of bed, threw her arms around me as she sobbed. I held her, and for a second I could convince myself nothing had changed. I breathed in the clean scent of her hair, held her so tightly I thought she might break. When I pulled back, the tears on her cheeks shone like silver, and reality fell back in.

"We need to get you out of here, okay?" I took her by the hand and dragged her towards the door.

"What about Chrys?" she asked, her heels dug into the carpet.

I pulled her harder into the hallway. I looked at Chrys' bedroom door, left ajar. Lavender squirmed, wriggled out of my grip. She pushed open Chrys' door, turned her head side to side. Dread pricked at the back of my neck as I followed her in.

His bed was empty, the covers thrown back, pillows discarded on the ground. It looked as if there had been a struggle, books knocked on the ground, a glass shattered by the door. Lavender bent, picked up a wad of paper, unravelled it. I snatched it from her, looked at the words scribbled there.

Chrys,

I don't know if we can keep on like this. I love you, but we have to think of our families.

Darwin

I turned towards the door, strained to listen past the howling outside. Lavender looked up at me, her glistening eyes as large as the moon, her lashes wet. We heard it then, the thump from our fathers' study, the cry of pain, and suddenly I was there, a knife in my back, my world shattering before me.

I would not let him suffer the same fate.

367

"Go wake mum and get out of here," I instructed as I walked back into the hallway.

Lavender grasped hold of my hand, her thin fingers cold and slim.

"Please, Callie. Don't go again," she begged.

I took her face in my hands, pressed my lips against her forehead. I forced her to look at me as I brushed the tears from her cheek.

"You have to be brave for me, alright? Go get mum and leave," I stroked her hair gently.

She nodded, sniffed a snot bubble back up her nose. I smiled at her, before I moved down the stairs. My father's study door loomed in front of me, and that same reluctancy crippled me like it had my whole life. Another thump rattled against the polished oak, and my hand moved to the gun. It was cold and hard in my hand, a daunting decision of life and death.

Lavender emerged at the top of the stairs, mother in tow. She looked barely awake, her eyes squinted against the darkness, but when she saw me, they shot wide open. Her hand went to her mouth as she gasped.

"Calluna," she breathed.

I nodded them towards the door as I moved to fathers' study. I pressed my ear against it, waited for them to leave. Mother hesitated, caught on the threshold, framed in the flames of the street. She reached for me, her feeble hands shaking. I shook my head once. There wasn't time. Lavender tugged her out into the street, and I kicked open the study door.

Chrys lay slumped on the ground, his arm held up to shield his face. Blood poured from a gash on his cheek, one of his eyes swollen shut. Father stood over him, his knuckles red with blood, the same penknife that had marred me held between his fingers. His eyes shot up at my intrusion, and for a moment, everything was still.

We stared at each other, a thousand words and memories flowed between us, filled the room until there was no air. I held my gun with both hands, its ugly mouth pointed at his chest. My arms shook as his eyes widened. Chrys looked up at me, relief and shock washed over his beaten face.

"Calluna," he cried.

Father took him by the neck, pulled him to his feet, pressed the edge of the penknife against his pale throat. Chrys struggled, but our father was stronger than either of us.

"Let him go," I commanded, but my voice betrayed me.

It shook where it needed to be strong, and as I took a step forward, our father dug the tip of the blade into Chrys' neck. Blood slipped from the scratch, a red tear that fell and stained his white shirt. Chrys hissed, grit his teeth against the pain.

"Don't come any closer or I'll kill him," he hissed.

My chest rose and fell hard with fear. Chrys looked at me, his eyes terrified. I could hear the fight outside growing louder, the heat of the fire filled the study as I heard crackling in the kitchen. It wouldn't be long until the house was consumed.

"Please," I begged.

I couldn't bear to see him in pain. Guilt clawed at me, threatened to drag me to the floor. I'd left this place to protect him and it hadn't changed a thing. Father laughed, a cruel, soulless laugh that froze my blood.

"Look whose returned home to play the hero," he spat.

He narrowed his eyes at the gun, his lips pressed thin.

"You don't have the strength to use that," he hissed, that same demeaning voice that had haunted my childhood.

He pressed the knife deeper into Chrys' neck, sent blood spilling down his skin. I stepped forward, pressed my finger over the trigger despite the trembling of my arms.

"Stop it!" I cried.

I couldn't stop shaking. Chrys squirmed, tears fell down his cheek as he tried to break free. Father tightened his arm across his chest, jerked Chrys' head back by his hair.

"It would be a kindness, to relieve him of his sins," he growled.

"He's your son," I said, but he shook his head.

"He's no son of mine," he hissed into Chrys' ear.

"You'll let me take him, let us leave," he continued, took a step towards the patio door.

"Calluna," Chrys pleaded.

I followed him with my gun, shook my head. Everything that had happened, every day in training, it had all been leading up to this moment. Protect my brother, kill my father.

Save a life, take a life.

"Let him go," I repeated, firmer this time.

He looked at me, his eyes filled with hatred, his lips peeled back from his teeth in a snarl. His black eyes reflected the flames that consumed the garden, and he coughed against the smoke that swirled above us.

"You won't kill me. One thing I know is I raised you to be complacent. To be subservient." He pushed Chrys towards me.

I stumbled back; my heart thumped in my ears. Sweat dripped from my forehead, the heat from the fire so intense my veins were beginning to bulge. He took another step towards me, closed the gap between us. My back pressed against the boiling wall, and I heard the glasses in the kitchen shatter from the flames.

"You will always be perfect. No matter how hard you try, you will always be my creation." His voice rose as he pressed Chrys forward, within reaching distance now.

Chrys whimpered, his eyes squeezed shut, his face bright red from the heat. I wanted to reach for him, to hold him, to protect him the way no one had ever protected me. A tear slipped down my cheek as my fingers wavered. I wanted to pull the trigger, I wanted to kill my father more than anything, but my finger refused to squeeze.

"Kill me. Do it," my father dared, stooped so I had a clear shot between his brows.

Chrys pleaded with his eyes, the tears on his cheeks shone in the dim moonlight as his lips wobbled. I grit my teeth, willed my finger to squeeze as my father smiled.

All my life, I had belonged to him.

All my life, he had broken me, moulded me, forged me into whatever he wished. He had owned me, and I'd allowed Theo to own me too.

I fought against everything that I'd been taught from birth, fought against my basest instinct. If I could kill my father, if I could save Chrys, then I could survive alone. I could be free of Theo, free of everyone.

A whimper of frustration and pain rose in my throat, tore from my lips as my fingers trembled.

You are nothing alone.

You will never be more than someone's property.

You will always be owned.

You will always serve.

My whole body convulsed as I sobbed, lowered my gun.

"That's what I thought," he whispered, a hint of disappointment in his eyes.

The front door slammed open, and we both started. My father panicked, and the blade sunk deep into Chrys' neck.

For a blinding second the world stopped.

I opened my mouth to scream, but no sound came out. Chrys fell to the ground in slow motion, his eyes widening with realisation. I dropped my gun as I sunk to the ground, cradled Chrys in my lap. Blood spurted relentlessly from the wound, his life slowly dripped down the front of his shirt. He gurgled as more blood spilled from his lips. I pressed my hands to the wound, tried to staunch the blood flow.

"Chrys please, please hold on. Chrys," I whispered.

"Calluna." I distantly recognised the voice, but all I could see was Chrys.

His lips moved soundlessly as his hand came to rest on my cheek, soaked with his blood. My heart cracked into a million shards as his fingers traced the line of my jaw. I shook my head as he blinked.

"Please," I begged.

His hand fell from my face as his eyes went blank. I removed my hands from his neck, my shaking fingers drenched almost black. There was a hand on my shoulder, it tried to drag me up, but I couldn't move. I looked down at Chrys' body and a wave of darkness rose up to consume me whole. It took my heart between its fingers and yanked it out whole, left a squirming, angry, empty mess in its wake. I wailed, a guttural scream that left the taste of blood on my tongue.

I'd failed.

"Calluna." The voice came again, and I looked up to see Alfie.

"We have to get out of here," he said as he hauled me to my feet.

I picked up my gun, looked around the room for my father. The patio door was open, the curtains billowed into the night sky. He was gone.

I struggled against Alfie, tried to reach for Chrys. I couldn't leave him here to turn to ash. I couldn't let him rest in a room that had caused him so much pain. I threw my head back, clawed at Alfie's hands, but he was relentless. Flames licked at the kitchen and living room, danced on the stairway. I coughed through the thick black smoke as Chrys' body disappeared from sight.

"I can't leave him here!" I yelled as I tried to pry free.

My feet dragged along the ground, tried to find purchase. My lungs burnt, and I found myself breathless as Alfie dragged me onto the front law. I threw my weight back into him and we toppled over. The grass was wet under my back, and I rolled over, got to my knees.

"Calluna no! You'll die!" Alfie grabbed me, wrapped his arms around my chest.

I screamed and screamed until my chest felt hollow. My eyes burnt from tears and smoke, and as he held me, the weight of what had happened crushed me. I stilled, turned into his chest, wrapped my arms around him.

"He's gone," I whimpered.

He pulled back, looked down at me. His eyes were misty, but he shed no tears. He brushed my hair from my face, and my withered heart gave a beat.

Alfie.

373

Alfie was alive.

A shadow rose behind us, and I looked up to see Theo.

He loomed above us, gun drawn, eyes dark, and as Alfie turned, his eyes widened.

It was like watching some distant movie, the way the jealousy and possessiveness shaped his face. His lips pulled back from his teeth in a snarl, and I lunged as he pressed his finger over the trigger.

"No!" I begged, but it was too late.

The bullet pierced Alfie's stomach, and he fell back with a cry. Theo aimed again, but I crawled in front of him, thrust myself between them.

"Please, he's my friend," I begged.

Theo looked from me to Alfie, his eyes narrowed. He didn't lower his gun.

"Get up," he said sharply.

I gaped up at him, at his lack of regret, at the hardness in his face. I shook my head, lips pressed tight. I turned back to Alfie, ripped a shred of my shirt free and pressed it against the hole. I refused to lose someone else.

"I won't let him die," I refused.

Alfie squirmed under my hands; his eyes squeezed shut as I peeled back his shirt. The hole was small, clean, but blood was already oozing from the wound. I pressed the fabric back over it, looked over my shoulder at Theo. His face was cold, his jaw set. He'd sheathed his gun, but his shoulders were still tensed, ready for a fight.

"Help me get him up. We need to take him with us," I said as I looped my arm under Alfie's shoulder.

Theo made no move to help. He crossed his arms, shook his head as he averted his eyes.

"No."

The word cut through my chest like a blade. He reached for me, grabbed me by the shoulder, pulled me to my feet. Alfie slumped back on the grass, groaned in agony.

"Get off of me," I hissed, but his grip intensified.

His eyes were as dark as night, and the anger in them turned my legs to jelly. He yanked me towards him so hard pain shot through my shoulders.

"You do as I say. Leave him to die," he said through gritted teeth.

I threw back my head, crushed his nose with a single blow. He hissed and let me drop.

"You do not own me. Touch me again and I will kill you," I promised.

I didn't give him the chance to reply. I dropped back to my knees, pulled Alfie into my lap with shaking hands. My whole body vibrated, every fibre sung and tore and writhed. Alfie looked up at me, tears on his face, and I swallowed past the image of Chrys that threatened to send me to a place of no return.

A cry made me turn my head, and Kellan ran down the street, his face drenched with sweat. He spotted us and turned, ran to my side. He looked up at Theo, who stood deathly still by my side, and he frowned.

"What's going on here?" He said as his hand found my shoulder.

I wouldn't leave without him, and if that meant staying here, if that meant the Emperor killing me, then so be it. He deserved that, he deserved the chance at a better life after everything I'd done. As he writhed, tears spilling freely down his cheeks, I stroked the hair from his face, held his hand.

I would die here with him if I had to, and maybe then I would feel peace.

"I won't leave him," I said as I stroked the sweat from his forehead.

"I already said no-" Theo began.

"I don't care what you have to say," I snapped back.

Kellan moved to kneel opposite me. He reached out and removed my hands from Alfie's stomach. He lifted the torn shred of my shirt, inspected the wound. Alfie groaned, but Kellan hushed him, pushed the fabric back down. He looked up at me, at the redness of my eyes, and then looked to my house, now engulfed by flames. He took a breath, before he pushed his arm under Alfie's shoulder.

"Support him, help him walk," Kellan instructed.

I rushed to comply. We dragged him to his feet despite his groaning. The windows shattered from the house, sent glass raining down onto the grass. Theo opened his mouth to say something, and I thought I saw regret flash across his eyes, but I pushed him out of the way.

"Soldiers a street away!" Ahzani cried as she barrelled out of the house.

I looked behind us at the hoard of Hovears, their headlights blinding. Kellan broke into a jog, and I struggled to keep up, Alfie's weight pressed against my back.

"Where... where..." Alfie tried to talk, but his limbs were growing leaden.

We reached the opening and Kellan hauled Alfie away from me.

"Go first. I have him," he reassured as a bullet pierced the brick.

Bodies littered the ground around our feet, fallen Mai-Coh who hadn't been quick enough. I took one last look at Alfie, hesitant to leave him. Kellan met my eyes, gave a nod, and I pushed through the wall.

On the other side Ahzani was reversing a truck closer to the wall. I flung open the backdoor, the sound of gunfire like the beat of a heart on the other side. I waited, and waited, each second agony. After a moment, Kellan emerged with Alfie stumbling after him. Kellan was sweating, his brow shone as he hauled Alfie to the truck.

"Get in... the back," he panted.

I pulled myself into the back seat, held out my arms to help Alfie in. Kellan picked Alfie up by the waist, laid him carefully in my lap. Alfie cried out, a pained shout that pierced through my heart. I pulled him close, tried to still his restless limbs.

Kellan pushed Ahzani into the passenger seat, and as he settled behind the wheel a bullet shattered the back window. I ducked, sheltered Alfie's head from the debris. The truck roared forward; tires skidded against the dirt as we followed the others. I kept my hands pressed against Alfie's stomach, my palms sticky with blood.

I looked back through the shattered glass at the burning Hollow, watched the flames climb into the sky. There were Pioneer's on the wall, shooting after us, but their bullets skimmed into the grass as we tore away.

I watched the wall grow smaller, unable to tear my eyes away from the burning remains of my old life. A part of me shattered and burnt too. The part that followed, the part that owed and trusted and bent. The other part of me that had begun to grow, the part that was beginning to love and want and need, splintered and broke into darkness.

And I was terrified of what might rise from the ashes in its place.

Acknowledgements

To Josh, my partner, for reading this in its very early stages and for following along through all the name changes, tears and heartache. Thank you for talking me down every time I wanted to delete the whole thing. Without you, I wouldn't have had the confidence to publish, and I am eternally grateful.

To my nan, who has always encouraged me to live my dreams. Thank you for letting me write at your dining room table when I was young, and for supporting and encouraging me when others didn't. You are my light.

To my beta readers, especially Jasmine Watson, for helping my characters to grow and change. I'm grammatically inept and your help was beyond words. Thank you for being my hype woman and helping me through the self-publishing journey.

To Sara Oliver, who designed the cover that made me cry. Your art and talent bought this book to life, and you made thirteen-year-old me very happy.

To veronikawunder, who designed the map to my world. How you made such beauty out of my horrific sketch is mind-blowing.

To Angela Silva, for creating the most beautiful bookmarks and stickers. You made me feel like a real author, and I won't ever forget that.

To all the artists who made wonderful art for my novel (Myriam Strasbourg, ampalayeah, alana.rene.art, clairosene), you all bought my characters to life in such different and breath-taking ways. I will never stop being in awe of you all.

And to you, reader, who stuck with me through this novel's twists and turns. Through its highs and lows. I will always be your biggest fan.

CPSIA information can be obtained
at www.ICGtesting.com
Printed in the USA
LVHW040835251121
704251LV00002B/4

9 781739 987503